1

0948 13 AUG 2002; NUBIAN DESERT, SUDAN
CAMP ALI

(Taubah, Sura 9:5)
Fight and slay the infidels wherever you find them,
and seize them, beleaguer them,
and lie in wait for them in every stratagem of war.

Fifteen-year-old Bassam Amin breathed slowly and deeply through a plastic straw. He'd become oblivious to the burning, itching discomfort of being buried under hot sand for hours. His secret was meditation.

Bassam's meditation had nothing to do with the Koran, nor the teaching of the holy men. He concentrated, instead, on remembering the belly dancer he'd seen on Egyptian television two years ago. His mind painted her every contour, her every expression, her every mesmerizing motion. Every smile, every wink, every toss of her hair. Every jiggle of flesh and every wag of the hips. He rotated her image to view her at all angles, stripping away her costume and dressing her back up again.

He'd never met the woman. He'd never met any woman who wasn't married, betrothed to another, or of too high a station to concern herself with an impoverished Palestinian bastard. With the changes happening in his body and mind over the last couple years, the wonders he'd never tasted became all the more alluring. Females were all he could think of sometimes.

Besides killing infidels and liberating his homeland.

Whump! A trainer's foot stomped on the sand over his chest.

Bassam exploded out of the ground, spitting out the straw and sand from his lips. He hyperventilated while sprinting at full speed, eyes not even open until he brushed the sand from them on the run. He risked tripping and injuring himself this way, but it would get him off to a quick start.

His eyes stung. The structures of the obstacle course appeared as translucent outlines against the blinding white light of the day. His skin itched terribly all over but he dared not slow down to scratch.

As he approached the rope, he planned out the trajectory of his jump--the higher he caught it, the shorter the climb and the less time it would take. He measured his stride so he wouldn't need to slow down. He hit the log and sprang into the air. If he missed the rope at this speed and angle, he would hit the side of the pit hard enough to break something.

He didn't miss. He caught the rope high and his arms took over as his legs now hung limp. Here's where the hyperventilating paid off-- his muscles had plenty of oxygen. If he used his legs on the way up, he'd be penalized thirty seconds.

Hand over hand, he pulled himself toward the thick beam from which the rope hung, back muscles popping painfully. At the top, he held on with one hand while his other felt around for the knife he knew should be lying on the beam. His fingers closed around the blade of the bayonet and he put the handle between his teeth so both hands were available to suspend his weight.

Now his arms and shoulders ached, but he knew the longer he waited the weaker they would grow. He hyperventilated again, then reached out for the first monkey bar.

The bars were fastened between two shipping ropes extending, at a shallow angle, diagonally out and down from the wooden beam. The structure bounced and swayed crazily. Cautious trainees gripped the bars with both their hands, then waited for the swinging to stop before moving to the next. Bassam swung straight from one bar to the next but couldn't help breaking rhythm due to the dangerous undulations of the hanging bridge. Now his wrists and forearms ached, too.

The last bar hung over a narrow plank atop a fence eight feet high. He waited until the swaying of the bridge positioned him directly over it, and let go. His feet hit the plank and his legs bent to absorb the shock. He struggled to gain his balance, gasping for breath.

He had to pause a moment--his lungs were burning and he felt light-headed. Trainees who'd made good time up to this point usually fell here, too exhausted to maintain their balance.

Hell and Gone
Henry Brown
Copyright © 2010 Virtual Pulp

Cover art by Logotecture (Fourth Edition)

For SFC Bob Krahn
A leader good soldiers gladly followed.

Bayonet still in his mouth, now dripping with his saliva, he held both quivering arms out at shoulder level and walked the plank.

The fence made a sharp left-hand turn ahead and Bassam slowed to a snail's pace before he got to it. He almost lost his balance making the turn, anyway. But he stayed upright, regained control and picked up speed.

At the end of the fence a tire swung back and forth from a rope tied to a horizontal pole with a sand-filled duffel bag on the other end. The pole balanced atop the notched end of a swiveling fulcrum. A thick, round rubber slab filled the center of the tire. Bassam took the bayonet from his mouth and wiped the handle on his pants, then gripped it and watched the swinging tire. He had to strike hard and accurately, or the knife wouldn't support his weight.

As the tire arced across his front, he swung downward with all his might. The blade sunk into the rubber slab only about an inch-and-a-half. It would have to be enough. He stepped off the plank, the one hand still clutching the bayonet, his other hand grabbing his wrist. This was Bassam's favorite part of the course. His momentum made the fulcrum pivot while his weight gradually overcame the weight of the duffel bag at the other end of the pole and he was eased forward and down to earth.

He wrenched the blade loose and fell upon a straw dummy, his legs wrapping around the torso. The bayonet slashed against the straw neck while his free hand squeezed what would be the lower third of the face. He half-severed off the head, but his weight and inertia were too much for the dummy. He and the dummy went down, its supporting post uprooted from the sand.

He panted and cursed, looking around to see if he was disqualified. His eyes locked with a judge's. "Go! Go!" yelled the judge.

Bassam thrust the bayonet into the chest and left it planted there, reached down into the hole where the neck had been and extracted two training grenades. Holding one in each hand, he rolled off the dummy and crawled toward the concertina wire before him.

He flattened against the sand, turned his knees out and pushed with his legs, plowing a furrow in the sand with his cheek and ribcage. He pressed himself down as hard as he could, and still the razor barbs of the concertina tore at his shirt. He had to lift his head up several times to adjust his direction, and each time he did, the concertina pricked his head and neck.

Finally he crawled into open space. Here he struggled to work the pins out of both grenades. He let the spoons fly and cooked them off for three seconds, then sprang to his feet facing right. A mock building wall stood twenty yards away. He slung the first grenade through the window, transferred the remaining grenade to his throwing hand and whirled to the left. On this side loomed an open-top oil tank some fifteen feet tall. He lobbed the second grenade and dropped back to the ground between the banks of the crawling trench. He heard the grenade bounce off the side of the tank--his angle hadn't been high enough--and the pop of the fuses blowing to his right and left.

"Go! Keep going!" shouted one of the trainers.

Bassam crawled forward under more concertina. The trench dropped deeper into the earth. His cheek plowed sand again, so he couldn't see ahead very well. But the coolness and the stench told him the "swamp" lay just ahead. Rumor had it the trainers relieved their own waste into this water. It certainly stunk as if they did.

Now Bassam's hands were wet. He was at the swamp. He took a deep breath and slithered into it. The wire hung so low it touched the surface of the water--there was no possible way to avoid submerging oneself in the disgusting muck and still make it through the course.

The swamp was deep enough for Bassam to crawl a little more comfortably without getting snared by the wire. If comfort could, in any way, be associated with this liquid hell. At the bottom of the swamp, his hands closed on a heavy object of metal and wood. He scooped it up and kept going.

***

Khaled Ali found it a bit disturbing to see Jan Chin laughing. The portly Chinese advisor's normal expression was a scowl that made Ali suspect he was always on the brink of maniacal wrath and any little thing might push him over the edge. But watching a trainee's face prune up in disgust at the horrible smell of the swamp, then crawl through it, always delighted Chin.

Ali, too, enjoyed pushing the trainees beyond their normal tolerance. He'd seen and smelled death, mutilation and many things a weakling couldn't bear to think about, all without blinking. But to see Chin grinning made him squeamish.

The two men stood upon the wooden tower overlooking the obstacle course, from which every part of the camp--and miles of landscape beyond--could be observed. But neither the Nubian Desert to the west nor the Red Sea to the east commanded their interest just now.

The young trainee made it to where the concertina wire ended and rose out of the swamp, dripping with scum of unspeakable origins. He cocked the slimy Kalashnikov and opened his eyes. He fired a burst at the target to his left (a life-sized cardboard effigy of an Hasidic Jew), stitching a line of bullet holes center-mass, then swung to his right and emptied the magazine into the last target (a cardboard Uncle Sam with fangs and devil horns). He then fell face-down on the sand, sucking hard for air.

Ali clicked the stopwatch. Chin, scowling again, leaned over to look at the elapsed time.

"He failed to get the second grenade inside the oil tank," Chin said. "Penalize thirty seconds."

Ali snorted. They could give Amin three such penalties and he would still hold the record for this course. Ali descended the tower, walked over and kicked the exhausted trainee in the leg.

"Go clean that weapon and yourself," Ali said.

Bassam rose wearily and staggered toward the field showers.

Chin nodded at Ali. "He has the sort of motivation you want."

"Everyone here is motivated," Ali said.

"He didn't hesitate at any obstacle. He showed no fear. No concern for life or health."

Ali nodded. "I have found my volunteer."

2

0932 13 AUG 2002; LEUCADIA, CALIFORNIA USA

Dwight Cavarra snap-kicked against the current. With knee still raised, his planted foot pivoted in the sand while his hips adjusted for the follow-up roundhouse kick. His foot knifed through the water only slightly faster than slow-motion replays on ESPN. In the follow-through, he dropped his lead foot, satisfied with the timing: the undertow didn't catch him standing on one leg. His lead hand arced down from the high guard into a low block, then his other hand extended in a leopard-paw strike.

Lungs burning, he squatted on the ocean floor, then sprang, hands and feet propelling him upwards. When his head broke surface, the lungful of stale air exploded from his mouth.

He treaded water while catching his breath. After a few moments of mentally prodding himself, he dove down to execute one more kata.

Air had seemingly never felt or tasted sweeter when he ascended for the final time that morning, and swam for shore. Once his five-foot-ten body could touch the bottom with his head still above water, he waded the final stretch, fatigued muscles straining against the pull of the sea.

Just past the mark of the tide's farthest advance, he removed his weight belt before kneeling to pull a bottle of water from the knapsack he'd left there.

How many years could he keep doing this? At fifty-two, or sixty-two, would he still be swimming around the buoys at sunup, then practicing martial arts underwater?

Bunch of Zen ego-pumping. And I've got a masochistic streak— that's what it is.

In younger days, he'd been impressed with a legend about a great master who fought a hurricane—punching and kicking into the deadly blasts of wind. He developed his own, safer exercise routine when fitness was almost a religion to him. He couldn't even remember that legendary master's name anymore, but Cavarra's tradition lived on.

Cavarra drained the bottle. He rose, slinging the knapsack and weight belt over one shoulder, and trudged inland.

Two early risers...attractive young women not yet warm enough to strip to their bikinis...unfolded lawn chairs next to a pile of umbrellas, towels, lotion bottles and paperbacks. They glanced at Cavarra as he passed, but the spark was dull: no magnetic head-turning; no nigh-unperceivable glow; no whispered comment or giggle to a girlfriend. Not that long ago, he'd taken for granted those primordial signals of superficial attraction from most of the women he encountered.

I'm disappearing off the female radar.

Another forty yards and he was out of the sand. He turned his back to the sun while slipping his sandals on. Instead of stealing another peek at the nubile beach bunnies, he studied his shadow.

It was a thick shadow. He no longer had a "powerful physique"—just a "stocky build."

Age was an ugly beast. His once jet-black hair was now salt-and-pepper. He avoided wearing hats lest his bald spot grow faster than nature intended. On the bright side, the morning cool didn't chill his wet skin much and the salt water irritated his eyes only moderately.

Cavarra turned back toward the sun and trudged on. He cut through parking lots and across asphalt roads, reaching his adobe house in less than ten minutes. After a quick shower and change, he shoveled himself a dish of fruit salad and sank into the swivel chair at his computer desk.

I'm gonna be brain-dead by noon, he thought, already growing mentally numb counting the email messages he had to sort through.

Then he noticed, buried in all the orders for ammo and gear, a message without a "Fwd" prefix. The subject line read: "Heads up, Rocco."

Cavarra's nose had been broken and set crooked, way back in ancient history. That and his cauliflower ears inspired the "Rocco" nickname his old acquaintances still used, because he resembled hired Sicilian muscle from some Prohibition-era gang. He opened the message.

Commander Cavarra:
Possible job for you. Real work. Respond A.S.A.P.

It was from a National Security Agency desk jockey he met years ago when assigned to Fort Meade. They'd kept in touch, mostly by forwarding jokes to each other. The humorless tone of this message was noteworthy. Plus, nobody addressed Cavarra by rank these days.

He clicked on "reply," typed "Wazzup?" and clicked "send."

He stepped outside and crossed the back yard to the huge sheet metal shed which served as both warehouse and workshop. Seagulls called, a neighbor's dog barked and a semi truck horn dopplered by from the highway. The salt air and sound of crashing waves carried by the breeze reminded him of the muscles still aching from the laps and the underwater workout. They also reminded him of a hundred other beaches in a dozen different countries, which he'd ran or crawled or otherwise snuck inland from, usually at night and a couple times, when best laid plans got FUBARed, under hostile incoming fire.

Fort Meade, Maryland. Six years ago, when Cavarra was ordered to leave his command position and his beloved Pacific Ocean to play glorified secretary for the pseudo-civilian spooks there, he was not a happy camper. Now he looked back on the leisure time, booze, golf, and sharing of war stories fondly. Maybe college would have been that way, had he not gone to Annapolis. Meade was a pleasant epilogue to his career. In fact, he'd gladly trade this civilian atrophy for another tour in Spyland.

He sighed, entered the shed and began assembling orders for shipping.

The E-mail must be some sort of prank.

He filled orders on auto-pilot, packing boxes with Ching-Slings, brass-catchers, scope mounts and Skin-So-Soft. Then the suspense grew too much to bear. He marched back to the house and checked for new E-mail.

A response awaited him in his "in" box. Now he felt that familiar old thumping in his veins.

Keep a phone with you today.
You might be called soon.

3

2321 13 AUG 2002; MCLEAN, VIRGINIA USA
"LANGLEY"

The activity level at headquarters was higher approaching midnight than at most office buildings on a Monday morning. Lights burned from every window. The security officers were far too busy screening people to be in danger of falling asleep at their posts. Coffee pots were never washed out, it seemed; just refilled. This was normal, though, in the intelligence business.

Bobbie Yousko checked her hair as she stepped off the elevator. The Big Guy calling her in at this hour meant something reasonably important. And given the state of current events, Operation Hot Potato was the most likely topic.

Her flats clicked on the polished floor as she strode down the white, antiseptic corridor to her office. There was nothing on the outside of her door to suggest her room was in any way unique; but when she waved her key card at the lock and pushed the heavy door open, the clutter on display inside contradicted the methodically-earned image of an Agency planner. Drawings from her children, portraits of her husband and of her father in dress uniform surrounded an American flag pinned to the wall. A scale model of the cruiser her father once commanded rode waves of backlogged paperwork atop the scarred desk. Bobbie collected the decoded messages from Crypto, a small stack of dossiers and a DVD-ROM into her laptop bag, and hustled back into the hallway toward the Big Guy's suite.

"Sir?" she called, into the huge office.

"Come on in, B.Y.," the Big Guy said.

Being called "B.Y." was a good sign. If things were already ugly, the Big Guy would have called her Mrs. or Ms. Yousko.

Bobbie stepped in and saw that her colleagues were already seated, facing the Big Guy's desk. She nodded to them and they nodded back.

"Have a seat, B.Y."

Bobbie sat in the Hot Seat--the chair dead center, flanked by Wilson (Special Activities Division) and Boehm (the Sudan desk).

The nickname "Big Guy" was typical American humor. Eric Varney was short, thin, and frail-looking. His eyes were rheumy and skin so pale Bobbie wondered if he'd ever been outdoors in his life.

Now his desk...that was big. It reminded Bobbie of an aircraft carrier. And it was immaculate--everything perfectly arranged and polished to a sheen. Curiously, it didn't face the picture window but sat perpendicular to it. No big loss: the view looked over the parking lot.

"This is quite a situation we've got here, B.Y."

"Yes, sir."

"Normally I don't stick my nose into the business I've delegated," he lied, "but this is a bad situation. A bad one."

"It's been brewing for some time," Boehm said. "We had our chance to intercept most of those hot potatoes years ago--"

Varney glared and interrupted. "Thanks for sharing, but we need to deal with right now." He turned back to Bobbie. "I'm not trying to micro-manage, here, but I want a broad-brush concept of the operation."

Bobbie rose and pulled out the decoded messages.

"Current location of the hot potato," she said, handing him a message. "Satellite confirmed on Saturday." Before he had a chance to question the first one, she handed over the second. "Probable target—known hostile operatives have been evacuating, quietly but quickly."

Bobbie always dutifully passed intelligence up the ladder, but in this case there was no telling when Washington would make a decision, if they'd make the right decision, or if they'd make any decision at all. She had to sell her plan to Varney, here and now.

"Pentagon brass will lick their chops at a counter-terrorist opportunity like this," Varney said.

"Their first instinct will be to cover their own backsides," Boehm said.

"You know that 'safest alternative' mantra they sing down from the State Department," Wilson chimed in.

"Same mantra they kept singing for Vietnam," Boehm said. "Good thing Charlie didn't have nukes."

Varney let Boehm's cynical observation go unrebuked this time, perhaps because he considered criticism of any rival organization to be loyalty to himself and the Agency.

"Disaster is almost certain if we wait for the Pentagon, sir." Bobbie stepped over to the computer against the wall next to the refrigerator, jiggled the mouse to cut off the screen saver, and loaded her DVD. Boehm hurried to pull down the screen at the back of the office while Wilson turned on the overhead projector. They returned to their seats, rotating their chairs so they could all watch the screen. With a few key strokes and mouse clicks, Bobbie brought up the map.

"Our hot potato is inside this camp," Bobbie said. "Soft facility with hardened positions guarding all land approaches. Flat desert terrain, so they can spot an approach for miles in every direction."

She opened the MPEG of the satellite footage showing training in the camp. Dozens of people fluttered around the facility. "The man in charge here is Khaled Ali--*Fedayeen* veteran with probable thirteen hits and participation in multiple successful terrorist bombings and rocket attacks. No conventional military experience, but some combat in Lebanon and the West Bank. His alter ego, unofficially, is a Chinese arms broker, Jan Chin."

"Chin worked with the African National Congress for about nine years, off-and-on," Boehm said. "Lots of Cuban military advisors on the continent have relied on him for ordinance and equipment. Solid background in the People's Army slaughtering demonstrators in Tibet, so he's become a trusted advisor himself."

"Ali seems to respect his ideas," Bobbie said. "The training camp has been set up accordingly."

"The Sudanese People's Liberation Army has mustered about three hundred volunteers for us," Boehm said. "One of my guys is arranging transportation for them up into the northern Sudan. If they hit the camp from the land side with the element of surprise intact--"

"People's Liberation Army?" Varney interrupted.

"Rebels," Boehm said. "SPLA. Tough little guerrillas in the south. Seen their families raped, shot, gassed, burned, starved and what-have-you, but they're still resisting."

"You're saying a bunch of illiterate African banditos are going to save the day?" Varney asked. "They're probably no better than terrorists themselves. I'd hardly trust them with a nuke."

"We weren't finished, sir," Bobbie said, ignoring the prejudice of his remark. "The rebels would attack from the west. Ali is still acquiring a boat for transport, but he does have a couple speedboats here at the dock already. His probable contingency, if attacked in force, is to put the hot potato in the best craft available and escape into the Red Sea."

Wilson cleared his throat. "Bobbie and I have put together a team of shooters. All combat veterans. All but two served with our own armed forces. The long-and-short of it is, each of them is well-suited to the specifics of this mission. More so than if we'd simply designated a SpecOps team on active duty."

Varney cocked an eye at Wilson. "Why not a SOG team?"

"We're stretched too thin already," Wilson said. "And frankly, sir, this calls for a team that's expendable."

Varney sighed. "But these has-beens haven't been training together?"

"No." Bobbie shrugged to concede the point. "But we've recruited somebody I consider the right person to ramrod this outfit: Dwight Cavarra--SEAL with medals from Grenada, Panama and a whole jewelry box from the Gulf. Some experience in military intelligence over with the NSA. Annapolis grad. Retired for personal reasons as an O-five."

"Never heard of him," Varney said. "Did you get his name from Soggy?"

Bobbie shook her head. "Most of the vets with that much eggplant are busy flying desks for the company, or being hired as military experts for the news networks."

"This isn't because he's ex-Navy, is it?"

Bobbie reddened. Varney knew all about her proud Navy family. But she'd second-guessed herself already. "First people I thought of were ex-Army Rangers. But Cavarra's just as qualified for this kind of mission... and his personal leadership style is exactly what a team like this needs. I think he can get our ducks in a row in a couple of days. And this has to be done in a couple days, sir. I'd give us no more than a week."

"How about the mission itself?"

"As simple as can be: This team is provisional to the rebel force we mentioned..."

She paused the satellite footage and pointed at the still image.

"The hot potato is probably inside one of these structures, here. Our team is to insert into a blocking position here, between the dock and the camp, just before the main attack. Blow the boats and hold the dock until relieved by the rebel force."

"Extraction?"

Bobbie bit her lip, then said, "Those who survive will be folded into the main force and moved back into southern Sudan where we can pull them out quietly."

"What about the hot potato?"

"Bring it back here," Boehm suggested. "Show it to the Senate, and CNN."

"Honestly, sir," Bobbie said, "I don't know and don't much care. As long as we get it away from Ali, we can let Washington worry about what to do with it."

Varney pursed his lips. His gaze bounced around the room.

Wilson, Boehm and Bobbie all knew he was thinking about pulling the plug, just to make sure his own yellow carcass was safe from any potential backlash. But far more than a CIA pension was at stake here.

"If we don't act pronto," Wilson said, "the Israelis will deal with it their own way."

Boehm struggled to keep from adding, yeah, and they actually weigh national security as more important than their own careers. Instead, he said, "The FBI has been taking some heat for not anticipating the 911 attacks, sir."

"B.Y.," Varney said in that patronizing tone of his, "I'll trust your judgment. The Pentagon doesn't know what you're up to and I'll keep it that way because I don't know either. Do I?"

"No sir. I'm acting on my own initiative."

Varney turned to Boehm. "Who's in charge of your rebel rabble?"

"He's a local," Boehm said. "Been fighting in the civil war since he was thirteen. Lots of command experience. The men will follow him. He's conducted successful raids into--"

"Chop him," Varney said.

"Sir?"

"Tell him to take a hike. We don't want an idealist in charge--no telling what he'll do. Hire a mercenary. When money is the motive, the person's behavior will be nice and predictable. Compare what Executive Outcomes accomplished, compared to all those nappy-headed Angolans."

"Sir," Bobbie said, aghast, "we only have a week. We need somebody who can--"

"There's bound to be mercenaries in the region," Varney said. "Find one who speaks the language, with command experience, who needs money. Come on; use your head."

Bobbie, Boehm and Wilson stared at each other, eyebrows stretched taut.

"I'm feeling a little peaked," the Big Guy said. "I think I'll head down to the spa for a few days. It would be nice if you'd check in with me every couple hours or so."

4

0957 13 AUG 2002; LEUCADIA, CALIFORNIA USA

(At the quick-time.)
Hi-ho diddly-bop
Wish I was back on the block
With that discharge in my hand
I'm gonna be yo' lovin' man.
Re-up? You crazy.
Re-up? You outa' yo' mind!
Hi-ho diddly-bop...

Cavarra hustled through the house switching on the ringers to his various phones. He had no call-waiting or answering machine, voice mail or cell phone; nor did he desire the cursed contraptions. He called Melissa to ask if she could bring the kids to him this time.

"You said you were going to pick them up," she said, her tone ugly.

"Yes, and now I'm saying I need you to drop them off," he replied.

"Why?"

"I'm expecting a call."

Amazingly, she didn't make any scathing remarks about his parental deficiencies, his friends or the nameless bimbos she imagined him fooling around with. She sighed and said, "Fine. I'll bring them over now."

"Fine," he said.

The phone still hadn't rung by the time he heard the Minivan crunching the gravel on his driveway. He opened the front door to see his kids standing on the porch, but only got a glimpse of the back of Melissa's head as she sped away. Her hair was short and blonde again.

Justin wore sweatpants, a tank-top, and a sneer Cavarra had noticed becoming more and more commonplace. He all but ignored his father's greeting while sidestepping him into the house. Just the hint of a perfunctory nod.

Jasmine was in sweats also. She smiled and gave her father a hug. "How are you, Pumpkin?"

"I'm okay," she said. "Mom is mad at you."

What else is new, he thought. "You guys hungry?"

Both were dark like their father, but Justin had his mother's pale blue eyes. At fifteen he wasn't yet old enough to drive himself and his sister around, but he was capable of taking care of her in nearly every other way.

Justin made varsity in his sophomore year as a tailback who occasionally played tight end. He was a borderline phenomenon this year. Cavarra hadn't run quite as fast at Justin's age. The boy was good-looking, self-confident and respected by his peers, but still somewhat a loner. Cavarra guessed the sneer was more individualistic egomania than typical jock elitism.

At thirteen, Jasmine was already a knockout and very sweet-natured. Cavarra had mixed emotions about the tomboy phase she was going through. On the one hand, it might just be her trying to imitate her old man--and the baggy androgynous clothes hid her figure enough to maybe fend off attention from the wrong kind of boys. Still, she was a beautiful girl and Cavarra wished she would be proud of that.

They ordered a pizza delivery and had an XBox tournament in the living room while Jasmine filled him in on every detail of her life since he'd seen her last. Cavarra tried to pay attention, but kept glancing toward the nearest phone, willing it to ring.

After Justin trounced his father at *WWF Raw*, then was pummeled in turn playing *Mortal Kombat*, he began to lighten up a bit.

"Have you been practicing every day just so you could beat me?" Justin asked.

"You forget I beat you last time, too, punk," Cavarra replied.

"Yeah, one game...pure luck! And you've never beat me at the wrestling game."

He mussed Justin's hair. "And I probably never will. Wrestling is for phonies, anyway."

Justin rolled his eyes, but grinned. The old man was still cool, after all.

***

Butch called to see if Cavarra was up for racquetball. A potential customer called to check when Cavarra would be teaching his next class. He dismissed both abruptly, trying not to let his disappointment result in rudeness.

The third call was paydirt.

"May I speak with Mr. Cavarra?"

"Speaking."

"Dave over in Maryland gave me your number."

"Yeah." Cavarra's voice was calm, but his knuckles whitened around the receiver.

"I'd like to have an interview with you, if you're game."

"When?"

"I can be in San Diego in three hours."

"San Diego to here is another hour or so. There's a restaurant just down the road from me." Cavarra didn't want to go any farther than that, with the kids at his house.

"You understand that the utmost discretion is required."

"Roger that."

Cavarra gave him the name of the restaurant and they agreed to meet there in four hours.

"Who was that?" Jasmine asked.

"Grown-up stuff, Pumpkin," Cavarra said.

Justin's smile faded. "Are we going to war with Iraq, Dad?"

"What makes you ask that?"

"You have that look again. Are you coming out of retirement or something?

5

1102 13 AUG 2002; BEERSHEVA, ISRAEL
BEN ARRI KIBBUTZ

Yacov Dreizil was far from overweight, but his shirt and pants felt uncomfortably snug. Perhaps he was just spoiled from the bagginess of IDF fatigues. He'd considered buying some better fitting civilian clothes for the last few years, but a little discomfort seemed inadequate justification for a complete wardrobe overhaul.

Besides, the tight clothes--and the weight of his *Uzi* machine pistol--kept him from relaxing overmuch.

He left his jacket in the car but carried a newspaper, some film rolls and a box of print paper to the one-story house hiding amidst a grove of banana trees. Just an ordinary citizen with a harmless hobby about to spend a quiet afternoon developing and printing some amateur photos.

More eyes might be watching him than the friendly ones he knew of.

Once inside the house, he deposited the photographic materials in a locker. Dreizil was one of the few ever to enter the amateur darkroom at the Ben Arri Kibbutz. The dim, red-lit interior always alerted him that he was leaving the make-believe, fantasy world and entering the blood-tinged reality that few people knew existed. It reminded him he was not just some common Israeli Defense Forces reservist packing an automatic weapon.

The film-loading booth doubled as an elevator which took him down to one leg of the maze-like catacombs leading to the central bunker. He pulled at his harness until the Uzi was centered against his back--the clearance in the tunnel was tight. This exposed a sweat stain in the shape of the Uzi shoulder rig. He enjoyed the coolness of the wet pattern on his shirt, accentuated by the breeze of his movement. He strolled to the first checkpoint humming the theme from Get Smart.

He stopped and held up his identification badge when his progress was blocked by a mirror. The lights here were so bright he had to squint.

"Jawbone," crackled a flat voice from behind a pattern of holes in a chrome plate mounted flush in the mirror.

"Honey," he replied.

The mirror--actually a thick pane of ballistic one-way glass attached to a skeletal steel door--swung open. Dreizil escaped the blinding lights and the door swung to lock closed behind him. An IDF trooper in battle garb with a full-sized Uzi nodded at him from behind what looked like a concrete information desk from some spartan indoor shopping mall. The structure was half of an octagon in shape, each of the four sides facing a door identical to that through which Dreizil had just stepped.

The bored-looking trooper lifted a telephone receiver to his ear, nodded to the video camera and said, "Moab Widow Ninety-One. Cart to South Junction for personnel."

Dreizil blinked to speed his adjustment to the dimmer light and hopped up to sit on the concrete desk. He would have offered the trooper a cigarette, but he didn't smoke. In all probability, the trooper didn't smoke, either, or he might not have made it through the training for the elite unit from which he'd been recruited for this duty. Instead, Dreizil unfolded the current edition of *Haaretz* and slid it across the desk.

"Couple good cartoons," Dreizil said. "And the crossword is untouched."

The trooper eyed both Dreizil and the newspaper warily.

Dreizil made a waving gesture. "I'm not a snitch. This isn't a trap. I pulled this duty myself, once upon a time."

The trooper glanced up at the camera, now panning across the two-way mirror doors, grabbed the paper and spread it out on a shelf out of sight under the desk top. "Thank you, sir."

Dreizil waved carelessly again, and looked down at his hands. They were long, thin, dark and deceptively strong. But his cuticles were peeling, just like when he was a kid. He tore and gnawed at the skin with his teeth. What was it about active duty that put a stop to the peeling for three decades? Was it the no-frills diet or the constant friction of rappelling gloves and sand?

His fingers bled where the hangnails were the most obstinate. If caught in a nuclear, biological or chemical war, a battle wound wouldn't be necessary for him to be infected quickly. Stupid cuticles would peel; bad news would enter his bloodstream; game over.

An electric whine announced the arrival of his chauffeur--another trooper, driving a golf cart. Dreizil slid off the desk and hopped in the passenger seat.

"Where to, sir?" asked the driver.

"Central bunker. Command room."

"Yes, sir." They took off.

"Been a busy day," the driver said. "Busy week, actually."

Dreizil played dumb. "Has it?"

"Yes, sir. But I'll take busy over boring any day. You can only make a golf cart and a weapon so clean."

Dreizil chuckled. He made small talk with the driver en route to the next checkpoint. The driver hailed from the *Golanis* and Dreizil had cut his teeth in the 35th Paratroop Brigade. Having learned this about each other, some ingrained rivalry surfaced, hiding the mutual respect.

The narrow tunnel opened into a cavernous space where the roof domed up some forty feet overhead. Dreizil stepped off and the cart whizzed away with a polite goodbye from the driver.

Dreizil stood before a bunker of steel-reinforced concrete rising out of the floor, with an outer layer of sandbags and Claymore mines. Several IDF troopers sighted their weapons on him from inside.

"Clear your weapon and present!" rasped an NCO's voice. "Pistol grip up! Palms up! Fingers curled in!"

Dreizil obeyed. Two troopers climbed down to him. One covered him while the other took Dreizil's machine pistol and patted him down. They escorted him up the front of the bunker to where an iron hatch opened on top. They all climbed down through the hole, Dreizil first. His Uzi was placed beside other weapons on a rack while the NCO examined his I.D.

Dreizil repeated his destination and the sergeant assigned one of the troopers to escort him. Behind the bunker a heavy vault door opened after the proper protocol. Dreizil and his escort stepped through into a huge, brightly lit, noisy room bustling with men and women, all in uniform.

The trooper took him to General Dahav, who shook Dreizil's hand.

Dahav turned to the escort. "You're dismissed." The trooper saluted and left.

The command room swarmed with IDF brass. Dozens of radios hummed. Aides adjusted the position of symbols on the huge topographic maps. Rows of computers bleeped and clicked. Doors opened and shut in the soundproof booths buttressed up against the walls of the enormous chamber. The place had a plastic smell, almost like a toy store.

Dahav was tall, but unlike Dreizil, showed every strand of his European DNA: fair hair, fair skin, hazel eyes. Dreizil had inherited his mother's Sephardic looks--darker than the average Bedouin.

"All the command infrastructure in place?" Dreizil asked.

"We've got all we can spare down here for now," Dahav said. "Too much of the General Staff disappears from upstairs and...you know: Opsec."

Dreizil nodded. Opsec--Operational Security. The rank-and-file didn't yet need to know something big was brewing. And the world at large didn't need to know the Israeli High Command knew it.

"You won't be staying down here with us," Dahav said.

"Didn't think I would, sir." He was a field operative, after all.

"We know the target, and we know the staging area," Dahav said. "As of Monday, the Americans do, too."

"The plot thickens," Dreizil said.

"Yes. And it looks like they're going to make a move."

Dreizil thrust hands in pockets and squinted up at the clusters of floodlights.

"We're not standing down, Yacov. But we're going to let the Yanks take a shot at it."

"I've got reservations, sir."

"So do we all. At least it's not Jimmy or Willie or Al at the wheel over there."

"No," Dreizil agreed. "But neither is it Teddy Roosevelt or Dirty Harry." They could use an ally like that, on the verge of nuclear war. "This isn't a couple of Scud missiles we can laugh off for fear of alienating their precious Jew-hating 'allies'."

"None of us 'laughed' about the Scud attacks. And the Yanks did knock most of them down before they got to us. I know how you feel about them, Yacov. And I understand. We're not standing down, but we've got to let them try to resolve it their way. Who do we have on our side, once they are gone?"

"Only God."

"I'm not a religious fanatic, Yacov. And I know you are not."

Dreizil nodded and shrugged, with a fatalism second-nature to so many men who visited this facility. "Are they going full-tilt?"

General Dahav's gaze dropped as he shook his head.

Dreizil made a sound that might have been a sardonic laugh or a disgusted scoff. "Of course not. They are Americans, after all."

"Looks like they're going to farm it out," Dahav said. "And that's where you come in, Colonel Dreizil."

6

1440 13 AUG 2002; LEUCADIA, CALIFORNIA USA

(At a double-time.)
Singin' one, two, three, four...
Somebody, anybody, start a war...

Cavarra felt confident the Mexican restaurant was safe, but he performed a cursory check around the table anyway. Then he sat back and waited, watching the front door. Business was slow, so the nearest patrons to this table were on the other side of the room, partially hidden by the mock-up adobe oven on the bandstand.

He searched for faces that might match the voice on the phone. He'd been able to tell undercover cops from normal civilians since his early adulthood. And the intelligence people he'd rubbed elbows with in Maryland fit a stereotype, too. Cavarra wondered if a field agent could conceal that straight-edge nature enough to fool him.

The spook spotted him before he spotted the spook. Maybe because there were pictures of Commander Dwight Cavarra, United States Navy, retired, in their files. Maybe because a former SEAL was just as easy to spot as a plainclothes cop, to an experienced eye.

The spook was lightly tanned with auburn hair bleached blond in streaks. He had a ponytail, goatee and pierced ears, and wore one of those expensive suits with shorts. About as Californian as should be legal to dress.

"Is the table clean?" asked the CIA man, whipping out a cellphone, punching buttons.

"I didn't find anything," Cavarra said.

The agent ignored his answer and watched the screen of his "cellphone" until he was satisfied. He set the device on the table and punched a few more buttons. No bugs in the immediate area.

"Kurt Hendricks," the spook said. "Let's order."

Hendricks got the waitress' attention by snapping his fingers like he owned the place. She brought tortilla chips, dip, *sopapillas* and a bottle of honey. Hendricks ordered a basket of *flautas* and Cavarra chose *chili rellenos*.

"Are your children with their mother?" Hendricks asked, after the waitress disappeared.

Cavarra nodded. Justin could take care of his little sister, but that was nobody's business. And the boy knew who to call if anything happened.

Hendricks tilted his head slightly. "You waited 'til late in life to have kids, didn't you?"

"Late twenties," Cavarra said. "A junior officer doesn't have a lot of time to chase girls and start a family. Not in the Teams."

"Even at that, it often doesn't work out, does it?"

Cavarra let the comment go.

Is he getting personal just to irritate me? Why?

Hendricks didn't shrug, but wore an expression that should accompany one. "Have you kept in shape?"

Cavarra hesitated. Not because he wasn't in shape--racquetball kept his feet tough, he swam laps five days a week and went diving nearly every weekend. He hesitated because the words were spoken in Arabic.

"Better shape than most eighteen-year-olds," he said, in Arabic.

Hendricks raised an eyebrow. "You've kept up your languages."

Cavarra had kept in practice, probably for the same reason he stayed in shape: Because he nursed a secret fantasy that some day a meeting like this would take place.

"Let's switch to Italian," Hendricks said, in that language. "I doubt our waitress speaks it."

"No problem," Cavarra said, in national Italian.

"Why did you choose to retire after only twenty years?"

"I figured my career in Hollywood had been on hold long enough."

Hendrix didn't even have the decency to smile at his razor wit. "Did your wife appreciate it?"

It was hard to say which irked Cavarra worse--Hendricks' question, or the piercing look in his eyes as he asked it. The creep was practically smirking.

Cavarra let out a deep breath and measured his response. *It's only natural for them to examine my background and motivations.*

Standard Operating Procedure. He swallowed his pride and answered honestly: "I thought she would appreciate it. But it turns out nothing I could do would please her--even retiring early to play Mr. Mom. Or maybe it was too late by then."

"You abandoned your career for her," Hendricks said, "and ultimately, she left you anyway. How did that make you feel?"

"What are you, a psychoanalyst?"

Hendricks ignored the remark. "After your divorce, it looks like you started hanging out again with the kind of men you knew in the Navy. Opened a 'tactical shooting school' for civilians. Became a dealer in ammunition and paramilitary equipment."

Cavarra dipped a chip in the sauce and took a crunchy bite. "I guess you can take a man out of the SEALs, but you can't take the SEAL out of the man."

"Have you ever done business with domestic terrorists?"

Cavarra's face contorted. "What?"

Hendricks eyeballed him like a teacher who knew a pupil was cheating. "You deny that you sell military gear to right-wing extremists, or train them at your shooting school?"

"Not that it's any business of yours, or your boss's, but some of the guys I know do have some radical political ideas. But you know doom-well they aren't terrorists." Cavarra's voice dripped with disgust at the accusation.

"Doom?" Hendricks echoed. "You said 'doom,' not 'damn'."

"I'm impressed by your attention to detail. Want me to draw you a happy-face?"

Hendricks held Cavarra's glare without blinking.

After a long, uncomfortable silence, Cavarra dipped another tortilla chip. "I thought this was about a job, not my personal life. Do you have work for me or not?"

Hendricks wasn't quite ready to let go. Almost like he knew how desperately Cavarra yearned for an old-school operation. "How familiar are you with their 'radical politics'?"

Cavarra rolled his eyes. He didn't see how this was necessary. "They believe in freedom of speech, freedom of religion, the right to bear arms... You know: the same stuff Jefferson, Madison and all those 'right-wing extremists' did. Those guys even put their radical ideas in writing, by the way—the original's in a glass case in DC. Maybe you oughta read it some time."

"Those same ideas have motivated some people to bomb government buildings and shoot at federal agents. In my book that makes your buddies potential revolutionaries." He squirted some honey into a sopapilla.

Cavarra stared at Hendricks for almost a full minute before saying anything. "You look like a potential child molester to me. Is somebody keeping tabs on you?"

"So you're a sympathizer, then?"

"To be honest, Mr. GQ Secret Policeman: Coming face to face with your attitude, they seem less and less like paranoid whackos every time you open your mouth."

This time Cavarra stared him down.

Hendricks smiled and hunched his shoulders. "We're actually just as concerned about domestic terrorism as we are with another Middle East-sponsored threat. I had to be sure where your loyalties lie. It's S.O.P."

"Are you sure now?"

"Nothing personal, Commander. You'll see how it's relevant in a minute."

The waitress returned with their orders and winked at Cavarra.

Roberta had flirted with him a few times...enough to know his full name, ethnic background and marital status. She was pretty, seemed to be both sensible and nice, but was probably too young for him. She must have sensed the importance of the conversation with Hendricks, because she offered nothing extra beyond the wink. Cavarra smiled at her, then unwrapped his utensils and tucked the napkin in his shirt. Roberta sashayed back to the kitchen.

Hendricks' voice dropped to a calm, discreet volume. "Since the collapse of the Soviet Union, control has been split in two. The Russian Mafia--formerly known as the KGB--runs the show in Russia, the Ukraine and Belarus. The southern states are under Muslim government."

Cavarra knew this, but listened anyway, relieved that the subject had finally changed to business. He chewed his first mouthful of rellenos... then reached for the sopapillas. The chili was hotter than usual today and he needed something to absorb part of the fire.

"All those governments are broke," Hendricks said. "Plenty of weapons; no money or food. Thanks to the increased American aid, they've been deploying approximately three new *Topol-M* sixth-generation ballistic missiles every month, and building Typhoon Class nuclear attack submarines non-stop."

Cavarra frowned. He gulped down some icewater while his brain calculated. The US had built its last MX over ten years ago. The Clinton administration had scuttled the US ballistic missile defense program while simultaneously replacing the "launch on warning" doctrine with "sustain a first strike," then neutered the most potent American counterstrike assets: attack subs and bombers. *So the money we've saved by gutting defense is being given to people who'd rather starve than miss the chance to amass more strategic weapons than the rest of the world combined. Makes as much sense as throwing away the Panama Canal.*

"Their Moslem brothers in the Middle East, however," Hendricks said, "have all kinds of money, but no nuclear weapons. At least they didn't before the status quo was disrupted."

Cavarra rolled his eyes and shoveled in another mouthful of tasty napalm.

"An awful lot of deliverable megatonnage has been unaccounted for in those former Soviet states over the last several years--even though their arms production has remained at Cold War levels. And what most people don't realize about nuclear warheads is that they have a limited shelf life. American warheads are good for maybe twenty-five years. But if you have a brand-new Soviet warhead, you've got about seven years to use it before it becomes ineffective."

Hendricks paused to gulp down some flautas. "Among the weapons we know to be missing are eighty-four suitcase-sized atomic warheads. Each one of them could destroy a city if detonated above ground level. What the blast doesn't incinerate, the fallout will poison. Perfect terrorist weapon...if the terrorist is willing to commit suicide."

Cavarra had watched footage of passenger jets hitting the Twin Towers over and over and over again. He'd been surprised there were no WMDs aboard either plane. "How old are those missing suitcase nukes?"

"Some of them are coming up on seven years old," Hendricks said. He let that sink in before continuing. "There's a high probability that some have already been placed in key US locations."

Cavarra's eyes narrowed and his jaw muscles bunched up.

"Saturday a field agent saw one of these devices being transported. We're confident it is now located inside a terrorist training encampment north of *Hala'ib* in the Sudan. Yesterday, several known and suspected *Hamas, Hezbollah* and other Islamic terrorist cells began evacuating *Tel Aviv*."

"Tel Aviv? Israel?"

Hendricks glanced around the room, then nodded. "Transport will probably be a small boat. Fishing trawler, maybe. We suspect they've already bribed their safe passage through the Suez Canal. From there a short trip up the Mediterranean, dock in Tel Aviv, move the bomb inland on foot or by car and detonate."

"Why Tel Aviv?"

"You mean besides the fact that these guys love to kill Jews?"

Even more than they love killing Americans--I know that, pencil-neck. "I mean why, strategically?"

"Jerusalem is out of the question. It's sacred to the Moslems as well as the Jews and Christians. But Tel Aviv used to be the Israeli capital and is their largest city, so it has symbolic value. And our embassy is still located there. It's a win-win situation for radical Islam. It starts an Arab-Israeli war no matter what. If the US supports Israel, Dubya's coalition against Iraq falls apart. In fact, the whole Muslim world might unite to turn on us, at that point. You think our economy is unstable now? Wait 'til gas is fifty bucks a gallon. They can do that without setting off any nukes in our country--should they be disposed to show such restraint. They destroy the US, and Israel is fresh out of allies."

The potent fumes of his entree now had Cavarra's nose running. He pinched it with the napkin.

"Or the US opts to hold the coalition together," Hendricks said, "and turns against Israel when they retaliate. Either way, Israel's enemies get their way."

"Why not let the Israelis beat the stink out of them," Cavarra said. "While they're making greasy spots in the sand, we put Saddam down for good this time, along with every cutthroat pimp government that takes his side. We could sustain ourselves twenty times over if we'd use some of the oil up in Alaska."

Hendricks looked as though he'd just caught whiff of a pungent odor. "I doubt that's ever going to happen."

"Then let the Israelis intercept the boat and deal with it."

"Our current peacekeeping policy forbids aggressive patrols by the Israeli Navy. In a nutshell, it prevents aggressive patrolling by our own Navy around the Suez, as well."

"That's just great."

"An *Entebbe*-style raid by Israeli forces in Muslim Sudan could just as easily touch off the powder keg over there. Sudan is considered a neutral, and there are no sympathetic hostages."

"There's no such thing as a neutral Muslim nation."

"You made a great commando, Cavarra, but you'd never cut it as a policy maker. Our government wants to forge a strategic partnership with the Sudan, once Iraq is dealt with. The bottom line is this: Somebody needs to defuse this situation before the Israelis do it, or all hell breaks loose. With a nuclear threat facing their country, they're not going to walk on eggshells. US sanctions, UN condemnation and world opinion all lose their relevance once Tel Aviv is a radioactive parking lot."

Cavarra cleared his throat. "Which team would I be going in with?"

Hendricks searched Cavarra's eyes, then forced a phony smile meant, probably, to soften the blow. "You won't be going in with a SEAL team. You're not being called up."

"What?"

"There's no time to get UN permission for a SpecOps insertion. Israel could be blown to hell and gone before they'd agree to it...if then. We're asking for volunteers. Arms, equipment, transportation and intel will all be provided. Lump sum payments will be arranged. But once you hit the ground over there, you're mostly on your own. If killed or captured, we've never heard of you. Me and my beer buddies will trade theories about what that old has-been Cavarra was doing way over in East Africa. That's if enough pieces are found to identify your body."

7

0124 14 AUG 2002; MIRAMAR NAVAL AIR STATION, CALIFORNIA USA

(At the quick-time.)
Around the block, she pushed the baby carriage
She pushed it in the springtime, in the merry month of May.
And if you ask her why she pushed the carriage
She pushed it for her Navy SEAL, far, far away.

Cavarra smiled to himself when the smell of tarmac, still blazing-hot from the day, filled his nostrils once again. He carried his stuffed sea bag across the field to the waiting aircraft. It was a small turboprop utility plane, normally used to shuttle flag officers hither and yon for tea parties or golf matches crucial to national security.

A haggard sailor pushed the steps up to the cargo door and opened it for him. Cavarra entered, stowed his bag, sat down and buckled up.

He knew Melissa would have pitched a fit if he'd asked her to pick up the kids, especially after making her drop them off. So he'd tucked Jasmine in, went over the shotgun, emergency phone numbers and so forth with Justin, and told him to call his mother the next day to come pick them up. He checked the fridge and cupboards to ensure there was plenty of food, and left some cash just in case. He'd deal with their mother when he got back.

If he got back.

Cavarra was tired, but decided to wait until the plane was at altitude and his ears had quit popping before racking out. Instead, while the air crew went through the pre-flight, he looked over the files Hendricks had given him.

Sudan was the largest nation in Africa. Mountain ranges lined the eastern and western borders, with mostly featureless plains in between. In the north, savannah dried out into desert approaching the Egyptian border. Rain fell nine months out of the average year in the tropical south, which boasted the world's largest swamp: the *As Sudd*. This year, however, *El Nino`* had brought droughts upon the mostly agricultural region.

Sudan's most profitable natural resource was oil.

The population was predominantly black in the south, Arabic in the north. Islam was the state religion and Arabic the official language, but many blacks were Christians who spoke English, while others spoke tribal languages or practiced tribal religions.

Sudan gained independence from Britain and Egypt in 1956, but suffered civil wars repeatedly up to the present. The twenty-year conflict still raging now pitted Islam against all non-Moslems.

Since the mid-1990s, Saddam Hussein had been hiding stockpiles of chemical and biological weapons in the Sudan, with Khartoum's unofficial blessing. The Sudanese Army sometimes used these weapons against the blacks in the South.

Egypt disputed ownership of the Hala'ib Triangle with Sudan. By letting Khaled Ali run his camp inside this demilitarized zone, the Sudanese could plead ignorance if any Western nation made an issue of it.

Sudan hosted an estimated thirty terrorist training camps like Ali's. Whether Khartoum knew about the hot potato or not, Cavarra wasn't told; but its placement in the Hala'ib Triangle suggested complicity.

Typical Washington pussyfooting around meant the most effective assets wouldn't be employed: DEVGRU/SEAL Team Six, Delta Force... or a Ranger Battalion if they really wanted to stomp it flat. The dossiers Cavarra held represented what CIA brass considered the next best thing: Ten has-beens and two never-weres.

His second time through the photos, Cavarra realized every Swinging Richard in this unit was either black or could pass for an Arab. Good: they shouldn't draw undue attention by appearance alone. Two were Navy Special Warfare vets. One was a former SeaBee--the Navy's version of a combat engineer. Three were ex-Special Forces, which was fortunate--Green Berets were highly cross-trained in combat fieldcraft and fluent in at least one foreign language. Two were Force Recon vets, which was also welcome news--marines were trained as infantry before moving on to their primary specialty; and as reconnaissance scouts, their stealth and navigational skills should be finely honed. Two were decorated snipers from Desert Storm. Two were mercenaries.

Come to think of it, it could be argued that all of them were mercenaries, now.

One has-been was none other than Zeke the Greek: Chief Petty Officer Ezekiel Pappadakis from the Special Boat Squadrons and the only man of the twelve Cavarra knew. They'd eaten some of the same sand at Grenada, Panama and the Gulf. Zeke was intelligent, dependable and admired by peers and subordinates alike.

Pablo Fava-Vargas was a Puerto Rican ex-SEAL from Team Two. Cavarra had never met him--Teams Two, Four and Six worked out of Virginia, while odd-number Teams were headquartered on the West Coast. Fava-Vargas became a SEAL between Blue Spoon and Desert Storm, when Cavarra took over Team One and finally returned to California. Fava-Vargas was highly decorated for his work in the Gulf, but left the Navy during the Clinton years. He had children, and was currently working on a masters degree in psychology.

Two of the three marines resumed civilian life ahead of schedule by way of the Uniform Code of Military Justice. Both had a history of alcohol abuse and one had a violent streak displayed under inappropriate circumstances one time too many. This didn't bother Cavarra too much--the best men to have in combat were often the worst to have in peacetime.

His team included a bona fide Shawnee brave, complete with authentic Native American name: Tommy Scarred Wolf. Cavarra pictured a wolf with scars festooning its head and body--from a ferocious fight with another wolf, probably--prowling outside a river camp where the Green Beret's great-grandfather was born. Cavarra had wanted to hold off naming his own son until he'd had a chance to observe some personality traits: Indian-style. But Melissa and everyone else considered this notion ridiculous. It simply wasn't done in civilized society.

The guys with cool names usually turned out to be wimps, morons or queers, anyway.

Cavarra spent extra time examining the dossier of the African mercenary. His nationality was listed as Sudanese, but he'd worked all over Africa, it seemed, including Angola, Sierra Leone, Chad, Rwanda, Somalia and Sudan. Those countries had seen some heavy action, so his experience could be extensive. The widespread demand for that experience might indicate that this merc was something special and not a "never-was" after all.

The American merc had a lot of baggage stamps, too, but mostly from "warm" spots with low-intensity conflicts. A Lebanese mother had passed down fluency in Arabic, plus the brown eyes and dark skin to qualify for this crew.

A third mercenary would lead a small Sudanese rebel force in a conventional attack on the terrorist camp. To Cavarra that meant an under-trained, undisciplined, poorly-motivated gaggle led by some wannabe with questionable integrity and motives.

Just before the Sudanese mob hit the target, Cavarra and his freshly-slapped-together squad were to infiltrate, take the dock, blow the boats and prevent anyone's escape with the hot potato. They'd be surrounded immediately and if the rebel attack didn't commence on time, every hostile in the camp would be on top of them. If the attack did come on time, the rebels might very well break and run upon encountering disciplined fire. But even assuming the assault was successful and the rebels pushed the hostiles into the sea, Cavarra's unit would be caught between hammer and anvil. If cornered terrorists didn't wipe them out, friendly fire might.

Only a maniac would volunteer to lead such an ate-up operation.

Or a has-been Special Operator.

Some part of Cavarra had always wanted a mission like this, though he'd prefer to undertake it with men he'd trained with for years.

Hendricks had been satisfied after Cavarra endured some vaccinations and a quick physical exam at a discreet location with an Agency physician. Then it was Cavarra's turn to get answers.

He got the personal compensation arrangements out of the way first. Then insurance coverage--he insisted Melissa and the kids be adequately taken care of should he never make it back. He made sure the men under him had been properly inoculated. He probed Hendricks about medivac and health contingencies. He hammered out the duration of the assignment, and transportation--both in-country and back to the States. He demanded, and received, a blank check for weapons, ammo, maps, equipment and food. He haggled over some finer details, then signed some papers and drove to his waiting plane.

Cavarra rejected the plan, as conceived by the CIA, from the very beginning. The bottom line was to prevent the terrorists from escaping with the nuke. To accomplish that without assuming his men to be expendable was the challenge.

The aircraft engines whined to life. The plane taxied, got clearance and lifted into the night sky. When they reached altitude, Cavarra leaned his seat back and closed his eyes.

Thousands of miles of land and ocean passed by underneath him.

***

Cavarra awakened twice: Once when the plane landed to refuel and change crews, and again to transfer from the US Navy craft to a smaller civilian seaplane.

When Cavarra stepped outside during the second stop, he almost got his feet wet. Around him was deep water in every direction. The distant sound of breakers teased his engine-numbed ears. He breathed deeply. Saltwater. The two planes were on an island...no, more like a sandbar--barely large enough to serve as an airstrip. He shook his head. Only a Navy pilot could bring a fixed-wing bird down safely on a sprinkle of dust like this.

He climbed into the seaplane. The pilot scowled at Cavarra's sea bag. "How much does that thing weigh?" He spoke with a New England accent, but was dressed in civvies and his hair was too long for any branch but the Air Force, if that. CIA, most likely.

"Maybe a hundred. Probably less."

"It better be less," the pilot said. "This is Gonna be hairy enough as is."

"Why's that?"

"Our refuel is at just about the maximum range for this crate."

Cavarra grinned and slapped him on the shoulder. "We can save some gas on takeoff: I'll steer, you push."

The pilot rolled his eyes and looked disgusted.

"So where are we, anyway?"

"In an airplane," replied the pilot.

Cavarra buckled his seat belt, dripping sweat. The heat was murderous.

The sea plane struggled to lift out of the ground swell, then leveled off at 150 feet.

Cavarra watched the plane's progress with one eye while reviewing the files with the other.

Dry land slid under them, but the plane kept low. Either they were staying under someone's radar or the pilot flew choppers in Vietnam. Green vegetation along the coast thinned out inland and finally gave way to desert.

"So where are we?" Cavarra repeated.

The pilot looked irritated. "Africa. That is what you signed up for, isn't it?"

"Africa's a pretty fair-sized piece of ground. It's sectioned off into smaller parts some people call 'countries.' I was wondering which one we're flying over."

"When you get off this plane you'll be where you need to be."

***

With too much time to think, Cavarra's mind drifted back to home.

After Panama Melissa begged Cavarra to take some cushy rear-echelon *pogue* assignment. He thought she'd gone crazy. His work in Panama earned him a crack at a command slot in the Teams. She wanted him to fritter the opportunity away in order to give her quality time.

Justin was only three when Saddam Hussein invaded Kuwait. Age three was about when a person started storing long-term memories, so the boy's earliest recollection could very well be of his father leaving him. Of course he couldn't have understood the reasons or the risks at the time, but certainly he felt the ominous vibes.

Looking back, Cavarra saw how selfish he'd been. The regular military was hard enough on marriages. An operator had no business starting a family.

Melissa never forgave him for that last combat deployment; for leaving her with Justin and baby Jasmine, flying halfway around the world to kill people and break things...and possibly be killed himself.

Cavarra thought his early retirement would make up for his previous mistakes, but by that time Melissa's heart was hardened and cold. She'd not only learned how to live without him, but seemed to prefer it. She discovered other men not only found her desirable, but showed it in ways Cavarra hadn't.

Other men also had a lot more time on their hands than her husband. Until he retired. Then his constant presence around the house only irritated her.

She got even with him--disappearing all day every day, leaving him alone with the kids. When she did spend time with him, it was only to complain or drop hints that he didn't light her fire anymore. Then he caught her lying about her whereabouts and activities.

The marriage fell apart. Jasmine seemed to be well-adjusted, for her age, but Justin had some issues. And here Cavarra was running off around the world again to put himself in harm's way.

Moth to a flame.

He'd examined his reasoning thousands of times and couldn't justify his lust for the warrior's life.

In time the heat and monotony got to Cavarra. He dozed off.

He awoke to the sound of the pilot cursing at the fuel gauge.

He rubbed his eyes and took a look around. The fuel tanks were almost empty and below them were some rough-looking mountains.

"Is it gonna be close?"

The pilot nodded. "Your adventure might be starting early."

Cavarra scanned the horizon for a flat surface to ditch on, seeing nothing that didn't appear fatal. Then a blue finger appeared between two mountain peaks. As they grew closer, the hills separated farther and beckoned them to a fat, calm lake just beyond.

"We can set down there, right?"

"That's our refuel spot," the pilot said.

Water was always welcome to Cavarra, so he felt home free. But the pilot didn't relax until his plane's pontoons began skidding along the surface of the lake.

When the engine stopped and the plane slowed to the speed of the prevailing wind, they spotted a heavy-laden flat-bottom boat chugging toward them from a far-off bank. On board were two thin African boys and a huge stack of jerry cans.

The boys helped the pilot refuel his plane, then he tipped them with canned goods and a pack of American cigarettes each. The most cost-efficient workers on the CIA payroll, Cavarra mused. They restacked the now-empty jerry cans in the boat and steered back for the shore.

Relieved now, the pilot got them aloft once again.

This leg of the journey was far shorter. The plane landed on a river so wide, it must have been a branch of the Nile. The pilot kept the engines running and used the propellers to pull them along the water to a dock projecting from an ugly city.

Even from a distance, Cavarra could see most of the buildings were in sad shape: Shattered windows, entire outer walls missing from apartment buildings...figures moving about in the cutaway rooms. The air stunk of garbage, rot, urine, feces and death. Dead animals and heaps of rubbish floated along the river downstream from the city. Groups of children played in that same water, oblivious to the filth floating by.

On the dock stood a black man in loose-fitting print cloth of an orange-dominated pattern. He helped Cavarra get his bag unloaded and extended his hand to steady Cavarra as he disembarked.

No sooner had Cavarra planted his feet on the dock than the door of the plane slammed shut and the engines throttled up. He turned and watched the sea plane turn, taxi and take off back in the direction they'd come from.

"Pilot's about a unfriendly mug," the man on the dock said, in what sounded like a Detroit accent. "Almost like he don't wanna stay here on the dark continent, huh?"

8

1805 14 AUG 2002; BOR, SUDAN

(At a double-time.)
Well, me and Superman had a fight
I smacked him in the head with kryptonite.
Busted his skull and pulped his brain
Now guess who's datin' Lois Lane?
Me and Batman had a fight too
His puny fists against my 7.62.
Riddled his body with lead and steel
Now guess who's drivin' the Batmobile?

Cavarra chuckled and slung his sea bag over one shoulder. "I thought it was my company he didn't like."

The terrain along both banks of the river was lined with exotic trees and tropical vegetation. Just beyond it was elephant grass as far as the eye could see--except east and south, where mountains broke up the horizon, and directly in front of Cavarra, where the dingy city of *Bor* marred the landscape.

"Welcome to the Sudan, Johnny Rambo," the man said. "Name's James--I'm your guardian angel. Call me 'Mugabe' when we're around locals."

"I'll just get in the habit starting now, Mugabe," Cavarra said. "Do you have the weapons I ordered?"

"Supposed to come in today. You know you only got twelve men, right?"

"Yup."

"Why all the extra artillery?"

"Mission specific."

Mugabe started walking. Cavarra followed him off the dock to dry land, then along a trail towards a reeking slum of mostly ramshackle huts with a few permanent-looking, stark block buildings thrown in.

They hopped in a black Dodge Ramcharger with water buffalo horns mounted to the hood. They left foul-smelling Bor and rolled down a rough country road through a vast expanse of grassland, spotted with blackened patches of scorched earth.

"What happened out there?" Cavarra asked, pointing at the burnt fields.

"Government troops burn the crops just before harvest," Mugabe said. "Infidels don't deserve to eat. Savvy?"

"How much of my crew is here, so far?" Cavarra asked.

"All present," Mugabe replied. "Some only been here a matter of hours, some longer. Brought in a few by the river on airboats, some overland by truck."

Several miles out of Bor they came upon a village. Mugabe steered them in between the mud huts and dilapidated tin and cardboard shacks. Malnourished children stared at them curiously as they passed. Some skinny adults whispered to each other.

"They dress nice enough," Cavarra said. One might expect residents of a place like this to wear tattered rags or something, but the women wore colorful dresses and the men nice shirts and slacks.

"Peeps here dress like this every day," Mugabe said. "What they wearin' right now is the only clothes most of 'em have."

"'Peeps'?" Glancing sideways, Cavarra imagined a tongue-sized dent in Mugabe's cheek. If he'd been in-country for any time at all, Mugabe should have lost the ghetto edge on his Ebonics. That it was still so pronounced when speaking English suggested self-parody.

The village was considerably cleaner than Bor, although half-wrecked recently, by the look of most of the huts.

Mugabe drove through the dirt streets to a church building that looked like it had been through a siege. Cavarra recognized bullet scars all over the brick. All the wood was fire-blackened, the windows broken and smoke-stained.

"What's this?"

"Your crib, for now--just call it Fort Rambo." Mugabe killed the motor, got out and strolled up to the front door. A pair of lazy brown eyes scrutinized them through a jagged hole where a burst of bullets had splintered through the wood.

Mugabe clapped Cavarra on the shoulder and said, "Here's da

man, fellahs."

The eyes stared hard at Cavarra. The door opened and Mugabe led the way in.

Cavarra stepped inside the vestibule and the door shut behind him. The interior of the building was lit with kerosene lamps. The plaster of the inner walls was cracked and pockmarked, and there appeared to be large blood stains on the floor. The man who opened the door was a tall, lanky black man Cavarra recognized from the photograph as Leon Campbell, one of his snipers.

Other men crowded into the room. "Fellahs," Mugabe said, "this here's Johnny Rambo Number-One. Your Commanding Officer from here on out."

Cavarra turned to Mugabe. "I need a word with you in private."

Mugabe nodded.

"Who's covering the back?" Cavarra asked.

"There's no window in back," someone said.

"Is there a door?"

A few men mumbled in the affirmative.

"Well, I want someone covering it. I also want a body at those windows on either side. I'll be busy for a few minutes. When I come back, I want it squared away. Then we'll break the ice."

Without waiting for a response, Cavarra walked into the worship area. In the dim light several pairs of eyes measured him, sizing him up as if they might have to fight him. It was something rough men from rough outfits did, and it could be unnerving.

Pews were overturned, shot and blown to pieces. The place reeked of old cordite. The floor was splotched dark brown with dried blood. Cavarra paused for a moment and Mugabe took the lead. Cavarra fell in step behind him and they made their way to the room behind the baptismal chamber.

Blood splatters decorated this area, too. Mugabe shut the door behind them and sat on a crate of charred bibles. "Private enough for you?"

"What happened here?" Cavarra asked, seating himself on a stepladder.

"There's a civil war goin' on here, Rambo."

"Yeah, no kidding. But this is a church."

Mugabe looked surprised at his naïveté. "Christianity's illegal. And here these folks had the audacity to practice it right out in the open in a big, fancy building. That's like showin' your hiney to Khartoum."

"Were these people armed? Did they resist?"

"They weren't armed, but I guess you could say they resisted. They didn't submit to Allah, now did they?"

Cavarra reached over to the wall and scratched at the dried blood with his thumbnail.

"Sudanese who practice tribal religions are the ones take up arms against the government," Mugabe said. "But most of the Christians are pacifists. The preacher here got hisself crucified--literally."

Cavarra decided he was naive, after all, and shook the impertinent thoughts from his head. "This building is un-sat. We need to get out of this town and secure an area out in the boonies."

"That'd draw attention, Johnny. Set up some tents out in the swamp, bunch of you corn-fed boys dittyboppin' around with weapons and gear--that looks too much like a SPLA operation. Save that for when you make your rendezvous with the rest of the posse."

"We got civilians crawling all over the place outside," Cavarra said. "We can't observe all the avenues of approach from here, and I don't have enough men to cover the entire town. Where's the main force holed up?"

"Can't tell you that. They don't know where you are, either. Opsec. You were briefed on where you be linkin' up, though."

Cavarra sighed.

"Look," Mugabe said, "nobody comes here, anymore. The other folks in town don't trust the government, so they ain't gonna drop the dime on y'all."

"Where can I find you?"

Mugabe laughed. "I get around too much for you to find me. But I be checkin' on you. Like I said, the weapons and gear should come in today. I'll holler at you then."

Mugabe rose and left. Cavarra breathed deep and remained seated while consulting his small spiral notebook. He had an overwhelming amount of tasks to accomplish in a short time, so he needed a moment to prioritize.

Cavarra reentered the main room of the church after a few minutes. Before he could say anything, a short, somewhat overweight man with a fat nose and crooked teeth approached and saluted.

"How you been, sir?"

Cavarra returned the salute instinctively, then extended his hand. "Hiya, Zeke. Long time, no see. How's civilian life?"

Zeke Pappadakis shook hands, then patted his beer belly. "A little too good, Rocco."

"I hope you're still sharp up here." Cavarra said, pointing to his temple.

"Sharp as a marble, sir."

"You can knock off the 'sir' garbage, Zeke. The buck stops here and I say forget the dumb stuff. Is the spook-puke gone?"

"Yeah. It's just us, now."

Campbell was still at the front door, and men were at each side, looking out the windows. Others gathered around facing Cavarra. "Who's got the back?" he called out, loudly.

"That'd be me!" a voice drawled back.

Cavarra looked over the men around him, matching the faces with the photos he'd seen. They all studied him the way wolves must eyeball new additions to the pack. They looked for signs of weakness, sure there must be some--visible or not. He almost had to fan the air to see through the testosterone cloud.

"Can you hear me back there?" he asked, toward the unseen man at the back door.

"Ooh-rah!"

"I'm Dwight Cavarra, and I'll be your C.O. for this operation. How much have you been told about what we're doing?"

Nobody said anything, so Cavarra pointed at tall, skinny Fava-Vargas, who had been singing an Enrique Iglesias song when Cavarra entered the room. "What do you know about it?"

Fava-Vargas widened his eyes and contorted his mouth. "We're supposed to insert into a terrorist camp and steal a bomb. That's all I was told."

Cavarra looked around. Everybody nodded. That's all anyone had been told.

"Mr. Mugabe's bosses have formulated a plan, but I think we're going to do it a little different," Cavarra said. "I'll give you a warning order tomorrow morning, most likely." He leaned back against the arm of a still-intact pew. "We don't have much time, so we're Gonna have to do a lot of stuff simultaneously, and I won't have time to explain every little thing. This isn't a regular military unit, obviously. I'm not gonna be acting like the typical officer, either--my involvement in this mission goes right down to every boot sole that touches the ground. Think of me as a non-com if that helps you.

"Outside of Zeke, here, I haven't worked with any of you before. And frankly, this mission would be hard enough to pull off even if we were a tight-knit unit. So we can't afford any BS, pissing contests or dissension in the ranks. Whatever petty differences crop up between us, we're gonna have to suck it up and drive on. So I need to know, right now, if there's any one of you that can't hang. Sound off now, and I'll have Mugabe arrange to get you back home *mos-koshee.* Otherwise, I expect loddy-doddy-everybody to dedicate yourself to this team, and the job ahead of us, a hundred-and-ten percent." His eyes locked on Zeke just to make it clear there would be no favoritism.

"With all due respect," said Force Recon vet Charles Mai, a Hawaiian with the build of a fire hydrant, "I myself can handle any mission that comes my way. But I don't know jack about you, who put you in charge, or if *you* can hang." His tone belied any pretense of respect.

Zeke rolled his eyes.

Cavarra stifled a groan. In *one ear and right out the other. We're off to a great start.*

"Okay," Cavarra said. "I retired from the US Navy at the rank of commander. That would be the equivalent of your rank of lieutenant-colonel, Gunnery Sergeant Mai."

Mai should be familiar with Naval rank, but men with ignorant attitudes ought to be prepared to have their intelligence insulted. Cavarra preferred to treat people like reasonable adults. Unfortunately, it wasn't always possible unless people behaved like reasonable adults.

"I've gotten wet in Grenada, Panama and the Gulf as a SEAL," Cavarra said, "and this is hardly the first time I've been in a command position."

Mai was undaunted. "Even if that's true, those are dubious

credentials: You squids screwed the pooch in Panama."

Cavarra stared at him. *Dubious credentials? Who's running around teaching jarheads big words like that?* Evidently Mai was determined to make waves.

"If you're asking to see my DD-214, Mai, I'm afraid I didn't bring it with me."

Zeke and a couple others snickered.

"If you want to discuss Panama, we can do that in private," Cavarra said, taking a few casual steps toward the marine. "Since you're questioning who's in command, here, I'll assume you missed my introduction by our CIA liaison. Who else missed it?"

"I *heard* it," said Carlos Bojado, a Mexican leatherneck, in a tone that suggested he didn't believe it.

"Then please get Mai up to speed," Cavarra said. "And I'll address this question to anyone else who doubts my 'credentials': Who recruited you? Who paid for your transportation over here?"

"The Agency," Zeke answered, for everyone.

"And Mr. 'Mugabe' is our CIA contact, right?" Cavarra scanned over the faces again. Few replied verbally.

Now he looked directly at Mai. "And did anyone hear our contact, or anyone else from the Agency, announce Gunny Mai to be in command of this gaggle?"

Nobody replied.

"Well?" Cavarra said. "Were you put in charge here, Mai?"

"No," Mai admitted, quietly.

"Well shazam. May I continue now, Gunnery Sergeant Mai?"

"Go ahead."

"May I have command of this unit back, Gunnery Sergeant Mai?"

"Hey, I--"

"Well thank you very much. Why don't you either shut that ugly scar under your nose or pack your trash for the next boat out of here."

Mai glanced around at the others and shrugged.

Inwardly, Cavarra was relieved. He had upped the stakes on Mai so quickly, it might have come to settling the matter outside. And had he been forced to thump Mai in front of everybody, the gunny would have become a liability to the team.

Cavarra made eye contact with all the men around him. "Now are we done with that, or does anyone else want to waste our time playing ignorant games?"

Most of the men looked down at the floor, embarrassed for Mai, except Mai himself; Bojado; Greg Lombardi--a man who'd earned both Special Forces and Ranger tabs in the Army; and Sam DeChalk-- a bejeweled mercenary from Illinois. No one spoke.

"Good. Where's my armorer?"

"Hup, sir." Former Special Forces Weapons Sergeant Tommy Scarred Wolf stepped forward. He wore a bright, lime-green sleeveless shirt, baggy print trousers and threadbare lime-green Converse high-tops. Lean muscle covered his average-sized frame. Blue veins pulsed down his long, sinewy arms and huge hands. His bronze face betrayed no trace of emotion, but his eyes burned with an intensity Cavarra liked.

"Our heavy metal is supposed to come in today," Cavarra said. "I'm gonna need some modifications done right off. You bring your tools?"

Scarred Wolf shook his head. "I told the suits back stateside what I would need. Tools are supposed to come in with the rest of the gear."

"Well, I sure hope they do," Cavarra said. "I ordered a few things, myself, you're gonna need. Pick out a work area in this building and get it squared away for when our trash comes in."

"There's a couple rooms in the basement that will work," Scarred Wolf said.

"Good. Make it happen."

"Hup, sir." Scarred Wolf grabbed a duffel bag on his way downstairs.

Now that was more like it.

"Where's my other sniper?" Cavarra called to Campbell.

Campbell shrugged, even as the voice from the back door answered, "Raat hyah."

"Somebody relieve those two," Cavarra said, pointing fore and aft. There was a moment of hesitation--most of these men were unaware of the others' respective ranks upon discharge and didn't want to volunteer if someone of lower rank was on hand. Finally Fava-Vargas and Jake McCallum, a six-foot-seven ex-Special Forces Engineering Sergeant, moved to take those posts. McCallum looked like Eddy Murphy's big brother, on stilts and steroids.

Campbell came front-and-center. Cavarra did a double-take when Cole appeared from the back. He was a former marine sniper from South Carolina and his dipped-in-pig-dung accent was something you'd expect to come out from under a pointy white hood. But he was darker than half the men present. His dossier listed his race as "other." Cavarra couldn't tell if he was of Native American, Arabic, or even Gypsy descent, but in any case he couldn't be called "white trash" or "redneck," despite the drawl. He had a lantern jaw, a unibrow and a fierce underbite. That and his husky upside-down-pyramid frame made him appear to be the missing link between man and bulldog.

Cavarra rested one hand on a shoulder of both snipers. "Soon as our trash gets here, I'm taking the two of you out to zero and do a little plinking. So get your gear together and stand by."

They grunted their acknowledgement and moved to comply.

"Where's my other engineer?"

Dwayne Terrell, the former SeaBee, turned from his post at the side window. He looked like a shorter, lighter-skinned version of McCallum, but no less muscular. "Right here."

Cavarra was about to assign someone to relieve him when Campbell returned with his web gear slung over one shoulder. "Suggestion, sir?"

"Go ahead."

"Rather than posting men on every side, why not just put one or two up on the roof? Better visibility up there, and less manpower needed. I can take the first watch until you need me on the range."

The suggestion was offered politely, in a humble way, but Cavarra burned with embarrassment. Campbell was absolutely right. *Why didn't I think of that? I'm tripping up, here.*

Several men watched Cavarra for his response. Undoubtedly, all of them had known officers too egotistical to acknowledge an enlisted man with a better idea, and waited for him to invent some lame excuse to nix Campbell's suggestion.

"Drive on, hero: Make it happen. Why don't you join him, Cole. I'll send your relief up, and I'll draft a duty roster tonight."

"Hoo-wah," Campbell said.

"Ooh-rah," Cole said.

"Heads-up play," Cavarra told Campbell, but the words were drowned out in the rustling of the two snipers moving out. Cavarra was glad it hadn't been Mai who thought of it.

He turned back to Terrell. "You go get with McCallum. First, I need you to build me a ladder for getting on and off the roof. Then I need you to put your heads together and draft a plan for a hasty rifle range. I want a zero range, a thousand-meter range, and see what you can come up with for pop-ups and moving targets from twenty-five to 200 meters."

Terrell looked like the weight of the world had just been dropped on his shoulders. "Sir?"

"See what you can dream up," Cavarra said. "I ordered some stuff you might be able to use. I need something safe, but quick. Copy?"

Terrell sighed heavily. "Copy that, skipper." He trudged back to find McCallum.

Cavarra kept firing off orders until every Swinging Richard was gainfully employed. Terrell muttered curses under his breath. Mai glared at Cavarra whenever he thought Cavarra wasn't looking.

One of the men remained silent the entire time. If Cavarra hadn't studied the photographs, his eyes might have passed right over him, so naturally did the man seem to blend into his surroundings. Cavarra knew the type. Guys like this could sham all the time and never get caught. They never got picked for scum details, CQ or guard duty. As long as they weren't stupid or weak, they could get away with murder until promoted into a leadership slot.

This particular chameleon was the African mercenary, Ehud Siyr.

9

1900 14 AUG 2002; NUBIAN DESERT, SUDAN
CAMP ALI

(Al Maidah, Sura 5:51-5:74)
Believers, take neither Jews nor Christians to be your friends:
They are friends with one another.
Whoever seeks their friendship shall become one of their number,
And Allah does not guide wrong-doers.

Bassam Amin stood outside the command post, playing with the selector lever on his rifle while drawing patterns in the sand with his feet. Commandant Ali's orderly had found him in the bivouac a half hour ago and told him to report to the CP.

Unlike the pup tents assigned to Bassam and the other trainees, most of the structures in the four acre camp were semi-permanent affairs of wood, plastic, metal and mosquito netting. The command post was sturdier, with walls of stacked sandbags and a heavy canvas flap for a door. Bassam could hear voices inside, but the drone of the generator behind the CP made it impossible to distinguish words.

He hadn't shown as much energy in training today as he usually did--his back muscles were quite sore from the rope climb yesterday. Perhaps he was to be reprimanded for his drop in motivation. That's the only reason he could imagine for this summons.

***

Inside the CP, Chin exhaled one last mouthful of smoke, dropped his cigarette onto the sand floor and waited for Ali to speak.

"I don't believe this is necessary," Ali said. He sat behind a crude desk of plywood and ordinance crates, enjoying the breeze of his small electric fan.

Chin struggled to keep his composure. All these years dealing with the savages of Africa and he still had trouble hearing his wisdom questioned. "Perhaps. And perhaps not. Wouldn't you agree that it's best to have all bases covered?"

Ali conceded the point by sucking his teeth.

"You won't be paying for it," Chin reminded him. "I will." Actually, the beauty of it was that the money ultimately came compliments of the capitalist enemy. But Chin still thought of it as his to allocate.

"It might make him soft," Ali said. "Weak. Spoiled."

Chin waved his hand. "Soldiers are like dogs. A dog is far more motivated to fight after catching the scent of a bitch in heat."

Ali drummed his fingers on the makeshift desk. Funny Chin should use the canine analogy--to Ali, Chin resembled a *Sharpei*. His face had more folds than a half-deflated air cushion and he spoke as if barking.

Jan Chin supposed that by Middle Eastern standards Khaled Ali was a handsome man. He approved of Ali's grooming, and dress. Ali eschewed the traditional Arab garments for a pressed-and-starched brown uniform. To Chin this bespoke much leadership potential. Chin could forgive lapses in judgment and occasional incorrect thinking when a man had the immaculate appearance Ali had.

The ugly young ragamuffin waiting outside the CP, however, appealed to Chin as the perfect candidate for a suicide mission.

Ali finally nodded agreement. Chin nodded back and left.

***

Bassam Amin stepped aside as the heavyset Chinese pushed through the canvas flap. Chin's eyes raked over Bassam briefly as he went by. There was power in those eyes. Bassam could see murder there, and rape, and things even worse. It was strength, but belied by the fat.

Bassam had never seen obesity first-hand. The closest he'd ever come before was when he met the overweight Yasser Arafat. Chin was heavier. He'd seen true obesity only on television and in newspaper photos--images of fat Jews and Americans, living luxuriously, amassing wealth by exploiting and manipulating those less fortunate. Soft, weak men whose biggest weapons were deception and greed.

Only hungry men possessed genuine strength. It was obvious Chin hadn't been hungry in a long, long time. Whatever strength appeared in his eyes was but a reflection of something lost long ago.

"Bassam Amin!" Ali's voice called from inside. "Enter!"

Bassam entered and stood before the desk.

Ali looked him over for a moment. He had an unnerving stare, and many trainees shrunk under it. Bassam endured it unflinching. In fact, his expression was blank, as always.

"Sit down."

"Thank you," Bassam said, and sat on the folding chair indicated.

"How long have you wanted to fight in the *jihad*?"

"Since I was nine years old."

"And what happened then?"

"Someone explained the nursery rhyme to me."

"What nursery rhyme?"

"First Friday, then Saturday, then Sunday."

Bassam had never known his father. His mother was killed attempting to mix TATP (triacetone triperoxide) explosives in southern Lebanon when he was five. He grew up in a refugee camp with a foster family for a while, but tired of the insults and beatings. The patriarch of the family detested the boy for some reason never voiced.

Bassam learned of an uncle he had in *Amman*. At nine years old, imagining this uncle would welcome him and raise him as his own son, Bassam ran away for Jordan. He was turned back at the border with no explanation.

He tried crossing again, this time explaining his motives to the guards. It did no good. Finally, he snuck across. But capricious Allah had the last laugh. A Jordanian soldier, who had been on border guard duty the day before, recognized Bassam asking for directions in a bazaar. He turned Bassam over to the PLO. The agents dragged Bassam to an apartment building where they slapped and punched and kicked him back and forth. They might have gotten carried away and killed him, but a superior officer happened on the scene and the men quit beating him.

The officer sat down and talked to Bassam. "First Friday, then Saturday, then Sunday," he said. "You've heard this, haven't you?"

Bassam had. All children were taught this saying, but nobody had taught him its meaning.

The officer explained:

"Friday is the Muslim holy day, Saturday is the Jewish holy day and Sunday the Christian holy day. Submit yourself to Allah in prayer and worship. Then take up the sword of jihad, and win the world to Islam.

"There are two types of people in this world--*Dar Al Islam*: the faithful of Islam, and *Dar Al Harb*: the infidels, with whom we are at war with until Judgment Day.

"The most dangerous infidels are the People of the Book. So push the Jews into the sea, then burn their brothers, the Christians, with holy fire. First Friday, then Saturday, then Sunday. After that, the godless and pagans will either convert or be put to the sword.

"Allah has placed you here for a reason, Bassam. You are to be a holy warrior and help drive the infidels out of Palestine. Allah has decreed it, and yet you try to run from your divine duty. Allah rewards the brave, but he hates cowards. Surely you don't want to be a coward?

"Boys your age have taken up the sword of Allah and died killing the infidel. And when you die killing the infidels, Bassam, you are guaranteed entrance into heaven.

"Why would you run like some coward from such an honorable mission and glorious reward? Are you a coward? My soldiers think you are because you tried to sneak out of your country and your duty. But Allah has prevailed upon me to give you a second chance. Will it be cowardice or glory, Bassam?"

The officer took Bassam back to the refugee camp, relieved his foster family of his guardianship and placed Bassam directly under the care of the Martyrs. Instead of humiliating Bassam for his cowardice, the officer praised him in front of the other refugees. He proclaimed Bassam a warrior in training.

Bassam understood very little about Allah or the teachings of Mohammed, but he knew that he lived under a curse, and he knew the curse was related to some Jew now occupying the land that rightfully belonged to him.

Bassam ran errands and did chores for the older Martyrs. In time, they taught him. They trained him how to scam and steal from tourists;

how to mix explosives; how to build booby-traps; how to carry a bomb into a big crowd of Israelis and set it off. But that assignment never came. Eventually he was recommended for advanced training, and he wound up at Ali's camp.

Ali beamed at the boy.

The Palestinian officer was truly an asset to jihad, Ali decided. United Nations relief fund payments were doled out to the PLO based on the headcount in the refugee camps. Defections would bite them in the pocketbook, but good leaders knew how to inspire potential Martyrs beyond such notions.

"Truly Allah's hand was at work," Ali said. "Have you abandoned the path of cowardice for good?"

Bassam nodded.

"That's good, Bassam, because Allah has given us a momentous task to undertake. It requires a man of tremendous courage and strength.

"At first I didn't think you had that strength. But I'm a fair man. Perhaps there is more courage inside you than I can see, outwardly. That is why I'm offering you the chance to strike a mighty blow for the jihad. If you volunteer for this holy mission, you will have the honor of delivering the most devastating attack ever against our oppressors."

"What is it?" Bassam asked.

"I will tell you right now that if you accept this mission, you will die. But you will die delivering the wrath of Allah on our enemies."

"Tell me what I have to do."

Ali smiled and pounded his desk, which wobbled from the blow. "Praise to Allah! I knew you weren't a coward!" He leaned back and clasped his hands behind his neck. "The details will be revealed to you in time. Right now, tell me what you know about Heaven."

"I know if I die killing infidels, I will go there."

"True. But what sort of place is it?"

"Paradise, I guess."

"What is paradise to you, Bassam?"

"I don't know. I don't understand the question."

Khaled Ali opened a drawer in his desk, pulled out a magazine and dropped it down where Bassam could see it. There was a well-endowed, naked woman on the glossy cover.

"Does this look familiar?"

Bassam was silent. They must have snooped around in his tent to find it. He was more angry than embarrassed.

"Don't worry," Ali said. "You're not in trouble. But tell me something: Have you ever bedded a woman?"

"No."

"Are you aware that when a holy warrior arrives in heaven, he is awarded a harem?"

Bassam's eyes glowed keen.

"A harem of wives far more beautiful and voluptuous than these women," Ali said, pointing to the magazine. "Wives who will serve you with every kind of pleasure you can imagine."

Bassam's eyelids twitched.

"It's too bad you've never had a woman," Ali said. "You can scarcely imagine how much pleasure even one can bring you."

Bassam felt light-headed, and couldn't help the dopey smile twisting his homely face.

Ali pretended to wrestle with an idea. "You know, in days of old, a general would bring in willing women to service his warriors on the eve of a great battle. So they could have a taste of the pleasures awaiting them if they died a hero's death."

Bassam's mouth moved, but no words would come out.

"Would you like that, Bassam?"

The boy's head bobbed vigorously.

"Very well. I will arrange this sample for you. I will trust that you won't let me down. That you won't let Allah down. That when the moment of truth comes, you will die bravely and honor all of Islam."

"I will do it!" the boy said. "I will not hesitate."

"Good. I will arrange a hero's brothel privileges. You are dismissed for now."

10

1929 14 AUG 2002; DINKA VILLAGE, SUDAN

(At a double-time.)
Early one mornin' in the drizzlin' rain
My first sergeant was raisin' Cain.
Kickin' in doors an' bustin' down walls
Droppin' lower enlisted like Niagara Falls.
He had NCOs all around his desk
And a leg lieutenant in the lean 'n' rest...

Jake McCallum and Dwayne Terrell took some scrap lumber found around the village, tied it together with 550 cord and covered the splintery rungs with hundred-mile-an-hour tape. Once done with the ladder, the engineers set out to scout a potential site for the rifle range.

Before the ladder was finished, the snipers found a way atop the building.

The roof was stucco, sloped only slightly. Obviously it never snowed here.

Campbell and Cole fashioned a couple hooches by tying ghillie ponchos between the small steeple and furniture scavenged from inside the church. The shade from the ponchos eventually cooled those sections of the roof enough to sit down.

"We could knock a mouse hole and some shootin' ports in that staple," Cole said, thoughtfully.

"Steeple's the first thing I'd shoot at if I knew a sniper was in a church," Campbell said.

Cole grinned. "Reckon even the Sudanese saw *Savin' Private Ra'an.*"

Inside, Cavarra oversaw reorganization of their temporary HQ. The men stacked pew fragments up by the windows to serve as shooting platforms. The intact pews were mated to form long rectangular trays in which two men at a time could sleep. Some men had brought hammocks, and hung these in the basement, the baptismal chamber and other out-of-the-way areas. They scraped as much of the dried blood as possible from the floor and walls with scrap wood, then swept it outside with brooms found in the basement closet.

Cavarra took over the office, where he hung his own hammock. After clearing the fire-blackened metal desk, he sat in the squeaky swivel chair, pulled out his spiral notebook and backward-planned the next day's schedule.

Sam DeChalk sauntered into the office and leaned against the desk grinning down at Cavarra. He introduced himself, then quickly found a pretense to start name-dropping and reciting his mercenary resume.

Cavarra knew from the dossier DeChalk had worked in Lebanon, the Balkans, Chechnya and even here in Sudan, but he'd never spent a day in a professional military outfit. Cavarra hadn't been all that impressed before. He was even less impressed now, since the merc seemed to be bragging about his "combat experience." Guarding roadblocks in Bumfuq, Egypt was hardly the sort of trigger-time Cavarra found useful for his current undertaking.

But the guy could speak Arabic.

"I've worked in-country before," DeChalk repeated. "So if you need any help finding your way around, talk to me."

"How much of the country have you seen?" Cavarra asked.

"South of Shambe, mostly. All the action is down here."

Not for long, Cavarra thought. "How are the roads? Are the rivers navigable?"

"The roads are pretty much like they are in all these jerkwater countries. Rivers are a hassle to cross. Especially the Blue Nile, from what I hear. It floods bad around September, though it's been a really dry year so far."

"What about dams? Falls? Rapids?"

"There's a couple dams on the Blue Nile, I think. One on the White Nile, just south of Khartoum. And there's some butt-ugly swamps down here."

Cavarra knew that much from the maps Hendricks gave him.

"You know what kind of weapons we'll be getting?" the merc asked.

Cavarra didn't answer. He was distracted by DeChalk's jewelry as the merc gesticulated. "You need to lose that trash," Cavarra said.

DeChalk was stunned for a moment. Then he said, "Don't worry. I'll take it off when we go tactical."

"Take it off now. Everybody needs to start getting in the tactical mindset. It won't be long before we're snoopin' and poopin'."

DeChalk reddened. "What about Mai and Fava-Vargas?"

"What about them?"

DeChalk held his hands up and fluttered his fingers.

Cavarra rose, stepped out of the office and, accompanied by DeChalk, tracked down the two men in question. Indeed, they also were decorated for the Pimp of the Year Contest.

Cavarra raised his voice. "Mai and Fava-Vargas, that goes for you, too...and anybody else who's bling-bling: All jewelry comes off, now. I don't want to see it again."

DeChalk looked angry.

"Did I stutter?" Cavarra asked. "Lose it before I melt it down into something useful."

With sullen glares, DeChalk, Mai and Fava-Vargas did as they were told. But Cavarra didn't stop there. "In fact, everybody get out of your civvies. Put your boots on, and whatever duds you'll be wearing in the field."

Lombardi, an ex-Special Forces Medical Sergeant who'd spent his first three tours in the Rangers, looked bewildered. "What's the uniform?"

"No uniform," Cavarra replied, loud enough for all to hear. "As long as it's subdued, with no shiny buttons or zippers exposed. And no unit patches or nametapes, if you brought your old duds."

Lombardi fairly sneered with distaste. "This unit isn't going to have a uniform?"

Cavarra hadn't expected this flack from a Sneaky Pete. "No uniform per-se. But no doomed neon tee-shirts or purple parachute pants either...which reminds me: Somebody go down and get Scarred Wolf up to speed. He's the biggest offender in the clothing department. And you all might as well get your web gear out now. Fill your canteens with fresh water. I've got some two-quart canteens with covers, and some iodine pill bottles for everybody."

Lombardi's expression read something like: What kind of incompetent Limp-Richard are you?? Mai had a very similar look.

"You expect us to provide our own equipment?" Lombardi wondered aloud.

"You didn't bring yours?" Cavarra asked. "Anyone else not bring their own web gear?"

No one responded. Most were digging it out. The snipers on the roof already wore theirs.

Cavarra nodded for Lombardi and Mai to follow him over to a secluded corner. He dropped his voice. "What the hell? You two were senior non-commissioned officers. How could you forget your load-bearing equipment?"

"Troops aren't expected to provide their own gear, sir," Lombardi informed him with an impatient, caustic tone as if addressing the idiot child of royalty. "They're issued what they need. I always told my men, 'if we don't issue it, you don't need it'."

"Amen," Cavarra said. "Thanks for sharing the LIFER Gospel of Braindeath. But in case the Agency misinformed you, you're not back on active duty. This is not the regular military and every man here is going to be expected to think for himself."

Mai was suffering a brain hemorrhage. "This isn't the way you do things! You issue the same LBE to everyone! Everyone is outfitted the same exact way!"

"That way if one man reaches for his LBE..." Lombardi began.

Cavarra interrupted, "...But grabs his buddy's by mistake, everything will be in the same place, blah, blah, blah. That garbage never works, men, even in the regular military where every effort is made to destroy individuality and build a hive mentality. Even if it could, some senior non-com would rewrite the S.O.P. every five minutes until nobody knew where anything was supposed to be packed, anyway.

"I ordered vests with the other gear, in case some half-stepping Richard-heads didn't have enough sense to bring their own. If we get them, you can have one apiece. Otherwise, you'll have to stuff what you can in your pockets."

"This is un-sat," Mai grumbled.

Cavarra stood nose-to-nose with Mai. "Did the Agency not tell you to bring everything you might need, short of weapons and ordinance?"

Neither NCO offered an answer.

"Well, shazam," Cavarra said. "Now I know where my weak links are, don't I?"

Campbell yelled something from up on the roof. Soon they heard the clattering growl of diesel engines and grinding of gears outside.

Everyone in the church mobbed outside to see what went on. Mugabe's Ramcharger led two big old trucks through the village to the church. Mugabe directed the drivers to back the trucks up against the rear of the building. The weapons and supplies had arrived.

Mugabe strolled up to Cavarra and said, "Here y'go, Johnny Rambo. Merry Christmas. The trucks are yours, too. I'ma' go drop the drivers off. You might not wanna unload 'til we're gone."

Cavarra wondered how much the drivers knew. He also wondered how many townsfolk would be watching them from their darkened doorways. "Just how secure are we here?"

Mugabe grinned. "Relatively secure. This is about as safe as it gets in the Sudan."

Cavarra and Mugabe discussed logistics privately for a few minutes, then the agent collected the truckdrivers and left.

Cavarra didn't want to unload everything, but he had to unload enough to find what equipment he needed right away. He got a relay-line going on both trucks, then pitched in himself.

Once the weapons and ammunition were found, the men hauled it down to the church basement where Scarred Wolf had set up shop. The tools, generator and arc welder followed. The food was also relayed into the church, from man-to-man. They dug out the spare web gear, so Lombardi and Mai would have some, and the tools and materials for the rifle range. Everything else was loaded back in the trucks.

Cavarra made sure DeChalk, Mai and Lombardi did their fair share of the work.

11

2044 14 AUG 2002; WHITE NILE RIVER, SUDAN

A tiny pinpoint of red light winked in the night. He was at the right spot.

Ehud Siyr rotated the paddle, changed his grip, and steered the dugout canoe for the bank. He ran the canoe aground and hopped onto dry land. Before he could regain his balance, the *Mossad* agent had pocketed his laser pointer, stooped down, grabbed the canoe and halfway pulled the heavy vessel onto the bank.

Between the two of them, they managed to hoist the dugout onto a level earthen shelf where the tall grass would make it hard to spot, even in daylight.

"Were you followed?" asked the Mossad agent.

Siyr shook his head. The Americans hadn't noticed him leave. Chances were, they'd never even been aware of his presence amongst them...except Cavarra. He'd locked eyes with Siyr at one point. He hadn't said anything, but he looked, and he'd remember.

They climbed the bank and got in the agent's Jeep Cherokee. The agent started the engine and drove north with the lights off. The vehicle was quiet, thanks to the heavy mufflers. Both men agreed that it was more difficult to surprise or eavesdrop on two people in a moving vehicle than two people chatting in the dark at a static location.

"Report," ordered the agent, in Hebrew.

Siyr answered in the same language. "Twelve of us total, until today when the C.O. showed up. All American, except me. One is a merc--don't know if he's trouble or not."

"Sam DeChalk?" The agent had received only sketchy information on the Americans.

"Yes, from Illinois. Seems more talk than action, but he's half-Lebanese."

"He worked for Major Haddad back during Peace in the Galilee, didn't he?"

"He guarded a few gates and target practiced on Spam cans, but talks about it like it was Mitla Pass or Omaha Beach. I'll bet the other 'action' he's seen was just as intense."

"He's probably harmless," the agent said. "The others are US military veterans?"

"Yes. Most of them look like pros. But they don't know each other, haven't worked together. Iron mixed with clay. Already there are petty arguments. Each one thinks he is tougher than the rest of them combined."

The agent shook his head. "American servicemen: Ex-high-school jocks who sign up to extend their adolescent machismo at four-year increments. How about the commander?"

"He seems pretty sharp," Siyr said. "He is doing well under the circumstances. Ex-Navy SEAL. Officer. Hard-charger. But not a primadonna."

The agent chewed his lip for a moment. "Dwight Cavarra. How does he lead?"

"From the front, I would guess, though only combat will tell."

"Can he do it? And will he do it?"

Siyr shrugged. "I think he is able, if anyone is, given these obstacles. Will he? I am uncertain..."

The agent picked up on a strange note in Siyr's words. "Does something bother you?"

A herd of zebras appeared out of the darkness and scattered before the bouncing vehicle. The Jeep swerved to miss the stragglers.

"He's failed to inform them of some important facts," Siyr said. "They know very little. He hasn't told them where the camp is, how many are in the camp, or about the attack by the Sudanese rebels. They know there is a bomb involved, but not what type of bomb or what its target is to be. At this point, however, maybe it's all just an opsec consideration."

The Mossad agent was silent for a moment. They drove on.

Ehud Siyr practiced what he considered "guerrilla Judaism." His mother taught him, when very young, that his lineage went from her all the way back to Solomon's Ethiopian wife. But few people knew this. He'd successfully masqueraded as a Sudanese, a Ugandan, a Somali, a Kenyan...and he knew enough about the enemy to convince outsiders he was Muslim even as he secretly worshipped the Mighty One who'd led his ancestors out of Egypt.

Siyr made his *alliyah* at sixteen, stowing away on a cargo ship to Haifa. His pilgrimage was disappointing at first, when he realized that most Israelis didn't worship the God of Abraham, Isaac and Jacob. Some of them didn't even believe in the Mighty One. Some actually wanted to surrender the Holy Land to the Philistines.

Siyr knew his Middle East history. When partition was decreed in 1947, the Jews were granted one fifth of the land promised them at *Versailles*. The rest was granted to the "Palestinians," who started out with everything Israel was now being told to surrender to them. Even that wasn't enough, so they attacked, along with the armies of five Arab countries. The nation of Israel consisted of a few shiploads of Holocaust survivors and the handful of *Sabras* who had survived various occupations of the Holy Land. A melting-pot militia with kitchen knives, museum-piece pistols and homemade Sten Guns, and an air force of two Piper Cubs, comprised Israel's military. Yet they fought off the invasion and not only survived, but held more land after the war than before it.

Historians attributed the War of Independence, and all the improbable victories since, to the Israelis' prowess in battle. Siyr knew better. Once the seed of Jacob was regathered from the nations, all the armies of earth and hell couldn't scatter them again. An inalienable Covenant guaranteed their place in the Land.

The very name "Palestine" came from the Roman pronunciation of "Philistine." The name was applied to Israel in order to deny the Hebraic connection to the Land. The same motive underlied renaming Judea "the West Bank."

The Palestinian Liberation Organization was formed in 1964-- three years before Israel captured the Gaza Strip, the Golan Heights and Judea. These were the territories the world Press now claimed gave impetus to the "Palestinian" cause. What, then, was the PLO's motive for murdering Jews when Moslems controlled all those territories? The Moslems' goal remained unchanged since their collaborations with Hitler: the annihilation of all Jews. But the Labor Party and the left-wing Press continually insisted that Israel's enemies harbored some unevidenced inner desire for peace.

Disillusioned but undaunted, Siyr joined the IDF as soon as they would accept him. Few Israeli soldiers were committed to the Mighty One, but at least they were committed to national survival.

Despite his skinny build, he made a tough, model soldier. When he volunteered for the Paratroops, his C.O. approved the request-- believing in the boy's willpower, if not his stamina.

The paratroop training almost killed him. He suffered heat exhaustion, heat cramps and even heat stroke. On the rare occasions he was allowed some sleep, he awoke so sore it took monumental willpower to move a single muscle. His feet grew blisters atop blisters, all of which ruptured during the endless forced marching.

His socks hardened and crusted with the dried blood and fluid, which glued them to his lacerated feet. A medic finally had to remove what was left of the socks with a scalpel. Pieces of the socks and the omnipresent sand had caused infections all over his heels, toes and the balls of his feet. The medic snipped away the flaps of shredded flesh, then scrubbed the raw pulp which remained. Siyr almost passed out from the pain. Then the medic sprayed some chemical on the open wounds which felt like a thousand white-hot razor blades, and bandaged them.

Still Siyr wouldn't quit. When his feet healed, he continued training.

The parachuting turned out to be the easiest part of the whole ordeal. The proudest moment in Siyr's life was when he first sported IDF jump wings on his chest.

When Siyr first met him, the Mossad agent was an officer in the *Sayeret Matkal*. He'd been with Yoni Netanyahu for Operation Thunderbolt and had a reputation as a hard man, even among the hardest of men. The next time Siyr met him, they sat side-by-side in front of General Shomron's desk.

Shomron and the officer asked questions about Siyr's religious and political beliefs, and were particularly interested in the languages he could speak. Siyr had a gift for languages and had mastered not only Amharic, Arabic, Hebrew and English, but also achieved fluency in Kiswahili, Nubian and some Nilotic dialects. Shomron congratulated him on his battlefield distinctions won in Lebanon, praised him for his reenlistment in the 35th Brigade, then proceeded to explain how he might serve Israel even more effectively than as an infantryman in an elite combat unit.

Since that day, Siyr had worn many uniforms, fought in numerous skirmishes, eavesdropped on countless conversations, observed manifold foreign officers and politicians, trained with several armies and rebel forces, and sabotaged various covert operations.

"Perhaps this Cavarra suspects a mole," the former commando officer suggested, his Jeep jumping a dune and landing with a violent shock.

"If so," Siyr said, "then he will be sure it is me."

"You have to win his trust."

Siyr shook his head. "You make me look suspicious by sneaking away to report to you, then tell me I must make him trust me."

"Americans are nothing if not gullible," the agent said. "I have some beer in the back seat for you to return with. Going AWOL for alcohol might prove you are worthy to be one of them."

Siyr doubted the plausibility of the story, but he couldn't think of a better idea. "What bothers me the worst," he said, "is that if I do gain their trust, it is only so that I can be in a position to betray that trust. These men are putting their lives at risk in defense of Israel, after all."

The agent frowned. He didn't want to argue. "The defense of Israel is **our** duty, Ehud. It is of utmost, immediate concern to **us**. The only trust that matters right now is our trust. Our faith in our country; our country's faith in us. That is the trust that can't be violated."

12

2136 14 AUG 2002; DINKA VILLAGE, SUDAN

(At a double-time.)
Old lady runnin' with a parachute...
She had a fifty-cal rifle and a ghillie suit.
Said, "Hey, Granny, where ya goin' to?"
She said, "Force Recon and sniper school."
I said, "Hey Granny don't ya think you're too old?
Ya better leave that stuff for the brave and the bold."
She said, "Hey little punk, who ya talkin' to?
I'm an instructor at the sniper school."
Hey-hi Semper Fi!
'Til the day I die...

The warning order was finished early, so why not give it early? No telling what could happen between now and the morning, Cavarra thought, and so led his men up onto the roof. They sat around him in a circle under the stars and the warm night air.

Cavarra struggled about whether or not to let them in on the gravity of the situation: All they knew, apparently, was that they were to intercept a bomb. They hadn't been told it was nuclear. It was something they deserved to know, given that they could be blown to atoms themselves if something went wrong. And yet he didn't know these men well enough to guess how they might handle the news.

Cavarra hoped they were the cool-headed killers the CIA thought they were. Most of them had been civilians for a while--including himself--but wimps or cowards couldn't have made it through the training these men had once undergone. Collectively, they represented the best fighting men America boasted--or at least once they would have. The elite of the elite. All except the mercenaries.

Mercenaries!

Cavarra looked around the group. Only eleven men. DeChalk was present, but the African merc was not.

"Where the hell is Siyr?" he demanded. "Has anyone seen him?"

They looked amongst each other, somewhat confused.

"Was that the skinny black guy?" Zeke asked.

"Kinda' black," Scarred Wolf said. "He looked mixed. Part black, part Middle Eastern, maybe. Strange accent."

"Yeah," McCallum said. "Real quiet guy. Did you talk to him?"

Scarred Wolf nodded, and turned to Cavarra. "Sorry, sir. I didn't think about him much. Guess I assumed you had him busy somewhere else."

"Me too," Cole said.

"I talked to him," DeChalk said. "He asked me some questions about Lebanon--"

"This is just great," Mai said.

Cavarra cursed. Accountability had to be one of the worst problems with commanding pseudo-civilians. "Who saw him last? And where?"

"Last I saw him was when the trucks arrived," Bojado said.

Cavarra sat silent for a moment trying to decipher what it meant. *Did he bug out? Did he get snakebit taking a leak outside? Is the mission compromised already?*

He couldn't afford to panic. "Alright, we're gonna have to find him as soon as we break up, here. Prepare to copy."

Most of them produced notepads and pencils, to copy by moonlight. A few used red-lensed flashlights, though the night was bright enough without them.

Cavarra nodded toward Terrell, then McCallum. "Did you find a good spot for the rifle range?"

"This whole country's a rifle range," Terrell said. "But to make one like you want, we're gonna have to bust our humps."

"I'll make sure you get the help you need," Cavarra said.

"I think we found a decent spot," McCallum said. "We came up with an idea or two for the fancy targets. Gonna be some work, though."

"Can you work in the dark?"

Terrell winced as if slapped. "You want us to work through the night, sir?"

McCallum looked at his ex-Navy counterpart and smiled while

shaking his head ever-so-slightly. *Relax, my brother. It won't kill us.*

"You can catch up on your sleep in the a.m.," Cavarra said. "I want to take my snipers out there at first light. I'll probably be a couple hours with them. Then the rest of us can go out there and zero our rifles. Two-at-a-time, I'm thinking. You two can go last, so you'll get more sleep. Soon as everybody's doped in, we'll move out."

"Will I be working through the night, too?" Scarred Wolf asked.

Cavarra shook his head. "Just get the M21s together tonight. You can knock out the rest in the a.m. But get started at, say, 0500."

Cavarra read the guard roster aloud. He had assigned himself the middle watch--this raised eyebrows but no comments. Officers and senior NCOs always excluded themselves from the scum details. But this wasn't the regular military and Cavarra had never been a typical officer.

Next he passed around the maps.

Cavarra went over some of the basic poop, omitting identification of their final objective and some other key info. He'd been struggling with whether or not to spill everything to them. On the one hand, everyone should know what he knew, so they could carry on if he got greased before reaching the objective. On the other hand, the CIA had only given them sketchy info for some reason, and if he kept them from knowing all the specific poop, there was less chance that one of them could compromise the mission if captured. Siyr might prove to be a case in point.

"I need a patrol," Cavarra said, once the briefing was complete. "Search this town for Siyr, and every nook and cranny just outside of town."

Every single man volunteered. Cavarra picked Bojado and Mai.

13

0329 15 AUG 2002; MALAKAI, SUDAN

Major Anwar Hasan of the Popular Defense Forces wore his night clothes. He pushed on his glasses and squinted through them at the thin, dark man outside his front door.

Hasan recognized the man, but it took his tired brain a moment to remember from where. He was black like a Nilote (southern Sudanese) but with Semitic facial features. A mixed breed. Now Hasan remembered: Bunty was an informant—an officer in the Regular Army had introduced them. Bunty hadn't given Hasan many tips, but the tips he'd given had paid off."

"Why do you wake me at this hour?" Hasan asked, with a tone that seemed to add *you half-breed filth.*

Bunty may have been a good informant, but he was still of inferior stock. Khartoum was finally cleaning them out of Darfur in the west, Muslim or not, because the Koran damned the black-faced savages. Not that Hasan needed religious teaching to realize they were only one step up from apes.

Bunty bowed. "Esteemed Major, you remember the Dinka village you raided last month?"

Hasan didn't, really. He'd raided so many villages in the last few years he couldn't remember the Dinkas from the Nuers from the Shilluks from the Mandaris from the Didingas. Doubtful he could tell one Dinka village from another.

"It was a village outside of Bor," Bunty said. "Infidels. They built a temple to the Christian God."

Now Hasan remembered. Their audacity had infuriated him. A few of the prettiest girls were spared for sale to the brothels in Khartoum. The other females, after his men had used them, were necklaced alongside the men and boys as an example that shouldn't be soon forgotten.

Hasan borrowed the idea from the African National Congress-- infidels were bound like mummies, then "necklaces" (tires full of gasoline) were placed on their shoulders and set afire.

"What about it?" Hasan asked.

"Many of the villagers escaped," Bunty said. "They've moved back into the village."

Hasan should have burned it to the ground, but he wanted the ghost town to serve as a memorial to the folly of resistance. Still, this news was hardly worthy of waking him at this hour. "Report to me in the morning. Now leave, before I have you flogged!"

Bunty bowed again. "That is not all, esteemed Major. There are men in the Christian temple. I think they are fighting men. Earlier, they received two truckloads of weapons, ammunition and equipment."

Hasan removed his glasses and rubbed his eyes. Could it be? Making war on the Christians had always been so easy because few of them bothered to fight back. The survivors showed their cowardice by forgoing vengeance in lieu of attempts at proselytization. Armed rebels in the church must mean they were finally preparing to actively resist.

Numerically, the Sudanese Christians had never been much of a threat. They were even less of a threat now, with so many of them wiped out over the last several years. But if they allied themselves with the rebels...

Either some Christians had decided to take up arms, or they'd hired someone to do it for them. Where had they obtained the weapons? What did they intend to do?

No matter. Bunty had presented Hasan with a golden opportunity. Hasan could destroy the nucleus of this new resistance faction before it had time to get organized. It could mean a promotion in the Popular Defense Forces, or even a commission in the Regular Army.

Two truckloads of weapons and ammunition meant a small force, depending on what their intentions were. A couple hundred men at the most. But Hasan only had 146 men under his command--if he could muster all of them.

"How many fighting men are there?" Hasan asked.

"Twelve," Bunty said.

It must be the command structure, Hasan decided. They plan to arm and train the Christians along the White Nile and in the highlands.

With twelve experienced soldiers, they could easily organize a few hundred rebels.

But Major Hasan had no intention of letting them organize anyone. He wouldn't need all his troops for twelve rebels. By dawn he could muster enough men for an attack that would make his earlier raid seem merciful by comparison.

"What else?"

"I've told you all I know, Major."

Major Hasan retrieved some dinars from inside, gave them to Bunty and dismissed him. He then returned to his bedroom, opened the closet and pulled out his uniform and boots.

14

0607 15 AUG 2002; DINKA VILLAGE, SUDAN

(At the quick-time.)
They issued me an M14 hurray, hurray.
They issued me an M14 hurray, hurray.
They issued me an M14, with FMJ loaded magazines
And they dropped me down right into the DMZ.
They issued me a blooper gun hurray, hurray...

The patrol returned after an hour without finding Siyr. Cavarra gritted his teeth but drove on with his original plans. He, Cole and Campbell were out on the makeshift rifle range as dawn broke.

The range occupied a neatly-plowed field lined with straight rows of charred stubble that once was a *sorghum* crop. The soil was burnt black.

The M21 sniper rifle was basically a scoped M14 with a match-grade barrel, capable of semi-automatic fire only. Their rate of fire, twenty-round box magazines and rock-solid reliability had prompted Cavarra to choose them for his "master mechanics."

Scarred Wolf had bore-sighted both the scopes and iron sights on the M21s. Cole and Campbell zeroed first with iron sights, then the scopes. Both snipers did so with an impressively small number of rounds fired. Apparently they hadn't gotten too rusty since doing this for a living. Their range estimation, elevation and windage adjustments were practiced and efficient.

The range was set up perpendicular to the prevailing wind, per Cavarra's instructions, which gave him a chance to see how the snipers would do with an unpredictable crosswind on the 1,000 meter targets.

They fired three rounds apiece, then Cavarra went down to check their groups and tape over the holes. He had them engage under time constraints, then fire at his command. After every three rounds he humped out to the targets to check the groups, running on the return trips to save time.

US Marines were traditionally better marksmen than shooters from the other branches. The USMC sniper school had a rep for being tougher than the US Army's counterpart. But Campbell was just as deadly-accurate as Cole, and a touch faster with iron sights.

Cole's rank upon discharge was lance corporal, the lowest of everyone in this group. He served with some distinction in Desert Storm. But repeated drunk-driving arrests and other alcohol-related misconduct back on the block had kept him from advancing in rank and, ultimately, resulted in a General Discharge Under Less than Honorable Circumstances. Too bad. He was one fine instrument of warfare.

"Where'd you learn to shoot, Cole?"

"Daddy taught me," he said, squirting tobacco juice through his teeth. "Got mah first squirrel with a twenty-two when Ah was seven. First Deer at fourteen with a thirty-ought-six. Ah still prefer notch sats over these here pape sats."

Cavarra never had a problem with military peep sights, but knew many shooters who did.

"How about you, Campbell?"

"Never shot a rifle 'til the Army taught me."

The Army was a huge organization, with units running the gamut from pathetic to hardcorps. It was easy to ridicule, because the reputation of the former got more attention than the performance of the latter. But assuming every soldier to be a lazy incompetent pogue was like assuming every Chicago native was a gangster or every Californian a surfer.

"What outfit were you in?"

"Recon Platoon. Second of the 504th P.I.R. Devils In Baggy Pants."

Cavarra knew enough about ground forces to understand the nomenclature meant Second Battalion of the 504th Regiment or Brigade. "What's the 'P.I.R.' stand for?"

"Parachute Infantry Regiment."

Airborne Infantry. This was no ordinary grunt, with or without the sniper training. Campbell had an Honorable Discharge, and had sniped with distinction in the Gulf.

Cavarra moved them over to the pop-up/moving-target range.

McCallum, Terrell, DeChalk and Bojado had labored through the night to put this one together. They'd dug pits downrange, in which one man could lie safely, operating the silhouette targets with ropes and pulleys while the other man tried to engage them. Most of the targets merely swung up on their hinges in fixed locations, knocked back down when hit. But one popped up and moved laterally along a track before disappearing again. Cavarra was impressed with what his sappers had been able to accomplish in one night.

Once again, both Cole and Campbell showed outstanding prowess with the M21, easily engaging every target. They returned to the church with Cavarra so pumped up, Siyr's disappearance almost didn't bother him.

In the church basement, Scarred Wolf was busy with the other weapons. Cavarra knelt to watch him work. Scarred Wolf heard him come in, but only glanced up for an instant.

"How's it going, Chief?" Cavarra immediately regretted using the term--it was probably considered a racial slur these days. "Sorry. No offense intended."

Scarred Wolf grinned. "It's okay, boss. I actually am a chief, so it's no insult."

"No kidding? Aren't you kind of young for that?"

"There've been younger Shawnee chiefs," he said, "back when the nation was free. All the *Galils* are bore-sighted."

"Grenade launchers?"

"I've got them off the M-shit-teens. But four of our heroes are still sleeping so I didn't want to fire up the generator just yet."

Cavarra had resembled the kid in the proverbial candy store when first told he had *carte blanche* in weapons selection. However, twelve Stoner 63s was too tall an order on short notice, even for the CIA. He considered the Smith & Wesson 76 and other superb submachineguns, but he wanted range as well as select-fire capability. He opted for the Galil.

After extensive testing, the Israelis had settled on the AK47 as the platform for the IDF's main battle rifle. It could be fired semi or full-auto all day long in any environment, then left to freeze or rust or be buried in sand or even submerged in saltwater; then without any cleaning, reloaded and fired some more without a jam. They chambered it for 5.56mm NATO, improved the accuracy with a hammer-forged, cold-swaged barrel, flip-up rear sight and a Tritium-lighted front sight, gave it a sturdy steel folding stock and built-in folding bipod, a swivel-up carrying handle, a muzzle brake/flash-suppressor, ambidextrous safety and charging handle, and a thirty-five-round magazine. The Galil was far more expensive than its Kalashnikov grandfather, but worth every penny. The flat trajectory of the .223 caliber round made for decent accuracy, and its weight was about the same as a pistol round, so a man could carry enough ammo to make its firepower comparable to that of a submachinegun.

The one problem Cavarra had with the Galil was that he wanted half his men to have grenade launchers. For a man with no stubborn ingenuity, that meant his grenadiers would have to hump M79s along with their normal weapons, or fire rifle grenades from the muzzles with blanks, reducing firepower and probably tweaking the barrels in the process. So Cavarra had ordered six 40mm M203 bloop guns, the welder and generator, in the hopes that his armorer could mate them to the Galil effectively.

Unfortunately, even though he'd specified that he wanted only the grenade launchers and handguards, he got them still attached to the M16s. This made extra work for Scarred Wolf.

Cavarra pointed to the fifty caliber Dover Devil machinegun Scarred Wolf was assembling. "Once you get that thing squared away, fire up the generator and put my bloopers together. The men will just have to sleep through it." He'd probably had less than four hours of sleep himself.

***

Siyr was still missing. Another patrol went out to look for him, even stopping to question villagers who didn't flee upon sighting the heavily-armed Americans. Nobody had noticed Siyr at all. Like he was some sort of phantom.

Cavarra took the next two men out with their Galils. He picked out a rifle for himself and zeroed along with them. They engaged the pop-up and moving targets, but didn't waste time launching varmint bullets at the 1,000 meter silhouettes.

The villagers quickly got used to seeing the Americans around town. After Cole had given out most of his rations to the kids, and Bojado had shown some of the skittish adults his crucifix, they seemed to accept that the Americans meant them no harm.

Two-by-two, Cavarra saw all his men qualified. Mai and Bojado didn't ace the pop-up targets as the snipers had, but they shot very well.

Not as well, however, as Scarred Wolf. Not only did every single shot he fired hit its mark, but he did it lying prone, sitting, squatting and standing offhand. His position didn't seem to matter--he could hit anything he could see. So far he was living up to the cool last name.

"You hunt a lot on the reservation?" Cavarra asked.

Scarred Wolf winked. "A little hunting; a little poaching."

"Yo' daddy teach ya?" He tried to imitate Cole's accent, but couldn't even come close.

Scarred Wolf shook his head. "Brother."

In between escorting pairs of shooters to the range, Cavarra delegated, inspected and supervised. Zeke took the initiative to set up the field stove and prepared a breakfast of T-rations. The smell of this...not the noise of the generator...awoke the men who'd worked all night putting the rifle range together.

As the men ate, Cavarra passed lurps out for everyone to stash in their buttpacks.

The "lurp" had been developed for members of Long Range Reconnaissance Patrols (LRRPs). Theoretically, after eating one, a man could hump through the bush for days on end without stopping for chow. It hit your stomach still dehydrated and gradually expanded as you drank water, keeping your stomach full. Cavarra had never known anyone who could eat an entire lurp at one sitting. And he'd known some big, hungry dudes in the Navy.

Cavarra had everyone's rifle zeroed ahead of schedule. Scarred Wolf had the six M203s remounted by 0845.

They still had time to dope in the machinegun and get some practice with the grenade launchers before moving out. Cavarra put Zeke in charge of a detail to accomplish that, told McCallum and Terrell to make sure the trucks were ready for the trip, and sat down to finish writing out his op-order.

Siyr's whereabouts were still unknown.

15

0907 15 AUG 2002; PORT SUDAN, SUDAN

(An-Naba, Sura 78:31-34)
As for the righteous, they shall surely see paradise.
Theirs shall be gardens and vineyards,
and full-bosomed virgins: a truly overflowing cup.

The drive south from the camp was silent, but for the Hillux truck's engine. Ali's orderly said very little to his passenger, Bassam Amin.

That was fine with Bassam. All he wanted to think about was losing his accursed virginity. Any discussion would be an irritating distraction.

Bassam ignored the miles of desert creeping by and watched, instead, the progression of vegetation along the coast. Suddenly, the city appeared over the top of a hill. It grew uglier, and smellier, as it drew closer.

The truck slowed approaching the city limits. Ironically, the trail became more rough as it gave way to paved road. Some of the potholes threatened to snap the Toyota's springs.

Pedestrians stared at the truck as it passed. Bassam stared back. Everyone he saw was as skinny as he. The stink from their hovels offended him. The squalor here was as pronounced as that in the refugee camp he grew up in, though the structures were intended to be more permanent.

The truck maneuvered through the narrow streets, mirrors scraping buildings on either side. It stopped in an alley behind a long, low block building with several loading docks.

A red light bulb glowed above one doorway set flush in the flat, barren wall. The number "1317" was painted above the bulb, but no words or names.

"You wait here while I go inside," the driver told Bassam. "I'll come back out to get you."

Bassam wanted to ask several questions about what was going to happen, but felt too embarrassed.

The driver jumped out of the truck and knocked on the door. After a long pause, the door swung open, framing the driver in a black rectangle.

Bassam faintly saw a face in the dark opening, and the driver's mouth moved. Bassam strained for a better look at the face inside, but the driver then blocked his view while entering. The door shut behind them and Bassam sat alone in the alley, staring at the door.

His heart raced as he imagined what was beyond the door in that wicked darkness.

After an hour, his heart resumed a normal cadence.

After another hour of sweating in the truck, uncomfortable with nothing to do, Bassam grew angry.

It wouldn't happen. Ali had changed his mind without telling him and this wasn't even the brothel; the whore wanted too much money; or it was all a cruel prank.

He waited and grew angrier. He rammed his fist into the dash repeatedly to see how deeply he could dent it with bare knuckles.

Being left alone to wait always angered him. His mother had done it to him hundreds of times. The Martyrs thousands. He was fed up with being left to wait in hot, uncomfortable places. He would almost prefer crawling through the swamp.

The door opened and the driver came out. His expression was blank but his posture seemed straighter. "Come on," he said.

Bassam threw the passenger door open and hit the ground racing toward the red light bulb.

The driver opened the door and pushed Bassam inside. "I'll pick you up tomorrow," he said, and the door shut behind him.

Bassam couldn't see much in the darkness, but he heard soft murmurs and whispers. Female whispers. He smelled many aromas. Strong. Sweet. Exotic. Alien. Female odors.

A voice called him by name, from close by. He blinked. Before him stood a figure of exquisite curves. He couldn't make out the face, yet, or the breasts, but it was unmistakably feminine. The figure reached out to him.

A cool, soft hand closed around one of his. Strange sensations shot up his arm. The hand was so unlike his own! Small, soft, fleshy. It tugged him forward.

He followed eagerly, through the frightening, wonderful place of murmurs, whispers and intoxicating scents. Soft music played somewhere. *Sitars* and flutes wove rich melodies to the hypnotic jangle of cymbals and tambourines.

His eyes adjusted to the darkness as he walked. Oil lamps cast pools of light onto walls and floors--windows through the darkness, through which he spied rugs, pillows, furniture, clothes, feet, legs...

Before him, the hand holding his tapered to a petite wrist, thickening into an even softer arm with dimples in the elbow and cushions of flesh jiggling slightly with movement. The arm blended into a small set of round shoulders below a shower of inky black hair. Bassam could make out voluptuous hips wagging as short, curvaceous legs with bare feet led the way.

Bassam's escort led him through a beaded curtain into a small room with incense burning.

She stopped and turned, letting go of his hand.

He saw her now in the golden glow of the room's oil lamp. She was about five feet tall, maybe a little more, clad in silk and satin. She was in her mid-forties...late-thirties at the youngest. She had a soft, oval face with pouting lips and dark eyes under long, thick, half-lowered lashes. Bassam admired her large, round breasts, wide, curving hips and sculpted legs. She wore many jewels and her eyelids were painted dark purple. Oh, how she thrilled him! A real woman.

"This is your first time, Bassam?" She asked, with a voice like velvet. Hearing her pronounce his name gave him chills all over.

He nodded. She smiled. It was a knowing smile. Then she touched him.

16

0948 15 AUG 2002; SOUTHERN CLAY PLAINS, SUDAN

Major Hasan saw the shape of Bor appear on the horizon, had his driver veer slightly eastward, then signaled his convoy to fan out. They spread from the road into the fire-ravaged sorghum fields and clay patches spotted with elephant grass.

Hasan had managed to muster some 120 of the troops under his command.

An attacker should outnumber the defender at least three-to-one, if the defender was dug in. These defenders weren't dug in, and Hasan always used overkill when he could. He felt good about the pending operation.

At first only about thirty men answered his alert, which was close to all he needed, technically. But as daylight broke, word spread rapidly among the villages in his jurisdiction. Many men recognized the historic potential of Hasan's battle to extinguish the Christian resistance, and wanted to be involved.

The radio came to life. The armored car on the left flank reported an unidentified vehicle moving parallel with Hasan's formation. "Looks like a civilian truck," the gunner said.

Hasan stood up in the gunjeep's passenger seat and looked over his column, to see if it was someone who'd fallen out of formation. The halftrack rolled along directly in front of his gunjeep, wheeled APCs (Armored Personnel Carriers) on both flanks and cattletrucks trailing behind. Everyone just where they were supposed to be.

Hasan didn't see the civilian vehicle, but he saw the dust geyser it kicked up.

"Do you recognize it?" he asked.

"No, Sir!"

***

Siyr and the Mossad agent both braced for the fire that could come at any second from the armed vehicles. The agent sped the Jeep as fast as he dared over the rough terrain, chewing on his lip wordlessly.

On their way back to the location of Siyr's dugout canoe, a fan belt had slipped off the alternator pulley. Thankfully it didn't break. But the engine had begun overheating and the alternator, of course, quit charging. By the light of a small flashlight, they attempted to loosen the alternator brackets enough to slip the belt back on, but this proved far more difficult than it had any right to be, and a crucial bolt was lost.

When they found the bolt, dawn was breaking. By the time the belt was back in place and the alternator tightened down, there was no chance of slipping Siyr back into the village undetected. They forgot about the canoe and drove straight for the village.

They overtook the PDF column just a few klicks from Bor.

***

Bor loomed closer ahead on the right. The Dinka village was only twenty minutes away.

The unknown vehicle sped forward, passing Hasan's formation.

Hasan's convoy rolled along at sixty KPH, about the fastest the cattletrucks could move over the rough terrain. The unknown vehicle was doing at least ninety, probably more. If he could see it, then its driver could definitely see his formation.

Most civilians ran in the opposite direction when they saw the Popular Defense Forces on the move. This one seemed to be trying to beat him to the village.

Is he racing to warn the enemy?

Hasan raised the radio microphone to his mouth. He was about to order the armored car to take out the civilian vehicle, but he hesitated. Sound carried fast and far across the plains, and they were close enough to the village that opening fire now would jeopardize the element of surprise. The sound would warn the rebels faster than the civilian vehicle could.

"Let him go," Hasan said. "Maintain present course and speed."

0950 15 AUG 2002; DINKA VILLAGE, SUDAN

From the church, Cavarra heard the heavy thudding of the machinegun on the range. Then the blooping of his grenadiers practicing with the M203s, using smoke shells.

Those left behind with him all looked ready to go. They wore old uniforms, stripped of all insignia. DeChalk had on some British desert fatigues and Herman Survivors. Terrell sported olive-drab fatigues and flight-deck boots. Cole wore old ripstop woodland-camouflage BDUs and speed-lacers. Lombardi wore tiger-stripes with spit-shined jungle boots.

Cavarra, reclining on a pew with notebook out, shook his head upon noticing the latter. He wasn't sure whether to laugh or curse.

Cole meticulously cleaned and oiled his M21. Terrell, DeChalk and Lombardi stood around one of the improvised bench rests, mating short-range radio headsets and shock pads to the "fritz" helmets Cavarra had ordered.

Campbell came in holding his M21 muzzle-down. His "chocolate chip" desert BDUs were dark with sweat under his load-bearing vest. On his feet were khaki-colored canvas boots, probably the smartest footgear imaginable for this climate. He shucked his boonie hat, wiped his brow with it and asked, "Who's turn up top?"

Nobody answered at first. Cavarra unfolded the guard roster.

"I believe it's Pappadakis," DeChalk said, around a cigar.

Cavarra looked at the roster, saw DeChalk was right and cursed. Zeke couldn't be in two places at once. Cavarra would have taken his place but needed to finish writing the op-order.

"He on the range," Cole said, spitting a brown stream of tobacco juice into a canteen cup. He stood and stretched, lower lip bulging out from the wad of chaw behind it. "Ah'll go back up thar for a spell."

"Thanks, Cole," Cavarra said. "I'll send Zeke up to relieve you when they get back. Shouldn't be too long."

"Ooh-rah." Cole shrugged into his web gear, reassembled his M21 and stepped outside.

Cavarra almost smiled. Alcoholic or not, Cole was a hard charger.

"What goes on?" Campbell asked.

"Grab a screwdriver and I'll show you," Lombardi said. "Take that helmet and that radio, and do what we're doing."

Campbell laid his M21 gently down on a pew cushion, as if it were a delicate infant. Then, somewhat less carefully, he removed his LBV and set it on the floor. "High-speed. Commo gear for the common man."

Lombardi looked at Campbell's boots. "Were you a tanker, hero?"

"Naw. These are Israeli desert boots. Light as go-fasters and fairly comfortable with arch support inserts. Pretty high-speed."

"That's not what I mean," Lombardi said, reaching down to hook the laces with his finger. "Only tankers are authorized to ladder-lace their boots."

Campbell grimaced. "Lawdy, lawdy, top! Guess I better go find myself a tank, then."

Lombardi either ignored the sarcasm or didn't recognize it. "No. I guess you better take them off and lace them properly--left-over-right."

Campbell looked lazily into Lombardi's eyes. "And I guess you can kiss my fourth point."

Lombardi's face first turned red, then ghostly white.

"Knock it off," Cavarra said, glaring at Lombardi.

Lombardi whipped his head around to glare at Cavarra.

"You were a first-sergeant when you got out, weren't you?" Cavarra asked.

"That's right," Lombardi said through gritted teeth, clean-shaven jaw bunched up.

"Well you act a lot more like a first shirt than you do a Special Forces vet," Cavarra said. "You should worry about your own doomed boots."

"My own boots!" Lombardi said.

"Yeah. Have you been outside yet? Is the ground spit-shined glossy black out there so your boots will blend in with the environment?"

Lombardi sputtered but had no reply.

"Maybe you need a better look at our surroundings," Cavarra said. "Should I issue you a rake and have you go out there to rake all the dirt into nice, straight lines?"

Campbell burst out laughing. "Hoo-wah, sir! That'd give him a

good look at the environment. Too bad there ain't any forests around--
he could go police up pine cones."

Lombardi swung around to face the sniper, livid. "There's a
reason we polish our boots, hero. It's to take care of the leather."

Campbell laughed some more. "Sure, top. So does spit-shining
take better care of the leather than brush-shining?"

"No wonder you got out, you little Limp-Richard," Lombardi
said.

Campbell was taller than Lombardi and found the "little"
adjective funny. "Tell me somethin', topkick: How come, when you
strac LIFERs see brush-shined boots in garrison, you say, 'why didn't
you shine your boots?' I mean, it's obvious the boots've been shined.
Maybe not spit-shined like yours, but shined. But you always gotta say
it like they ain't been shined at all."

"I ain't never said jack to you until just now," Lombardi said. But
he was guilty, hundreds of times over, with hundreds of different
soldiers, of exactly what Campbell accused him. He felt absolutely
justified in his actions, but didn't want to debate it with Campbell. The
ex-paratrooper seemed eager to tear into him with that accursed
civilian logic. Lombardi's best riposte against logic was to simply pull
rank and threaten disciplinary action. But he had no chain-of-
command to back him up, here. And no rank, for that matter.

"Lombardi," Cavarra said, "just stow the spit-and-polish garbage.
What do you call that in the Army?"

"Strac," Campbell said.

"Stow the 'strac' cheese-eating garbage," Cavarra went on. "This
ain't the Buckingham Palace Guards. You're here to move, shoot and
communicate; not to look pretty. If you'd channel all that attention-to-
detail into something practical, we'd probably know where to find
Siyr."

Lombardi hadn't been defied like this in so long, he had no clue
how to deal with it, short of violence. He was no stranger to violence,
to be sure. He'd kicked *boocoup* butt and enjoyed it. But he was no
spring chicken anymore at forty-six.

He'd never been called a "LIFER" to his face--to him it meant
"Lazy Ignorant Fool Expecting Retirement." He certainly wasn't lazy
and, so far as he was concerned, Campbell and Cavarra were the

ignorant fools.

DeChalk tried to defuse the situation. "Commander Cavarra," he asked loudly, "what's going to happen to the M16s?"

"We'll take 'em with us, for now," Cavarra said. "Ultimately, I don't know."

"May I trade this rifle for one?"

"No."

"Why?"

"Because we're not Gonna have time for you to clean it after every five shots. There's a good chance we'll be throwing some lead downrange, and we'll be in a sandy environment."

Campbell didn't miss this--sand meant their target was north a good ways.

"I've used one in the desert before," DeChalk said.

"Yeah? And how many caps did you pop, total? And how many between jams?"

"I burned a whole magazine off without a malfunction and without cleaning it."

Cavarra gasped in mock awe. "Well, rat spit! We'll have to engrave a plaque for you when this is over--it's long overdue."

"What do you call an M16 in a desert deployment?" Terrell asked. No one responded. "A combination tent stake and fly-swatter," he said.

There was a commotion outside, then someone burst into the church.

Siyr.

He swung something down toward the floor and released it to go sliding across the church, as if bowling. It was a case of German beer. He looked around frantically for the pile of his gear.

Cavarra put away his notebook. "Where the hell have you been?"

"No time...!" panted the African merc. "Village...under attack...halftrack...armored cars...heavy weapons...coming from the north..."

"Slow down, man," DeChalk said. "What'd he say?"

Cavarra heard what he'd said. But was it for real?

"At ease!" Lombardi cried. "Listen!"

They all listened. Cole shouted something from the rooftop.

Cavarra and Lombardi rose with rifles in hand.

Cavarra, Lombardi, Terrell and DeChalk poured out of the church and looked up.

Cole stared down at Cavarra, eyes bulging out of his bulldog face. "You expectin' company, suh?"

Inside, Campbell hastily donned his web gear, grabbed his M21 and loaded a round in the chamber. He removed the magazine, dug a .308 round out of his pocket and topped off the twenty-round box before locking it back into the rifle. He looked for his bush hat, found it, and slapped it on his head.

Siyr finished strapping on his own gear, grabbed the rifle nearest him and looked around for ammo. He saw a stack of loaded magazines and stuffed them into his mag pouches.

Outside, Cavarra yelled up at Cole, "What is it?"

"Light armor," Cole said. "I see four...five vehicles...maybe more. Comin' straight at us!"

"How long before they're here?" Cavarra asked.

The sound of automatic weapons fire answered him.

17

(At a double-time.)
Well, up jumped the grunt from a paddy of rice
Was a cold mamma-jamma you could tell by his eyes.
Had a Grease Gun, Ka-Bar by his side
Those were the tools that he lived by...

THE RIFLE RANGE

Scarred Wolf was pleased with his work on the M203s. They functioned perfectly without interfering in the handling of the rifles, and his welds held up through the launching of grenades. The only drawback was that the built-in bipods had to be reversed so that they folded forward past the muzzle rather than back to sink flush into the foregrip.

He was impressed with the Dover Devil machinegun, too. Scarred Wolf had fired the M85 and M2 Browning, but had only heard of the Dover Devil from the gung-ho old-timers. It had never graduated from the prototype stage, though tested extensively in the early eighties and found to be an awesome weapon. That Cavarra knew enough to request one was almost more impressive than its successful procurement.

The Devil was lightweight for a large-bore belt-fed weapon (forty-five pounds lighter than the M2) and beautifully efficient in design. The headspace and timing were fixed, so neither a gauge, nor a man qualified to use one, were necessary. The barrels interchanged simply, and best of all, the dual-feed mechanism meant the gunner could keep firing with a belt on one side while the assistant loaded the next belt from the other. Zero reloading time. High speed, low drag.

When finished at the range, every weapon was locked and cleared and Pappadakis did a quick safety check. Then they saddled up and headed back for the village in a grabasstic gaggle. There was some smoking and joking, but not as much as there might have been among men who knew each other better.

When Scarred Wolf stopped in his tracks, the others froze,

following the line of his eyes with their own, as if some unseen orchestra had begun playing suspenseful music, signaling imminent danger.

Heading toward the village from the north was a fast-moving Jeep.

"Is that Mugabe?" Asked Zeke.

"It's that Limp-Richard from the CIA," Mai said.

"Mugabe is the CIA guy," Fava-Vargas said.

McCallum reached behind himself to wriggle a hand into his buttpack. He extracted a small pair of rubber-armored binoculars, held them up to his eyes and brought them to focus. "That's a green Jeep," he said. "Mugabe drives a black S.U.V. with waterboo horns."

The Jeep slowed to walking speed just inside the village. A black man jumped out of the passenger door and hit the ground running toward the church. He was carrying...a case of beer...? The Jeep accelerated, blazing through the village, out the other side and off into the horizon. The view of the running man was obscured by the buildings of the village.

Villagers, young and old, burst from their huts and ran for the river like lemmings in overdrive.

Now Scarred Wolf pointed to a growing tsunami of dust on the horizon.

"What the...?" Zeke muttered.

"Now that can't be good," McCallum said.

Bojado locked-and-loaded.

Mai whirled on him. "You best re-clear that rifle, marine," he said, with a few expletives thrown in for emphasis. "Nobody told you to lock-and-load."

"Everybody lock-and-load," Zeke said.

Actions slammed home in a metallic cacophony. It would have been a humiliating moment for Mai, but things were happening too fast for embarrassment.

McCallum surged forward, range-walking for the village. Zeke did likewise, and the rest followed. Without a word being spoken, the men fell into a wedge formation, McCallum on point, five-to-ten meters between each man.

Scarred Wolf set down the machinegun, slung the Galil around his back and called to Bojado, "Give me that ammo can."

Bojado trotted over and dropped the heavy can. Scarred Wolf knelt, popped the lid open, pulled the first few links of the belt out and loaded the machinegun.

Zeke, unaware of this activity behind him, pumped his fist up-and-down twice in the signal for "double-time." Maintaining the wedge formation, the men ran toward the village.

"Want me to get the tripod?" Bojado offered.

Scarred Wolf started to disconnect the tripod from the gun, then stopped and shook his head. The gun would be almost useless without it--which meant he and Bojado couldn't be separated. He'd never worked with Bojado and wasn't positive they could stay together in the impending action.

Bojado shrugged and sprinted to catch up with the others.

***

Major Hasan's column bore down hard on the village. His radio squawked. This time the call was from the halftrack.

"Major, I see men with rifles at the edge of the village. They are running toward the church."

"How many?"

"Four...five...yes, five."

"Pincers!" Hasan ordered. "You may fire at will."

The heavy machinegun atop the halftrack opened up. The long burst demolished some villager's erstwhile home.

***

At the first explosion of gunfire, McCallum dove to the ground. The others were only a split second behind him

"Hit the dirt!" Mai yelled.

A mud-and-tin shanty at the edge of the village shook violently as large-bore MG bullets tore through it. The whole structure disintegrated in a shower of clods and dust.

McCallum stuffed his binoculars inside his shirt and plucked a smoke grenade from his vest. He assessed the direction and speed of the breeze while working the pin loose. He let the spoon fly and tossed it a short distance away.

***

Hasan's gunjeep and one APC swung around to skirt the west edge of the village while the other armored car split off with the halftrack to skirt the east edge. One cattletruck followed each element. The gunner on the halftrack was thrown off-balance by the force of the turn and his bucking machinegun sent a heavy stream of lead skyward.

DINKA VILLAGE NORTH

Cavarra glanced around quickly. The best thing to do would be jump in the trucks and unass the area, but the gear wasn't loaded and his force was split. They'd have to fight it out. "Grab your trash!"

Lombardi, DeChalk, Terrell and Cavarra ran inside the church.

"Let's get outside!" Cavarra said, pulling on his web gear. They wouldn't suffer the same fate as the previous occupants of the church, if he could help it.

DeChalk spun in circles, a panicked expression on his face. "Where's my ammo? I had nine loaded mags!"

Cavarra glanced around. "There's ammo down below. While you're down there, grab some LAWs. And move with a purpose!" Cavarra followed Lombardi back outside.

Terrell found his magazines, but his rifle was missing. He raced DeChalk down to the basement. Both men cursed inventively on the way.

***

Campbell slung the M21 over his back and scurried up the ladder. As he hoisted himself atop the roof, Cole looked back toward him with a lost expression.

"What's our orders?" Cole asked.

"It's opfor," Campbell said. "Engage targets of opportunity...I guess."

There was no shortage of targets. Cole turned back around and put his cheek to the stock, released the safety and centered his crosshairs on the driver of the cattletruck. He squeezed the trigger. The M21 bucked in his grip.

The cattletruck windshield spiderwebbed around a small, neat puncture and the driver spasmed in his seat. The cattletruck creaked to a stop some hundred meters from the edge of the village.

Campbell pulled the ladder up after him and laid it on the roof.

Cole fired again and a front tire on the APC flattened. It swerved and almost hit the gunjeep. This threw off the aim of the gunner on the armored car's recoilless rifle (a mounted single-tube rocket launcher). His rocket missed the church and hit the building just beyond.

The jeep gunner opened up toward the church. Campbell unslung his rifle and dove to a prone firing position a few meters from Cole.

Cole fired again and the man at the recoilless rifle was twisted in his station as if struck by a wrecking ball.

The gunjeep swung into the village, between a row of buildings. The gunner had placed Cole's rifle report and adjusted fire. Heavy slugs slammed into the church just below the roofline, gouging out chunks of the wall.

Shards of brick pelted Campbell in his forward hand but he tried to ignore it as he tickled his trigger.

Crack!

The gunner's head split open as his now-limp body did a backwards somersault off the speeding jeep. The gunjeep was about to disappear behind a building when Campbell and Cole fired simultaneously. The driver took one round in the chest and one in the face. The jeep swerved wildly and tipped over.

***

Siyr found cover on the concrete steps leading down from the rear of the church. He readied his rifle, sighted down between two buildings into the swarm of troops unloading the cattletruck, and opened fire.

Lombardi charged around the corner, heard the whine and snap of bullets splitting the air around him, skidded to a stop, fell on his butt and scrambled backwards for cover. He rolled to the prone position, sighted around the edge of the steps and fired.

***

"Where's the .223?" DeChalk shouted, charging into the basement.

"Where are the rifles?" Terrell demanded. No sooner had he asked than he spotted a Galil still dripping cosmoline. He grabbed it, slapped in a magazine and worked the charging handle. "Check the crates," he said, bounding up the stairs.

Terrell ran out the back door, saw Lombardi shooting around the corner, saw dust kicking up on the street, heard the ricochet of live rounds, and dropped with his back against the wall.

Lombardi yelled back at him, "Secure the other end of this building, or they'll come around behind us!"

Lombardi was right. Terrell ran to the front of the church, dove to the prone and peeked around the corner.

Cavarra made a note of where his men were and sprinted for a position where he could see Terrell, Lombardi and the top of Siyr's head simultaneously. "Campbell!" he yelled.

"Hoo-wah!"

"What's the situation?"

"Enemy split up," Campbell called down from his vantage point. "We got an armored car still mobile on this side, and troops pouring out of the cattletruck coming this way--I'd say about fifty of them!"

"Where's the truck? I don't see it!" Cavarra's view was blocked by a building.

"Your one o'clock! Hundred and fifty meters!"

The opposing force were trying to envelope the village. Six of Cavarra's men were on the opposite side of town and, for all he knew, had been caught out in the open and mowed down.

Cavarra cursed. If he had a high explosive shell for his M203, he could take out the cattletruck and a lot of the enemy with it. But he'd told Scarred Wolf to secure them until further notice, afraid some knucklehead might waste one for target practice.

He had let the weaponeer issue hand grenades--each man had one smoke, two fragmentation and one incendiary.

He also cursed Mugabe for not delivering the commo gear earlier, because he really needed radio contact with Zeke and the others now.

And where was DeChalk with the LAWs?

***

DeChalk looked desperately around for the 5.56mm NATO ammunition. Feeling as if in slow motion, he went around to every crate. Of course it was the last one he found. *Now where in blazes are the Galil magazines?*

DINKA VILLAGE EAST

Scarred Wolf got the machinegun loaded and, at first, attempted running after his compatriots. But the belt of .50 caliber SLAP (Saboted Light Armor Penetrator) rounds unfolded out of the box as he went and the weight of it slowed him down as if the gun was tethered to a heavy log. He considered that the belt might get tangled and twisted dragging over the ground, and the gun with tripod was already more than a handful.

Cover was scarce out here. He'd have to settle for concealment. He dropped behind some scrub brush and let the weight of the MG barrel divide the foliage, giving him a narrow opening to sight through. He gripped the spade handles, traversed until the cattletruck fell into his sights, and ripped off a burst.

Thubthubthub! The SLAP rounds stitched a line across the ground in front of the cattletruck. The driver chose the absolute worst option available to him: he hit the brakes.

Scarred Wolf corrected and cranked off another burst. The truck vibrated, lurched and stopped as the powerful SLAP rounds mangled the engine. Sparks flew from under the hood. Oil and coolant gushed out. Then the engine exploded.

***

McCallum heard the heavy pounding of the Devil behind him and figured Scarred Wolf's covering fire just might give them a fighting chance. The smoke from his grenade was about chest-high now and spreading, though not fast enough for his liking. It would have to do. "Follow me!" he said and rose sprinting for the nearest intact building in the village.

The others rose and followed his lead.

"Let's go! Move it! Move it!" Mai shouted.

They reached cover and positioned themselves to face the attack. The halftrack roared right at them, machinegun chopping the town to splinters.

***

Scarred Wolf raked fire back and forth across the cattletruck. The unarmored vehicle winced as metal and wood flew from it like shell fragments from a pecan in a nutcracker. The fifty caliber slugs shredded the truck, sliced through the solid meat packed inside and blasted out the other side sucking pulverized human flesh along behind.

A chorus of human screams joined the symphony of gunfire. Body parts splattered inside the cattletruck like an enchilada left too long in the microwave. Most of the men inside were soon dead or mortally wounded--those who still even resembled men. The survivors who could make it to the side or rear doors, or squeeze out the windows, fought like wild animals to escape further horror. But some were trapped inside by the weight of surrounding bodies and theirs was perhaps the most gruesome fate that could be suffered by soldiers in combat.

Scarred Wolf swept back through the vehicle with the gun and made their immobility permanent.

***

Zeke and the men with him held their fire--engaging the halftrack with .223 would accomplish little but giving away their position. The halftrack roared past and turned into the village, machinegun blasting an indiscriminate swath through the town.

They cheered when they saw Scarred Wolf had neutralized the bulk of the opposing force before it could unass the cattletruck. Most of the PDF troops who managed to get out ran like scalded dogs away from the village, shedding weapons and gear in shameless panic.

Without discussion, the Americans opened up, dropping the deserters in flight. Then an APC careened around the corner right next to them and roared toward the center of the village. The gunner had his recoilless rifle aimed rearward.

DINKA VILLAGE NORTH

"Mag change!" Cole drawled.

"Gotcha'!" Campbell said, and picked off a soldier exiting the cattletruck. "Work from the rear forward!" If the advancing soldiers didn't realize the men bringing up the rear were dropping, they likely wouldn't start looking for the snipers' position.

"Ooh-rah!" Cole said.

Crack! Campbell dropped another man, whose comrades were oblivious.

Cole locked a new magazine in the mag well and jacked a round into the chamber. "I'm up!" he said.

When Campbell's magazine ran dry, he yelled, "Mag change!" Then the process was reversed. They paced their fire so that they were never caught reloading at the same time.

In some morbid way, they enjoyed their work. The threat of being overrun by a numerically overwhelming force didn't spoil their cocky fun for one second.

Below them Siyr tapped a man with every round, using a sightless firing technique he'd learned many years ago. Some of them dropped, but the .223 was a varmint round--better for wounding men than killing them--and didn't have the knockdown power of bigger projectiles. Still, once a man's vital organs had been punctured by a supersonic pellet, he wouldn't be an effective combatant for long.

The armored car with the blown front tire swung the corner and blocked Siyr's firing lane. Troops from the cattletruck used the armored car for cover as they advanced toward the church. Some of them tried to stand in for the dead gunner, but Lombardi and Cavarra sprayed them off with full-auto bursts.

Still, Siyr's position had become virtually useless. He loaded a fresh magazine and sprinted across the street.

"Where you going, hero?" Lombardi asked.

Siyr was already thirty meters away and oblivious to the question.

Lombardi rolled over and scrambled up the steps to Siyr's abandoned position. He quickly realized why the merc had left and considered returning to his previous spot.

Cavarra saw Siyr run toward the direction of the attack and disappear behind a building. What was he up to? Making a break to join the attackers? But he'd been shooting them down just a moment before.

Cavarra popped smoke, called to Lombardi and Terrell, "Flanking position! Let's move!"

***

In the church basement, DeChalk finally found some magazines. After another painfully fruitless period of time he abandoned his search for a speed loader and resigned himself to loading the magazines by thumb.

The sound of the firefight outside was awesome. He'd never heard anything like it up close.

In his haste to get loaded, a handful of .223 rounds slipped from his hand and clattered on the floor.

He cursed.

He cursed the ammo, he cursed the hidden speed loaders, but most of all, he cursed whoever had swiped his stack of loaded magazines.

DINKA VILLAGE EAST

The armored car driver saw dust puffing up near a bush out in the open. That and the hard, pounding sound told him there must be a machinegun firing there. He informed his gunner, continued south a good distance, then turned into the village. His gunner whirled around with the recoilless rifle to scan for the bush in question.

***

The cattletruck was destroyed and the former passengers were no longer a threat to anyone. Scarred Wolf let the barrel cool while looking around to assess his situation.

Something made him glance toward the APC plunging away into the village. He found himself staring down a loaded rocket tube.

The recoilless rifle fired with a *Fwoosch*.

Scarred Wolf was already up, running with the gun and tripod, trailing a belt of SLAP rounds, when the rocket plowed into the ground just beyond his former position and detonated. The concussion lifted him up and forward, slamming him down on his face.

18

(At a double-time.)
Slap another magazine... in your trusty M14
All I ever wanna see...are bodies, bodies, bodies.
Lock-and-load that fifty gun... watch those big bad commies run
If there's one thing I like ta see... it's piles of punctured pinkos.
Fire off another LAW... send Bin-Laden to Allah
If there's one thing I like ta see... it's flame-broiled Ayatollahs.

Zeke and the others got back in position once the armored car had passed. They poured fire after the gunner and saw him dance with the impact of several dozen varmint rounds.

"Somebody needs to go back for Chief," Zeke said, thumbing back over his shoulder.

"I'll go," Bojado said, but then saw Scarred Wolf rising out of the dust cloud, waving them off while checking the gun for damage. "Never mind. He's cool."

The others glanced back to confirm this. Then McCallum turned to Zeke. "We need'a link up with our buddies. They're probably in deep dooky about now."

Zeke grimaced. "Wish we had a LAW or two."

"We'll have to take out those vehicles, somehow," Mai said.

McCallum looked skeptically at the baseball frags hanging on his ammo pouches. "I don't see any way but the John Wayne method."

Zeke absently tapped Fava-Vargas on the shoulder with the back of his hand. "We'll go after the halftrack."

McCallum nodded and jerked his head toward Bojado. "We'll take the armored car--"

Mai slapped Bojado's shoulder. "As you were. **We'll** take the armored car. It's not a job for John Wayne--it calls for somebody who knows what they're doing."

McCallum cocked an eyebrow at Mai. He shrugged. "Fine. I'll trail and make it an inverted wedge. I'll try to keep all of you in sight, and provide cover fire as needed."

"You do that," Mai said, sneering. "Try not to shoot us in the back, all right?"

McCallum regarded Mai coldly. "Try not to let that bug crawl out of your fourth point of contact. It might block my line of sight."

"Knock it off," Zeke told them. "Let's get this party started." He made eye contact with Fava-Vargas, and the two of them moved out at a crouching run.

Mai and Bojado followed suit, in a slightly different direction. McCallum hung back for a moment, then adjusted his position and followed, keeping both pairs of men in sight.

DINKA VILLAGE WEST

One moment Major Hasan was in control, leading the western pincer of his enveloping maneuver, with his forces deploying according to standard practice. The next moment his command vehicle was on its side and he lay dazed on the ground with the wind knocked out of him. At first he realized only that his uniform was now dirty and his arm hurt.

Gradually, sounds registered. He heard gunfire and yelling from all directions, yet where he lay, near the wrecked jeep, there seemed to be an almost peaceful quietness.

Ridiculous.

Trailing from the jeep was the body of his driver, part of his head missing, dark, thick pools of blood soaking into the dust. There was a firefight in progress. The peaceful sensation was some sort of insane distorted perception. He sat up and blinked his eyes several times. He tried to focus past all the banal details, now vying for his attention, to the big picture.

He heard engines in between the gunfire, but didn't know where his other vehicles were. He crawled toward the jeep and found the radio mike. It was smashed.

He heard voices to his rear. Lots of them. His men must be behind him.

Hasan rose and staggered back through the village until he found them.

He was confused. There weren't as many as there should have been. They were just now entering the village when they should have been in position to storm the church by now. They all either babbled incoherently or stared at him like idiots. He screamed orders, trying to get them organized. His men kept falling, sometimes two at a time.

One of his lieutenants found him.

"Where is my armored car?" Hasan asked.

The lieutenant had a radio and located the APC. They had it advance into the village toward the church, with most of the men using it for cover walking behind. Hasan dispatched the lieutenant with some men to move down a parallel street which led past the church, not directly to it. They could probably move undetected up to where they could turn into the defenders' flank.

***

Siyr crept toward the enemy with his back to a hut. He heard their voices, their shuffling and the chatter of their weapons. They were a reserve outfit, not used to organized resistance. Still, he had no intention of getting cut off from the Americans or letting these clumsy killers get within arm's distance. He just wanted to find a good position with a clear field of fire.

A handful of PDF guardsmen, in a skirmish line, moved into the street only one building down from Siyr. They saw him the same instant he saw them.

With no aforethought and no hesitation, Siyr ran. But not away from the enemy--straight at them, firing from the hip and roaring some incomprehensible exclamation.

For an instant the PDF lieutenant and his men were surprised into paralysis. One of Siyr's wild shots dropped a man who screamed and clutched at his stomach, writhing in the dust. By the time the men recovered, Siyr was upon them.

The lieutenant leveled his weapon, but the steel buttstock of Siyr's Galil bashed in his face and he collapsed unconscious. Siyr stomped his neck on his way to the next man.

***

Cole and Campbell saw Siyr's situation unfolding and exchanged a look.

"Let's give him some help," Campbell said.

"Ooh-rah!" Cole said, already taking up trigger slack.

***

By the time the halftrack reached the center of town, Zeke and Fava-Vargas had nearly intercepted it. The driver concentrated on the action to his front and had no reason to believe men on foot were running his vehicle down.

The two men ducked behind a hut to catch their breath before one last rush.

Fava-Vargas leaned back against the mud wall and fumbled for one of his grenades. Zeke put a restraining hand on the younger man's wrist and shook his head. Fava-Vargas looked at him quizzically.

Zeke slung the rifle over his back, drew his SOG fighting knife and panted, "Let's get wet... see if we can save that 'track for ourselves."

Fava-Vargas' throat tightened, but he nodded, slung his rifle and drew his own knife.

Zeke peeked around the corner, then turned back to his comrade, hyperventilating. He gesticulated as if turning a steering wheel and jabbed a thumb toward his chest. He mimed firing a machinegun and pointed at Fava-Vargas, who nodded. They took more rapid breaths, then burst around the corner and sprinted up the street.

Even with Zeke's head start, his younger partner reached the vehicle first. Fava-Vargas tried not to think about getting his foot caught and mangled in the treads. He vaulted over the side of the halftrack, rifle butt banging on the armored hull even as his body cleared it.

The gunner whirled at the noise, saw the American and began to traverse the machinegun. Fava-Vargas blocked the barrel with his body. His blade arced over the gunner's head and sunk into the upper back.

The gunner cried out and clawed at his assailant's face. Fava-Vargas struck him with the heel of his free hand while yanking the blade out. The gunner was stunned, but kept flailing, and bit down on the American's arm. Fava-Vargas winced, drove a knee into him, pulled back, drug the blade across the gunner's neck. He severed the carotid artery and blood spurted everywhere in incredible volume. The gunner lost his strength, stopped resisting and crumpled.

Fava-Vargas struggled not to vomit as the reality of what he'd just done sunk in. This was the first time he'd ever "gotten wet." He grabbed the gunner by his blood-slick uniform and heaved him over the side.

The driver noticed the man running up beside him right before Zeke stepped onto the running board, reached in and clamped a strong hand over his mouth. With his other hand, Zeke slit his throat. The driver slumped forward, gurgling.

Zeke yanked the door open, flung the driver out and took his place behind the wheel. A quick glance over his shoulder informed him that Fava-Vargas had dispatched the gunner.

***

Mai and Bojado readied grenades when they got within range of the APC.

"Now!" Mai commanded, and they let fly.

Their frags rolled underneath the car and detonated, lifting it a foot or so off the ground, blowing the tires, puncturing the torque converter, melting the clutches and severing the layshaft.

Now the APC was going nowhere.

Mai sunk down behind cover, gulping for air.

Bojado dropped to the prone, watching the APC's top hatch over his rifle sights while groping for a grenade with his off hand.

"You having a nice little rest?" Mai asked. "How 'bout you get off your lazy butt and secure the target?"

Bojado studied Mai, who squatted on his ostensibly non-lazy butt leaning back against the outer wall of a hut, sucking wind.

Bojado shook off his thoughts, rolled to his feet and ran to the APC. He jumped atop, let the spoon fly on an incendiary grenade and dropped it down the portal from which the dead gunner's body sagged. He jumped off and ran for cover as the armored car became the world's largest pressure cooker.

***

Scarred Wolf's arms and back ached from humping the gun and tripod. But the belt was short enough now that he was able to keep it from dragging the ground by hanging it over his shoulder. His face felt raw and there were several stinging areas on the back of his legs, but he ignored them and tried to concentrate on his buddies up front in between spinning to check his six-o'clock. Lagging so far behind, he saw both the halftrack and armored car dealt with.

Some forty meters ahead, McCallum turned to check behind him and they locked eyes.

Scarred Wolf's mind raced. McCallum had rear security covered. With the firepower of the halftrack, Zeke and Fava-Vargas could probably rescue Cavarra and the others if it wasn't too late already. If Scarred Wolf could get around in the enemy's rear, he might be able to break up the attack completely.

Gasping for breath, he turned north and kept running.

DINKA VILLAGE WEST

Terrell and Lombardi took positions on opposite sides of a narrow street, belly-down, poking out the open doorways of unoccupied huts. Cavarra dropped down in the center of the street, behind the stinking carcass of a death-bloated camel. Some thirty meters away, the smoke in the intersection swirled and parted before the slow-moving armored car.

All three had caught their breath, but were sweating from the anxiety.

Cavarra's plan was to wait until the armored car left the intersection and the kill zone was packed with live meat. But the wait was nerve-wracking.

They pulled baseball frags and worked the pins out, glancing at each other, then back toward the intersection.

Terrell cursed softly. One leg of the cotter pin broke off and his sweaty fingers were too slick to muscle it out. He tried to seize the looped end with his teeth, Hollywood-style, but found the effort both painful and futile.

The vehicle was fully exposed now. The first few soldiers followed it into the intersection. Cavarra could make out their faces. Nervous faces. Confused faces. Young faces. Some coughed and swatted at the smoke and dust, but all of them looked straight ahead...as if death could only come at them from the front.

What if Sudan was his native home, he thought. It would be perfectly normal for a boy like Justin to be drafted into some warlord's little army. Instead of playing football and trying to earn his driver's license, he'd be killing, raping, and possibly getting shot to pieces in an ambush like these boys were about to. He shook the thought away.

Cavarra locked eyes with Terrell, then Lombardi. Each worried that one of the others would panic and trip the ambush too soon. The older men worried more about Terrell, still struggling with the pin, than they did each other. They turned back toward the enemy.

The trailing edge of the APC disappeared behind the edge of a building. The three men exchanged looks once again. They nodded at each other and rose to their knees.

Lombardi flung his grenade at the kill zone, the spoon separating from it as it hurled toward the target.

Cavarra let his spoon go and cooked off for three seconds before throwing.

Terrell whipped out his multi-tool and used the pliers to violently extract the stubborn cotter pin. He reared back and slung his frag with gusto.

Lombardi's grenade hit the ground a little short, bounced once and rolled right into the midst of the enemy. The PDF guardsmen looked at the round, smoking object at their feet, then glanced around to see where it had come from.

They don't even know what it is, Cavarra thought, as time slowed down so that a split second seemed to take minutes. These kids have never encountered organized resistance.

Now Terrell's frag arced through the air like a major league fastball. It smacked right into the head of a guardsman, knocking him cold.

Lombardi's frag detonated just before Cavarra's went off in mid air above the disoriented guardsmen. The enemy was sandwiched between two furious blasts. Arms, legs and heads were ripped from the limp rag-doll bodies sailing in all directions. Just as the blast was settling, Terrell's grenade went off and stirred it all up anew.

Few survivors could be seen through the smoke in the intersection, but the American trio poured fire in just the same.

When each had emptied their magazine, Cavarra yelled, "Fall back!" He wanted to withdraw before a counterattack could cut them off from the church.

They ran east for a block, then cut south, changing magazines on the run. One more block and they would hook west again. Hopefully the wide arc would get them back safely before the enemy could interdict.

**

Siyr was vaguely aware of enemy soldiers dropping all around him, but had no time to ponder it. He focused on the man nearest him. Life existed one split-second at a time.

With the PDF lieutenant down, there was enough empty space between Siyr and this man to use their weapons as intended.

The guardsman hesitated. Fear contorted his face. He made to run, stopped himself, then made to aim and fire. But Siyr eliminated that costly first step and fired twice without hesitation.

The man went down. Siyr readied for the next attacker...but there was none. Suddenly all was still and silent in his tiny corner of the universe. He was the last man standing.

He had only accounted for three of them, himself. He was sure of it. Yet the others had fallen as surely as if the Angel of Death had swung his scythe at their ankles.

Then he remembered the snipers--it must be their work. He waved at the church rooftop. A head bobbed acknowledgement.

Now alone with his thoughts, in the hyperawareness that follows a close brush with death, his own behavior perplexed him.

What he'd done was insane.

**

Cavarra saw two men ahead, running perpendicular to his present course. He dropped behind a pile of garbage. The two men saw him and did the same.

"They look like friendlies!" Lombardi said, rolling for cover himself.

Cavarra thought so, too--one wore "chocolate chips" and the other the new US desert cammies. "Crash!" he called.

An anxious second passed, Cavarra hurried to change magazines, then a Hispanic accent replied, "Burger!"

"Who's there?"

"Sergeant Bojado and Gunny Mai. Who is there?"

"Cavarra, with Lombardi and Terrell. We're comin' out."

The five men rose from cover and moved toward each other. When close enough, they all pressed their backs up against the same wall and sucked wind.

"Glad you guys made it," Cavarra said. "What happened to the others?"

"That dogface sapper is behind us," Bojado said. "We took out an APC."

"Good job."

"You mean McCallum?" Terrell asked.

"Yeah," Bojado said.

"What about Pappadakis and Fava-Vargas?" Cavarra asked.

"And Chief?" Lombardi added.

"Your squid buddies went after the halftrack," Mai said.

"Yeah," Cavarra said, skimming sweat from his forehead, "how 'bout Scarred Wolf?"

Bojado shook his head and shrugged.

"Does that mean he bought it, or you don't know?" Cavarra asked

"I dunno," Bojado said.

Cavarra cursed.

"He wiped out an eighty-pax full of opfor over there, before they could unass the truck," Bojado said. "Single-handed, man. I offered to stay back with him, carry the tripod..." He shrugged and shook his head again.

Cavarra was thoughtful. *Dinky dau* redskin, playing Crazy Horse. But God bless him. He'd put half the enemy infantry out of commission, if this was true.

A block over, McCallum stepped into view, spotted them instantly, recognized them and found temporary cover while waving to get their attention.

The men spotted the movement and rifles were leveled.

Cavarra extended his arms and knocked muzzles down. "It's our other sapper," he said. The dark giant in OG-107 "jungle fatigues" and unflashed khaki beret could only be one man.

Cavarra tapped Terrell and Bojado. "You two go join McCallum. Follow his present course to the church." He nodded to Mai and Lombardi. "You two follow me."

***

DeChalk finished loading, finally, his thumb raw from the friction, and stuffed the magazines in pockets and pouches. He almost went upstairs, then remembered Cavarra's instructions to bring LAWs.

The M72 Light Antitank Weapon was a collapsed fiberglass tube with 66mm rocket preloaded. Not nearly as large as its grandfather, the bazooka, but still large enough that they shouldn't be too hard to find.

***

Zeke drove the halftrack around the side of the church yelling, "Friendlies! Friendlies!"

Cole and Campbell scooted back from the edge of the roof and exchanged a look. Below, the APC had reached the church. Cavarra's ambush had brought smoke on a dozen or more enemy, but a handful of them had made it out of the kill zone beforehand, and followed their rolling shield safely up to the church. The crew, sans driver, also dismounted with submachineguns ready. They sprayed the roof, keeping the snipers at bay.

"They gonna man that rocket," Cole said. "Then our crap is weak."

Campbell pursed his lips and looked around. Then his eyes widened. "Man, I forgot we had these!" he groaned, fumbling for a grenade.

Cole had forgotten, too. Snipers didn't ordinarily use them.

Zeke's halftrack roared around the corner. Zeke saw the armored car--a modified *Al Fahd* reconnaissance APC--less than twenty meters away. "Holy...!" He cut the wheel hard and the halftrack swerved violently away.

The crew members had removed the body of the dead gunner. One of them was taking his place, reloading the recoilless rifle.

Fava-Vargas saw this and yelled, "Rocket!"

The new recoilless rifleman knew the halftrack's driver and gunner. He didn't recognize the men now in the halftrack. He screamed to his comrades and swung the rocket tube to bear.

Zeke cursed and floored the accelerator.

Fava-Vargas traversed the gun and opened up.

The recoilless rifle fired.

The PDF Guardsmen around the *Al Fahd* scattered.

Grenades dropped from the roof and landed on either side of the car.

Heavy slugs hammered through the hull of the APC and mangled the gunner.

The vehicle rocked from explosions on either side. More tires blew. Metal fragments whined and whacked into the steel armor.

The driver was far forward of where the armor was torn by machinegun fire, but fully enclosed, and thus deafened and terrified by the thunderous, shrieking hailstorm. He stomped on the gas and tore off for the edge of town.

The rocket streaked right for the side of the halftrack. Fava-Vargas didn't know whether to jump out, rattle off a hasty prayer or try to shoot the rocket down--it didn't seem so ridiculous an idea at the time. But he had no time to do any of those things.

His world was blinding light and crashing thunder. Like the mother of all lightningbolts had struck him right in the face.

The blinding white turned to bright crimson. No shapes. No texture. Just red. As red as the blood from the man he'd knifed.

The world roared. Roared like a jet engine's afterburners were aimed point-blank at his head. It roared and rang and vibrated. The fury of the noise was threatening to rip his brain loose, spin it inside his skull and crush it. The violence so terrible he could only conceive

one thought:
  I'm in Hell.

19

(At the quick time.)
I'm a steamroller baby, and I'm rollin' down the line.
I'm a steamroller baby, and I'm rollin' down the line.
So ya better get outa' my way now
Or I'll roll right over you.
I'm a jackhammer baby, and I'm hammerin' down the line.
I'm a jackhammer baby, and I'm hammerin' down the line.
I'm gonna rock, I'm gonna rock yo' soul
With a little rock'n'roll.
And a little bit mo'...

McCallum walked point. He saw the muzzle flash. Something grabbed him by the hip and spun him to the ground.

Terrell and Bojado saw him go down. They dropped, returning fire.

McCallum checked himself. He didn't feel any pain, but his side was wet. He rubbed it, then brought hand up to eyes. He figured he could judge the seriousness of the wound by how dark and thick the blood was.

There was no blood. He looked down. A bullet had gone through his canteen cup, canteen, and carrier. The canteen lid had blown right off. He rolled to his stomach. "Opfor in the church!" he yelled. The muzzle flash had come from a window.

***

Cavarra spearheaded the other contingent. He saw PDF guardsmen running for the back door of the church. He fired on the run. Mai and Lombardi shot from the hip on their way to cover.

All three had targeted the same guy. Red splotches appeared all over his uniform and he fell, convulsing violently. The others made it inside untouched.

Cavarra cursed. Then he saw a strange sight up the street--one man staggering toward them, another following, dressed in Rhodesian fatigues, rifle muzzle nudging the first man in the back. "Hold your fire! It's Siyr!"

"You better step it out!" Mai screamed at Siyr. "There's an APC behind you and ragheads inside our building!"

The enemy in the church fired out the windows. McCallum's voice bellowed something from the next street over.

Siyr continued calmly guiding the PDF lieutenant toward them. Amazingly, they made it to cover unscathed.

"What's this?" Lombardi asked.

The PDF officer's breathing was labored, rasping. Blood streaked outward from his nose and mouth. He sported two black eyes. The lower half of his face was swollen and, where blood didn't cover it, yellow, purple and black. He looked like a raccoon with a balloon for a jaw.

"Prisoner," Siyr replied.

***

Using the pitiful buildings for concealment, McCallum, Bojado and Terrell leapfrogged around each other up to the church, two firing while the third rushed. When they could advance no further without crossing the open ground around the church, McCallum posted Bojado where he could watch the front door, Terrell watching the rear.

"Hello, friendlies!" he called up to the roof. "Friendlies! Friendlies?"

Campbell had taken up position on the east side of the roof. Cole still faced west. "Hoo-wah! Who is there?"

"It's Mac and two friendlies. Who's up there?"

"Snipers Campbell and Cole."

"We got opfor in the church."

"No foolin', man! They're shooting up the roof at us."

"Can you see any more targets to engage from up there?"

There was a brief, muttered exchange between the snipers. "Not really."

"Then come on down. Where's the ladder?"

"Up here."

"Good. Come down the northeast corner. There's no windows

there."

"Hoo-wah!"

"And be advised, there's another group of friendlies over there somewhere."

"Hoo-wah, Mac!"

***

The red faded little by little and Fava-Vargas made out a faint outline. It was the shape of a human face. He blinked. Blinked again. A little less red. Closer to orange, now. It looked like the face of Senior Chief Petty Officer Ezekiel Pappadakis, US Navy, retired.

Zeke's lips moved; eyes staring intensely at him. Fava-Vargas blinked. Zeke's lips continued to move. He could still only hear roaring and ringing. The orange gradually lightened to yellow, and Fava-Vargas could now focus. He saw the pores in Zeke's skin. He saw blood on his face and a swollen, crooked nose.

Zeke shook him a little. He felt it, and laughed. I'm alive. It's Earth--not Hell. Not yet.

Zeke's bloody face smiled at him. He laughed, too. His lips moved some more.

"I'm alive," Fava-Vargas said. He couldn't hear his own words, but he felt his mouth move. Zeke's mouth moved, too.

Fava-Vargas had never been a lip-reader, but now, out of necessity, he tried. He watched Zeke's lips. "*Que*?" he asked.

Zeke's mouth repeated the pattern.

"*Que*...say again?"

"Can you man the gun?" That's what Zeke was saying! He was asking if he was able to drive on with the mission. The machinegun. The firefight was still in progress. But the halftrack...the rocket...

"Help me up," Fava-Vargas said. At least he thought that's what he said.

Zeke maneuvered behind him, grabbed him under the arms and lifted.

Dizzy. Painful.

The world rocked and swayed around him. His legs and back were rubber. No...rubber was sturdier than that. He hurt all over, especially his head and left hand.

Zeke's mouth was still moving. Fava-Vargas pawed weakly at it. *Shut up. I'm having enough trouble without trying to read your lips.*

The gun loomed before him. He reached out, miscalculated the distance and fell into it. He slumped over the gun, closing his eyes. Had he been inside a room, it would be spinning.

Zeke shook him again. Fava-Vargas waved him off, trying to curse but hearing nothing.

The world gradually stabilized. Fava-Vargas got his feet under him and stood up straight.

He was standing in the halftrack. He looked around.

The back of the vehicle was partially missing. Most of the tailgate was gone. The remaining armor was twisted at the edges. The rocket had only clipped the trailing edge of the vehicle. Fava-Vargas laughed again. The warhead detonated in the air after glancing off the rear armor. The blast force pushed against the tailgate in one direction, but against empty air in every other. Explosive force follows the path of least resistance, and isn't nearly as powerful when given room to expand. Only a fraction of the warhead's concussion had reached Fava-Vargas, and that fraction had deteriorated considerably by the time it reached him.

Had Zeke been a split-second later in reacting, or had the halftrack's carburetor bogged, or a cylinder in the engine missed, the rocket would have pierced the side armor. The warhead would have detonated inside the halftrack. It's power multiplied by the confinement of the surrounding armor, it would have blown him sky-high. It would have rained Fava-Vargas for several days.

He kissed the halftrack. He kissed Zeke the Greek.

Zeke grabbed him by the shoulder, gave him a playful shake, and returned to the driver's seat.

***

"So they captured the halftrack," Cavarra said, "but are they alive?"

Siyr shrugged. "As of a minute ago, yes. But the vehicle took a hit from a rocket. I think one of them went down."

Cavarra nodded. It figured. So Scarred Wolf and at least one other man were probably dead.

Some opfor were now bottled up in the church. Less than a dozen, probably. But how many were still on the loose west of the village? And would they press the attack, or had they had enough? He dispatched Lombardi and Mai to recon the western edge of the village. He posted Siyr, with his prisoner, on the side of the church opposite McCallum. Now the building was surrounded. If they could mop up this pocket, they'd be in much better shape.

Cavarra yelled in Arabic for the Guardsmen to surrender. McCallum joined in. Bojado and Terrell echoed the demand in English. Siyr commanded his prisoner to order the men inside to give up. The lieutenant attempted to comply, but he could barely breathe, much less yell. Siyr yelled into the building in a strange tongue. He was answered with shouts and gunfire.

***

DeChalk slung four LAWs around his back, grabbed his rifle and ran for the stairs. The firing outside had died down considerably, but he could still hear an occasional shot...fired from inside the church, by the sound of them. He also heard voices shouting in some Nilotic dialect very near. So the building was surrounded.

Maybe he shouldn't be mad. There must be only a few Americans left, and they were trapped inside the church. Maybe if he'd got in the firefight earlier, he'd be dead or wounded. But his arrival now could turn the tide. Maybe with the LAWs and the added firepower of his rifle, the survivors could break out of the church and escape with their lives. And that would make up for missing most of what sounded like one whale of a shoot 'em-up. Maybe.

He rounded the corner and ascended the second flight of stairs.

***

Seven PDF guardsmen remained in the church. They argued amongst themselves in panicked tones, wild-eyed and hoarse from the dehydration of fear. Each of them had an opinion about the best course of action and tried to scream it over the voices of his peers. There were men outside both doors, ready to shoot anyone who stuck his head out.

A month ago, they had butchered the infidels right here in the temple of their Hebrew/Christian God. Now the same fate awaited them. Was it some ironic joke by Allah?

They considered surrender, but didn't want to die disgracefully as the Christians had. And surely the men outside with strange accents, telling them to surrender, would take revenge.

No, a couple guardsmen argued, if they were Christians, then they were weak. They would show mercy, and let them live.

"Christians don't fight like these men have," one of them said.

The others cursed him for a coward.

One of them noticed a staircase leading down. Maybe there was a way out down there...a tunnel to another building or something. After all, some of the infidels had escaped the purge of last month. Maybe they escaped through a tunnel. He swung into the staircase.

***

DeChalk and the guardsman almost ran into each other. They came to a stop so close their noses almost touched. The guardsman shrieked and ran back up the stairs. DeChalk realized it was an enemy, leveled his rifle, and squeezed the trigger.

The trigger wouldn't budge. The safety was engaged. In the instant it took to correct that, the guy was gone.

The guardsman ran screaming from the stairway door. The enemy was downstairs, too! They were outside, pushing in! They were underneath, pushing up! They were everywhere!

He bolted for the back door. The others saw his white-faced terror and ran with him.

They exploded out the back door and scattered, running in seven directions. Terrell was so surprised, the first few got by him before he fired and dropped a man.

A few of the guardsmen fired as they fled. One of them hit his own fellow in the back.

McCallum yelled toward the front of the church, "Bojado! They broke out! Sweep through the building and link up with me at the back door!" Then he peeled off from his position.

Cavarra drew a bead before they all disappeared into the village. He winged one.

Cole dropped his man.

Campbell drew his pistol and popped one point-blank.

Bojado burst through the back door, eyes darting around wildly. McCallum arrived simultaneously. "Clear?"

Bojado nodded. "DeChalk's in there. I almost greased him. Otherwise clear."

McCallum took off after the three hostiles still running. Bojado followed. Terrell hesitated, then ran after.

Bojado fired from the hip. The limping guardsman winced and clattered to the ground. McCallum and Bojado ran past him, after the remaining two.

The wounded guardsman watched the two Americans running past, and thought it would be a good chance to kill one of them. He knew he was dying, but if he could die killing one more infidel, Allah was sure to reward his valor.

Terrell saw the downed guardsman move, scraping his submachinegun along the ground in order to point it at Bojado's back. Terrell yelled and adjusted his stride. One foot came down on the weapon. It smashed the wounded man's fingers against the ground and he cried out. Terrell's other foot swung up as if kicking a field goal, catching the man in the face. The force of the kick knocked the man unconscious while flipping him over onto his back. Terrell pumped two rounds into the man and took off after the others.

Adrenaline gave the guardsmen speed they ordinarily wouldn't have had, but the Americans ran them down and brought them back as prisoners.

***

The halftrack bounced out the western edge of the village and Zeke turned it north.

Now he saw the *Al Fahd*, speeding north as fast as it could move with mostly flat tires.

The surviving guardsmen, who had fled after Cavarra's ambush, ran the same direction on foot. They waved wildly and screamed for the APC to stop and pick them up, but the car passed by without slowing.

Fava-Vargas blinked his eyes, sighted the gun and fired. Geysers of dirt spouted from the ground behind the armored car. Zeke got the halftrack straightened out and accelerated.

Hunks of metal flew off the *Al Fahd* as it swerved left, veered right, straightened out, slowed down...then it cut hard to the right while accelerating, and flipped.

Then Zeke heard the report.

Thubthubthubthub!

The deserters changed directions and ran for the river.

Thubthubthubthub!

The capsized car shuddered and spun on it's roof.

Zeke moved his foot from the gas to the brakes. That was the sound of the Dover Devil. From some unseen point north of the village, Scarred Wolf must be laying down fire. But likely he didn't know friendlies were in the halftrack.

Zeke threw it in reverse and backed up as fast as the halftrack would go.

Thubthubthubthub!

The bodies of the Popular Defense Force guardsmen were flung, flipped and ripped apart like some invisible child were throwing a tantrum with his marionettes.

***

Mai and Lombardi returned from their recon and found Cavarra.

"It's over," Lombardi said. "The only ones left are running back the direction they came."

Cole and Campbell exchanged a silent look, then bumped fists.

Cavarra felt enormous relief. "Let's get the radios finished and pass them around. Mai, Lombardi, see if you can find the halftrack and our two guys. Cole, Campbell, see if you can find Scarred Wolf. Last anybody saw him, he was on the east side. Siyr: front-and-center. And bring that sorry dirtbag with you."

DeChalk emerged cautiously from the church, saw Cavarra, then hurried over with a clattering sound. "I found the LAWs," he said.

20

1335 15 AUG 2002; BEERSHEVA, ISRAEL
IDF CENTRAL COMMAND BUNKER

A female lieutenant approached General Dahav, who was looking over the target maps of Iran and Syria.

"Sir, Operator Twenty-Eight is on the land line with a status report for you."

The timing of this call spelled unforeseen complications. Dahav tried not to show his alarm, but dropped what he was doing and followed her to a small booth with a single telephone inside. He thanked her and went in, closing the door behind him.

The soundproofing of the booth was less to keep the staff from overhearing than to filter out the ambient noise of the bunker. He picked up the telephone receiver.

"This is General Dahav."

There was much static on the line, and the voice was faint. "Things are not going well, sir. The merchants had been here less than twenty-four hours when a robbery was attempted."

Dahav's chest tightened. "The merchants" were the American team in the Sudan. Had Sudanese intelligence discovered them so quickly? How could that be?

"Was the robbery successful?"

"Unknown. But the bandits had a large force. I'll know more if our consultant can meet with me tomorrow night."

"You keep your distance," Dahav said. "Even if he didn't make it, don't risk falling prey to the bandits. You're all we have over there."

The static fluctuated for a moment. "Yes, sir. I'll find out what I can and let you know as soon as I can."

"Make it by 0600 on *Shabot*. If I don't hear from you by then..."

"Understood, sir."

"Very well," Dahav said, and hung up. He sat down and rubbed the bridge of his nose. He felt tears building up behind his eyes. He cursed himself. *Get it together. You're a soldier--act like it. You always knew this day could come.*

He left the booth and marched across the bunker. Officers and aides parted before him, giving him strange looks. He felt light-headed and weak.

General Hiram Ben-Gadi, chief of the I.A.F. Bomber Command, was addressing a group of his subordinates over tea. One look at Dahav's pale face and glossy eyes, and he dismissed them quickly.

Even after the two generals were alone, they remained silent for a long moment.

"Arm the Doomsday Machine?" Ben-Gadi finally asked.

"I must speak with the Prime Minister," Dahav said. "You should issue Target Allocation One to your wing commanders. All passes canceled or revoked, indefinitely. Cancel all training now in progress. Let the pilots and crews rest, as possible, but be sure every one of them is accounted for on a minute-by-minute basis."

Ben-Gadi nodded--he knew the drill. He'd seen it in 1973 when he himself was a pilot. His own aircraft had been prepared for delivery of a single bomb. A dreadful, terrifying bomb. Thank God, the order to deliver it never came.

Dahav left him, and Ben-Gadi stared at three buttons on the console near him. One would send his bomber groups a discrete General Quarters alarm. One would activate sirens at airbases and Civil Defense shelters throughout the land. The other would once again call forth those abominable warheads from the Abyss. He pushed the first button, careful not to even breathe on the other two yet.

Ben-Gadi wished he could call his wife, talk to his family once again. But that was impossible once sequestered in the bunker.

***

Dahav met with more commanders, issued more orders. The wheels of an efficient, deadly machine began to turn.

SAM batteries deployed around military installations and major population centers. The Armored Corps went on full alert. Reserve divisions mobilized. General Quarters sounded in every Navy vessel. Three Dolphin Class nuclear attack submarines assumed radio silence, submerged and commenced maneuvers to escape Egyptian tracking. Israeli paratroopers were issued live ammunition, field rations and parachutes; mustered to the tent city just outside the airfield where flight crews hurriedly checked and re-checked their C-130 Hercules transports.

All these forces awaited the relay of information from two men in the Sudan. Should Operator Twenty-Eight fail to report by 0600 on the Sabbath, or report that the American team was compromised, the Israeli paratroopers would load up and lift off for the Hala'ib Triangle. Should their mission fail, General Ben-Gadi would push the other two buttons.

21

1342 15 AUG 2002; INGESSANA, SUDAN

(At the quick-time.)
When I was just a little boy... Mama bought me a brand-new toy
Hey! It was a G.I. Joe... With combat gear from head to toe.
Then one day I turned eighteen... They shipped me off to Fort
Benning
Hey! Now I'm a G.I. Joe... In combat gear from head to toe...

Cavarra drove the halftrack, leading the small convoy north. It was an old US eight-ton, probably given to the British during Montgomery's campaigns against Rommel, or a lend/lease hand-me-down from the Soviets to the Sudanese. A sixty-five-year-old testament to the pride Americans once took in what they built.

Campbell dozed in the passenger seat. Perched behind them, at the gun, was big Jake McCallum.

Zeke drove the rear truck, with Cole riding shotgun. Most of the gear was in this vehicle. Mai drove the middle truck, with Bojado beside him in the cab. In the back rode the wounded Scarred Wolf and Fava-Vargas, with Lombardi, Terrell, Siyr and DeChalk.

Zeke had a broken nose from the steering wheel. Fava-Vargas had some burns, a broken hand and a severe hearing loss. He still seemed rattled, but otherwise good.

Even the suicidal Scarred Wolf, whose John-Wayning probably saved everybody's bacon, had cheated the Grim Reaper. When Cole and Campbell found him, he had his own rifle, two MAT49s and an M1928 Thompson slung around his back, towing the Dover Devil behind him, tripod and all, on a makeshift gurney of PDF uniforms tied together. He was cutting uniform insignia off fallen PDF troops. He wouldn't return to the church for medical treatment until they'd helped him salvage the recoilless rifle and what rockets they could from the *Al Fahd*.

He had some flesh wounds, but nothing incapacitating.

Cavarra had a good idea what all his has-beens were made of, now. They came through like pros in the firefight.

All except DeChalk. The CIA probably picked him for his language skills and mercenary experience. But a man had to be measured by his actions, not his reputation or baggage stamps. DeChalk was just a hopeless wannabe with an active travel record.

Siyr was something different. He handled himself well in the fight, but Cavarra didn't buy his story about wanting to scrounge some beer just so he would be welcome in the otherwise American group. If Siyr hadn't put himself in harm's way a number of times, Cavarra might seriously wonder if he hadn't been the one to tip off the enemy in the first place.

Cavarra had followed a hunch and drafted Mai to assist him with the interrogation of the prisoners. Mai's inherent cruelty was well-suited for such jobs--he would have made a perfect North Vietnamese P.O.W. camp commissar. With adequate persuasion, the prisoners sang like opera stars.

It seemed that the attack was due to a mistaken conception--not because anyone guessed their purpose here. The Popular Defense Forces had rolled into town expecting to find a few rear-echelon pogues and maybe the women and children they'd missed the first time around. Thus the element of surprise had quickly shifted from attacker to defender. The effect was like a diver swimming into the mouth of a sleeping shark.

Still, Cavarra had learned his lesson: Each of his men now had a LAW, his grenadiers had High Explosive and White Phosphorous rounds for the M203s, and everybody had a short-range radio headset. Lead could fly at any time, any place, for any reason in this country. He had to get out of the linear mission mindset. The operation hadn't officially kicked off yet, but they were in Indian Country just the same.

Siyr's disappearance, then reappearance right before the attack, kept bothering him. He would keep a close eye on the African from now on.

The halftrack was jarred going over a bump, and Campbell stirred.

"Sorry to disturb your nap," Cavarra said. "Would you like some milk and cookies now?"

Campbell rubbed his eyes, looked around and smiled sheepishly. "I used to think joining the infantry would turn me into a light sleeper. You know--like the slightest little sound would wake me up, ready to fight." His normal voice was a slightly marble-mouthed drawl. Now it sounded as though course gravel had replaced the marbles. "Just the opposite. A grunt can sleep anytime, anywhere, through **anything**. I guess it's because you get so little sack time in a line unit, you learn to appreciate it more. Your body takes it whenever it can get it."

Cavarra nodded. Sleep deprivation could do that. He'd been the same way after BUDS. "I used to think, to be a commando, I'd have to be trained by some Ninja assassin how to move through the bush in absolute silence. Part Apache, part ghost. When I first became an operator, I couldn't believe how much noise we made on a tactical movement."

"We're always in a hurry," Campbell said. "A lot of men, humpin' a lot of gear mos-koshee. It ain't quiet."

"Fortunately, enemy infantry sleeps just like you do," Cavarra said. "You just gotta' make sure your gear doesn't rattle. And don't talk. Human voices will carry, out in the bush. That's the number one bolo."

Campbell stretched. "Thanks for the tip, boss."

Cavarra felt embarrassed. *Preaching to the choir, genius. Like a sniper wouldn't understand noise and light discipline.* He'd always made an effort to avoid the elitist arrogance of his fellow officers, yet he often slipped easily into a lecturing mode. Insulting men's intelligence had become second nature to him, partly because it was S.O.P. for officers and NCOs to do so; partly because he'd served with many men who had no intelligence to insult.

"I understand you jumped into Panama," he said.

Campbell nodded.

"First combat jump since World War Two, wasn't it?"

Campbell shrugged. "Rangers jumped in Korea. Into Grenada too, from three hundred feet with no reserves. Division was air-landed after they took *Point Salines* Airport."

"That's barely enough elevation for a parachute to open," Cavarra said.

"That's why they didn't bother with reserve chutes. Anyway, I wasn't there."

They rode on wordlessly for a moment. Clouds gathered over the plains, but the heat was still oppressive.

"You were in Urgent Fury, right?" Campbell asked.

Cavarra nodded. "SEAL Team Four." His team blew up a radio station. It was his first taste of combat. One of the transport planes completely missed the drop zone and put its SEALs from Team Six over the ocean. Some of them got tangled in their chutes and drowned.

"With all due respect, sir," Campbell said, "what was Mai referring to about Panama?"

Remembering Mai's comment made Cavarra want to stop the convoy, get out and beat the ignorant jarhead to death. He sighed and forced himself to calm. To let someone anger you to that degree was to let him control you.

"He was talking about the mission to disable Noriega's private jet," Cavarra said. "Given the terrain, the enemy strength and the size of the airfield, the brass should have sent in the Rangers to secure it. Or some of you guys."

"Oh really?" Campbell was surprised he would admit that.

"Different forces are good for different missions," Cavarra said. "Take me, or McCallum, or Fava-Vargas back there. We're all operators. A whole lot badder than some gunner's mate on a destroyer. But who can bring more smoke on a target--us or that tin can?"

Campbell didn't appear to be following his logic.

"Take you," Cavarra said. "You're badder than any crewman on an Abrams tank, right?"

"Hoo-wah."

Campbell was no musclepig like McCallum or Terrell, but he was hard as woodpecker lips. He had the perfect build and metabolism for an airborne grunt--he could run all day and run all night, humping eighty pounds of whupass; dig a fighting position in frozen mud with a small entrenching tool; catch maybe an hour or two of sleep in a freezing rain, then fill in his hole and start running again.

"But can you outrun an Abrams?" Cavarra asked. "Can you wipe out a formation of T72s in five minutes while taking the best their main guns can dish out?"

Campbell shrugged. "I can drop behind enemy lines, capture a bridge, fight off enemy sappers and hold the bridge so that tank can drive over it."

"Exactly. That's my point. I wouldn't hand you a T.O.W. missile and ask you to attack a Republican Guard armored brigade, just like I wouldn't drop a tank out of an aircraft behind enemy lines. I wouldn't try digging a trench with a sponge, and I wouldn't clean the bathroom tub with a bulldozer."

Campbell understood now. "I copy. Right tools for the right job."

"There was only so much combat to go around in Panama," Cavarra explained. "Navy brass wanted to make sure we got a share. To blazes with whether or not the mission suited us. The planner of the operation was a commodore with as much imagination as a plankton. One of his subordinates suggested some alternate plans far less suicidal, but he nixed them.

"We blew the aircraft, accomplished the mission, but got shot to pieces in the process. Four of us never came back. Eight seriously wounded. And it was all avoidable at the planning stage."

"No offense," Campbell said, "but that's what I hate about officers...most of them, anyway. Their own reputation, their own 201 File, their own ego is more important than the welfare of the troops. Why is an officer considered brave because he's willing to sacrifice his men in any old hare-brained operation? And what's worse, he'll talk like he's doing his men a favor: 'My boys are itching to prove themselves, General. They just won't be able to live with the disappointment if you don't let my boys frontally assault that hardened enemy position. Artillery? Air support? Sure, that would be nice, General, but my boys couldn't bear the shame of waiting around for all that'."

Cavarra was conflicted. Having been an officer himself, he felt a bit defensive. But he'd often choked down the very same thoughts.

Still, they weren't thoughts an officer shared with an enlisted man.

Yet he was no longer an officer, and Campbell was no longer an enlisted man. They were two civilians, two veterans, sharing war stories.

"A combat commander needs to be decisive," Cavarra said. "He has to be able to put his men in harm's way without hesitation. You can't win a war without officers who will."

"Custer was decisive," Campbell said. "So was the chairborne commando who dreamed up your mission in Panama."

Cavarra squirmed. "The decisiveness has to be married with good judgment. Knowledge, initiative, imagination. common sense--"

Campbell laughed. "Common sense? I don't know about the Navy, but I think that's what they try to destroy in all that officer training. NCO leadership courses, too. Lombardi's a good example. Check your brain and sell your soul at the E-Five Board."

Again, Cavarra inwardly agreed, albeit grudgingly. "Is that why you got out?"

Campbell nodded. "Part of it. Wanted to be a free man for a while. Finally took advantage of the G.I. Bill. Working on a degree, taking some R.O.T.C. Figure maybe I'll become an officer myself, if my common sense doesn't disqualify me. Be the kind of officer I would have liked to follow."

Cavarra thought he might make an outstanding leader. But that didn't mean he'd go far in today's military. Too much depended on luck--what chain of command he would fall under, what quotas needed filling and what policies would be in effect. And even if he got lucky, his ability to brown-nose and shuffle paperwork would prove more important than his actual leadership aptitude. Equally important would be his willingness to stab his buddies in the back to earn cheese points. The Army was probably the worst branch for that.

The Navy had its share of BS, but in balance there were many factors to make it worth the hassle. Serving with good men was one of them--men like Campbell and Cole, Scarred Wolf, Zeke, Fava-Vargas, McCallum...these were men he could count on when rounds were flying uprange. To Cavarra this was the only genuine friendship in life.

"So how'd you go from college student to mercenary?" Cavarra asked.

"Got a call Saturday from some suits at Soggy. They offered to pay me for time and travel just for driving up to meet with them."

"Who?"

"S.O.G.I. I'd never heard of them, either. But I think they

recruited McCallum, back there, and most of the others. Captain Stone remembered me... he works for them, now. They've got a rifle range, and they put me through the paces with a Barrett fifty to see if I still had the right stuff."

A water buffalo grazed on the plain, oblivious to the vehicles until they infringed on its invisible comfort radius. It trotted another sixty meters away, then stopped to watch the convoy pass.

"So I guess they're not the ones who invited you here," Campbell said.

Cavarra shook his head. "Somebody dropped my name to the Agency, and they recruited me directly. Wish I'd have known about this other outfit." He wondered why he hadn't been recruited through the same channels the others had. "What's their name again?"

"Special Operations Groups, Incorporated. 'Soggy' for short."

Why had the Agency chosen him to lead the team over somebody already in S.O.G.I.'s database? Was it because someone appreciated his abilities, specifically? Or because he was simply considered more expendable than the more orthodox retirees with command experience?

"Couldn't stand retirement, huh?" Campbell asked.

Cavarra grimaced. He didn't think of himself as a warmonger. But being a SEAL was the most fulfilling thing he'd ever done. He'd never felt so alive as he did after a firefight or a tactical dive. It was what he did best. Melissa had been attracted to that aspect of him, at first. Later she came to hate it.

"Guess I'm having trouble adapting," Cavarra said. "How 'bout you?"

"Can't really say why I'm here. Money's good, but that's not it. Might not live to spend it, right?"

Cavarra nodded.

Campbell fell silent, experiencing contradictory thoughts he'd suffered many times.

War was an ugly, dehumanizing evil. He acknowledged this, intellectually, yet didn't feel the horror of it like he knew he should. Unlike most of his friends and family back in Valdosta, Georgia, he appreciated America enough to believe it was worth fighting for. But that didn't change the fact that he was just an assassin, when it came right down to it. He took human lives by puncturing vital organs with jacketed lead balls flying at the speed of sound, launched from such great distance that his targets were rarely even aware of his presence on the battlefield.

He'd reentered the civilian world with a newfound appreciation for life...and freedom. At first he'd done what he could to wash the stench of death from his conscience. But after the terrorist attacks in New York and DC, dormant instincts reawakened in him. After Americans were deployed in Afghanistan to hunt down Bin Laden and overthrow the Taliban, he started having dreams about it.

In his dreams, he was back in the Airborne with his old buddies. Bringing smoke and taking names. Jumping into the capitals of terrorist-sponsoring countries and kicking some serious *cundingy*. He didn't tell anyone about the dreams, for fear it would betray some despicable psychological ailment.

He awoke some mornings with an impulse to call the recruiting station, but would talk himself out of it before breakfast. Yet when his old company commander asked him to volunteer for this covert mission, he hardly hesitated.

He hadn't kept in touch with Captain Stone, didn't know if he was still a captain or even still in the Airborne. Hadn't thought about him at all, really, for years. But when Stone said, "We can really use your help, son," he was flattered. And he felt strangely obligated--he didn't want to let Stone down.

***

Riding behind them, standing by the gun, unable to hear their conversation, McCallum's thoughts traveled down parallel tracks.

Mac had loved being an A-Team operator. He'd had every intention of making a career of the Special Forces. When he made Delta Force--the elite of the elite--he figured his future would just keep looking brighter and brighter. Then came the catastrophic gagglejerk in Somalia.

He did his job, like the rest of the men on the ill-planned raid into Mogadishu, but he'd made it known from the beginning he thought the mission was ate-up like a soup sandwich. The ensuing debacle proved him right, but this hardly made him popular with his superiors.

His disillusionment and bitterness were hard to contain after that. He admitted, now, he'd been too loose with his tongue on a number of occasions. But to send America's best into the bowels of Perdition with one arm and a leg tied behind their back was an inexcusable offense. His disgust for the Limp-Richard politicians--both in and out of uniform--was no secret, and made him enough enemies up high that when he refused to re-up, nobody tried talking him into it.

Once a civilian, he looked into law enforcement as a new career, but found too much red tape between him and a position on a SWAT team, or any other slot that could utilize some of his skills. Instead, he founded his own construction business.

His company was struggling to turn a profit when he got his first call from an S.O.G.I. recruiter. They had a "client" in Bosnia who could use a sapper with combat experience. They didn't have to twist his arm. Afterwards, he told them to keep him in mind if more work came up. They were happy to oblige.

***

In the back of the middle truck, Scarred Wolf absently watched Lombardi put a cast on Fava-Vargas' hand. Fava-Vargas was covered with dried blood and looked like something from a horror film. He was one of those guys who sang all the time, and seemingly had every Top Forty song memorized. This was annoying enough before his hearing loss. Now he **sounded** like something from a horror film, too.

Lombardi had pulled dozens of tiny shell fragments out of Scarred Wolf's buttocks and legs. The shrapnel wounds burned constantly, but flared sharper with every jolt of the truck's suspension.

Like McCallum, Scarred Wolf was infuriated by the Somalian nightmare. He hadn't been involved, personally, but that didn't diminish his outrage.

Tommy Scarred Wolf's father was an alcoholic, so he never was taught of his warrior heritage. But he knew it was there...could feel it in his blood. His older brother was the same. Vince was smart, and spent a lot of time at the library. He researched all he could about the Shawnee way of life before it was corrupted by the white man, and passed the knowledge along to Tommy. The two young boys would try to reenact glorious exploits of Tecumseh on the plains behind their mother's trailer, with car antennas for spears and beer bottles for tomahawks. They played a violent version of hide-and-seek around the reservation, in which the hider would ambush the seeker if he got too close. Vince taught him how to wrestle, how to shoot a rifle, a pistol, a bow, how to stalk game, and later passed along the martial arts he picked up when he found a job and could afford lessons.

One of their uncles was a Vietnam veteran, who had a television. He never missed a war movie, unless two were being broadcast simultaneously. Vince and Tommy spent many hours watching reruns of Combat and war movies with Uncle Jay. One time Vince got some money for a birthday and used it to buy two bags of army men and some plastic tanks and deuce-and-a-halfs. They staged pitched battles in the grass, using dirt clods for ammunition...bottle rockets in July. Tommy assumed he and Vince would one day serve in the military together and distinguish themselves in battle.

When Vince was old enough, he chose to join the tribal police instead.

Tommy Scarred Wolf carried out his childhood plans, joined the Army and volunteered for Special Forces. He was almost as proud to see his name on the new BDUs issued him in basic training as he would be later upon winning his green beret and Special Forces tab

The training was rough, but Scarred Wolf made a natural Sneaky Pete. He excelled at land navigation and all the weapons training. His endurance was remarkable--possibly from all the running he did on the reservation growing up with Vince. The only part he had major trouble with was the swimming—his body had the buoyancy of a rock.

Scarred Wolf's instincts and fast thinking during covert operations in the Gulf got him decorated and promoted. He achieved the distinction in battle he'd always wanted. But return to peacetime operations was a tremendous let-down. Not just because it was boring, by comparison, but because he once again had to kowtow to the bean-counting chairborne commandos who shoveled out mountains of chickenshit from behind their armor-plated desks. Putting themselves in for medals while inventing idiotic busywork for the troops; harassing good operators to the point of AWOL with scum details for wearing non-issue underwear or failing to polish the soles of their boots... It was sickening.

The scuttlebutt from Somalia--and the image of American bodies being desecrated and dragged naked through the streets of Mogadishu--only confirmed what he'd been thinking already: that the people he worked for had no honor, no loyalty to their troops, their country, or anything but their own careers. If capturing warlord Aidid's henchmen was important enough to send Delta Force and the Rangers into a place where they'd be completely surrounded and outnumbered by hundreds-to-one, the relief should have deployed in tanks and APCs, with gunships in support. But instead, politics dictated the extraction be performed by HMMWVs, with air support from only a few scout choppers.

Scarred Wolf rethought letting his life be controlled by a constantly changing chain-of-command who thought of men as "assets at our disposal" rather than "warriors on our team," with integrity that fluctuated with the political winds.

He took leave to visit the reservation.

His people had mixed reactions to him. They admired his accomplishments as an elite warrior, but didn't approve of him serving the Federal Government. His brother was a big shot in the tribal police by then, and said he could get Tommy hired easily.

Also, Scarred Wolf saw the adult version of Linda Dunning. She'd been barely a teenager when he left, but a fully blossomed woman now.

Scarred Wolf's superiors and all his fellow Sneaky Petes talked themselves hoarse trying to convince him to reenlist when he returned from leave. But his mind and spirit were in harmony. His ETS date arrived; he tossed his boots over the wire and drove back to Oklahoma.

Vince not only got him hired, he pulled a few strings and got him a detective's badge.

Scarred Wolf won respect among the people by making drug busts and working homicides. In his free time he chased Linda. She was not an easy catch, and he had to start learning the old language just to keep up with her. Through her he met many others who'd grown up just as he had...starved for a connection to their own heritage, their own culture, but with no parents around or sober enough to teach them. Now, as adults themselves, they sought to reclaim it together.

At the powwows, Scarred Wolf was welcomed into the select "forty-nining" circle. Warriors like his Uncle Jay met with the old ones who'd fought in Korea; in North Africa, Italy, France, Belgium and Germany; on Guadalcanal, Tarawa, Iwo Jima, Okinawa and Corrigidor... They taught him one of the honor songs from back in the days following WWII, when forty-nine out of the fifty warrior brothers who'd shipped out to fight Hitler and Tojo regathered to share that special bond that only warrior brothers know.

Linda became his woman. She was a good companion, a good lover, and before long, a good mother. They had three strong children.

He was elected war chief, which meant mostly sitting in on tedious political meetings. But it also gave him the opportunity to drill the Shawnee Militia and pass along some of his experience. It was a good life.

At night, though, Scarred Wolf was teased by dreams of being an operator once again. Especially after September Eleven, 2001, and all the white man's talk of war.

He confided in the old ones while forty-nining one night. They discussed his dreams amongst themselves. Michael Fastwater, a marine who'd lost an eye and part of his hand in the South Pacific, said the dream meant Scarred Wolf still had unfinished business. His spirit knew there were more battles in his destiny and was trying to tell his mind. The others agreed. Scarred Wolf asked them if he should leave his family and join back up. They discussed this and decided he should not. He should wait because he would be called to war when the time was right.

When the man from S.O.G.I. contacted Scarred Wolf, he knew the time was right.

"How can you bear to sit down?" DeChalk asked, jarring him out of his thoughts. "Doesn't it hurt?" DeChalk had seen some of the shrapnel Lombardi pulled out of Scarred Wolf's backside.

"Of course it hurts," Scarred Wolf said.

"You think he doesn't feel pain 'cause he's an Injun?" Lombardi snapped.

DeChalk wanted to protest, but Lombardi said, "We all feel pain, we just don't hide in the basement to avoid it."

"I wasn't hiding!" DeChalk said.

"That's right," Lombardi said, "you just lost your rifle."

"It was my ammo, not the rifle. And I didn't lose it--Siyr took it."

His words were drowned out by the jeers of the others--even Fava-Vargas, who couldn't hear what was being said, but only knew that DeChalk was the subject of discussion, joined in. This infuriated the merc. Siyr had admitted to grabbing his loaded magazines, but DeChalk suffered all the ridicule. He thought they were finally done breaking bad on him once the trucks were loaded, but now it looked as though they might never tire of it.

The hostility directed at DeChalk, however, was not a sign of low morale. To the contrary, spirits were quite high.

Prior to the attack on the village, conversation amongst the group had been stilted and sporadic, limited to sports, reality TV shows, or speculation about Cavarra's leadership ability.

Now they all shared a common experience. The doubts about Cavarra fizzled away. He was "Rocco" now, not just to Zeke, but most of them.

There was plenty of fuel for conversation, now. Most of the men were intent on delivering, with gusto, a blow-by-blow account of where they'd been and what they'd done in the firefight. Each of them portrayed their own behavior as fearless, but in a circumspect manner so as to disguise their attempts to impress the others.

Siyr recognized the backhanded bragging as being universal among professional soldiers.

Interesting that Scarred Wolf didn't take part. In fact, he said very little at all. Partially due to the pain of his wounds, no doubt...but Siyr suspected something else as well: For one thing, he didn't need to boast. Everybody knew his actions had proved instrumental in the team's survival.

Nobody came right out and praised him openly--in the testosterone-blinded ego of a self-proclaimed stud, to do so was akin to admitting some inferiority or weakness in one's self. Instead, they made a joke of it--portraying Scarred Wolf as insane, not heroic. "That dinky-dau redskin," they called him. It was all code talk for grudging admiration.

They called Siyr crazy, too. Cole told him, when Siyr had charged the PDF squad, it was the first time he'd "evah seen a colored man give a rebel yell." Siyr didn't know what a "rebel yell" was, exactly, but he knew Cole was expressing respect according to unofficial custom among men like these. And besides, maybe he was crazy.

Siyr still didn't know why he rushed the PDF squad. Had he taken time to think, he'd have run the opposite way. Had the enemy not been so hesitant, and had the snipers not made a heads-up play, he could never have survived. And with him gone, the Mossad lost any modicum of control over this mission. A stupid, stupid risk.

"A hundred troops against twelve of us," Terrell said, again, this time slapping Siyr's back. "Hoo-yah! Next time they better bring more men."

Terrell was a minor celebrity himself, now, thanks to his memorable grenade throw.

The others chuckled. Siyr thought Terrell's newfound machismo was the most interesting. He'd been such a gloomy, exasperated type before, always accentuating the negative in every situation. The only time he opened his mouth, it seemed, was to complain about all the work he had to do putting the rifle range together, standing guard on the roof, missing a night's sleep, and so on. He seemed like a different man now.

Terrell wasn't high on an adrenaline rush like the others.

Unknown to anyone else, he'd never killed anyone before today. During Desert Shield/Storm he'd nearly broken his back building roads through the desert and erecting various buildings, but never fired a shot in anger. As he followed McCallum and Bojado from the church, he'd been struck with the notion that he didn't belong here with all these super-commandos. He didn't measure up.

Then he'd saved Bojado from being shot in the back. He'd looked right into another man's face while taking his life: his initiation.

Now he ran his mouth like the others, but mostly to avoid thinking about what he'd done.

Scarred Wolf lightly thumped Siyr on the arm.

"What's going on in this country?" Scarred Wolf asked.

"What do you mean?"

"The blood all over the church back there," Scarred Wolf said. "All the burnt crops. The way the opfor opened fire on the town before they even knew what they were shooting at."

Siyr gave him a condescending smile. "The government in Khartoum has a goal to become the first completely Islamic nation in Africa. The problem is, twenty percent of the population is Christian. Or they used to be, some years ago. You heard what the prisoners said: Villages like this are put to the sword. Some of the villagers escaped last time. The PDF intended to kill the survivors along with us."

"Genocide." Scarred Wolf had suspected this, but wasn't quite ready to believe it. It was too doomed medieval.

"*Theocide* is a better word, maybe. Is there such a word in English?"

"I don't think so."

"There should be. This is nothing new. Khartoum declared jihad in 1983. It's the Turkish Inquisition all over again. Don't Americans watch the news?"

"Sudan isn't in the news," Scarred Wolf said.

***

Up in the cab, Mai and Bojado rode silently. They hadn't said more than three words to each other since the trip started.

At first Bojado sought out Mai as a fellow marine and therefore a comrade he could trust. He had even shared Mai's contempt for Cavarra. But now he understood Cavarra--and Mai--a lot better.

Bojado liked Rocco's leadership style. The man knew his stuff. He wasn't like other officers--and not just because he was retired. When Bojado was active duty in the Corps, he thought of officers as a third gender. They obviously weren't female, but they sure weren't men, either. It had something to do with their aloof, elitist attitude. Rocco didn't have that. He left no doubt about who was in charge, yet he treated his underlings like adult human beings. He might be the commanding officer, but he was still one of them.

Mai, on the other hand, treated everyone as if subhuman. Maybe he'd been a drill instructor...but that was no excuse. *Get over it*. Mai despised everyone, including fellow leathernecks Bojado and Cole. He just hated them a little less when in the midst of non-marines. He was possibly the most hateful, bitter man Bojado had ever met--including the D.I.s on Parris Island.

Bojado had reversed his initial impression 180 degrees. He would gladly follow Cavarra into combat. But he didn't look forward to fighting beside Mai.

***

Mai did, in fact, hate everyone. No matter how dark their skin may be, they were still a bunch of *haoles* to him. He regretted taking this job. He should have just stayed on the island...but he hated most of his fellow Hawaiians, too. And he couldn't seem to hold on to any decent civilian jobs.

Five years. He'd only had five years to go when that incident occurred. He could still see the little bastard's face, too.

Officer Candidate Trevor Banks was everything Mai hated about haoles--blond haired, blue eyed, tall, handsome, muscular but trim... Mai just knew he was some snotty rich kid. And smart--probably a teacher's pet. But Mai couldn't intimidate him, no matter what he did.

Banks was Jewish or Protestant or one of those other weirdos. And prior service, but not in the Marines, which made it even worse. Mai broke bad on Banks before PT every morning so the kid would already be smoked and unable to keep up on the runs, but the kid sucked it up and hung tough.

Mai tried to embarrass Banks one time by lumping him in with the morons who couldn't field-strip the M16A2 and put it back together. The little smarmy freak stripped it down and reassembled it faster than anyone Mai had ever seen. Much faster than Mai himself could do it. Boy, did that ever piss him off.

It was the breaking point.

Mai made Banks stand at attention, then punched him in the stomach in plain sight of the rest of the platoon. "Think you're pretty smart, don't you Banks?"

The other candidates were stunned. So was Banks, who doubled over but said nothing.

Mai slapped his face repeatedly, screaming at him to straighten up and stand at attention. Bewildered and dazed, Banks didn't cry out. That angered Mai all the more. He screamed louder and struck harder.

Finally, Banks defended himself. The two of them were rolling around on the deck when the platoon commander and some of the other training NCOs came on the scene.

An investigation was launched. The smarmy little haole college kids in the training platoon snitched on Mai...testified he had laid hands on the candidate. Banks was "boarded" out, but Mai had to stand before the commander of Officer Candidate School and undergo an interrogation.

Mai explained that it was no big deal for instructors to administer a beating back when he was a recruit. The C.O. didn't buy it.

In desperation, he admitted his wife had left him for some haole and it had upset him tremendously. It might have saved him from hard labor, but it didn't save his job. They booted him out of the Corps.

Mai begged everyone to let him back in, from the marine recruiters to his Congressperson. They wouldn't even discuss it with him.

He was sleeping at a Honolulu flophouse, panhandling and mugging tourists to supplement his welfare check, when another skidrow veteran told him about a group that hired ex-servicemen with special skills for mercenary jobs around the world.

***

The convoy came to another wide river. Hendricks had provided them with maps denoting the location of bridges across the Blue Nile, but Cavarra thought there might be guards posted at all bridges now, since the battle at the Dinka village. He didn't want to tangle with the Sudanese again before it was time, so they looked for a spot to ford.

They found an area of semi-rapids, and the halftrack got across easily. With the winch, the trucks were helped across with no mishaps.

Cavarra was pleased with the spirit of teamwork growing and strengthening ever since the firefight. The men were really starting to work together, it seemed. Maybe the surprise attack in the village was the best thing that could have happened to them.

They were good men. Most of them. Even Mai and Lombardi had proven themselves good to have in a fight, if good for nothing else.

***

The black sky sparkled with stars when they rolled up to the rally point. Concertina wire surrounded a crude airstrip, three strange fixed-wing aircraft, two large canvas tents and a few smaller ones. The whole compound was about two acres in size. A tawny, muscular, short-haired terrier watched their approach for a while, then bolted for one of the tents.

In a moment the dog reemerged and returned to the gate where he watched the convoy approach with ears forward and tail down. A man came out of the tent wearing a loud pair of shorts and holding a pistol.

Cavarra came to a stop just outside the gate and dismounted to meet the man walking up. The dog watched Cavarra's every move but didn't make a sound.

The man was tall, with a lean build and an enormous wristwatch. *Must be a pilot.*

"Arkansas," challenged the man.

"Locomotive," Cavarra replied.

"Tell me about the Superbowl."

Cavarra hesitated, then said, "Gotta give the Patriots credit for some inspired defense. But then the Rams played their worst game of the season that day."

The man grinned and extended his free hand. "Gordy Puttcamp. Good to meet you."

"Dwight Cavarra. What if I didn't know anything about football?"

Puttcamp shrugged. "I guess I could let that go. But if you told me Tom Brady was some kinda' phenomenon at quarterback, I'd have to shoot ya. How many guys with you?"

"Thirteen men, counting me. Three vehicles. Lots of equipment."

"Pull on in. There's only four of us here--two other pilots and a mechanic. You and three others can bunk with us in that big tent on the right. The rest of your guys can take the one on the left. Off-load your gear there where that tarp is suspended, then park the trucks back here in the southeast corner. Cool?"

Cavarra nodded and climbed back up in the halftrack.

22

1653 15 AUG 2002; KHARTOUM, SUDAN
WAR DEPARTMENT HEADQUARTERS

General Anwar Moussaoui of the PDF stepped inside the wood-paneled office and saluted General Rahim of the Sudanese Army.

Rahim returned the salute and bade him sit down across from his desk. "I'm afraid I don't completely understand. Something about a major who deserted and some Dinka rebels?"

Moussaoui shook his head. He'd never said Hasan deserted. Hasan had run to Bor on foot after his unit was wiped out in an ambush. He was wounded and hysterical.

"Hasan got a tip that some Christian resistance cell was arming and training Dinkas," Moussaoui explained.

"Christian resistance?" Rahim laughed.

Moussaoui hunched his shoulders. "This is what he was told, sir. Only a small force of them, but armed and equipped, nonetheless. Hasan mustered his men and went to investigate. But he was surprised by a much larger force and sustained heavy losses...including two of the new *Al Fahd* armored cars."

Rahim groaned. "This is what happens when I give good equipment to amateurs. We should put you all back on horses. Where is the enemy force now--are they still with the Dinkas?"

"Hasan doesn't know. I will find out, though, you can be certain."

Rahim waved his hand, irritated. "No. This is an Army matter now. We'll clean up your mess, General. But I want a full report on my desk tonight about how you will deal with Major Hasan's incompetency."

"Uh...yes, sir..."

"This is probably a unit of a new rebel guerilla force calling themselves the 'Sudan Liberation Movement.' They split off from the SPLM because of Garang's rapprochement."

John Garang, leader of the Sudanese People's Liberation Movement, was currently showing a willingness to cooperate with

President Omar Hassan Ahmad El-Bashier. Bashier was trying to negotiate a cease-fire now, with the carrot of a strategic partnership with the US dangling before his nose. He would dial down some of the violence and terror against the infidels, agree to halt his military cooperation with Uganda, and in return sanctions would be lifted, the extermination of two million black Sudanese would be forgotten, Egypt's hegemony in the region would be checked, and billions of American dollars would come rolling into Khartoum.

Once this budgetary precedent was established, the religious and racial cleansing could resume. Garang and his naive cronies would be dealt with quietly. But the rogue SLM could potentially spoil things, if they found some way to focus American attention on the scorched earth policy, the slave trade, or the inquisition by the Muslim regime. Washington would gladly look the other way, as long as no significant voting bloc in America took notice.

"Perhaps they are working with rebels from Darfur," Moussaoui said. "They certainly fight with strength, as you would expect warriors of Islam to do."

"Perhaps," Rahim said. "Our dilemma with those black devils will get worse before it gets better. But we need to resolve this specific problem now, regardless of its origin. I'll dispatch my armored strike force to hunt them down."

Moussaoui nodded. The *Murahaleen* Scouts. However large this new rebel unit was, the Strike Force would find them and crush them.

"Now," Rahim said, "follow me to the map room and show me where Major Hasan was ambushed."

23

2218 15 AUG 2002; TEKEZZE RIVER CAMP, SUDAN

The Allman Brothers' "No One Left To Run With" bumped from a boom box. The men had broken up into cliques and sat around the pilots' tent doing what fighting men do during downtime: drinking, playing cards and grabassing. Cavarra figured they could use some unwinding time before they got busy rehearsing for the mission.

Cavarra sat with Puttcamp and Phil Jenkins, both former Air Force pilots, and Wade Haugen, a Harrier driver from the USMC. With their assistance, Cavarra built a sand table with a scale model of the terrorist camp.

Campbell, Terrell and McCallum played spades while Siyr looked on.

Cole and Bojado talked girls and cars. Fava-Vargas, starting to get a little of his hearing back but still functionally deaf, tried to follow their conversation by watching their mouths move.

Lombardi spit-shined his boots. Mai sat nearby nursing beer, borrowing some Kiwi for his own boots. They spoke in low tones, with occasional glances around the tent.

Zeke knocked back some beer himself, losing interest in the dry, humorless conversation of Mai and Lombardi...centered around the lives of lower-enlisted men they'd managed to ruin.

After cleaning the Dover Devil, Scarred Wolf flopped belly down on a cot and was now busy inspecting the inside of his eyelids.

Sentry, Puttcamp's no-nonsense terrier, kept watch around the camp outside. But Cavarra supplemented the canine security by ordering DeChalk to walk the perimeter...mostly so he wouldn't have to hear the know-it-all's big mouth. And because the chiding and jeering directed at the merc had been getting too personal.

DeChalk was ate-up like a football bat. Cavarra probably despised him more intensely than anyone, but he hated scapegoating even worse. Every military unit produced at least one individual who became the target of universal scorn. Sometimes they deserved it.

Sometimes they just happened to be the most convenient focal point for everyone's aggressions. After the firefight, DeChalk was the natural shoo-in for Team Scapegoat. And his juvenile need for recognition only made it easier.

Part of Cavarra's aversion to scapegoating was due to experience. He'd been raised primarily by his grandparents, who could barely speak English. Though a native of California, he struck his Annapolis classmates as just-off-the-boat.

The other plebes were from privileged, hoity-toity families, mostly back East. They'd always worn designer clothes and shoes (hand-me-downs were unthinkable), had perfect haircuts and even manicures. Never had to walk to school or take a sack lunch. Never had to take out the garbage or mow the grass. Never had to work at a gas station to help support the family. Their mothers had never clipped coupons and their fathers never had to fix the car.

Other people--lesser people--attended to those menial chores. The only economic hardship they'd known was settling for a Mazda when Daddy wouldn't spring for a Porsche.

After all the class warfare and lionization of the poor promoted by public school and TV, Cavarra had imagined his shabby upbringing would be a point in his favor in the adult world. If it didn't bring sympathy, it might at least make up for his heavy accent.

He'd been rudely surprised.

The classism of the other midshipmen was only slightly less pronounced than that of the capitalist caricatures on TV sit-coms. And though he wouldn't have guessed it, shallow rich kids were exactly what the military wanted for the officer ranks. They already had the primadonna elitism deeply ingrained. Their superficial "clothes-make-the-man" orientation was tailor-made for the peacetime military's obsession with appearance. They already knew how to hob-nob with snobs. Gossiping was second nature, as was mercurial personal politics. They were accustomed to backstabbing their peers and saw nothing wrong with it, so long as it worked to their own benefit.

Cavarra was lost. The harder he tried to fit in, the more he stood out. Being a football player only made the non-jocks resent him more.

To make matters worse, the brass hats at the Academy took an instant dislike to Cavarra as well. They'd just booted some hopeless screw-up in the class before him. Another swarthy, ethnic plebe. One of the Yard officers decided Cavarra not only resembled him, but must also be just as unfit for the Navy. Fueled by the prevailing attitude of the other midshipmen, this officer's hostility to Cavarra spread around the Yard. His scapegoat status became official.

Had he not been on the football team, strong academically, and hard as woodpecker lips during whatever PT they could dish out, the Academy would have separated him.

Still, they almost did it.

Cavarra's roommate, Oscar Kelly, was a charismatic young midshipman who fancied himself a tough guy. He boosted his own popularity by insulting and provoking the scapegoat. Even after advancing into the second year, Kelly tried to brace him as if Cavarra were still a plebe. Cavarra tried to ignore him, but his restraint only encouraged Kelly to assume he was intimidated. The more Cavarra tolerated, the more aggressive Kelly became, until enough was enough. Cavarra offered to meet Kelly somewhere off-base during weekend liberty and settle their differences face-to-fist.

Somebody--probably Kelly himself--snitched to the upperclassmen, and Cavarra found himself standing before the Honor Board. The Board was the official proceeding preceding a swift kick back to civilian life. Some cadets referred to it as Kangaroo Court.

Only certain specified criteria from a list of recognized clout could save you from the Board back in the Carter years, when the paltry military budget inspired a high separation rate at the training stage. Parents who were flag officers or high-ranking government employees were the most common forms of salvation. Privileges of the nobility. Cavarra's recognition as a defensive back both in high school and on the Navy team was one of the few achievement-based tickets, and it was enough.

In a way, going before the Board was a godsend. The officers presiding, while attempting to amass evidence of his unworthiness, were forced to confront his exemplary performance. Their attitude about him changed after that.

Cavarra graduated at the top of his class. But he never forgot the lessons learned at Annapolis.

He worked as hard at losing his accent as he did to earn a slot in

BUDS. And he wore his uniform properly. But that's where his conformism stopped. He saw nothing worth emulating in the typical officer and made every effort to distance himself from the caste. He mutated from scapegoat to maverick. But oddly enough, he made just the right sort of leader to advance quickly in a small, tightly-knit unit like SEAL Team Four.

By the time a command slot opened in the West Coast SEALS, Cavarra was custom-fit for Team One's skipper.

"What are you Gonna do with the hot potato once you have it?"

The question came from Phil Jenkins. It snapped Cavarra back to the present.

"I hope you don't plan on bringing it aboard my crate."

Jenkins was the designated pilot for the Fokker F27 cargo plane parked outside. His task was to transport Cavarra's team to the target.

"I guess we turn it over to the Agency and let them worry about it," Cavarra said.

Haugen looked as grim as a man could, blowing bubblegum. "What if we miss a bunker and drop one of our bombs on the hot potato? Won't that set it off and blow us all into outer space?"

"I don't think nukes are triggered that way," Jenkins said.

Cavarra flinched at the word "nuke" and looked around. He still hadn't told the men, but the pilots had been briefed as he had. Nobody seemed to notice.

"Excuse me if I don't trust what you think," Haugen said.

"The Israelis took out a nuclear reactor in Iraq way back when," Jenkins said. "They bombed the place, and it didn't start a *Chernobyl* or anything."

"Just to be safe," Puttcamp said, "let's not drop any bombs on it."

Cavarra shared Haugen's concern. What was to keep the hot potato from going off if hit by shrapnel or a stray round? Just to be safe, indeed.

The other two aircraft outside, in crude, hasty revetments, were funky old relics: A1E Skyraiders, antique even when used in Vietnam, and ugly as sin.

Since Puttcamp had piloted F15s and Haugen had hopped Harriers, Cavarra had no doubt they could handle the old propeller-driven beasts. He did wonder whether the CIA planners were out of their minds, choosing those rickety old aberrations for his support aircraft.

Well, better than no air support at all. It's not like he expected a squadron of A10 Warthogs or Apache gunships. And Puttcamp, himself hardly thrilled at the selection of the Skyraiders, assured him the A1Es could take a terrific beating flying low and slow, carrying a huge payload, and stay up a long time on not much fuel...compared to a jet. He and Haugen had been acclimating themselves to the Skyraiders as much as possible.

Over at the card game, Siyr used the Galil's bipod to open a bottle of beer, and took a swig. His mind was also burdened by the possibility of a nuclear detonation during the operation. Though not necessarily by accident.

McCallum pointed at Siyr's rifle. "Now them Israelis, they try to think of everything, don't they? Built-in bipod, works as a wire-cutter and bottle opener. High-speed."

"They've got a pretty high-speed main battle tank, too," Campbell said, dealing cards to each, aces high trump. "Versatile."

"M1A1 Abrams they got from us," Terrell said, gathering his cards up.

Campbell shook his head. "Not those--I mean the ones they designed themselves."

"The *Merkava*," Siyr said. "It is combination tank and armored troop carrier."

McCallum looked his hand over and rearranged some of the cards. "Gotta' hand it to them: Dollar for dollar, they build better weapons than anybody. Even us."

"They fight the same way," Campbell said.

"She-it," Terrell said. "Y'all outa' your mind. Americans got the best equipment and the best training in the world."

"Most expensive," McCallum corrected. "That don't make it the best. I'll bid eight."

Campbell raised his eyebrows.

"Doom, niggah," Terrell said.

"Are you aware of what your British allies say about you?" asked Siyr.

"I'll bid six, and I thought that was brave," Campbell said. He turned to Siyr. "What?"

Siyr assumed a surprisingly authentic English accent. "The Yanks have great kit. They just don't know how to use it."

Terrell laughed derisively. "Board. And I got Club Deuce." He tossed down the two of clubs.

Campbell swallowed some beer and said, "Limeys still got a case of cundingy over that friendly fire in the Gulf."

"Friendly fire is an oxymoron," McCallum said, eyes hidden behind his cards. "You know why we don't fight as well as the Israelis, proportionately?"

"Lots of reasons," Campbell said. He looked over his cards and laid down his lowest club.

Zeke appeared with a freshly opened bottle, and unfolded a camp stool in their midst. "For one thing," Zeke said, "we always think the answer is money. We think, if we spend more money, the results will automatically be better. That's not the way it always works, though. It's not just the amount of money you spend, but how you spend it."

Silence ensued for a moment while the others watched Zeke.

"What'sa matter?" Zeke asked. "No white folks allowed here?"

Terrell slapped him on the arm. "Naw, Boss." He pointed at McCallum and Campbell. "They just wanted to keep the Navy outnumbered at this table. Now it's fair."

McCallum dropped his lowest club. "Roger on the spendthrifting, Zeke. But it ain't the reason. It's because we always pull our punches. We're always more worried about not hurting our enemies too much than we are about winning."

Terrell took the trick, marked the score and dropped the Jack of Hearts.

Siyr nodded. "I notice this about Americans. I think Americans feel guilty when they win. Most people in the world interpret this as weakness and cowardice."

Terrell wasn't drunk. Just a little buzzed. But this ruffled his feathers. He stiffened and glowered at Siyr. "We ain't no cowards, man."

"Be cool," Campbell said. "That's not what the man said."

"Not at all," Siyr said. "I only mean that most people around the world look at things more simple...in 'black and white.' They don't understand the American preoccupation with...with..."

"With restraint," Campbell finished for him.

"Pussyfooting around," Zeke said. "Handicapping ourselves. Bleeding-heart *caca*."

"Yes," Siyr said. "They simply see it as weakness."

"It ain't weakness," Terrell said. "We could wipe all you pissants off the map if we want."

"Well, once upon a time we coulda'," Zeke said.

"Now your country is in much trouble," Siyr said. "You disarm yourselves while the Russians and Chinese prepare for war with you. In fact, you give them even more money. You don't build a ballistic missile defense because your enemies don't want you to have one. But the Shanghai Pact powers have a ballistic missile defense. They also have a functioning civil defense infrastructure. Should that not teach you something?"

"The Cold War is over, man," Terrell said.

Siyr smiled sardonically. "Evidently no one has told the Chinese this. They have threatened to destroy you over Taiwan, remember? And thanks to the guided missile technology you gave them, this is no empty threat."

"Yeah, but it was worth it," Zeke grumbled. "In return, they paid to get our Draft-Dodger-In-Chief reelected."

"Your economic policies are suicidal," Siyr continued. You strangle your own businesses with taxes and environmental regulations...is it any wonder nothing is produced in your country anymore? But you refuse to tarrif Chinese products. Foreign industry doesn't let environmental concerns affect production, yet you buy their goods while you destroy American companies for the same environmental infractions."

"There's the labor cost, too," McCallum said. "The Chi-Coms pay out three bucks a day to their assemblers, and can kill or torture them if they don't make quota. American companies are expected to pay sixty bucks an hour for the same work, then suffer lawsuits if a union assembler is asked to work a different line one day."

McCallum took the trick, updated the score and laid down the first card of the next trick.

"I was in America once," Siyr said. "when the Summer Olympics were taking place. You know, I was simply amazed... All the talk was about the 'Dream Team.' You remember this?"

They all bobbed their heads.

"I tell you, most of your nation was ashamed that you would field such a basketball team. You talked as if it were unfair."

"It was unfair," Campbell said. "That team was rock-steady."

Siyr's eyes widened and he pointed at Campbell. "You see? Every other country sends it's best basketball players, and Americans accept this. But you act as if it is wrong to send your own best players. You feel guilty that your best athletes are better than their best athletes. You conduct foreign policy with the same mentality."

Terrell followed suit and Campbell took the next trick.

Siyr's pager vibrated. He slipped a hand into his pocket and pushed the button to make it stop.

The Mossad agent wanted to meet him tonight.

24

2004 15 AUG 2002; LODWAR, KENYA

Mugabe knew something was wrong when Kabiu tried to avoid him.

Kabiu's farm occupied a thirteen-acre stretch of grass roughly outlined by mangrove and acacia trees, just two miles outside city limits. Lions sometimes prowled through his place.

Kabiu was an intrepid businessman in these parts. His farm also served as a junk yard, used car lot and tire retreading facility. His goats used the wrecked vehicles for shelter and climbing practice.

Mugabe didn't see his trucks anywhere.

Kabiu ducked around the back of his house, presumably to help a customer look for something. Mugabe cut around the opposite side of the house and trapped him.

"Where are my trucks?"

"I am busy," Kabiu said. "Wait your turn, please."

Mugabe stepped up and gave the customer a hard shove. The customer left without protest.

"Where are my trucks?"

Kabiu tried to meet his glare at first, but gave up after a few seconds. "The agreement was, you pick them up tomorrow."

"Which means," Mugabe said, "that today you're gassing them up, checking the oil, checking tires, making sure they are ready for tomorrow. Only I do not see this happening."

Kabiu had always known Mugabe to be a good-humored chap, joking and making light of everything. Now he was a completely different person. His eyes were cold and humorless. His mouth was hard and tight, as though it had never smiled.

"Perhaps this will teach you not to attempt premature collection," Kabiu said, weakly. He forced a laugh, hoping good humor was contagious.

Mugabe's furious expression didn't change even slightly.

"Would you like some tea?" Kabiu offered.

Mugabe just stared.

Kabiu's throat tightened. His heart thumped harder by the beat. "I'm sorry..." he said.

"WHERE ARE MY TRUCKS?"

Kabiu winced at the force of the shout. "It was my assistant's fault," he said. "An official of the government needed them. My assistant didn't know you wanted..."

"I paid half in advance, Fred Sanford!" Mugabe pounced like a striking snake. In less than a second he had the thin man face down on the ground, arm wrenched behind his back, knee mashing down on his spine, and a straight razor against his neck.

"I will give your money back," Kabiu said.

Mugabe put more pressure on the man's arm. "You will give me the trucks."

"I don't have them anymore! Surely the safari can be postponed?"

"This is how you treat your customers, Sanford?" The razor bit slightly into his skin. Blood trickled down Kabiu's neck. "Do you know what customers do who are cheated?"

"I don't know anyone named Sanford," Kabiu protested, shrilly. "Please, take anything on my lot and I will return your money."

Mugabe wanted to kill him. The greedy little thief's compulsion to turn a quick buck meant that the Sudanese rebel force now had no transportation.

He eased the razor away, folded and pocketed it. Killing Kabiu would only jeopardize his effectiveness as an operative down here, and the Agency would have to spend years planting someone else.

He ground Kabiu's face into the dirt. "I won't kill you right now, Sanford. It's something I will contemplate, though. You had better think of a way to make me happy very quickly."

He released the terrified Kenyan, who hurried to refund Mugabe's down payment.

Kabiu gave him keys to a couple dilapidated vehicles the government man had left behind.

25

2349 15 AUG 2002; TEKEZZE RIVER CAMP, SUDAN

(At the quick-time.)
I don't know but I been told...
A nuclear winter is mighty cold.
I don't know but I hear tell...
Nuclear summer is a burnin' hell.

Stars and moonlight painted the small encampment blue-white. A jackal sang a lonesome song that carried for miles across the valley.

Pete Baker, the mechanic, walked the perimeter with an Ingram MAC Ten machine pistol, glad to be stretching his legs after a long, hot day busting his knuckles on ancient aircraft. He stopped at the northeast corner to relieve himself, and looked up at the alien constellations.

Sentry sat near the center of the camp, lazily playing with a chipped, scarred and slobbery bowling ball, a little large even for his monstrous jaws.

Everyone else stood around Cavarra in the pilots' tent for the op-order.

He spread out a topographical map next to his sand table.

"When I first got here," he said, "I gave you the opportunity to quit before the mission began. We've already eaten some of the same mud, back in that village, so you could argue that the mission's already started. Even so, I'm Gonna give you one last chance: Anybody wants to quit after what I'm about to tell you, sound off quick and I'll deal you out."

The tent was quiet enough to hear a sand flea fart. Cavarra scanned over their faces. He had an idea what they were made of, but he wasn't sure how they would react to his bombshell.

He motioned to the pilots and himself. "I don't know why, but for some reason, the people who hired you didn't tell you everything we've been told. Well, I say you deserve to know."

Cavarra unsheathed his black anodized Trench Master and pointed with it at the model tents in the sand table. "This is our target: a terrorist training camp in the Nubian Desert." He shifted the full tang fighting knife from the sand table to point at the map. "It's located in the Hala'ib Triangle--a demilitarized zone that Egypt and Sudan don't completely agree on the ownership of. In other words, both countries can deny knowledge of, and responsibility for, what comes out of there." The knife pointed back to the sand table. "Somewhere in this camp is a tactical atomic weapon small enough to fit in a suitcase, a knapsack, book bag, laptop case or even a large purse."

Cavarra paused. Twelve pairs of eyes looked from him to the pilots, to the sand table, and back to him.

"That's the bomb we're supposed to intercept," he said. "So not only is it likely that some of us won't come out of this alive, it's possible that none of us will. That there won't even be enough of us left to bury."

Mai exploded. "You weren't Gonna bother telling us about this?"

"I'm telling you now. And you can quit now."

Mai looked around at the others, hoping to see the same outrage he felt.

Some mouths hung open, many eyes widened. A couple men stared keenly at Cavarra, but otherwise looked blank.

"That's just brilliant," Mai said. "How the hell do we get out of here now?"

Cavarra nodded toward Jenkins. "You can stay on the bird after we deploy. Captain Jenkins will be heading from the target directly to a friendly airstrip."

"What airstrip?"

"Don't worry about what airstrip," Jenkins said.

"What if we get shot down?"

"Then I guess we crash," Jenkins replied.

"You can *didimau* right now if you want," Cavarra said, "and find your own way home. Is that what you wanna do?"

Mai opened his mouth again, then closed it. His eyes shifted back and forth.

"What's the target for the nuke?" asked Scarred Wolf.

"Intel thinks it's Tel Aviv," Cavarra said.

Mai cursed a blue streak. A couple others expressed their own surprise.

"It's not even Gonna be used on an American target?" Lombardi asked. "We're risking our lives to save a foreign city?"

"It ain't just any foreign city, top," McCallum said. "This could start World War Three."

"That's right," Haugen said. "This ain't just any old bomb, either."

"When you signed on for this," Cavarra asked, "was it to fight terrorists? Or was it only to fight terrorists who plan to directly attack the US?"

"They didn't specify," Terrell said. "But they also didn't say anything about an A-Bomb."

"That makes this job all the more important," Bojado said. "If there's a nuclear war, our shit is weak no matter what city gets blown up first."

"You got a point," Campbell said. "But what if it touches off while we're in the camp?"

"Then it blows up a bunch of terrorists," Scarred Wolf said, "and thirteen other men, plus a chunk of worthless desert. But it doesn't kill millions of civilians."

This spawned a whirlwind of comments from every quarter, born of shock and anxiety. Everyone had an opinion to offer, and Cavarra let them get some of it off their chests for a moment. Only Cole remained silent through all the verbal pandemonium.

When the din quieted to a dull roar, Cavarra waved his knife for silence. "Okay. Everybody here has put in their two cents--"

Terrell clapped Cole on the shoulder. "Not Bulldog, here."

"True that," Campbell said. "I'd like to hear what he has to say."

Cole shrugged and shook his head, slightly.

"C'mon, Bulldog," Fava-Vargas said, moving to where he could watch Cole's mouth.

Cole shrugged again. He sighed, then spoke softly. "Reckon Ah'm as scared as any man here, 'bout that bomb. Maybe mo'. I don't wanna die. Ah got an old lady and young'uns back home Ah'd laak ta see again--"

Mai moved restlessly, as if ready to storm out of the tent. "You're breaking my heart, redneck. This whole deal is--."

McCallum whirled on Mai. "Why don't you shut that hole in your face, before I close it for you? You've been shooting off your mouth enough for ten people. Let the man say his piece."

Mai glared up at McCallum, violence in his heart.

McCallum recognized the wild look and wished Mai would try to get rough.

"Look, guys," DeChalk began, but was silenced by a chorus of scornful voices.

"We heard enough of your mouth, too, you worthless slab of meat," Zeke said. "Let him finish. Go ahead, Bulldog."

Cole spat chaw juice into his canteen cup. "The way Ah see it, Ah knew back when Ah joined the Corps there was a risk. If we go to wo', marines fight, marines kill, marines die. Well, we went to wo'. Them Iraqi sojahs didn't invade ma home state. They invaded some little place Ah never even heard of. But ma country asked me ta help kick 'em out, so Ah did.

"Those A-rabs didn't fly no airplanes into ma house. They knocked down a couple buildin's in New Yoke City. Ah never been ta New Yoke; don't know anybody from New Yoke; don't have any kin there. But if Ah was still in the Corps, I'd be over in Afghanistan, or wherever they wanna send me, 'cause you just don't let folks get away with that.

"Now the same fellahs recruited me who recruited y'all. They told me right up front this'd be dangerous. Ah knew Ah maat get killed, and so did y'all. I signed on anyhow, and so did y'all. Truth is, Ah wanted the money. Now if'n Ah get shot in the haid, or if'n that bomb kills us, we just as daid. So Ah don't understand why summa' y'all so bent outa' shape.

"Ain't nobody promised me these A-rabs was Gonna bomb ma house if'n we didn't stop 'em. Whoever they Gonna bomb, it ain't Gonna be good, an' it ain't Gonna be raat. So scared as Ah am, y'all, Ah'm a'thankin' it might be a good thang Ah'm here. Ah believe Ah'll stay on this team, and see this mission through."

They all kept their quiet for a moment, except Lombardi, who muttered, "Anybody wanna translate that into English?"

"Now we've heard from everybody," Cavarra said. "You still wanna quit, Mai?"

Mai glowered at McCallum, and at Cavarra, but said nothing.

"Anybody else wanna quit before we go any further?" Cavarra asked. "Now's the time to sound off. I don't want anybody going in with me who won't go all the way."

Some locked eyes with him. Some looked at their feet. Nobody spoke.

"Okay then. Prepare to copy and save all questions for the end.

"Enemy: Approximately a hundred terrorists--jihad veterans and their paramilitary trainees. Their camp is inside this quarter-mile square." He pointed toward the red square on the map. "Concertina wire links these four concrete pillboxes that cover all land approaches. We can assume there are mines laid outside the camp. Pillboxes are not camouflaged at all--wind blows the sand right off them. They're likely equipped with heavy machineguns and Sagger missiles, at the least. Behind the barbed wire, in between the pillboxes, are these foxholes. Satellite recon tells us they're unmanned most of the time, except for random drills."

He pointed to the models on the sand table as he spoke. "Covering the sea approach to the camp, they've got these machinegun nests which do seem to be manned constantly, though by skeleton crews. The good news is, this is a training camp, where the emphasis is on teaching individuals and small groups how to conduct terrorist ops, so they're not well-organized as a combat unit, and they haven't trained for a stand-up fight. And besides the hot potato, all they have are infantry weapons. The bad news is, these guys have loaded A.K.s with them at all times--no matter when we hit them, we won't catch them with all their rifles locked up in the armory."

Cavarra stepped aside and motioned toward the pilots. "Friendlies: These dudes behind me with the gigantic watches. Lieutenant Colonels Haugen and Puttcamp will be prepping the camp immediately prior to our insertion. Hopefully they'll be able to flatten those pillboxes and catch most of our welcoming party asleep in their tents.

"We've also got friendlies on the ground. There's a Sudanese rebel unit should be meeting up with us here tomorrow, and we'll have a chance to look them over. They'll be attacking the camp just after we insert, if all goes according to plan.

"I'm thinking about detaching one of you to the rebel unit, but we'll see."

Most were too busy scribbling in their notepads to think about this, but McCallum looked up curiously. Would this detachment merely be an excuse to get DeChalk out of their way? Or was there a legitimate reason they would need eyes and ears in the larger force?

"Mission," Cavarra continued: "We are to invest the eastern side of the camp and prevent any terrorists from escaping with the hot potato.

"Execution: As this operation was handed to me, we were to insert here, just southeast of the camp. Our sappers would breach the defenses for us, we'd pour in, secure a position guarding the dock, blow the boats and hold our position until the rebels break through to relieve us."

A few throats were cleared. A few men looked horrified. The plan was suicidal.

"You get the idea that the Agency considers us expendable?" he asked. "Well, I made a few changes. Here's my concept of the operation:

"You all saw the Para-Foil TMCs. And you're all HALO qualified." HALO meant "high altitude, low opening" parachute deployment. "TMC" stood for "tactical main chute."

"At 0330 Sunday morning, Puttcamp and Haugen will prep the camp. They'll bomb the bunkers and bivouac area while laying down strafing fire across the target. The door will be opening on our transport bird as their attack takes place. At 0335 we'll put our knees in the breeze. The last bombs should be detonating as our last man hits the silk. Captain Jenkins here has been keeping up with the weather, and assures me we'll have clear skies, low winds and a bright moon. So none of us should have any trouble avoiding the water."

Mai shook his head and muttered something about drowning.

"Jumpmaster Lombardi is gonna give us a HALO refresher class tomorrow," Cavarra said. "He'll also supervise us packing our chutes. The rebel force commences the attack on the western side of the camp at 0340. Hopefully, that will draw any attention away from us."

He pointed at the beach area on the sand table. "We're Gonna drop in right here. Inside the camp, so we don't lose the element of surprise getting through the minefield and concertina."

He waved a hand at Jenkins. "While all this is going on, our bird racetracks after dropping us, comes back in low over the beach and heavy-drops the rest of our trash.

"By now we've cleared the machinegun nests and secured the DZ, such as it is. We don't blow the boats, we sweep them. As a backup, though, part of the heavy-drop will be a couple rubber ducks —'inflatable rafts' for you land-lubbers. Rather than wait for someone to attempt escape with the hot potato, we send a team in to secure it and bring it back to the boats while our sappers rig the dock with C-four. We load ourselves and our trash in the boats and shove off. Once we're a safe distance out, we blow the dock.

"Originally, extraction would be accomplished via link-up with the rebel force and movement overland back to the south. I never did like that plan. I like it even less since our little warm-up this morning. I've been talking it over with our pilots here, and we've got some alternate plans we intend to propose to Mugabe. There's an American sub prowling around the Gulf of Aden that might be able to pick us up. Lieutenant Colonel Haugen is aware of some Marine Corps Chinooks at the US Combined Joint Task Force HQ in Djibouti that could just possibly stray off course on their next training sortie, and accidentally pick up some stowaways. Failing that, Captain Jenkins is willing to fly back in for us."

Cavarra next went over the sub-unit tasks. He kept it as simple as possible, because the details of any plan are the first casualties in combat. But he did go over his organizational breakdown.

He subdivided the squad into two-man teams: McCallum and Terrell were the easiest to pair, since two engineers cooperating could accomplish four times as much as any lone sapper. Snipers Campbell and Cole were another natural team. He paired Zeke with Siyr, needing his most trustworthy man to keep close watch on his most suspicious. Similarly, he teamed the reliable Bojado with the hapless DeChalk. Ignoring their senior ranks, he put Mai and Lombardi together. Now the LIFERs could gig each other on sleeve-rolling procedures or LBV configuration...maybe kill each other off over some heartfelt uniformity issue...but in any case, stay out of everyone else's way. Scarred Wolf and Fava-Vargas made up his weapons team.

"Service and support: Mr. Baker, the aircraft mechanic--he'll be shoving off the heavy-drop. And Mugabe--our official link back to the World.

"Command and signal: Chain of command is as follows...myself, McCallum, Pappadakis, Scarred Wolf, Lombardi."

As expected, there was some grumbling over this. He knew Zeke was a competent NCO, but the firefight had told him something about the others, as well. McCallum was a natural leader, knew his tactics and could think on his feet. Scarred Wolf was the model fighting man and, with instincts like his, would make the right calls. Lombardi was no genius--of a military, or any other variety--but he kept a cool head when bullets were flying.

"Challenge is 'loiter,' password is 'scramble.' Running password is 'razorback'."

The radios they'd be using amongst themselves were short-range, on a fixed frequency. He now gave the frequency for the team radio they'd use to keep in touch with the other friendlies.

He asked for questions.

"Why are we blowing the dock?" Zeke asked.

"While we're floating out into the Red Sea," Cavarra explained, "that dock would make a nice platform for them to set a heavy weapon on. Depending on how industrious they are, they might even break it loose from shore and use it as a raft to pursue us."

Lombardi indicated himself and Mai. "Why did you pick us to handle the nuke?"

"Why?" Cavarra sang, "because we like you. M-O-U-S-E."

"That's something for the lowest ranking man," Mai complained, "not the highest."

Cavarra opened his mouth to reply...

"I volunteer to retrieve the device," Siyr said.

Everyone stared at him.

26

At 0300, Siyr completed his second round through the camp. He peeked inside the tent and counted the sleeping forms. Satisfied, he stalked toward the front gate.

Sentry stood stiff-legged in between the tents. He watched curiously as Siyr approached.

Siyr knelt beside the dog to pet him and be sniffed. If he had to kill it coming back into camp, things would get rough.

Sentry followed him almost to the gate, then watched him disappear into the darkness. He trotted back to the center of camp and, following his nose, entered the pilots' tent to sit beside his master's bunk.

Puttcamp didn't stir. He slept heavy with a few beers in his system. Sentry fidgeted for a moment, then nudged Puttcamp with his nose and licked his eyelid.

Puttcamp started. In a short moment he remembered where he was. He rubbed his eyes, swinging up to a sitting position.

Sentry sat with his back to his master, ears down as if expecting a reprimand.

"What is it, boy?"

***

Siyr walked south along the river, sticking close to the foliage so as not to silhouette himself. A few klicks out, he gradually saw the outline of the Jeep emerge from the blackness.

The Mossad agent recognized Siyr and felt relief. He'd made it. Last he'd seen Siyr, he was running into a village about to come under attack. Possibly running to his death.

The agent nodded for Siyr to get in the Jeep with him.

"We'd better not," Siyr said, softly. "There's a dog in the camp and driving around tonight would be pushing our luck."

"I didn't hear him bark when I parked here."

"He doesn't bark. He appears to be extremely well-trained. I tried to make friends but he only tolerated me. I think it would be safer if we just stay here."

"Well, we can at least sit in the Jeep so our voices don't carry as far."

Once inside with the windows rolled up, the Mossad agent asked, "How many survived?"

"All of them. Two have minor wounds."

Siyr told his incredulous superior all about the firefight and the other pertinent developments since then.

"So the mission is going ahead as planned," the agent said.

"Yes, sir. And I believe they have an excellent chance at success. Cavarra is a shrewd commander. He's scrapped the CIA plan and made his own."

The agent listened to him explain the plan, then considered it silently for a time. A jackal yipped in the night. Something splashed in the river.

"Still, there are no guarantees," the Mossad agent said. "You must be ready to do what we discussed."

Siyr nodded. "I am."

"And what might that be?"

The voice came from outside.

They peered into the darkness outside the agent's door and into the muzzle of a Galil. Holding the rifle was a dark figure with night vision goggles protruding from his face.

Keeping his exposed upper body perfectly still, the agent reached for the knob on the side-spot lever hanging over the edge of the dash.

Cavarra saw movement on the corner of the cab, but didn't recognize exactly what it was in the murky green light of the PVS5 display. It was a small object rotating. It wasn't the door opening or a weapon being leveled...

By the time he understood, the spotlight beam caught him right in the goggles. Everything washed out. He was blind.

In a split second, the doors flew open, the driver tackled him and brought a tanto blade to his neck. Siyr came around behind and covered him.

"Do you recognize him?" the agent asked.

"It's Cavarra," Siyr said.

"Don't try anything stupid, Commander Cavarra," the agent said.

"Put 'em down and cut that light," Puttcamp said, in English, from behind Siyr. "I can pop both of you before you turn around."

A leopard screamed, far off. Something scurried in the brush.

The man with the knife withdrew it, stood and backed away. "Remember," he told Cavarra, "I could have killed you."

Siyr lowered his rifle.

Cavarra slowly sat up and removed the goggles. The spotlight was switched off as he blinked his eyes several times.

"That's good," Puttcamp said. "Now you two move away from the vehicle. But first, Siyr, set that weapon down on the hood."

Siyr looked at the agent, who nodded. They did as they were told.

"Thanks, Gordy," Cavarra told Puttcamp, climbing to his feet. "What is this, Siyr?"

Siyr took his time answering, and then did so softly. "Commander Cavarra, this is Colonel Dreizil."

"Who do you work for, Colonel?"

"Mossad. Israeli intelligence," Dreizil said. "You speak good Hebrew. When did you learn it?"

"On my own time. But let's all be polite and talk English so my buddy doesn't feel left out, okay? Why are you interfering in this mission?"

"Not interfering, Commander," Dreizil said, in English. "We want to help."

"Is that why you've got Siyr spying on us? Is that why you tipped off the PDF about us?"

"The PDF raid was not our doing," Dreizil said, "though it's understandable how that might occur to you. I'm trying to find out who tipped them off, and why."

Cavarra had no idea why the Israelis would want this mission compromised.

"Since your country has chosen to act without the cooperation of mine," Dreizil said, "we wanted 'ears on the ground,' so-to-speak. That's why Mr. Siyr has been reporting to me."

"My sincere apologies, Commander," Siyr said. "I regret I had to deceive you, but I must follow orders."

Cavarra brushed himself off. "And what are your orders, exactly? And what happens now that your cat is out of the bag?"

"Good question," Dreizil said.

"I've got another one," Puttcamp said: "How many men are working for you?"

"Just we two," Dreizil said.

"Okay," Cavarra said, "let's go back to the big question, then: Why are you spying on somebody trying to save your country?"

Dreizil chewed his lip. "Have you ever heard of Masada?"

Cavarra shrugged. "Yeah. I watched the miniseries."

"Cute. How very American. What do you know about it?"

"Roman garrison on a steep hill. Jewish guerrillas...Macabees, right?"

Dreizil sighed. "Not really. But go on."

"...Jewish guerrillas captured it. Roman Army laid siege. When they finally breached the walls, they found the defenders had all committed suicide rather than be taken prisoner." He reached behind himself to pull a thorn out of his upper thigh. "At the beginning of the series, they showed Israeli soldiers visiting the place, taking a vow that it won't happen again...or something like that."

Siyr shook his head. "We resolve to die before we let Israel fall to her enemies."

"We?" Cavarra echoed, looking closely at the African. "Who are you--Sammy Davis the Third?"

"Once," Dreizil said, "Israel's contingent strategy was built atop what some called the 'Masada Complex.' But we've had atomic weapons for some time, now, and our defense forces are guided by a 'Samson Complex'."

"Samson? From the Bible?"

"He died killing as many enemies as possible."

A baboon shrieked in the distance.

Cavarra felt just a touch queasy.

"When Egypt and Syria surprised us on *Yom Kippur*," Dreizil said, "the situation looked very grave for the first few days. With a country as small as ours, national survival can be determined in a matter of hours. Maybe even minutes."

"Had the Moslems defeated us," Siyr said, "there would be no Israel today."

"Most of the world never suspected how close we came to nuclear war in 1973," Dreizil said. "But our air and ground forces managed to turn the tide. By the time it was over, we could have rolled through Cairo and Damascus...but then your beloved United Nations intervened. They ignored the war while we were overwhelmed. It was only when we began winning that they cried for peace."

"So what you're telling me," Cavarra said, "is that you'll blow 'em to hell and gone before you'll let them drive you off the land."

"If they destroy us," Siyr said, "they will be destroyed, too."

"It is beyond even that, now," Dreizil said. "Thanks to you Americans and your U.N. designed 'peace process,' Israel is being forced into a policy of a preemptive nuclear first strike."

"Crucial defensive terrain," Siyr said, "which we paid for in blood, has been handed over to our enemies."

"In exchange for your empty promises of peace," Dreizil said. "Jericho, the Gaza Strip, the Sinai...and of course you want us to surrender the 'West Bank'."

Cavarra had nothing against the Israelis. If anything, he admired them for their tenacity and combat record. But he didn't like hearing anybody break bad on his own country. He knew Dreizil didn't mean to insult him personally...but it felt as though he was spitting all over Cavarra's very identity. "Don't talk like the United Nations is some ally of ours," he said. "It's as anti-American as it is anti-Semitic."

"Ah, but when have Americans ever hesitated to feed the mouths that bite you?"

"Ask Fidel Castro or Saddam Hussein," Puttcamp said.

"Or the Russians or the Red Chinese or the North Koreans or the Saudis or the Afghans," Dreizil said.

"The point is," Siyr said, "the bomb in the terrorist camp is intended for an Israeli target. Israel will not allow it to reach that target."

"That's what I'm here to prevent," Cavarra said. "Remember?"

Dreizil nodded. "And your victory back in the village was most encouraging. But you must admit, the possibility of failure is substantial."

"That doesn't mean we will fail," Puttcamp said

"But if you do," Dreizil said, "Siyr and myself are in a position to report it while there is still time for Israel to take action."

"Take action..." Puttcamp said. "You mean nuke 'em 'til they glow, then shoot 'em in the dark?"

"We would probably pursue a conventional solution first," Dreizil said. "But that will prompt an ugly situation. Bush's precious 'coalition' might self-destruct. It would likely lead to a nuclear confrontation anyway. Russian warheads have been smuggled into the hands of many of our enemies, and Iran is close to developing its own nuclear capabilities."

Cavarra exhaled heavily. "Look, I want to get the bomb away from the bad guys, too. We all do. I don't want terrorists to nuke Tel Aviv, Jerusalem, New York...or even Cleveland. And I'm Gonna do everything I can to stop 'em." He pointed to Siyr. "But I'm not jumping into a hot DZ with your stooge behind me. If we fail, fine...do what you gotta' do. Chances are I won't be alive to care. But watch from the sidelines, 'cause I won't tolerate your interference."

"I'm afraid that's unacceptable," Dreizil said.

"I don't know what to tell you, then," Cavarra said.

"Perhaps there's a suitable compromise," Siyr said. The other men broke eye contact and looked to him. "You mentioned detaching a man to the Sudanese rebel force," he reminded Cavarra. "Make me that man. Then you needn't worry about me sabotaging your mission. Plus, I speak a few Sudanese dialects--I might be the best choice for a liaison."

This suggestion jarred Dreizil. Cavarra didn't miss his apprehensive look.

They all had the same goal: Keep the terrorists from using the bomb. So Dreizil and Siyr had no reason to sabotage the mission. And what damage could Siyr do to Cavarra's team if he was with the rebel force? After all, the rebel force had the same goal, too. The fact that Dreizil seemed to dislike the idea made Cavarra like it even more.

Why?

He didn't doubt much the Israeli had told him. Yet he still didn't trust him.

"Why did you volunteer to grab the nuke, Siyr?"

Siyr shrugged. "It doesn't matter if I am carrying the bomb, or half a mile away. If it explodes, I am dead either way."

"Everybody on the team knows that. Their concern with handling it is the radiation. They don't want to catch cancer or grow a third eyeball or have both their arms fall off. Why doesn't that concern you?"

"It does concern me," Siyr said.

Dreizil watched the African just as intensely as did Cavarra.

"I am an Ethiopian Jew, Rocco. I'm also a patriot and soldier of Israel. To protect Israel, I will risk not only death, but radioactive infection."

Cavarra believed this, but had the impression something important was left unsaid. Dreizil seemed satisfied with Siyr's answer, but still upset about something else.

"What were you two talking about when I got here?"

They both played dumb.

"You said, 'you have to be ready to do what we discussed'."

Dreizil thought fast. "We weren't sure we could trust you. Trust that you would, or could, pull off this mission. We planted Siyr in your team to handle things if you couldn't. Or wouldn't."

"You mean frag me?"

"To do whatever had to be done. And you aren't the only question mark--you've got quite a few dark, Arabic-speaking men on your team. How much do you really know about them?"

"There's a couple Richard-heads, but they're not *Al Qaeda* spies," Puttcamp said.

Dreizil looked a little too smug. "We try to prepare for every contingency. We can't afford to let anyone betray us, for any reason."

"Then you'll understand why I can't let your boy jump in with us," Cavarra said. "He goes in with the Sudanese, or he doesn't go."

27

0525 16 AUG 2002; NUBIAN DESERT, SUDAN
CAMP ALI

A camp trainer kicked Bassam awake.

"Report to the medical tent immediately!" the trainer yelled.

Bassam scrambled to get dressed, sleepiness flooding quickly away from the shock of the kick. He'd got back to camp less than an hour ago.

What an incredible day--the most spectacular day of his life! He hadn't wanted it to end.

All his life he'd been treated roughly. Rough physically; rough verbally. The beatings from his foster family, the beating from the PLO, the beatings of the *Mujahedin*, the kicks and slaps from the camp trainers... But in that wonderful place of sweet smells and pretty music, a gentle creature caressed him with soft words and tender touches. It was incredible. Woman.

On the ride back to camp, he replayed those wonderful hours in his mind over and over.

Bassam was physically exhausted, but the fire in him burned hotter than ever. Other men, some even younger than himself, tasted those pleasures whenever they desired--maybe even took them for granted...because they were born wealthy, privileged, and/or handsome. Some boys his age had never received a single beating--boys who actually deserved punishment. Boys who had no excuse for their shameful behavior.

He hated them all: everyone more fortunate than he. That included other Moslems. It included other Palestinians. It included the man who'd just kicked him.

Surely Allah could differentiate between the true warriors and the spoiled hypocrites. Surely Bassam would be rewarded some day for enduring all the cruelty from those who surely would be punished.

Bassam found the medical tent brightly lit. Commandant Ali waited there for him, with a doctor. Bassam started to ask what was going on, but was hushed.

Ali told him to cooperate with the doctor in every way, then left.

The doctor examined Bassam extensively, especially around the privates. He had him urinate in a jar. He inspected his rectum. It was all quite humiliating.

When the exam was finally complete, the doctor told Bassam to go wait outside the commandant's tent.

***

Bassam waited for hours. The sun was up and burning hot before Ali called him in.

"Sit down, Bassam."

The boy did so.

"We've discovered something unfortunate," Ali said. "The woman you were with..."

"Shondana?"

"Yes. It seems she has entertained some Jews, in the past."

Bassam bristled at the thought of those fat, spoiled pigs touching his woman.

"The filthy animals brought with them a symptom of their depraved culture. The woman carries a disease."

Bassam's gaze roamed around the tent, then rested back on Ali.

"Had we known of this before, we wouldn't have allowed you to consort with her. As soon as we learned, we brought a doctor here to see if he could help you."

"You mean I...she..."

Ali nodded gravely. "She has passed this horrible disease on to you."

"So fast? But--"

"It is a fast acting disease, Bassam. The Jews and Americans, in their boundless debauchery, have spread the most horrible diseases known to man. If it were anyone else, Bassam, I would try to protect them from the truth of it. But because of your courage, I know you can handle it: It is fatal and irreversible."

Bassam pursed his lips for a moment. "How long do I have?"

"You probably won't feel any different for a week or so. Then your insides will start rupturing. Your private parts will swell, twist, then shrivel. There will be excruciating pain with no relief, and a foul smell that will grow worse and worse. You won't be able to urinate. Many infections will occur within you. Your bladder will swell and burst. The pain will be too great for you to walk or even crawl. You'll likely contract more diseases, since your body will be too weak to fight them. Death will be slow and very painful."

Bassam imagined the humiliation of living in his own filth, unable to even use the latrine on his own; covered by flies and maggots, too weak to fend them off. "How long will the suffering last?"

"Someone as strong and courageous as you...maybe weeks. Of course, it will seem like centuries to you, with all that pain. We'll have to remove you from the camp, of course, to some spot out in the desert. Perhaps we can send a holy man out there to pray for you once a day or so. Once you die, we'll have to incinerate your body, so no uncleanness spreads. If you wish, we can bind the woman who gave you this disease, throw her at your feet and stone her to death while you can still hold your eyes open to see it?"

Bassam shook his head firmly. "Please don't. You say my body must be burnt?"

Ali nodded gravely. "To ashes. Fire is the only way to be sure."

"Would the explosion of a bomb work as well?"

"What do you mean?"

"The mission you told me about. I was to deliver a bomb, right?"

Ali arched his eyebrows. "Oh. Well, yes. I suppose an explosion would do it. But you will be too sick to carry out the mission. We've decided to give the honor to another volunteer. I'm sorry, Bassam."

"But you said I won't feel any different for a week. So I will be able to carry out the mission until then."

Ali raised his hands, fingers spread. "I'm sorry, Bassam, but the mission is scheduled for later. Maybe a month or more. I'm sorry."

Bassam slowly lost his color. "But I am ready to go, Commandant. I can accomplish this mission. I am ready to go right now. This very minute. I know I can do it."

Ali shook his head sadly. "I'm sorry, Bassam..."

Bassam's eyes glassed over. He trembled visibly. "Please...why must we wait? What is the target?"

"An office building in Tel Aviv."

"Give me the bomb, Commandant...I will take one of the speed boats to the target...I will leave right now...please..."

Ali stroked his chin. "Well, we have acquired a fishing vessel to smuggle the bomb through the Suez...no. No, that would mean moving the schedule forward... I like you, Bassam. I would like to do this for you, but it would disrupt too many plans."

Bassam slumped in defeat.

Ali chewed on his lip as if wrestling with some great dilemma. "Bassam...if I do this for you...can I trust you?"

The boy came back to life. "Yes, Commandant."

"Will you do whatever it takes to deliver the bomb?"

"Yes! I swear it!"

"Will you fight off whatever infidels try to stop you? Will you detonate the bomb as soon as you place it?"

"I swear it!"

Ali sighed. "Very well. I will move up the schedule. I will arrange it for this week. I hope you won't disappoint me, Bassam. I'm counting on you, as is all of Islam."

***

When the boy left, Chin strolled over from the mess tent and entered the CP to sit with Ali. "Is he primed?"

Ali nodded. "He was already primed. I still think this ploy was unnecessary. But yes: he thinks it is his idea, and I'm doing him a great favor."

Chin nodded, amused. "Aren't you?"

"Of course I am. I don't know why I went along with this. Maybe your soldiers need this kind of deception, but warriors of jihad are proud to give up their lives without it."

"You went along," Chin said, "because with an operation of this magnitude, it is best to leave nothing to chance."

28

0700 16 AUG 2002; MCLEAN, VIRGINIA USA
"LANGLEY"

Bobbie Yousko had barely sat down with her coffee when John Boehm entered her office and shut the door behind him.

Bobbie read the look on his face and asked, "What is it?"

"Your team got hit yesterday."

Bobbie forgot the coffee and stared at him. "Hit? Who? How?"

"Don't know the details yet. Haven't heard from my guy in country...maybe they got him with the rest. The crypto lab pulled it out of the radio traffic."

Bobbie felt sick. "How bad is it? Any idea?"

"Some of them must've survived," Boehm said. He took a seat facing Bobbie. "Sudanese Army dispatched the Murahaleen Scouts to hunt them down."

The Murahaleen Scouts were Sudan's version of an SS Panzer Battalion. They were equipped with M60 tanks and M113 APCs donated by Uncle Sam. They had the range, speed and firepower to erase fifty commando teams.

The whole mission required stealth up until the hour of the attack on the terrorist camp. Even then, the team would be relatively safe from overt Sudanese threats while inside the Hala'ib Triangle. But if exposed inside Sudan proper, the commando team was worse than helpless. The US would be unable to deny involvement if the Agency offered any assistance to the mercenaries now.

Bobbie had avoided this danger--or tried to--by recruiting operators who could blend in with the local population and carefully selecting the muster points in war-torn southern Sudan. She consolidated her merc operators in a village just outside Bor, rendered a virtual ghost town by a recent Popular Defense Force raid. Khartoum had no reason to pay attention to a village it had just had annihilated, and the Dinkas in surrounding areas had no reason to look twice at a small group of armed men who spoke Arabic.

Cavarra wasn't the type to pull some stupid stunt that would blow their cover. Then how was it blown? Was there a leak? Where?

"Are you sure about all the operators we hired?" asked Boehm.

Was she? She wondered about DeChalk. He was half-Lebanese, but both parents were Protestant and he'd never worked for a Muslim employer. He hadn't been back to Lebanon since the Syrian occupation began.

Siyr? He was the only non-American on the team. But Bobbie had checked and re-checked him. Not only was he not Muslim, but he'd done some work for the Israelis and was still in good standing with them.

"They're in the middle of a civil war," Bobbie said. "Maybe there's no leak at all. Maybe something just happened and our shooters had a case of bad luck."

"I can have my crew look over all the intra-office activity for the last week," Boehm offered.

This was no small chore. Bobbie couldn't possibly get it done without Boehm. "Please. Please do. I appreciate it."

"Uh, B.Y...?"

"What?"

"Whether we find the leak or not...whether there is a leak or not...your boys are in a pinch over there. It probably won't help them much at this point."

Bobbie nodded. "It won't. In fact, there's almost nothing I can do to help them now."

She had to get in touch with James "Mugabe" Harris. But to do it faster than normal channels risked blowing the man's cover.

29

0726 16 AUG 2002; TEKEZZE RIVER CAMP, SUDAN

Sentry stood stiff-legged at the gate as the Jeep rolled to a stop before it. Zeke approached, rifle leveled.

As Cavarra opened the passenger door and stepped out, he shook his head at Siyr in the back seat with Puttcamp and pointed at the dog. "You were Gonna try to sneak past that monster? He uses bowling balls for his chew toys."

"What goes on, Rocco?" Zeke asked.

"It's cool," Cavarra said. "Let us on through."

Zeke stepped aside. Sentry recognized Cavarra but watched him closely as he got back in the Jeep.

Dreizil drove them over to the motor pool area, hoarse from arguing all night and more than a little annoyed that the Americans were now aware of his presence.

The men coalesced into a mob around the trio as they walked from the Jeep to the center of camp. Cavarra stopped to address them.

"This is Mr. Dreizil from Israeli intelligence." He didn't allow time for the murmuring to grow into Twenty Questions. "As you can imagine, the Israelis are quite concerned with our mission here. Mr. Dreizil will help us to succeed in any way he can."

McCallum and a couple others stared with a skeptical keenness.

"I'll be discussing with him just how he can do that, so you'll be seeing him around. I'm detaching Siyr to be our liaison with the rebel force. So Zeke and DeChalk are buddies, now. Bojado, you're with me."

***

Lombardi had everyone lay out their parachutes on the nylon "instant runway" staked out inside the camp. The men re-packed their own TMCs, with his assistance. When done packing, they cleaned their weapons and configured their gear while conversing in the cliques they'd established. The most popular topics were Dreizil and Siyr, and speculations concerning them.

Some suspected Cavarra had either withheld some pertinent poop about Dreizil, or had lied to them outright. Lombardi and Mai were the primary proponents of this theory. DeChalk also subscribed to it, but nobody cared what he thought.

Dreizil had left camp not long after his introduction. Several men recognized his Jeep as the vehicle which had dropped Siyr off just before the firefight, so it was no longer a secret that Siyr had some connection to the Israelis. Cavarra banished him to the supply tent, forbidding him to participate in or observe the actions of the others.

Siyr obediently kept to himself. He cleaned, checked and re-checked his rifle, sharpened his sawtooth bayonet, unloaded his magazines to let the springs rest and re-taped down everything on his web gear that might rattle.

He prayed, then opened his Bible.

Now the temple was crowded with men and women; all the rulers of the Philistines were there, and on the roof were about 3,000 men and women watching Samson perform. Then Samson prayed to the Lord, "O Sovereign Lord, remember me. O God, please strengthen me just once more, and let me with one blow get revenge on the Philistines for my two eyes."

He removed boots and socks to smear petroleum jelly on the bottom of his feet, then elevated his legs.

Siyr knew all the subterfuge wasn't necessary. Israel's survival was guaranteed by the Creator, not by anything as fickle as US foreign policy. The Mighty One had used the Americans from time to time, but even they would feel His wrath if they defied His Covenant.

Siyr was bound to obey Dreizil's orders; yet he knew Dreizil didn't believe literally in a God who intervened on Israel's behalf. Dreizil didn't believe in much anything he couldn't see, hear or touch. But many things couldn't be seen, heard or touched—gravity, magnetism, radiation, love for Israel—and they were no less real for their intangible inaudible invisibility.

Thoughts were always gloomy before a mission, but this time it was worse. Not because of the danger. Not even because of Dreizil's concern that he wouldn't be able to carry out his mission. What made it bad was that Siyr still had a chance to carry out his mission.

No matter what happened to the Sudanese rebels during the attack, Siyr could get inside the camp. He was armed to the teeth and he'd pulled off rough missions armed with little more than his wits. He could get inside, and he could find the bomb.

When Dreizil first briefed Siyr on the mission, he'd been up front about what was expected of him: If the Americans aborted or double crossed them...if they appeared to be in danger of failure...if they were compromised at any point near the target...if they initially succeeded but were intercepted with the hot potato before extraction...if Siyr even had a bad premonition...he was to secure the device and manually activate it.

He was to detonate the warhead--blow the terrorists, the Americans, and himself, into atoms.

Then Samson reached toward the two central pillars on which the temple stood. Bracing himself against them, his right hand on the one and his left hand on the other, Samson said, "Let me die with the Philistines!"

The threat would be neutralized a safe distance from Tel Aviv and any other Israeli target. Israel wouldn't have to take any overt action, and could deny any knowledge of it after the fact. "The terrorists blew themselves up. That's what they get for fooling around with nukes." Sudan couldn't raise a too big a stink without drawing attention to her harboring of active terrorist cells.

The Americans would also deny knowledge, of course. Americans let their own soldiers be starved and tortured to death in Asian P.O.W. camps for decades with little protest. They wouldn't even peep about the loss of some mercenaries.

So Israel would be saved, the American-led coalition would hold together--maybe even be strengthened, and the next nation planning to host such an operation would have something to think about.

Dreizil was worried Siyr wouldn't be in a position to do this now, separated from Cavarra's team. Siyr had the opposite worry.

Then he pushed with all his might, and down came the temple on the rulers and all the people in it. Thus he killed many more when he died than while he lived.

30

0903 16 AUG 2002; DINKA VILLAGE, SUDAN

Lieutenant Colonel Qawi adjusted the *agaal* and *shumagg* on his headdress as his command vehicle followed the lead tank into town. The village was almost destroyed and no living creature stirred. Flies, birds, jackals and hyenas had gathered for the great feast. He saw dead bodies everywhere. Most--or perhaps all--seemed to be Popular Defense Force personnel.

"Sir," announced a voice over the radio, "we've found some wreckage east of the village. A PDF cattle truck, I believe. There are many dead."

Another voice announced a similar finding west of the village. Still another reported a wrecked gunjeep with PDF markings.

"We'll continue our sweep," Qawi said. "Once we've passed through, A and B Troops will secure a position south of the village. I want two squads of infantry to dismount and search the village thoroughly. C Troop will recon in a spiral from here."

His troop commanders acknowledged his instructions and the Murahaleen Scouts kept rolling through the war-ravaged pattern of rubble that only resembled civilization. Qawi's own vehicle passed the burnt-out hulk of an armored car. After his footsoldiers had searched and secured the village, Qawi himself dismounted and took a look around. He could make little sense of the carnage, and the stench of the decaying bodies almost made him nauseous. He held one side of the shumagg over his mouth and nose while examining the gruesome scene.

Qawi had never been this far south before. General Rahim liked to keep his elite units close to Khartoum, and refused to risk them in petty engagements.

With an approximate body count of the PDF soldiers rotting in and around this village, Qawi understood why Rahim had deployed the Scouts here--it was a matter of pride.

The Popular Defense Forces had never suffered a massacre like this. They were dealing with more than just some gang of primitive tribesmen armed with antiquated or improvised weapons. President El-Bashier needed to save face.

***

C Troop reported footprints along the river bank leading toward Bor. Qawi briefly considered chasing down the survivors and forcing them to dig mass graves for the PDF, then seeing what intelligence he could squeeze out of them. But that ugly task was hardly worthy of his Scouts. He radioed Rahim's staff to suggest something be done about the bodies.

The enemy had at least one tracked vehicle which left distinct imprints in the ground. Qawi ordered B Troop on point to follow the tracks, and the Murahaleen Scouts were on the move again.

B Troop set an ambitious pace. Too ambitious: in areas of hard ground, the tracks were harder to see. They lost the trail a couple times and had to send wide arcing patrols out to pick it back up. Qawi rotated A Troop to the point and ordered them to slow down.

They proceeded at a snail's pace north. Qawi knew his quarry had moved at a much faster rate, but they couldn't run forever. There would be no refuge for them to the north. Sudan was the largest country on the continent, so they would have to stop somewhere inside it.

Wherever they stopped, the Murahaleen Scouts would find them.

31

1153 16 AUG 2002; TEKEZZE RIVER CAMP, SUDAN

(At the quick-time.)
As I was boppin' down the street, what did my eyes meet?
A grunt with jumpwings standin' tall
Baddest dude I ever saw
Like my recruiter said to me, "Be all that you can be."
As I was humpin' through the sand, I came upon a rag-tag band.
Freedom fighters, lean an' mean
Baddest dudes I ever seen
Like my recruiter said to me, "Go and save democracy."

The chutes were all packed and all bellies were full. Now Rocco's Retreads stood burning under the late morning sun, stripped down to T-shirts. Cavarra led them in rehearsals of the actions to be taken on the objective.

Jenkins burst out of Pete Baker's workshop tent and marched up with an excited look on his face. The anomaly of seeing a jet jock lose his practiced composure was enough to get everyone's attention.

"There's something you all want to take a look at," Jenkins said.

They followed him into the tent where Baker's tools were kept. The mechanic had some electronic gizmos hooked up to his solar-charged batteries, with a small computer monitor. On the screen was footage of the devastated Dinka village from the day before. There was excited murmuring as the men recognized what they were seeing.

"At ease!" Lombardi barked, pushing forward to hear what was being said.

"Turn it up!" somebody said.

"...once-peaceful village in the Sudan," the commentator's voice was saying as the camera panned over the devastation, then zoomed in on men working to bury some mangled corpses, "in an attack that left hundreds dead. Local sources report that this is the work of Christian rebels who want to overthrow the Sudanese government. Southern

Sudan is no stranger to violence, having suffered civil war for many years, but the brutality of this attack on the Muslim population has led Khartoum to appeal to the United Nations--"

"What!" cried Terrell. "**They** attacked **us**! What kind of--"

"Shh!" Mai hissed.

The scene changed to a studio where male and female anchors turned from the teleprompters to face each other, shaking their heads with dour expressions. "What connection, if any," the female asked the male, "might this have to President Bush's 'War on Terror'?"

"That can't be established concretely at this time," the male replied. "But it's possible that, despite the President's public assertions that we are not at war with Islam...he's even admitted that it's a religion of peace, if you recall...some radical, pro-western factions in various parts of the world have taken all the saber-rattling for a signal. These Christian fundamentalists may very well have decided that the political climate is right for their own war of terror on their Muslim neighbors."

The female frowned sadly. "Just because Islam is a peaceful religion, that doesn't mean every religion is peaceful."

"Exactly," said the male. "In most parts of the world, religion is just one cultural aspect of society. It's when the religion becomes the primary focus that these fundamentalist groups are able to thrive and atrocities like this become just an everyday fact of life."

McCallum cursed. "What is this? One of the Arab news agencies? The BBC?"

Baker shook his head and forced a laugh. "This is network news from the World, man."

"How 'bout Fox News?" Zeke asked. "What are they saying?"

Jenkins shrugged. "The commie asswipe says pretty much the same thing. The neocon asswipe says things like this happen because the US doesn't have a strong enough presence in the region."

The reporters now invited a retired officer into the conversation, as their military adviser. He explained that such an operation was the work of a well-armed, highly-motivated unit, working with deadly precision. Perhaps the Sudanese People's Liberation Army had hired some outside help.

The sound of a gasoline engine lured Cavarra outside. The men's outrage was interrupted by the arrival of Mugabe.

Mugabe swung out of his Dodge and said, "Our peeps are comin', Johnny."

Mugabe's tone was more serious than what Cavarra had come to expect.

"Who?"

They stopped face-to-face. Mugabe looked worn out.

"The rebels. They less than a mile out."

"I don't hear anything." Cavarra looked around for Sentry.

As if reading his mind, Mugabe nodded toward the gate. "The dog hear 'em. He up front waitin'. They on foot."

"On foot? What...?"

Mugabe shrugged. "Unexpected difficulties procurin' transportation."

They walked to the gate where Sentry sat watching the horizon. "We had some unexpected trouble of our own," Cavarra said, and brought him up-to-date on recent developments.

Mugabe grimaced upon hearing of the firefight, then grew even more serious when told about the news program.

"Ain't that some mess? Complete news blackout for twenty years on all the black folks gettin' murdered, here. Then the PDF get they ass kicked good one time and 'stop the press!' Mean old rebels oppressin' the government. The horror!"

Some of the men gathered near the fence to watch the growing line of specks on the horizon.

"Infantry?" Campbell wondered aloud. "We're gonna assault the terrorist camp with straight-leg infantry?"

McCallum shrugged, but looked somewhat concerned himself. "Old School warfare. Happens a lot in the Third World."

As the rebels grew closer, details became clearer: Most carried AK47s. Some had RPGs slung around their backs, some mortar tubes, some machineguns. Aside from their weapons, no two of them were dressed or outfitted the same. They were tall, rawboned black men, shiny with sweat. They numbered around 300.

"What a bunch of douche-bags," Mai said.

"Where did they hump in from?" Bojado asked.

"We're still a long shot from our target," McCallum said. "These jokers are Gonna be smoked if they have to hump there by tomorrow night."

Cole asked the obvious question. "How they Gonna have the stren'th ta fight once they get there?"

"They don't look like they could fight off an old lady even now," Mai said.

McCallum wondered. He could tell a lot about a man just by how he carried himself and his gear. Even if the man was only a silhouette in the distance. These men had their heads up and appeared alert. They maintained reasonable intervals on the march. They carried their weapons at the ready, not like burdensome luggage they'd just as well discard. They'd obviously been marching long miles across the hot wilderness, but they weren't broken.

The rebels drew closer. A white man wearing a garish uniform and hat emerged from the ranks. He walked with a painfully erect posture. He wore shorts that reached almost to his hairy knees. Around his bulging waist was a lacquered pistol belt. Hanging from the belt was a chrome-plated Beretta in a lacquered holster.

Cavarra groaned. "Please say that's not the rebel C.O."

Mugabe flashed him a wiry grin. "That's Chargin' Charlie Thibeault."

"Looks like Inspector Clouseau in military drag. Is he French?"

"French, Belgian...one of those pansies. That's good, though: 'General Clouseau.' I like it."

They went through the gate and walked out to meet the European mercenary.

***

Cavarra, Mugabe and Thibeault sat alone in the motor pool.

"Seems to me," Cavarra said, "you should circle the wagons out there. Secure the area 360 degrees around this camp, until you're ready to--"

Thibeault made a spitting sound. "You need my men to protect yours? After we marching for three days, we no exhausting enough?" He turned to Mugabe. "And where are promise trucks?"

Mugabe replied in a calm, measured tone, "Like I said, I need some volunteers from your men to drive. I got five trucks stashed about an hour from here--"

"Five! Five trucks? How to pack all my men into five trucks? We feet already blisters!"

He had a point, Cavarra realized. Those poor bullet-stoppers wouldn't be in any shape to attack the terrorist camp after four straight days of humping through this heat. "You can have our two trucks. And our halftrack--it'll serve well as your command vehicle. It's got a Browning M2 might come in handy for you. We got another M2 off a jeep you can have. One of my heroes also captured a recoilless rifle and some rockets. You're welcome to mount it on one of the trucks--"

Thibeault glared at him. "I have nine and three-hundred men. Seven trucks do not more good than five."

"Do you want the vehicles or not?" Cavarra asked.

"Whoa there, General Clouseau," Mugabe said. "Don't be lookin' the gift horse, ai'ght? I'll go find you some more trucks here in a minute."

Cavarra looked at Mugabe. "We got some M-shit-teens you could use for trading. No handguards, but otherwise they're complete."

Mugabe brightened. "M16s? I could trade for a whole fleet of trucks with a few of those! How many you got?"

"Seven. But like I said--no handguards."

"She-it. They can carve handguards outa' wood or bamboo or sumpthin'." He winked at Thibeault. "You'll get your trucks, Clouseau."

"How many?"

Cavarra cleared his throat. "Eight more would do it. If you have to, you can stuff all your men in ten trucks. It won't be comfortable, but it beats humping the rest of the way. Whoever can't fit inside can strap themselves to the hood, the roof, the fenders, and ride Russian-style."

Thibeault played with his moustache for a moment. "This situation much unacceptable. I can be expected to perform not effective."

Cavarra put a gentle hand on Mugabe's shoulder. "You probably need to get going. Go see Tommy Scarred Wolf and tell him I said to give you all our leftovers."

Mugabe hesitated, giving Cavarra a curious look. "Cool," he finally said, rising to leave. "I'll let y'all work it out. Just don't kill each other." He got the names of five men who could drive from Thibeault and left the motor pool.

Both men were silent for a moment after Mugabe left. Cavarra popped his neck and knuckles.

"I don't know what you're getting paid or what your agreement was," Cavarra said. "But you are getting paid, or you wouldn't be here. And I know they didn't promise you this would be a milk run."

"Don't dare to condescend me!" Thibeault exploded. "I am ranking officer here."

"Shut up and listen, before I condescend upside your pointy little head."

Thibeault's eyes narrowed.

"You know about the nuke. You know what happens if we don't get it away from the bad guys. Now I'll help you in whatever way I can, but I can't do my job if I have to fight you all the way, *capish*?"

32

1326 16 AUG 2002; MALAKAI, SUDAN

Yacov Dreizil sat alone in a cafe watching the rain through the window, sipping tea.

Tea. The British sure did leave their mark on this part of the world.

Even the Jews, who found themselves in a belligerent position against the United Kingdom after WWII, had picked up many British habits from the occupation.

Dreizil examined his hands. The cuticles not scabbed from his previous inspection were peeling anew.

Now, of course, the United States had replaced Great Britain at the top of Israel's "with friends like this, who needs enemies" list.

Israel was the first nation to volunteer to join the coalition for the "War on Terror," but was snubbed by the US. Some Israelis believed the Americans might quit criticizing Israel for her reprisals against Palestinian terrorists, after the attacks on New York and Washington last year. But apparently acts of terrorism were intolerable, cowardly atrocities only when they occurred outside of Israel.

American politicians who claimed, "We don't negotiate with terrorists," insisted that Israel negotiate with Yasser Arafat

Arafat ordered the murder of Israeli athletes in Munich. He ordered his "holy warriors" to bomb schoolchildren. He cut open the wombs of pregnant women and butchered the babies before their eyes. He hung his own people by meathooks through the neck. The Nobel "Peace Prize" winner had killed even more Arabs than Jews. And though appeasing him had never brought an end to the terror by his followers, the Israelis were expected to sit across the table from his puppets and give them more Jewish land every time they opened their mouths to lie.

Dreizil gnawed at the peeling flesh on his fingers. He stopped long enough to check the safety on the pistol under his trenchcoat for the umpteenth time.

***

Bunty emerged from the bazaar with a bulging burlap sack. He turned down an alley, unaware of the eyes watching him from the cafe window.

Dreizil paid for his tea and hustled outside to follow the informant. The sky was dark and the rain came down hard. Dreizil couldn't even hear his own footsteps over the constant splatter.

He shadowed Bunty through the alley and along a fenced-off drainage ditch strewn with garbage and animal carcasses. He was thankful the downpour suppressed the stench.

Bunty crawled through a hole in the fence, crossed a weed-ridden field and came to a half-skeletal building. Dreizil followed him to the unfinished warehouse.

Construction had been halted years ago on this place. What portions of the roof existed were in bad condition. Bunty sat down on a truck dock under one such portion and leaned back against the wall.

Dreizil emerged from the rain and loomed over him.

Bunty looked up at Dreizil and was transfixed by the silencer protruding from the trenchcoat.

"So you're not religious," Dreizil said. "You snitch to the PDF for money to buy drugs."

Bunty was speechless. He couldn't even find words to think.

Dreizil had found the driver, hired by James "Mugabe" Harris, who had tipped Bunty off to the men and weapons in the Dinka village. With adequate persuasion, he gave Dreizil a lead on where to find Bunty.

Dreizil knew assassinating collaborators in a country like this was like trying to plug the Titanic with a champaign cork. The driver was tied and gagged under a tarp in the Jeep.

"I-I don't...I didn't..." Bunty said.

Dreizil waved the pistol at him. "Toss the bag over."

Bunty complied.

Keeping his eyes on the frightened Sudanese, Dreizil squatted and dipped his hand in the bag. He wanted to see what kind of inanimate substance almost caused a nuclear holocaust. He expected to feel bundles of Somalian *khat*, but his hand came out with a sesame cake.

"Please, sir," Bunty said, "my family is starving."

Dreizil studied him. The man was ghastly thin and sickly-looking, like so many of the southern Sudanese. He hadn't come here to consume drugs in private--he'd merely needed to rest his emaciated body before continuing on the journey to take much-needed food to a malnourished family.

"Take your shoes off," Dreizil ordered, pulling some rawhide strips from his pocket.

33

1336 16 AUG 2002; AS SUDD, SUDAN

Qawi ordered a halt and cursed.

The drought was over. Rain poured down with the density of a waterfall and the river was starting to flood.

The tracks of his prey were being swept into oblivion. Had they crossed the river here and turned back north? Or had they driven along over the rapids to conceal their progress?

Wherever the tracks reemerged, they were disappearing with every liter of pounding water and it would be impossible to find them.

Qawi could now fully appreciate being stationed in the North. Down here it rained nine months out of the year. Even during a dry year, like this one, torrential rains weren't uncommon.

He closed the hatch, hunched down in the turret and opened his map case. Where could they be going?

Certainly they had no intention of raiding anywhere north of Rashad--that would be suicide for any unit the rebels could muster.

Just how large was this force? It was hard to determine since they traveled single-file. They destroyed a 120-strong PDF contingent. By conventional logic, then, that put their numbers at that many or more, depending on entrenchment, surprise, and who had surprised whom. Probably twice as large or larger, and with some respectable firepower.

What could the mission of such a unit be? Possibly to destroy a dam. Maybe ransack a government storehouse. Perhaps a reprisal torching of some Muslim farms...

That was it! The northward movement was just a ploy to throw off pursuit. The real target must be the oil fields across the Sabat River from Ethiopia. The Christians had dried up a portion of the As Sudd swampland adequately to farm. One of the farmers had discovered oil by accident. Within a week, the farmers were dead and the government was drilling there.

The clever rebels must have turned southeast once in the river, so they couldn't be trailed. Tracked vehicles were heavy enough not to be swept away by the current. They couldn't hope to hold the oil fields by themselves, but they could wipe out the crews and set the fields afire to deny Khartoum their use.

Qawi had C Troop cross the river. With A and B Troops on the southwest bank and C Troop on the northeast, his Scouts turned to follow the Sabat down toward the oil fields in the merciless downpour.

34

1641 16 AUG 2002; TEKEZZE RIVER CAMP, SUDAN

Puttcamp's Skyraider climbed at a steeper and steeper angle until it stalled. Then he performed a wing-over and sent the old bird into a spin.

Haugen dove after and quickly overtook him.

Puttcamp was only a thousand feet off the deck when he pulled out of the spin and swung onto Haugen's tail.

Haugen barrel-rolled and nosed down into a half-loop. Puttcamp followed.

Wingtip-to-wingtip, the Skyraiders dove another few hundred feet and pulled up to skim along the river at strafing altitude.

***

Cavarra called a break from the rehearsals and the men gathered to watch the aerobatics.

Scarred Wolf stood beside Jenkins, who shook his head and chuckled. "You ever hear the famous last words of a jet jock?"

"I don't think so," Scarred Wolf said.

Jenkins poked his tongue into his lower lip to simulate a wad of chaw and drawled, "'Watch this'!"

"Which fighter jock was that?"

"Any one of 'em," Jenkins replied. "Take your pick."

Scarred Wolf got it, now, and laughed. "Still, it's gotta make you a little jealous. I'm not a pilot and I'm jealous, watching them hot-dog up there."

Jenkins winked. "Oh, I'm jealous, all right. I've just had a lot of practice hiding it."

***

Mugabe's Ramcharger entered the camp, leading five old five-ton trucks. Scarred Wolf went to meet Mugabe, since the agent would now be needing the M16s.

Thibeault's men cheered when they saw the trucks. Mugabe turned them over to Pete Baker for refueling and a basic inspection.

Mugabe stored the rifles in the back of his Ramcharger and found the European merc.

"Here's sumpthin' to get you started, General Clouseau. I'm headin' into town to find some more. If any's available, I should be able to get plenty for you."

"This is... asinine," Thibeault said. "I no can explain you and this 'Rocco' to understand that I can possible not march 300 men to target by H-Hour with five trucks. We necessary must leave in some few hours. No time for rest. How you more trucks delivered us?"

"I'll try to get them back here before you leave. If I don't, I'll catch up with you."

Thibeault threw his hands up. "I no can believe! You just now arrive, and with only one third of minimum vehicles I require. Where have you been doing?"

Mugabe had meant to get back much sooner, but he'd been contacted by Washington, and had to ditch the volunteer drivers temporarily in a safe spot while he went off to take the call in private. If Bobbie Yousko was willing to dial his direct and unsecured, it must be important.

B.Y. had heard the team was compromised, and was relieved tremendously to learn that it was still intact and the mission going forward. Yousko instructed Mugabe to push the schedule up since their cover was blown, but this was impossible without the trucks for Thibeault's troops. In fact, the lack of transport was now the biggest obstacle to the mission.

B.Y. cursed Kabiu and told Mugabe to find some trucks in a hurry, however he could.

"Don't start trippin'," Mugabe warned Thibeault. "You ain't the only one with problems. You just gonna have to improvise."

***

The Skyraiders came in for landings on the nylon "instant

runway" and taxied to their revetments. Haugen and Puttcamp climbed out of their cockpits and swaggered toward the big tent, talking, nodding and symbolizing maneuvers for each other with motions of their hands.

Cavarra went to fetch Siyr, but the merc wasn't where he'd left him. He groaned. What now? Why had he snuck off again?

At first, he ignored the ruckus outside the camp amongst the rebels. Thibeault was screaming at somebody in Arabic. But in time Cavarra's curiosity got the best of him and he marched out to investigate.

There in the center of the disturbance he found Siyr.

Thibeault saw Cavarra arrive and grew even more enraged. "This is not your affair! I no will tolerate your interference! I am in command here!"

Cavarra held his hands up, palms forward. "Whoa. This is one of my heroes. What's the problem here?"

"One of yours? Why I am not surprised? He tries to have mutiny with my men!"

Siyr shook his head. "Not true at all. I only attempted to arrange the men into a more tactical posture. There is no provision for security here--the men are too close together and nobody is watching--"

Siyr's explanation was drowned out by Thibeault's screaming.

"Get back to camp," Cavarra told Siyr.

Siyr shrugged and headed for the gate. Some of the Sudanese smiled and called to him as he walked past.

When Thibeault calmed down enough to listen, Cavarra said, "I apologize. He didn't intend to usurp your authority."

The mercenary seemed thrown off-balance by the apology. "You sended him to do this?"

"I did not. He must've just noticed the same thing I did..."

"No more your lectures on security."

Cavarra hunched his shoulders. "Like you said, you're in command." He hoped the rebels wouldn't get wiped out because of that.

Thibeault was momentarily silent.

"His name is Ehud Siyr. He's your sergeant-major, and the liaison between you and me. I'll have a talk with him about not stepping on your toes."

"Liaison?"

"Right. He speaks a lot of languages, including some of the dialects your men speak. He'll be handy for you to have around. Not only can he communicate with your troops, he's pretty good in a fight."

"I am not too much certain..."

"Look: This is to be a coordinated attack, right? Now how am I supposed to coordinate with you if we don't have a go-between?"

***

Cavarra smiled to himself as the old familiar stress headache came back. I must be crazy to enjoy this. He caught up with Siyr back inside the camp. "I need a word with you."

Siyr shook his head. "What sort of imbecile has been hired to lead these men?"

"Knock it off," Cavarra said. "I don't care what you think of him. That's his unit, and you don't go stealing his thunder like that."

"I was only introducing myself among the men," Siyr said. "A few of them commented on the poor state of security, and I could see they were right. All I did--"

"Hey, I admit that's a gaggle out there. But you made him look bad and that's an unforgivable sin with most officers."

"Commander Cavarra, this man makes himself look bad. There is no way to make him look otherwise. He is either a reincarnation of Von Moltke's constipated nephew, or he learned all his tactical doctrine by watching *Starship Troopers*."

"What makes you say that?"

"Well, you see how he's deployed his men...if you can call it a deployment. Even a peacetime bivouac is more tactically sound. And these men he has? They are not stupid cannon fodder as he treats them. They are all volunteers from the SPLA. They've all seen combat...some have seen quite a bit, but he seems to think of them as basic trainees. You know how he selected his officers and NCOs from among them?"

Cavarra shook his head.

"When he took command, he gathered them together in a large

building and had each one of them stand up and introduce himself with a short speech. All 309 men. This is the means he used to pluck his chain-of-command from among them."

Cavarra frowned. If this was true, it was almost insane enough to be funny.

"They've not drilled together. He's told nobody of his plan, if he has one. Not even the officers he brevetted. I am afraid all he thinks they are good for is a frontal assault, and perhaps that is the only battle drill he is familiar with."

Cavarra had assumed the Sudanese rebels to be unmotivated and undisciplined. But if what Siyr said was true, they had remarkable reserves of both motivation and discipline just to march for three days with this slab of meat.

"He passed out the mortars and machineguns without bothering to find out who was experienced with them. Yesterday, he had the mortarmen on point."

Cavarra sighed. "How are his subordinate leaders? Hopeless?"

"Actually, no. Some could be better, but all could be far worse. A few have taken the initiative and shuffled the ranks around. They've also put the support weapons in the hands of experienced troops."

"Listen, Siyr: This makes it all the more important that I have you with him. But you've gotta walk on eggshells with this guy. Feed his ego a bit...that might win him over. Then see what you can do with the men and their appointed leaders. But discreetly."

"See what I can do?"

"Draw them a layout of the camp. Give them an idea of what they're up against--"

"They know nothing of the nuclear warhead."

"Not surprising. Well, don't go telling them now. But if you get the chance, drill them a bit in coordinated fire-and-maneuver."

"What about planning?"

"If he doesn't have one, then you might as well help the leaders formulate something tentative. Nothing fancy. Assuming the bunkers have been knocked out, a brief rolling barrage by the mortars right through the mine field and into the camp, followed by sappers to breach the concertina in three or four places. I'd attack from the south--their defenses seem weakest there. Once you breach, have the mortars fire flares over the camp. Emplace the machineguns on the high ground--on top of the pillboxes, whatever's left of them. Once you get that far, the worst should be over. But for the luvva' Mother, remember my guys'll be over on the eastern edge. Make sure they know that."

Siyr nodded. "I will do what I can, Rocco."

***

While the others checked and readied their night-vision goggles, Scarred Wolf blindfolded himself and arranged to have Cole act as his eyes for the rest of the day.

"What you doing, Chief?" Bojado asked.

"Low-tech night vision."

A few laughed. "It may look like night to you, now," Lombardi chortled, "but the rest of us have broad daylight to see you look like some jackass with a blindfold on."

More laughter.

"He's gonna take it off before the jump," Cole said.

"And he'll have the night vision of a cat," Campbell added.

Mai held up his goggles. "Hello? Earth to the Redskin? It's called 'PVS-Fives'."

"This doesn't require batteries, or throw off your depth perception," Scarred Wolf said.

"What is that?" Terrell asked. "Some old Apache trick?"

"I'm not Apache."

"Whatever," Mai said.

35

(At a double-time.)
He was a rough tough hard-chargin' US Marine
Loaded down heavy with bullets an' beans.
He lined a hundred 'jockeys up against the wall
Bet a thousand dollars he could grease 'em all.
Greased 99 'til his barrel glowed red
Stuck his Ka-Bar through the last one's head...

Dreizil returned as the men were helping Pete Baker load the heavy drop.

Cavarra was bewildered to see the Israeli pulling two gagged and blindfolded Sudanese out of the Jeep. They were barefoot and bound with wet rawhide.

"What's this?"

Dreizil forced Bunty and the driver onto their knees, then turned to face Cavarra. "I want to 'clear the air.' Is that how it's said? I don't want any reason for mistrust left between us."

"You lost me."

"This is one of the men who delivered your trucks. He described what he saw to this man here, and this man passed that information along to the PDF."

Cavarra looked them over. They both appeared malnourished and terrified.

Dreizil switched to Hebrew. "You were worried that me or Siyr had squealed to the PDF ourselves. You are free to interrogate these men until you are satisfied that I'm telling you the truth."

Cavarra locked eyes with the Israeli. "Thanks. But Siyr won't be jumping in with us."

Dreizil tried to look nonchalant. "How about myself, then? You have an extra parachute."

Cavarra's jaw dropped, not sure he had heard correctly. "**You're** asking to go in with us?"

Dreizil shrugged. "Yes. Most of my jumps were static-line, but I've had some HALO experience."

"You're serious."

"Yes."

"Just why would you want to do that?"

"My country needs to have eyes and ears on the ground during the crucial part of the operation. I've told you why."

Cavarra shook his head. "Stick around for a minute. I'd like to talk to you." He turned away to search the curious faces around the camp. "Mai! Lombardi!"

The two senior non-coms sauntered over. Cavarra pointed to the prisoners.

"Mr. Dreizil says these are the snitches who tipped off the opfor about us. Why don't you take them somewhere and see if you can confirm that."

They lifted the two Africans to their bare feet to escort them away.

"They're both almost starving," Dreizil said. "A little food and they will probably tell all."

Mai sneered back at him. "Oh, they'll tell all."

Cavarra motioned for Dreizil to follow him.

They entered the tent to which Siyr had briefly been banished, and sat down.

"You're not playing straight with me." Cavarra said. "What's really going on?"

"We've been over this," Dreizil said.

"Yeah, and you all but admitted you want to be there in case you have to frag me. As reassuring as that may be, neither you nor Siyr are jumping in with us."

Dreizil smiled weakly. "I guess I can't blame you. But there was no harm in asking."

"What's your real reason? Siyr will be able to tell what's going on just as easily with Thibeault as he would with us. We'll be in radio contact."

"Perhaps. But I have no confidence in either Thibeault or his men."

"What, like you trust me and mine?"

Dreizil sighed. "I have nothing personal against you, Cavarra. If circumstances were different, you and I might get along, you know?

We might even be friends."

"I guess that's a compliment," Cavarra said.

"I think you are an honorable man. I have no intention of killing you, or seeing you killed." This much was true, Dreizil realized.

Cavarra folded his arms and leaned back.

"However, the individuals you take orders from are not honorable. This has been proven time and again to my people." Dreizil scratched his chin and opened his arms wide for a moment, as if welcoming a blow to his head or torso.

"America?" Cavarra asked, flinching. "We're the best friends you've got. The only friends."

"Because you give to us with one hand while stabbing us in the back with the other? That doesn't make you our friend. And you give more to our enemies than you give to us. Would you like to compare American arms handouts to Egypt or Saudi Arabia with those given to us?"

"Backstabbing? You're calling us backstabbers?"

"The PLO was bankrupt until your President Clinton bailed them out with US money. He froze the loan guarantee for the Russian immigrants in order to influence our elections against the *Likud*. His predecessor, Bush the Elder, bypassed the legitimately elected *Knesset* and negotiated with the leftists of the Labor Party, who were not even in power--"

"Hate to bust your bubble, Dreizil, but there are non-Jews indigenous to Palestine."

"Who refuse to coexist peacefully. Perhaps you've forgotten their celebration after September Eleven? You certainly forget the atrocities they commit against us."

Cavarra never dreamed he'd be obliged to argue in favor of the PLO. "Hey, they want their own country, just like your *Hagannah* terrorists did during the British occupation."

"There has been a 'Palestinian' state," Dreizil said, "longer than there has been a Jewish state. It is now called 'Jordan.' Where is the worldwide pressure on that country to absorb Arafat and his murderers? Why does no one suggest that the 'poor Palestinians' are given territory from their Islamic brothers? Why must the land be taken from the only Jewish state, which is already the smallest?"

Cavarra's jaw twitched. "The Palestinians are orphans. The other Arabs don't want them."

"So how is this Israel's fault?"

Cavarra could see he'd opened a real sticky wicket, here. No good could come from arguing with Dreizil. How, then, to steer the conversation back to tangible matters? Like what was hidden up the Israeli's sleeve.

Two gunshots pierced the camp.

36

1755 16 AUG 2002; AD DAMIR, SUDAN

Atef Al-Dura was thickly built for an Arab, and obviously didn't bathe often. He handled the M16s roughly, almost angrily. Mugabe knew Arab traders often behaved this way to disguise their recognition of a great deal.

The two men stood in the hot evening sun between Mugabe's Dodge and a huge Mercedes diesel truck. Three of Al-Dura's men stood nearby watching lazily.

"What about handguards?" Al-Dura asked.

"I'm sure some can be found easily enough," Mugabe said. "Or improvised, if need be."

Al-Dura handed the last rifle to one of his men. "Come inside."

Mugabe followed him from the truck lot into the lavish (by Sudanese standards) adobe/stucco house.

Many lamps dimly lit the interior of dark wood and animal pelts. Al-Dura and an armed worker escorted Mugabe into a small room with a long table. They all sat down.

Al-Dura noticed the way Mugabe crossed his legs: American-style, with the ankle resting on the knee. He made no mention of it, and Mugabe seemed oblivious to his observation.

A veiled woman brought in refreshments, and left without a word, shutting the door behind her.

"Why do you need the trucks?" Al-Dura asked, lighting a Turkish cigarette.

"A safari," Mugabe said.

The armed worker gulped tea from the glass set before him.

"You have the necessary permits for this safari?"

Mugabe shrugged. "That's not my concern. I just procure the vehicles."

Al-Dura nodded. "Who are you procuring them for? Who is undertaking this safari?"

Mugabe smiled. "I'm sorry, but I can't disclose that."

Al-Dura leaned back in his chair and sipped from his own glass. "Please drink. We have much cold tea."

"I'm not thirsty," Mugabe lied. "But thank you. I'll drink some later."

The worker stood, stretched, walked to the door and exited.

"Where will your safari be going?"

"Jebel Marra, I suppose."

Al-Dura exhaled smoke through his nose. "I'm prepared to trade fifteen trucks for your rifles. Will that be enough for your party?"

Mugabe's chest tightened. That was too easy. No Arab offered a fair trade right up front. It took hard-fought haggling to get a square deal. "The rifles are worth twice that much," he said, distractedly.

"So you need thirty trucks to haul your party?"

James "Mugabe" Harris sat up straight and put both feet on the floor. An electric charge wrapped around his brain and tingled in his teeth. *Oh, snap. Is this it?*

As if in answer to his question, the door reopened. The worker came back in, followed by a man he hadn't seen before. The worker stood blocking the door while the stranger stood across the table from Agent Harris.

The stranger had "secret police" written all over his posture and blank countenance.

Agent Harris stole a glance at Al-Dura, who took another drag from his cigarette and flicked ash into a bronze tray.

It was the cellphone. Bobbie Yousko blew my cover with that phone call.

"You are under arrest for espionage, 'Mugabe'," the stranger said. "I don't have to tell you what we do with spies. But if you cooperate--"

In one fluid motion, Harris rose while throwing the table over and drawing his .44 Ruger Blackhawk.

He had a small automatic in his ankle holster--far more popular for spook work. But he liked the balance of the cowboy-style revolver. And if he was going out, he might as well raise some hell on the way.

The secret policeman slapped leather. Al-Dura's lot worker already had his pistol halfway drawn. Flame and thunder spat from the Blackhawk's muzzle. The worker's body slammed backwards into the door, wrenching it off the hinges.

Harris pivoted and fanned the hammer once with his free hand. The Blackhawk roared again. The secret policeman got a shot off, then half of his head disappeared as he backflipped to the floor.

Al-Dura was still seated, cigarette in hand. His mind still hadn't processed all that had just happened in the split-second whirl of violence.

Harris grabbed a chair and broke it across the man's face. In a blur, he whipped out and flipped open his straight razor. He stooped, dipping the blade carelessly downward, then folded and pocketed it. Al-Dura now had a new mouth under his chin.

"Smile, asshole."

Every bullet was precious, now. Harris ejected the empty casings from his smoking six-gun, dropped in fresh rounds, snapped the cylinder back in place and plunged through the door.

A shot rang out close on his left. A burning sledgehammer smashed into his side. He dropped, rolled and fired, punching a huge hole in the shooter.

Figures appeared in the front doorway. Harris fanned the hammer and the doorway cleared.

Blood gushed from him. The pain was incredible and he felt weak. *Game over. I'm not Gonna make it this time.*

He crashed through a side window backwards and landed on his back outside, somewhat tangled in the curtains. The Blackhawk bucked in his fist and flattened an armed but unsuspecting man.

It never looked this painful in those John Woo movies. Shards of glass sent fire into his spine. He struggled to his feet.

He was dizzy and his vision was washing out. He staggered toward the cover of his Ramcharger. He took a round in his calf and went down. Another shot tore his forearm.

He blinked, saw more men taking aim at him from the truck lot. He fanned the hammer until it smacked into a spent chamber.

He fumbled for the ankle holster, but his fingers wouldn't work anymore, and he couldn't see anything clearly. Gunfire sounded far away and a cold sensation climbed his body.

This is it.

James "Mugabe" Harris bit down on the cyanide capsule and relaxed.

37

1802 16 AUG 2002, TEKEZZE RIVER CAMP, SUDAN

Cavarra and Dreizil passed Mai on their way to where the shots had originated. The burly marine was stalking away with a scowl that looked even angrier than normal. Dreizil paused to stare after Mai and fell farther behind.

When Cavarra trotted around the side of the halftrack, he saw two dead bodies. Head shots. Lombardi knelt over one, checking vital signs for some crazy reason. He turned to face Cavarra, shaking his head, eyebrows stretched high.

"What happened?"

"Mai greased them and walked away," Lombardi said.

Others from all over the camp arrived to stare at the scene.

The Sudanese were still bound and blindfolded. Cavarra felt sick. "What did you do this for? I said interrogate, not execute!"

"I didn't do it," Lombardi said. "I didn't know Mai was gonna do it. Had no idea...he just did it."

Cavarra sank to one knee and fought to hold his cookies.

Dreizil turned to Lombardi. "Did they refuse to talk?"

"No," Lombardi said. "They told us everything. They tipped off the PDF, just like you said. They confessed everything."

Cavarra shut his eyes tight. *Now we're not just mercenaries. We're murderers, too.*

"Why were they shot?" Dreizil demanded.

Lombardi threw his hands up.

***

Bojado caught up to Mai and called out to him. "Hold it right there, Gunny."

Mai stopped and turned, irritable.

"What's your problem?" Bojado asked.

"You talking to me?" Mai asked, through stiff lips.

"I'm talking to you. Aren't you the sick scumbag who wasted two civilians in cold blood?"

Mai sneered. "Oh, spare me. You really Gonna cry about a couple dead sand-niggers?"

McCallum arrived and put one huge hand on Bojado's shoulder. "I got this."

Bojado was only momentarily distracted. "You're a disgrace," he told Mai. "You're a disgrace to the Corps."

McCallum placed himself between Mai and the smaller marine. "So why did you kill the 'sand-niggers,' Mai?"

"They ratted us out. We got what info we needed out of them. They were no longer useful."

"You are a sick puppy," McCallum said. "And a disgrace to...to everything. Whatever you are, you're a disgrace to it. You're a worthless slab of meat and a sorry excuse for a man."

Mai quivered with rage and pointed an index finger at McCallum. "You broke bad on me once and got away with it. Don't push your luck."

McCallum pointed back with a finger as big around as a broom handle. "I'm gonna do a lot more than push."

Bojado reluctantly backed up to give them room.

The others drifted over from the murder site and formed a circle around Mai and McCallum. Everyone but Scarred Wolf (still blindfolded in the tent) and Fava-Vargas (singing, unaware of the gunshots or the subsequent chaos) gathered to watch.

Cavarra made no effort to prevent the fight. If McCallum didn't do it, someone else would, and Mai had it coming. If Cavarra hadn't felt so nauseous, he would have taken care of Mai personally.

The circle of spectators reminded Mai of high school. He would pick fights with haoles in the parking lot almost every week. He was an experienced brawler even before joining the Marines. The angry black giant facing Mai only scared him a little. Mai had beaten big men before. Size and strength didn't necessarily mean a man knew how to fight. In fact, big dudes were often easy to take down.

"C'mon, dogface," Mai taunted. "Take your best shot. C'mon. I'll let you get the first one in for free."

McCallum took a shot.

Nobody present expected such a large man to move so quickly--least of all Mai.

McCallum's left jab smashed straight-on into Mai's nose. Cartilage busted and blood sprayed. Mai's eyes involuntarily shut for a moment. He never saw the follow-up right cross that nearly unhinged his jaw.

Mai fell hard. He instantly scrambled to regain his feet, but McCallum kicked him in the head and put an end to that.

The rest was an anticlimax. McCallum dove upon him, knees pinning his arms down and enormous fists battering his head, but Mai was already out.

Cole, Terrell, Zeke and Lombardi were able to pull McCallum off Mai. Probably because McCallum didn't want to hurt any of them.

38

1844 16 AUG 2002; AS SUDD, SUDAN

Qawi called a halt.

"Say again," he said. "I didn't copy. Over?" Something about a spy and a shoot-out in Ad Damir, but the rainstorm was making radio conversation difficult.

"Are you still tracking them?" asked the voice on the radio.

"Not exactly. The rain has destroyed their tracks. But I think their target is the oil fields. We're following the Sabat--"

"Negative! Negative! Their target is north. I repeat, north. Over?"

"North where, over?"

"Uncertain of specific target at this time. Regular Army divisions are spreading east from the Nile. You need to about-face and move north on the double. Over?"

"Wilco. How large is the enemy force, over?"

"Unknown. But the high command was very clear: You are to move north. Over?"

"Wilco. Request aerial recon across suspected enemy route. Over?"

"Birds are wheels-up already. Will inform on contact. Over?"

"Roger. Out."

The Murahaleen Scouts reversed direction and cut for the highway.

The deluge hadn't yet made the dirt road unnavigable. The Scouts strung out along the road and drove north.

Qawi wondered what the rebels could be up to. Was it some suicide mission? How big was their force? Was high command right about their target being north?

Just because a spy was caught trying to buy trucks in the North didn't mean the rebels' target was in the North.

Well, he would comply with orders. If high command was wrong, he couldn't be faulted.

Either way, they should be out of this accursed downpour in an hour or two. Then they could refuel and buckle up for a wild ride. It wasn't often he let his Scouts run the M60s at full-throttle, so this should prove a night to remember.

39

1958 16 AUG 2002; TEKEZZE RIVER CAMP, SUDAN

(At a double-time.)
When I was young I always wanted to say
"I'm a SEAL, I'm a Ranger, or a Green Beret."
Now that I'm here an' I'm fit to fight
I got a drop into Indian Country tonight...

"I know this would happened!" Thibeault complained. "No more trucks. I march all night must again. Four days consecutive!"

The sun sank low and a breeze swept the camp. Thunder rumbled in the distant South, but here only a hint of clouds showed on the horizon. The two men stood near the transport plane, watching Baker check and re-check all three aircraft.

"Look," Cavarra said, "you got seven trucks and a halftrack. Pack as many troops inside as you can. Have as many as possible ride Russian-style. The rest hump for a while, then ride while somebody else humps. Let your men take turns riding and walking, and they'll be fresher at H-Hour. Keep the mortars and other heavy trash on the trucks, though. But you gotta' leave now, to make the objective on schedule."

Dreizil had left some time ago, to see if he could track Mugabe down.

Cavarra's feelings toward the Israeli had softened considerably in the last couple hours. Dreizil saw him during a very weak moment-- right after the murder--but made no comment about Cavarra dropping the ball. He also refrained from taking any cheap shots about Americans, murder, civilian casualties or any other topic grazed during their conversations. The connection would have been so easy and tempting to make, thanks to the shocking actions of one homicidal sadist among them.

At the very least, Dreizil--or anyone else--should accuse him of stupidity for trusting Mai. In fact, one could argue that Cavarra caused the atrocity by encouraging Mai to exercise his sadism.

I didn't know he would go that far. How could I have known that?

"So easy for you to say me to march, when you will riding an airplane," Thibeault said.

"I've got a spare parachute, if you really want to ride like the big dogs."

Siyr stepped up and saluted Thibeault. "Would you like me to load the vehicles now, sir?"

Thibeault returned the salute, frowning.

"Your command vehicle is loaded, fueled and ready for you to climb aboard, sir."

Thibeault pursed his lips, then told Siyr, "Very well, Sergeant-Major. Draft rotational roster for men who no can to fit on trucks. They will take turn riding, to walking. Understand?"

"Yes, sir!" Siyr said, and hustled off to load the convoy.

In fact, Siyr had already worked out the roster, and many other details he would let Thibeault take the credit for.

Cavarra breathed easier, knowing Siyr could pull Thibeault's strings.

Siyr barked commands in Arabic, English and Nilotic tongues. Gas and diesel engines sputtered to life. Men ran and shouted. Weapons clattered. Trucks bounced from the force of men jumping aboard. Grim-looking Sudanese rebels tied themselves to fenders, hoods, bumpers and cab roofs while others squeezed inside the cargo holds.

"I'll meet you at the dock," Cavarra told Thibeault, unsure if this was true or not.

***

Cavarra entered the tent to find his men posing for a picture. At Jenkins' urging, three of them sat together on a cot, Scarred Wolf with hands over his eyes, Fava-Vargas with hands covering ears, and Cole with hands over mouth. All it needed was a "see no evil, hear no evil, speak no evil" caption.

The camera flashed and Jenkins said, "Thanks, monkeys. If it don't make the Stars *and Stripes*, it should at least make the cover of

National Lampoon."

Cavarra approached the cot where Mai lay by himself, and squatted next to him.

Mai's nose and lips were badly swollen and lacerated. Some of his teeth were missing. One eye was blackened. Dried blood caked his face in an irregular pattern.

"How's your head, Mai?"

"Fine."

"You gonna be up to speed tonight?"

"What if I'm not?"

Cavarra honestly didn't know. He wished he had a magic wand to just make Mai disappear. "Maybe I deal with you the way you dealt with those civilians."

Mai nodded and stared straight up.

"You got one chance," Cavarra said, "and one chance only: You keep that ugly scar under your nose shut and do exactly as you're told. Save your attitude for the enemy. If you cross the gray line in any way...if I see you so much as give a dirty look at Mac, or anyone else...I'm Gonna deal with you in a language you'll understand. Copy?"

Mai nodded.

"If, by some miracle, you make it through this alive, we'll go our separate ways and never have to see each other's face again. And count yourself lucky."

"Aye aye, sir."

Cavarra rose and returned to the men.

Mai silently cursed everyone and everything in existence.

It happened again. First his career in the Corps was ruined, and now even this mercenary business was ruined. He had no doubt Cavarra meant exactly what he'd said. *Haole squid bastard was up in my face from the very beginning.* If Mai made it out alive, he'd never work for Soggy again. And he'd never be a marine again, even with a war brewing.

So he was in a place he hated, surrounded by people he hated, on a job he hated. And he'd been humiliated by someone he hated, in front of witnesses he hated.

He had a rifle, a pistol, and live ammo. His gut instinct was to kill McCallum...and Cavarra, and maybe a few others. But McCallum hadn't taken his eyes off Mai for one second since he'd regained consciousness. Even now, across the expanse of the tent, McCallum sat glowering at him. His eyes challenged Mai to try something. Anything.

And Mac wasn't the only one. No less than four pairs of eyes had been watching him at any time. Even the dogface haole Lombardi, who at least seemed a little less of a loser than the others, now looked at him in a way that made Mai furious.

Even if he shot the giant sapper in the back, one of the others would surely kill Mai.

Mai didn't dare step out of line now. An opportunity might present itself when the shooting started, but it wasn't likely. And he didn't want to ever face McCallum again, even with a loaded gun. Someone who knew how to use his size and strength to fight like Mac could with bare hands would also be dangerous with a weapon. McCallum didn't overestimate the value of what nature had endowed him with, or neglect any aspect of a warrior's craft. Mai wanted to stay as far away from him as possible. He feared the nuclear warhead less than he feared Mac.

Still, there was no telling what opportunities fate might present.

40

(At a double-time.)
F27 rollin' down the strip
Twelve operators on a one-way trip.
Mission top-secret, destination unknown
Some might not be comin' home...

Dark amber glasses had replaced Scarred Wolf's blindfold when they loaded the bird that night. He didn't want the moonlight to spoil his vision just yet.

The scene looked otherworldly. A lone transport plane sat quietly on a synthetic runway in the middle of an exotic wilderness. Insects and strange animals sang to a huge, bright moon bathing the alien landscape with a pale, monochrome luminescence. A single-file line of oddly garbed humanoid creatures approached the winged craft, and disappeared into it. Radios squawked in the night. A few quiet voices carried through the air.

Scarred Wolf appreciated the surreal qualities of the scene as if he was not just part of it, but also observing it from some vantage point outside his own body.

Sentry watched the procession intently, as if appreciating it in the same exact way.

The Fokker F-27 seemed unusually roomy, although actually smaller than even the C130s they were all so familiar with. But there were only twelve jumpers, with the thirteenth man, Pete Baker, acting as loadmaster. Also, they didn't have to waddle under the weight of loaded ALICE packs. Their web gear bristled with ordinance and their stomachs stretched happily around the shifting lurps consumed two hours earlier. Scarred Wolf was jumping with the Dover Devil and his rifle/grenade launcher. Fava-Vargas and DeChalk would be jumping with the SLAP ammo. Cavarra had the squad radio, and Zeke had the back-up radio. Everyone else was "Hollywood."

The entire squad now wore Kevlar helmets with short-range headset radios attached. Most operators despised conventional headgear, but Cavarra knew of men who were still alive thanks only to these bullet-stopping brain buckets. They also wore flack vests under their web gear. Some had night vision goggles around their necks ready to slip on when the time came.

Lombardi, the designated jumpmaster, gave the eleven-man "stick" a final visual once-over as they lumbered onto the bird. He and Cavarra made sure seats were taken in assigned stick order. Once seated with belts fastened, Cavarra quizzed them on their sub-unit tasks.

When Jenkins cranked the engines to life, Cavarra left the men alone to their thoughts.

Mugabe had never returned to camp. Neither had Dreizil. Cavarra hoped they'd delivered the trucks to Thibeault's group. Siyr hadn't broken radio silence, which meant Charging Charlie was driving on with the mission.

Baker shut and locked the troop door. Now the red interior lights painted everyone's features a Martian hue.

Outside the transport plane, the A1E Skyraiders sputtered to life. Haugen and Puttcamp performed their own pre-flight inspections. Puttcamp carried Sentry to the cockpit of the Fokker and dropped him inside. Sentry whined. Flying scared him and made his ears hurt.

Lombardi watched the fighter jocks through the window for a moment. Flying scared him, too, but he'd never admit it. He used a signal mirror to help apply camouflage paint to his face. Dark brown on the peaks, light tan in the valleys, exactly as the desert warfare field manuals dictated. Cavarra had insisted he scuff the shine off his jungle boots this time. Saving the warpaint for now gave him something to think about besides the jump.

Lombardi was fascinated by fear. So few things scared him, he actively sought them out. That's why he volunteered for the combat arms. Also why he went Ranger, then Special Forces. It certainly accounted for his 147 static-line jumps and twenty-nine free-falls.

Even when experienced, fear was no big deal once he learned how to channel it. So he paid close attention to every dull smear he applied to his face. This would postpone the fear until it was inevitable. Until he needed it.

The first time Lombardi remembered being scared, he was six years old. He remembered the doorbell ringing. His father cursed and turned the volume down on the basketball game. He screwed the cap back on his beer, placed it in the refrigerator and re-tucked his t-shirt into his ironed jeans as he went to the door.

An irate big man stood on the front porch. Not just big, but tough-looking, too. He cussed at Lombardi's father, angrily. Lombardi didn't know until years later, but the big man was angry because his father had turned him in for letting the grass on his lawn grow too long.

The man was so angry and so large, Lombardi feared for his father. Then Lombardi's father pushed the big man and they began fighting on the front porch.

Though shorter and outweighed by at least 100 pounds, Lombardi's father destroyed the big man. Lombardi watched from the window, so caught up in it he didn't realize his hands were touching the glass, until it was too late.

His handprints were on the glass--there was no mistaking whose they were. He'd been warned a dozen times about touching glass with his bare hands. How the oil from his hands would smear it. He tried to wipe the prints away with his shirt but they only smeared worse. Then his father came back through the front door.

He ran back to the living room, hoping his father wouldn't notice the curtains swinging and look behind them at the smeared glass. When he heard the refrigerator open, he knew he was safe for a while.

He tried to sneak away to clean the window somehow, but every time he tried, his father would ask, "Where you going, Greg?"

"Nowhere."

"Then sit down."

He didn't get a chance for the rest of the day.

He got up late that night, moving slowly and quietly, because his father was such a light sleeper. He took the dishrag from the kitchen sink and wiped blindly at the window, not daring to turn the lights on.

At breakfast no mention was made of the window. Then, to his horror, while waiting for the bus, he looked back and saw that now the entire window pane was covered by a spiral smear.

All day at school he expected to be called to the office, and find his father waiting for him. But it never happened. He got home and found that his mother had cleaned the window spotless. Nothing was ever said about it.

Lombardi remembered that day every time something scared him. First he'd been afraid the big man would beat up his father. Then he was even more afraid that his handprints on the window would be discovered. So afraid that he wished once or twice that the big man had won.

***

Fava-Vargas dealt with fear the same way he dealt with just about everything...by singing.

"...Stand up, hook up, shuffle to the door
Leap right out and count to four.
An' if my main don't open wide
I got a reserve by my side.
An' if that one should fail me too
Look out below I'm a-comin' through.
Scrape my body off the ol' drop zone
Bag me up an' ship me home.
Pin those wings upon my chest
Bury me in the lean 'n' rest..."

Pablo Fava-Vargas had no delusions about ever becoming a pop singer. He knew his tenor voice was good--he'd been asked to sing at Mass and a few weddings. But he also realized he was no Michael Jackson. He sang because he loved to sing.

His was a large and very musical family. Not a silent moment ever passed in his house. When his big sisters weren't playing the radio or practicing for talent shows or school dances, his mother was playing the guitar and leading the whole family in Spanish folk songs.

He joined the Navy for job security and college money. He'd only heard of the SEALs from cheap action movies. It was Petty Officer First Class Brinkerhoff who made him want to be an operator.

Brinkerhoff had left SEAL Team Two due to some medical issue he never talked about, but he still had stars in his eyes. He was a man who commanded admiration just by his presence. And he saw some kind of potential in Fava-Vargas to be more than just a one-tour sailor.

Their relationship was closer than just that of an "old salt" to a "seaman stain."

Brinkerhoff enthralled Fava-Vargas with tales of his commando exploits. One time he said, "There's a lot more to being an operator than just being tough. You gotta' be tough, but it's a lot more than that. You've gotta' enjoy doing stuff that other men would detest. You've gotta' be at least a little dinky dau--off your rocker"

Fava-Vargas saw the truth in that now. Money alone would never have persuaded him to volunteer for this mission. He volunteered because...well, because he was at least a little insane. He had almost died when the rocket hit the halftrack. His hearing would probably never be the same. And yet when he looked back on the experience, he smiled to himself. Hell, it was fun.

***

Fava-Vargas' incessant singing reminded Campbell of another man who was more than a little crazy.

Well, "man" might be stretching it. They were all just kids in Panama, really. The oldest of them in their early twenties.

His platoon had just pulled back into a secure area in the jungle for chow and a short rest while awaiting orders. There was a cease-fire in effect, but they all still had live ammo. The platoon leader was at some briefing or after-action review, and T-Rex was the ranking NCO.

T-Rex was, by far, the coolest NCO in the company. He let them do a rucksack flop in place to eat chow, smoke, joke, and let off steam.

Briar was in one of his strange moods that day, and keeping mostly to himself. But he'd got a song stuck in his head, and kept singing the only lyrics he could remember out loud.

A psyops unit had been blasting music and other sounds up at Noriega's penthouse, and the noise carried all over Panama City. When the shooting stopped in their sector, all of them could hear Madness' "Our House" echoing through the streets.

"Our house," Briar sang, "in the middle of the street. Our house...in the middle of the street..."

Maybe it was Ghost's fault. He'd been singing some Spanish song when Briar first started. But who could predict what might set Briar off on one of his kicks?

"Our house...in the middle of the street. Our house..."

Woodstock and Nutsack were ignoring Briar, discussing bodybuilding, Van Halen's last album and all the usual stuff.

Briar wasn't exactly shouting, but he was singing much louder than anyone would dare back at Bragg, or if some power-tripping scumbag like the Weenie (SFC Green) was around. Weenie wanted Briar worse than Bush wanted Noriega. He'd recently punished Briar with a quarter-mile low-crawl through brambles and wait-a-minute vines for referring to his rifle as a "gun"--basic training BS.

"Our house...in the middle of the street. Our house..."

Butthall was off by himself, too, reading a letter from his young wife.

Driftwood and Meeshter were making fun of Thomas'n'shit for finishing almost every sentence he spoke with "and shit:"

"Don't be tryin' to switch your pork patties with my meatballs, 'n' shit."

"This wet heat is wearin' me out, 'n' shit."

"Ya got any more of that Break-Free, 'n' shit?"

Thomas'n'shit shrugged it off while trying to think up a good comeback 'n' shit.

"Our house...in the middle of the street..."

Chief, Splash, Old Man (he was twenty-four) and LaPenis were discussing the possibility that Operation Blue Spoon/Just Cause was pretty much over, and they'd soon be going back to the World.

"Our house..."

Campbell (A.K.A. Cannonball amongst Second Platoon) was watching Ears show him and a couple of the cherries how to sharpen a Ka-Bar.

"In the middle of the street..."

The platoon not only ignored Briar, they refused to even acknowledge his annoying behavior to each other. It was like some huge child were throwing a tantrum and everyone came to an unspoken agreement not to encourage him.

Crack! A rifle shot sent everyone diving to the prone, spilling canteen cups and half-eaten MREs.

The paratroopers grabbed for their weapons, looking out into the jungle for the source of the shot. Not a word was spoken, but they all inwardly cursed the idiot who declared this area secure.

Campbell thought the report sounded mighty close. And it sounded like an M16. Slowly, he turned from the jungle to look behind him.

"My gun..."

Still flopped comfortably, smoking M16A2 pointed skyward, buttplate on the ground, Briar left his finger inside the trigger guard and continued singing.

"...in the middle of the woods..."

He now had the platoon's undivided attention to share his new lyrics.

"My gun...just sent you all down to the prone..."

Once T-Rex realized what Briar had done, he went nutso. The coolest NCO in the company proved that he could be a rampaging jerk, too.

At the *Pacora* Bridge, Briar had used his body to bridge concertina wire for his buddies. In *Panama Viejo*, when a DigBat grenade landed in their midst, he ran toward it, knocked Driftwood and Tron out of the way, scooped it up and flung it back where it came from. On the way to the Mariott Hotel, he intentionally exposed himself to draw fire so Splash and Nutsack could cross an open space to set their machinegun in a good spot.

Briar was hell-on-wheels in combat. A great guy to have on your side in any kind of fight. But he was an embarrassment on a weekend pass, a disaster in garrison...and probably a sociopath in civilian life.

Not long after they made it back to Bragg, Briar was in trouble again. Drinking, fighting, whoring...and he got chaptered out. Campbell often wondered where he wound up. Probably some prison or the grave.

Maybe not all volunteer soldiers are as crazy as Briar, but aren't we all a bit dysfunctional?

Campbell didn't understand other civilians--"normal" people. And he knew they didn't understand him. He didn't fit in anywhere. Nowhere but in the middle of insanity like this.

"You were Eighty-Second Airborne, weren't you?" DeChalk asked over the noise of the engines.

Campbell nodded.

"I thought you guys jump static-line."

"We do. I learned HALO for Recondo School."

DeChalk nodded.

Campbell realized he could have said, "I did." But he hadn't. He used present-tense. Inclusive. As if he were still in the Eighty-Deuce.

The Skyraider engines roared louder and louder, then the roar died down a bit. The old fighters must have just taken off.

Now the transport began to taxi.

***

DeChalk envied these men around him, for the training they'd gone through, the weapons and equipment they'd been allowed to play with. At least once a day he wished he had joined the military. But the US wasn't fighting a war when Sam DeChalk came of age.

The American involvement in Vietnam was long past when he graduated high school. And judging by the US response (or lack of one) to the Iran hostage crisis, it seemed to him the American military wouldn't be involved in a shooting war any time soon. Boot camp and an enlistment of at least two years seemed like a heavy price to pay, just in case a war started somewhere and the US might get involved.

Africa and the Middle East, however, always had some fighting going on. Mercenary veterans of the Rhodesian conflict flooded the US with literature and "merc schools."

After paying to attend numerous paramilitary training courses, hanging out at surplus stores and gun shows, and poring over the classified ads in *Soldier of Fortune*, he made a contact that paid off.

There was a guerilla war in Lebanon. Both sides were hiring mercenaries who could provide their own weapons and gear. Thanks to his doting mother, money had never been a problem for Sam DeChalk: He had the weapons and gear. He could also speak Arabic. He was in.

Merc work was rather disappointing. Most deals fell through, and the jobs that didn't were usually boring. DeChalk fired very few shots in anger, even after the conflict started heating up in former Yugoslavia.

Still, he'd spent more time in combat zones than the rest of these men put together. It just wasn't fair that they disrespected him.

Tonight, though, he would allow no one to swipe his ammo or otherwise mess him up. He'd be dropping into a target-rich environment with nothing to prevent him from tasting a full dose of combat up-close-and-personal. Tonight nobody and nothing could stop him. Tonight, he'd show them all.

***

The Fokker lifted off and climbed at a steady angle. Outside, the old fighter-bombers fell into place on the transport's flanks.

Most of the men dozed off almost instantly.

Cavarra and Lombardi remained awake, as did Cole. Mai's eyes were wide open, staring at a spot on the opposite wall of the bird. McCallum calmly stared at Mai.

Terrell dreamed of falling. Falling for miles and miles while bullets riddled his body. Falling into a lake of atomic fire.

Bojado dreamed of Christmas with his family. The bicycle under the tree he hoped would be his.

Zeke didn't dream at all.

Scarred Wolf dreamed of sitting on the porch swing with Linda, watching their kids play outside, discussing her plans for the house and a surprise birthday party for Vince.

Campbell dreamed of being locked in a padded cell with Briar.

Fava-Vargas dreamed about his youngest sister entering American Idol.

DeChalk dreamed he was Chuck Norris in an action film come to life.

41

0149 17 AUG 2002; BEERSHEVA, ISRAEL
IDF CENTRAL COMMAND BUNKER

He rubbed his eyes and picked up the phone. "General Dahav speaking."

"I have good and bad news for you, Sir," Dreizil's voice said.

Dahav tried to focus his bleary eyes on the officers bustling by the booth he sat in. "Is the transaction going forward?"

"That's the good news. All the merchants survived the robbery."

Dahav sighed. "Good. Thank God."

"They may prove to be shrewd businessmen, sir."

"Go ahead with the bad news."

"First of all, the merchants have discovered our shareholding. Our consultant has been fired."

Agent Siyr was compromised. "Is he well?"

"Quite well. He's found employment with the parent company. But the merchants' own consultant was not so lucky."

That's the CIA operative...Harris was his name. "That's too bad."

"Yes, Sir. In fact, he hadn't completely secured distribution for the product."

Using this metaphorical device, Dahav was brought up to date. Before he hung up, Dreizil let him know he would be driving to the Hala'ib Triangle himself.

Dahav drummed his fingers on the desk for a moment.

Well, they had another three hours before the attack on the camp.

He stepped outside the cubicle and Ben-Gadi met his eyes.

Both of them glanced at the two unlit buttons on Ben-Gadi's console.

"We're holding what we have until further notice," Dahav said.

42

0256 17 AUG 2002; NUBIAN DESERT, SUDAN

Siyr led the Sudanese rebels at a fast trot, checking his GPS on the run.

The vehicles followed the men on foot.

They were actually on schedule. The target was only a few kilometers away. They might have a chance to rest before the assault.

"How is everyone back there?" Siyr called over his shoulder.

He heard grunts and heavy panting. It was probably time to rotate this group back into the trucks. Despite the daytime heat, the desert air at night was so cool he could see their puffs of breath in the moonlight.

Another three kilometers and everyone would dismount to cover the rest of the distance to the camp on foot.

The radio squawked: Thibeault, excited.

Thibeault had been content to ride along in the halftrack, letting Siyr and his officers attend to the details. The last time he said anything was several hours ago when a plane flew over. He was excited then, too.

"What if we are observed?" he had asked. "What if plane is reconnaissance and have the night vision?"

"We keep going, sir," Siyr had replied. "By the time ground forces arrive, we'll be gone."

Now Thibeault said, "Sergeant-Major, there is movement to our rear I think!"

"What do you mean?"

"I mean something moves behind us!"

"Can you confirm, sir?"

"No! You must confirm!"

Siyr groaned. "Sir, we are on foot. In your vehicle you could ascertain the situation and be back in formation quickly."

"I am in command! You will to obey orders!"

Siyr directed the men behind him to continue at the same pace and azimuth before he fell out.

I've had almost enough of this idiot. Is he a coward or lazy or both and more?

Siyr turned to face backward, catching his breath.

He scanned the horizon, and saw nothing out of the ordina...

The silhouette of a tank turret popped over a rise. Siyr's blood ran cold.

He spun in circles, looking for some kind of cover.

Running parallel to their line of advance, to the east, was a dried out riverbed. Perhaps a half klick or less distant.

Siyr tuned to the frequency he and the officers had agreed to earlier and said, "Enemy to the rear! Enemy to the rear! Run for the wadi on our right and spread out!"

For a moment the convoy continued on its present course as if they hadn't heard or understood him. Then suddenly the trucks veered and accelerated. One of them cut too hard and the top-heavy beast rolled, flinging off the men who'd been hanging onto the outside.

Siyr ran to the capsized truck and screamed at the men inside to get out and run for the wadi. The dazed men had no time to consider what was happening.

Siyr grabbed, yanked and kicked to get them moving. He was relieved to find that this truck was not carrying any mortars or baseplates.

The night erupted in flames as the first enemy shell landed and blew a handful of men into eternity.

Siyr sprinted for the wadi with everyone else.

***

Qawi saw several vehicles and perhaps hundreds of personnel scrambling for cover in the moonlit desert. The enemy force was a little larger than he had guessed. But still no match for his Scouts.

"C Troop form a skirmish line here," he ordered. "A Troop take the left flank. B Troop take the right flank. This is motorized infantry. All gunners load canister and fire at will."

***

The Fokker troop ship finally leveled off.

Lombardi watched Cole and Cavarra now starting to nod off.

Strange how fear affected everyone so differently. It kept him wide awake before a jump, but knocked most men out. Not the fear itself, exactly, but the exhaustion it caused.

Cavarra awoke with a start when the team radio squawked. "Has-Been Dog one, this is Has-Been Rabbit. Over?"

Siyr was breaking radio silence.

"This is Has-Been Dog One, go ahead Has-Been Rabbit. Over?"

"We are taking fire. I say again: We are taking fire. Over."

Cavarra sat up straight in the webbed seating, now wide awake. "Report, Rabbit. Over?"

"Uh...roger... Size: Maybe a battalion. Activity: Attacking us from the west. Location: Five klicks south of target. Unit: Heavy armor with mechanized support. Time: Now. Equipment: Unknown, but no air assets as of yet. Over?"

Cavarra heard explosions and screaming in the background. "How many casualties have you taken?"

"Light so far...but we're being encircled. It looks bad. "

Cavarra closed his eyes and thought. Sweat dripped off his face, splattered on his lap and moistened his shirt. "There's not much I can do, Rabbit...stand by. Over?"

"Roger...out..."

"Has-Been Bird, this is Has-Been Dog One, over?"

"Go ahead, Big Dog," Jenkins replied. "Over?"

"Did you copy conversation with Rabbit?"

"Roger that. "

"Bird Two and Three...change of plans: Break off from Bird One and provide air support for Rabbit. Communicate directly with Rabbit. Over?"

"Wilco, Dog One." This was Haugen's lazy drawl. "We're on our way. Out."

The Skyraiders banked over and accelerated westward.

Cavarra blinked hard. Justin could take care of Jasmine. He'd be like her surrogate father. But who would be Justin's father? Certainly none of Melissa's couch potato boyfriends.

How had Thibeault managed to trip over an armored battalion?

Well, the feces had officially hit the fan. What to do now? Should he scrub the mission altogether? Infantry didn't have a prayer against armor in the open field.

Tel Aviv. Poof. Holy war. The Samson Complex.

He shook his head and pinched the bridge of his nose. *Suck it up and drive on.*

***

Ali and Chin emerged from their tents at the same time. They looked at each other, then out into the dark desert from whence the noise was coming. Lights flashed in the distance, followed by the sound of explosions. Small arms fire chattered in the night.

43

Siyr ran along the wadi, yelling, "Save your ammunition! Spread out! Deploy the mortars!"

The trucks were parked at the bottom of the wadi. Men lay facing outward at the crest of both banks, firing into the dark.

Infantry doesn't have a prayer against armor in the open field. The best we can do is make a fight of it.

He located the recoilless rifle and the men who knew how to use it. "I need you up at the top of that berm. After every shot, slide yourselves down the bank to reload."

"Yes, Sergeant-Major!" The two men scrambled up the ravine to comply.

Siyr weaved through the chaos toward the heavy pounding of one of the M2 Brownings. When he found the gunner, he grabbed him by the shoulder and pulled him back.

"You're going to melt the barrel if you hold the trigger back like that," Siyr said.

The young gunner looked at Siyr with bulging eyes. He had a crazed look.

"Don't panic," Siyr said. "Panic won't help us. You're wasting ammunition--concentrate on the APCs and shorten your bursts. Repeat after me: 'Fire burst of six!"

"Fire burst of six..." the skittish boy said.

"Good. Say that every time you fire. Your bursts should only last as long as it takes you to say that."

The boy nodded. Siyr patted his shoulder. The M2 could handle longer bursts, but the instruction should compensate for the gunner's greedy trigger finger.

A rocket from the recoilless rifle scored a direct hit on a tank's side armor. A cheer swept through the ravine.

Siyr found the halftrack and a dismounted, panicking Thibeault.

"Why have you been doing, Sergeant-Major? What matter is bad your radio?"

"Sir, we need to get our mortars firing."

"We need retreat!" he shrieked. "Heavy armor! We are all killed!"

"Retreat to where, sir? This is the only defensible position for miles. There's no way we can outrun them, even if we hadn't lost a truck."

"Load everyone you can on the remaining trucks. Everyone else will have to surrender!"

"Surrender?" Siyr echoed.

The rebels within earshot all looked aghast at their commander.

Siyr decked Thibeault with his rifle butt and turned to the nearest man. "Tie and gag him, and put him somewhere out of the way."

"Yes, Sergeant-Major!"

He radioed his Sudanese officers. "This is Sergeant-Major Siyr. I have relieved Major Thibeault for cowardice under fire. I am now in command."

He addressed his officers by name, giving each of them a separate task. Nobody questioned his new authority.

Shells burst in and above the wadi. The blasts shredded men and equipment. A truck took a direct hit and burst into flames.

***

Qawi watched his tanks deploy with satisfaction. The enemy was completely bottled up, now. He kept his tanks out of RPG range, pounding the ravine with their main guns. Behind them, his infantry dismounted their M113s and prepared to move in for the mop-up.

Down from the sky came the scream of radial engines and the whistle of heavy objects splitting the air: A1E Skyraiders in a power dive.

Haugen released his first bomb at point-blank range. One tank exploded and another was knocked on its side from the blast.

Puttcamp came in behind him and scored a direct hit on another tank.

"Infantry in the open!" crackled Haugen's voice over the radio.

"Roger that," Puttcamp said. "I have a visual."

Heavy machineguns ripped off a harmony to the screaming engines. A hailstorm of lead rained down from the sky, chewing men and APCs to pieces.

***

Bojado's mother presented him with the bicycle, and he was overjoyed. The whole family was happy for him. They accompanied him outside and cheered for him to ride it.

He fell several times. Then his brother gave him a lecture about centrifugal force and he tried again. Just as he was getting the hang of it, the sky flashed red. A nuclear fireball rolled through the city, removing every structure from its place. He watched his family members reduced to skeletons, then ash.

"Game time, man! Game time!" Zeke the Greek elbowed him awake.

Lombardi was on his feet. Oxygen was being passed around.

Cavarra was shouting to them, "...everything just like we planned! We're not gonna wait around for the rebels! Copy?"

"Hoo-yah!"

"Hoo-wah!"

"Ooh-rah!"

They hastily re-checked their chutes and equipment. Each man snorted some pure oxygen.

The troop door yawned open and a tremendous rush of wind and noise clawed at them from the black, terrible sky.

The stick faced Lombardi, who showed them three fingers.

"Three minutes!"

Lombardi clamped hands on both sides of the doorway, wedged his feet solidly, then hung his body out in the roaring air. He looked all around with deliberate slowness, before his quivering muscles pulled him back inside. He faced the stick and held up one finger.

"One minute!"

He took a short glance out the door.

"Drop zone coming up!"

Bojado prayed.

Fava-Vargas crossed himself.

Scarred Wolf removed the dark glasses.

McCallum switched on his PVS5s and cinched them into place.

Terrell cursed.

DeChalk hyperventilated.

Mai wet his pants.

"Go!"

One by one, they shuffled up to the door and hurled their bodies out into the night. The last one out was Lombardi, who winked at Pete Baker and performed a backflip out the door.

Briefly, the loud, hot prop blast buffeted each man about. Everything beyond their hands was a dark blur.

Then, suddenly, the night was quiet.

The aircraft soared by high overhead.

Cold wind tore at them.

Cavarra put his arms against his sides and streaked down to the lead. The others sought out their buddies in the darkness and tracked into position.

Somewhere, thousands of feet below them, their target was a speck on the coastline too small yet to see.

THE BIVOUAC

The hoarse voices of trainers yelled throughout the camp. Bassam awoke and jumped up before anyone could kick him.

He heard the faint drone of an aircraft. He grabbed his rifle and stepped outside into a cold night. He could still hear the aircraft, but all he could see were stars.

Explosions and popping sounds wafted in from the south. He turned to look in that direction and saw flashes on the horizon. Trainees mobbed toward the gate to get a better look, as if gawking at a fireworks display.

THE WADI

Bedlam rolled over the airwaves. Qawi shouted into the radio to make his commanders shut up, but it took some time.

C Troop had lost three tanks, five APCs and probably thirty men or more. And here came the dive bombers again, spitting death.

"Spread out! All gunners man coaxial machineguns and engage those bombers!"

His words were drowned out in the roar and chatter as the

Skyraiders bore down on B Troop.

Haugen and Puttcamp had unleashed a tempest among C Troop. Now they concentrated on the formation moving into the rebel left flank with a perfect enfilade. More tanks went up in smoke. More APCs were hammered by machinegun fire.

A Troop, as yet untouched, scattered. The commander had witnessed what happened to his counterparts and wanted no measure of it.

Qawi switched radios and called for air support.

***

"Don't waste your ammo!" Siyr yelled to his riflemen. "And save the RPGs until they get in close! Then aim for the side, the rear, or where the turret meets the hull!"

His mortar officer had most of the tubes set up and aimed roughly at an enemy tank formation. He used one crew to bracket the formation, then told all his crews, "Correct fifty up and fire for effect!"

High angle hell whistled down on the enemy armor. One tank shuddered under a direct hit and the rebels cheered again.

Siyr cupped his hand to the mortar officer's ear and said, "Good job. But do you see that tank there?"

"Which one?"

"See the man with binoculars standing through the hatch?"

"How can...oh. Yes! I see!"

"That is probably an enemy commander. I suggest you concentrate fire on him."

"Yes, Sergeant-Major!"

Siyr strode to the center of a large concentration of riflemen and raised his voice over the battle. "I need six volunteers!"

Forty men raised their hands and shouted.

"Six brave men!" he amended. "Bravest of the brave!"

Only a couple dropped their hands.

"You probably won't make it back alive."

A couple dozen dropped their hands.

"You with the RPG, go get on the halftrack!"

The man indicated ran down the wadi and jumped aboard the

halftrack.

"Are there any experienced machinegunners among you?"

"I am, Sergeant-Major!"

"Go join him. How about drivers?"

"Here, Sergeant-Major!"

"Go get in the passenger seat. The rest of you take the magazines from your rifles and form a line here!"

One by one, he weighed magazines in his hand. When he found one that felt still fully loaded, he pushed that man toward the halftrack. When he had his six volunteers, he left the most experienced officer in charge and ran down the wadi to jump into the driver's seat.

With air cover, the rebels had a brief respite. But the enemy would regroup all too soon. And the chance of being killed was infinitely greater when standing still.

It's now or never.

44

(At a double-time.)
Parachute blossomed nice an' round
Released my ruck an' up rushed the ground.
Well I slipped to m'right an' slipped to m'left
Slipped right down to a PLF.
Slipped to m'left an' slipped to m'right
Slipped right down to a firefight...

Puttcamp's Skyraider came in so low the flames from busted APCs licked the fuselage. His guns ripped through sand, flesh, steel...whatever got in his way.

He saw two tanks collide in the chaos. He pulled up and banked slightly.

Bombs away.

His climbing A1E shivered in the shockwave. Direct hit. *Scratch two turtles.*

Another detonation. Haugen missed a zigzagging tank, but the concussion knocked it off its treads.

Puttcamp felt something tear through his wing. Then a machinegun slug punctured his altimeter.

He leveled off, then banked for another pass.

He quickly assessed a target and nosed down into a shallow dive with guns blazing.

Tracers crisscrossed all around him.

A hole appeared in the fuselage in front of him and wind whistled in. A bullet smashed the airspeed indicator.

Another bullet tore through the floor and punched through his horizontal situation indicator. Glass splintered above him. He glanced up and saw a bullethole in the cockpit.

"Jumpin' bugshit!" he exclaimed. "These guys got no respect for my equipment!"

He let another bomb go, and tracers chased him up into the wild black yonder.

Puttcamp's and Haugen's bombs hit simultaneously, about a half-mile apart.

"Afraid that's the last of my heavy ordinance," Haugen said, banking to see another tank busted, and one with its main gun bent.

"Roger that," Puttcamp said. "I'll stay here. You go see what you can do at the camp."

"I'm gone."

Haugen's Skyraider climbed eastward, leaving a thin trail of blue smoke against the stars.

CAMP ALI WEST

Jan Chin buckled a pistol belt around his big belly and called out to the trainees clustered around the fence, "Get back to your beds! Training will begin early tomorrow, just like normal! Don't worry about that...it's just some wargame exercises!"

Ali cried, "No! General quarters! Everyone, combat stations!"

Ali and Chin had some heated words. The trainees drifted away from the fence.

THE BIVOUAC

Bassam had never joined the mob of gawkers. But he wandered close enough to hear Ali's order.

Ali was probably right. There was no guarantee that the ruckus was an army exercise. Bassam followed the designated route to his combat station at a fast trot.

He stopped in his tracks and looked up. An ominous crackling noise rippled across the sky. It sounded like the electric rumbling that sometimes precedes a thunderclap. But didn't thunder require clouds? There were no clouds tonight--only stars. There was also no flash of lightning.

He resumed running for his general quarters station, then noticed something strange out over the sea.

Some stars disappeared briefly, then reappeared, in definite patterns. Like small clouds were passing in front of them--only these "clouds" were moving downward, not laterally as one might expect from a breeze. Then Bassam made out the figure of a man dropping from the sky...under a rectangular sail.

Cries and screams pulled his attention toward the other side of the camp. Some pointed up at the sky to the north. Bassam looked that way, wondering if men were falling from the sky over there as well. But it was no man. Rather, a roaring machine.

ABOVE THE CAMP

Haugen had plenty of fuel, but no more bombs and not a whole lot of machinegun rounds. His oil pressure was gradually dropping, and attacking the armor had thrown him off schedule. Cavarra's men would have popped their chutes by now. Haugen arced his Skyraider around to come in from the north, so Cavarra's men wouldn't be in his line of fire.

He came in low and slow, strafing the largest concentration of men he could see. He alternated left and right rudder to disperse his fire in a slight zigzag pattern. In a few seconds, the camp was behind him. He circled for another pass.

***

Cavarra pulled his rip cord. The harness tugged at his groin as the main canopy blossomed, drastically slowing his meteoric descent.

Above him the chutes of his team popped open in quick succession.

They floated over the Red Sea, but the target was clearly visible in the moonlight, now. He steered for the southeast corner of the camp.

There's no greater sense of tranquility than swinging under a fully deployed parachute. All is right in the world...at least temporarily. Even with chaos unfolding below, the parachutist is just a spectator for a few merciful seconds.

Cavarra had the best seat in the house to watch Haugen strafe the camp. The Skyraider swooped down for a second run when Cavarra's spectator time ran out.

He yanked down on both toggles as the ground rushed up to meet him. The Para-Foil set him gently down on his feet.

Cavarra stood in the corner of a gigantic sandbox. Probably a PT pit. He shed his harness and knelt to extract his rifle from the weapon carrier case.

Bojado hit the ground some twenty feet away.

Haugen's voice crackled from the squad radio. "Bird Three to Dog One, over?"

Cavarra pushed the mike button. "The beagle has landed. Go ahead. Over?"

"I'm spent, baby," Haugen said, in his best Austin Powers imitation. "I'm afraid you're on your own, now."

The rest of the team touched down while Haugen spoke.

"Roger. What's the status with Has-Been Rabbit, over?"

"We shook it up a bit, but it doesn't look promising. Over."

"Roger. Thanks, Bird Three. Drive safe, now. Out."

The A1E banked and climbed, disappearing out over the Red Sea.

"Has-Been Rabbit, this is Has-Been Dog One. Come in, over?"

THE WADI

The halftrack jumped out of the wadi and landed with a jolt, treads spraying sand like a rooster's tail. Siyr steered for the hulk of a burning tank at full-throttle.

"I'm busy, Dog One!"

"Status report, over?" Cavarra's voice persisted.

"Same as before. Will notify if significant change. Out! Has-Been Bird Two, this is Has-Been Rabbit, over?"

"Go ahead, Rabbit," Puttcamp replied.

"I'm breaking out, moving west from our position. Do you see me, over?"

The Skyraider maneuvered for a better view. "Roger, Rabbit. I have a visual. What are you doing, if you don't mind my asking, over?"

"I could use some cover, Bird Two. Over."

"You got it. Here I come."

Puttcamp sighed. It was still a target-rich environment, but the targets had a lot of distance between them now. *Oh well. No turtle shoot lasts forever.*

Tracers reached up at him from all over the desert. He swung low behind the speeding halftrack, buzzed it, then cut loose his guns when an enemy APC fell into his crosshairs. He had one bomb left, but he wasn't going to waste it on light armor.

***

Qawi saw B Troop Commander's tank disappear in a terrible flash.

A tornado of fire and sand rolled across the formation with a *crump, crump, crump,* sound: Mortars.

Not surprisingly, the B Troop Commander didn't answer his radio call. Qawi cursed. The leaderless B Troop was now in headlong retreat. He radioed C Troop commander to round up B Troop's survivors and reinforce himself with them.

It was a stupid mistake to have my gunners concentrate on the aircraft, he realized. That gave them time to set up their mortars. That was the difference experience could make.

He ordered his gunners to concentrate their main guns on the wadi once again, in the area he suspected the mortars to be.

He had a good plan, but he had to sort through the chaos first. A Troop was scattered to the four winds and it took costly minutes to regroup them. The Scouts had never taken fire before and B Troop's survivors were rattled. It took much screaming over the radio by C Troop's commander to organize them.

Qawi deployed A Troop in a crotchless "V" ambush formation on the left flank. C Troop, once reinforced and organized, would thrust into the right flank.

C Troop was the broom and A Troop the dustpan. Machinegunners could engage the remaining bomber until live meat was in range. Air Force High Command should be scrambling fighters now and the attacking aircraft would be scrap metal soon.

CAMP ALI EAST

The Fokker F-27 came back around over the beach, now only a few hundred feet off the deck. Bulky objects fell out the back. Huge cargo chutes opened behind them as they dropped. Then the plane shrank from sight and quiet fell over the camp.

"Dog One, this is Bird One," Jenkins said. "Your party supplies have been delivered. We're going out for dinner and drinks. You kids behave yourselves. Over?"

"Roger, Bird One," Cavarra said. "Keep in touch. Over?"

"Wilco. Good luck. Out."

Cavarra continued searching the southeastern corner of the camp until he located each of his men, then waved to get Bojado's attention.

"Dog Two, this is Dog One," he said, into his headset mike. "Radio check, over?"

"This is Dog Two," Zeke replied. "Loud and clear."

Cavarra was relieved by his post-jump head count. *At least nobody streamered in.*

He and Bojado stole along the fence toward the south-facing pillbox, with Cole and Campbell trailing some twenty meters back.

A burst from an AK47 sent the Americans scrambling for cover. Then the camp erupted with small arms fire.

45

(Hadith Mishkat 4549)
According to the venerable Abu Musa,
Allah's Messenger has said:
"The portals of heaven lie under the shadow of the sword."
On hearing this a lean and emaciated man stood up and said:
"O Abu Musa, did you hear this hadîth with your own ears?"
"Yes," said Abu Musa,
and then and there the man went up to his companions and said:
"I bid you salaam." So saying, he broke the sheath of his sword
and proceeded towards the enemies.
He killed many with that sword
and ultimately attained martyrdom himself.

THE MOTOR POOL

Bassam heard the sound of mass panic from the west side of camp behind him. He ignored it and ran toward the beach, trying to calculate where the flying men had come down.

The strafing airplane had erased his momentary confusion: The camp was under attack.

Jihad had come to him.

As he rounded the motor pool, he saw movement down by the boathouse. He pulled the rifle into his shoulder and fired on full auto. Within moments, dozens of his compatriots were firing in the same direction.

CAMP ALI WEST

Ali raged at Chin. "The camp is under attack, you idiot! Do you still want to argue?"

"General quarters!" Chin yelled to the confused trainees.

Trainees tripped over each other trying to reach their predesignated positions. Once there, they fired blindly out into the desert.

Ali hustled around the perimeter, looking for the enemy but not seeing them. The battle was still raging to the south...between whom he didn't know. But the dive-bomber had strafed the camp, making two deliberate passes. That meant an attack was coming here.

And that meant they were coming for the bomb.

He told Chin as much, and the two of them mustered a large force to lead to the armory, where the bomb was stored.

THE WADI

Dreizil heard explosions and saw flashes in the desert night. He steered toward them.

March to the sound of the guns...

His jeep topped a dune and he saw a battle unfolding before him. But his GPS showed he was still five klicks from the terrorist camp...and there were dozens of armored vehicles maneuvering in the moonlight.

We don't have any armored vehicles, he realized, with a chill.

The Jeep veered hard away, to skirt wide around the scene.

CAMP ALI EAST

Scarred Wolf lowered the gun, in its Javaline jump pack, a hundred feet above the beach. It hit the sand an instant before he did.

To his right, a shadow landed flat-footed on uneven ground, lost his balance and fell over. Scarred Wolf shed his parachute harness and ran to his side, pulling him to his feet. He was about to ask for the tripod, then realized this was not Fava-Vargas, but DeChalk.

"Where's Pablo?"

DeChalk shrugged.

"You're supposed to be with Zeke."

"Where's Zeke?"

Scarred Wolf snorted and used his Ka-Bar to cut the ammo box out of DeChalk's webbing.

Scarred Wolf found Fava-Vargas further down the beach. They ran together to the boathouse. "Here. Hold the gun."

Fava-Vargas took the Dover Devil. Scarred Wolf kicked in the door and rolled inside.

The interior was nearly pitch-black, but Scarred Wolf could see every shadowy shape. Nothing stirred. He came back outside--which was like daylight, by comparison.

"Gimme a boost."

Fava-Vargas squatted, and Scarred Wolf climbed his back. Slowly, the ex-SEAL stood, with his partner perched on his shoulders. It was more than a little painful. Scarred Wolf let go of his buddy's helmet, which he'd been holding for balance, grabbed the edge of the boathouse roof and hauled himself up.

Once atop the roof, Fava-Vargas handed the gun, SLAP ammo and tripod up to him. Both men tugged wads of empty burlap pouches out of their buttpacks and dropped them to the ground. Fava-Vargas unfolded his entrenching tool and worked furiously to fill the sandbags, ignoring the Fokker F-27 returning low for the heavy drop.

***

Zeke let go of the mike button and turned to DeChalk. "See the MG nest?"

DeChalk nodded and pointed at it. "Overlooking the beach, about twenty yards out."

"Shh! Keep your voice down. Follow five meters behind me. When we get there, cover me just like we practiced."

They dropped to the sand and crawled. First on an azimuth perpendicular to the nest, then they turned at a right angle to slither up behind it.

So far, so good. Zeke thought for sure the crew would open up on Jenkins' bird when it came back by for the heavy drop, but the guns were silent. According to satellite intel, there was usually only one or two men in the position. Maybe the dumb slabs are asleep.

DeChalk stopped when he reached his covering position. Zeke kept crawling, slowly, until he was close enough to peek over the edge.

In the luminescent green of his night vision display, Zeke saw that only one man was in the nest. That man was facing away from him, toward the sea, and was, indeed, too still to be awake. Zeke silently drew his knife and drug his knees forward until his leg muscles were bunched under him.

Zeke sprang from the back edge of the nest and fell upon the sleeping gunner. DeChalk saw this, surged forward and rolled into the southern edge of the nest, coming up with rifle leveled. Zeke cursed. His knife rose and fell several times, then he flung something out onto the beach. DeChalk crawled up beside Zeke to find him biting his wrist, then spitting. Biting and spitting, biting and spitting.

"What did he do? I thought he was asleep."

"So did I," Zeke replied. "But he wasn't. He was dead. Touch his skin."

DeChalk did. The body was cool. He'd been dead for a while. "What...?"

"A snake," Zeke said, biting and spitting.

"Did it get you?"

"Doom right, it bit me!"

DeChalk keyed his headset mike. "Dog Team Five, this is Dog Team Two. We need a medic, over?"

"Forget it. Get those guns turned around," Zeke said, then keyed his own team mike. "Disregard, Dog Five."

"But the poison.... Lombardi might have..."

"Son, we got a job to worry about right now. I'll get some help afterward. If there is an afterward."

THE BOATHOUSE

A bullet tore through Terrell's thigh and he went down with a yelp. McCallum came over, stopped short, then felt the rest of the way forward with baby steps until he was at his buddy's side. No matter how much experience you had with night vision goggles, they played hell with your depth perception.

"You hit? Terrell? You hit?"

"Hell yeah I'm hit!"

McCallum dragged him behind the boathouse, almost bumping into Fava-Vargas.

"Got me in the leg, man!" Terrell reached down and tore open his trouser leg, where the bullethole was. "I think it missed the bone.

Hurts like a blind mother, though."

McCallum removed his gloves, popped open a first aid pouch and extracted a field compress. "Okay. Let's patch it up. Think you'll be able to walk on it?"

"Yeah, man. Sorry. Didn't mean to be a baby."

"It's cool, bro. Looks like it missed the artery, too. We'll get Lombardi to take a look here in a bit."

"Our heavy drop came in," Terrell observed. "I can set the charges, but I don't think I oughta' swim out there to grab our gear."

McCallum slapped him on the shoulder. "I'll get it. First let me check the boats for enemy or booby traps. Then you wire the dock while I chase our trash down. Copy?"

"Hoo-yah."

CAMP ALI SOUTH

Cavarra and Bojado made it to the pillbox just as the heavy pounding of large-bore machineguns tore westward through the camp.

"Willie-Pete," Cavarra panted, back against the concrete wall.

Bojado nodded and struggled to free a white phosphorous grenade from his ammo pouch. He yanked the pin, sidestepped around the corner and let the spoon fly as he slam-dunked it into the firing slot.

Screaming, flaming apparitions ran out the back of the pillbox. Cavarra put a bullet in each one of them.

"Dog Team Six, this is Dog Team One. Over?"

"This is Dog Team Six," Campbell replied.

"The deer stand is all yours. Happy hunting."

Bojado and Cavarra rushed toward the motor pool to cover for the snipers.

THE WADI

The halftrack careened out from behind the burning tank and turned to run parallel with the maneuvering M60s.

"RPG up!" Siyr cried over his shoulder. "You have a perfect shot into the flank. Fire!"

The RPG man aimed and fired. The conical rocket caught a tank in the side and the shaped charge in the warhead blew through the armor.

Siyr drove into the middle of the tank formation, where they couldn't use their main guns without hitting each other. Behind him the M2 Browning hammered away, making the enemy tankers button up.

The formation scattered once again. Siyr singled out one tank and ran alongside it, using it as a shield. Rounds from coaxial machineguns whined and ricocheted off the tank.

Siyr turned to the man in the passenger seat. "Are you ready to drive?"

"Umm...yes."

"Good. Once we're off, head back to the wadi. Put that RPG to good use on the way!"

He stood at the wheel, motioning for the man to slide into the seat behind him. They switched places, and the halftrack lurched from the clumsy transition.

Siyr stood on the hood, holding onto the windshield for balance. "Riflemen! Come with me!"

The halftrack ran alongside the tank, and Siyr jumped from one vehicle to the other. The three men armed only with rifles stared at Siyr, then at each other, then at the space between the vehicles. Gritting their teeth, they made the jump.

Siyr climbed atop the turret and set his rifle down. He drew his . 45 and threw the hatch open. A curious face appeared in the hatch. He shot it.

Siyr stripped off the tanker's helmet, grabbed him by the collar and pulled him up and out. Wheezing from the Herculean effort of manipulating a limp, blood-slick body through the narrow opening, he slipped down through the hatch, pistol in hand.

Inside the noisy, claustrophobic machine, Siyr shot the unsuspecting driver, loader and gunner point-blank. The tank rolled to a stop.

With the help of his volunteers, Siyr got the bodies out. Then, in between shouting alarming, confusing messages to the Murahaleen Scouts over the captured radio, he gave his men a crash-course in driving, loading and shooting.

***

In scrambling around to obey the contradictory orders coming at them from seemingly all sides, a Scout M60 strayed in between two M113s. The three of them were close enough to fit inside a small parking lot. Puttcamp's A1E Skyraider came streaking in, dangerously close to the ground, and laid its last egg.

Scratch three enemy vehicles.

Puttcamp cranked off the rest of his ammo on the next pass, flattening another M113. A wisp of flame licked out from a pattern of holes in his wing, glowing blue in the night.

"Rabbit, this is Bird Two. That's all I can do. Over?"

No response. Well, Siyr must've bought it. Poor fool had more guts than brains.

Puttcamp banked hard one last time, eastward. He had been over the Red Sea only for a hot second when the radio crackled again. It was Jenkins.

"You been watching your radar?" Jenkins asked.

"No," Puttcamp said. "The old Mickey Mouse artifact is shot to pieces, along with most of the aircraft. Why?"

"Looks like we got fast movers coming in from the southwest."

Puttcamp nudged the stick forward. The old crate dove down to within fifty feet of the water before he pulled her out straight-and-level.

"Did you copy that Bird Two?"

"That's a good copy," Puttcamp said. "My butt is definitely hangin' out in the breeze. What are they drivin' these days? F5Es?"

"Tiger Twos? That was so last season. Try *Chengdus* and late-model MiGs."

"Gotta love what oil revenues can do for medieval gang lords, huh? You gonna make it?"

"I may have to ditch this thing on the first seagull turd I find," Jenkins said. "But I'll make it."

"I might be going in the drink myself, even if the MiGs don't find me. I'll meet you at Pharaoh's Chariot."

***

The halftrack returned to the wadi after RPG rounds had knocked one tank off its tracks, destroyed one APC and damaged another. But just as it got there, a direct hit from a tank's main gun obliterated it and everyone aboard.

Two hundred men, or more, lay dead or dying in the wadi. The mortar officer was dead and all but a couple tubes mangled. Wounded crews doggedly fired on, but were now having little luck scoring clean hits on anything. The first recoilless rifle crew was gone, but two replacements continued to load rockets and drag the tube up to peek over the berm for desperate long-range shots.

The enemy tank formation to the south seemed to be floundering in confusion yet again. It was the only reason the rebels hadn't been overrun.

The Skyraider was gone, but one of the M60s was now taking out other tanks from the rear.

The officer Siyr had left in charge called out to the survivors, "Listen up! None of us will live if we remain here. We have four trucks still operational--if we load up and retreat, we might be able to outrun our pursuit."

The general consensus was in favor of his idea.

"What about Major Thibeault?" someone asked, pointing to the bound, gagged and terrified European sitting at the bottom of the wadi.

"He would have us surrender," said the officer, contemptuously. "I say, leave him here to follow his own edict."

They loaded into the trucks. Four was enough to carry what men remained.

With a groan of straining old motors buried at redline, the trucks lurched up out of the wadi and sped off to the west.

***

Dreizil drove as close as he dared to the camp, then left the Jeep and continued on foot.

He walked upright in the draws, but crawled over the dune peaks to avoid silhouetting himself. Snails crunched under him as he went.

I'll never understand why there are so many stupid snails out in the desert.

It reminded him of Egypt. The Sinai glistened with their slime trails every morning. Dreizil and many older veterans had seen it first-hand, since Israel had paid in blood for the Sinai Peninsula three times. But it belonged to Egypt now. Again.

Dreizil grew angry every time he thought about the Sinai. Despite their investments, and the oil reserves there which could meet all Israel's energy needs, American politicians coerced Israel into giving over two-thirds of her land mass to a country that failed to take it by force twice in six years. And where was the peace promised in exchange?

The more Israel gave up, the more was demanded, but peace never came. Cavarra acted as if Dreizil were unreasonable for not trusting the Americans completely in this current crisis. How could he?

Cavarra himself seemed honorable, and so far had done right by Dreizil. But obviously there was much beyond Cavarra's control.

Dreizil wasn't sure what had gone wrong this time, and he didn't know what happened to Siyr or the others. But the mission had gone haywire, for certain. He cursed and spat.

It probably didn't matter, anymore, what had gone wrong or who was dead. What did matter was that he was going to get inside the terrorist camp and find that warhead.

THE MESS AREA

Behind Chin, people screamed and groaned as a hailstorm of lead tore them to pieces. Chin knew the enemy must have taken the machinegun nest and turned the guns around. There also must be another belt-fed weapon somewhere, but he couldn't tell where.

Survivors of the air strike ran to dive into foxholes around the western border of the camp. The holes were overcrowded with hysterical humanity. Some even sought refuge in the latrine pit.

Now strange *bloop*ing noises sounded from several places-- almost like the sound of mortars firing, but not nearly as loud. Explosions tore through the bivouac area, shredding tents and human bodies still in the open. The miniature mortars targeted the foxholes, and the slaughter was terrible.

The pillboxes were his best defensive assets, but they were useless, now. They would prove a formidable defense against attackers outside the wire. But when Chin laid out the plans for this place, he'd never dreamed an attack might come from **inside** the camp.

He led his gang of skirmishers toward the center of camp using first the mess tent, then the command post for concealment. Here he ordered them to spread out into the obstacle course and motor pool, and advance on-line.

He turned to Ali just as the camp commandant fell, holding his chest. Another man nearby fell, a small hole in his forehead and a huge hole in the back of his skull. Chin heard the rifle reports above the other battlefield sounds, and dove to the ground.

CAMP ALI EAST

McCallum swam sidestroke, towing the floating bundles to the dock, where Terrell pulled up what he needed. When the last of it was retrieved, McCallum hauled himself up onto the dock.

***

Atop the boathouse, Scarred Wolf fired the gun while Fava-Vargas finished stacking the sandbags in front of them.

"Did you check inside here?" Lombardi called up.

"For people. Not for nukes," Scarred Wolf said.

Lombardi and Mai entered the boathouse and scanned the interior with night vision goggles.

Cavarra had shown them a photo of the warhead, so they had an idea what to look for.

They turned the place upside-down, but found nothing.

Next they tried the supply tent.

***

"Rock & roll!" DeChalk cackled with glee as he raked fire

mercilessly across the north side of the camp. He now saw figures moving on the obstacle course, and scattered them like cockroaches. Then his belt ran dry and the bolt slammed home on an empty chamber.

"Got any spare ammo over there, Zeke?"

Zeke flopped on his back at DeChalk's feet, muttering softly.

***

Bassam crept slowly now, sensing the enemy was near. He moved from cover to cover, watching for tell-tale shadows, listening for some suspicious sound above the terrific noise.

Then he heard a staticcy voice say, "Dog Team Five, this is Dog Team Two. We need a medic ASAP, over?"

"What's up, over?" replied a live voice, very close.

"It's Zeke. He's down."

Bassam peeked around the corner and saw Lombardi emerging from the supply tent. He aimed and fired a long burst.

One round caught Lombardi in the neck. He hit the ground spasming.

46

THE WADI

Qawi braved the flying lead to stick his head out of the hatch for a look around. The destruction surrounding him was awesome. A third of his tanks were out of commission. Half of his APCs. And now C Troop was on the verge of breaking--from what he didn't know.

But the screaming jet engines overhead announced the arrival of the MiG23 Flogger squadron. Now he was safe from any subsequent air attack. And the enemy was running.

They were out in the open... sitting ducks for his main guns. He tried to give new orders to his commanders, but someone was burning up the air, jabbering away on his frequency again.

The strange voice ranted out a string of confusing orders non-stop, and Qawi's tanks were going crazy trying to comply.

Blang!

Something ricocheted off his cupola, inches from his face.

Then he heard the chattering of the M85, and looked around to place it.

It came from one of his own tanks.

A lone tank had broken out of formation, and raced north. He tried to raise it on the radio, but the same fool was still clogging up the frequency.

***

Siyr figured it was time to quit pushing his luck. He ordered the driver to disengage and head for the camp.

As they rolled away, he spun the turret backwards to maybe knock out a couple more tanks with the 105mm main gun.

He saw a hatch open and a head stick out. He cranked off a burst from the M85 cupola gun. But below him, the gunner and loader got into an argument over which shells were armor piercing discarding sabot (APDS), which were high explosive squash-head (HESH) and which were high explosive anti-tank (HEAT).

He quit broadcasting on the tanker radio long enough to say, over the intercom, "Load the APDS! It's the same kind you've been using!"

When he tried to resume his radio chatter, someone else was talking and he couldn't break in. Orders were being given to split the enemy force--one troop was to handle the rebels Siyr had left behind, and the other was to pursue him.

"Dog One, this is Rabbit. Over?"

"Hey Rabbit. What's up, over?"

"Our conventional attack is a little late. But it is finally coming."

CAMP ALI SOUTH

Once Siyr had explained his brainstorm, Cavarra had to smile. He shook his head with grim humor.

"What's up, boss?" Bojado asked, firing his M203 at a cluster of writhing bodies in the latrine ditch.

"That doomed psycho, Siyr," he replied, reloading his own grenade launcher.

"He's still alive?"

"I know, right? You heard of the fine line between genius and insanity?"

"Sure."

"Well, he's teetering on that tightrope. C'mon--let's go see if our sappers need a hand."

CAMP ALI WEST

Now that he was close enough to see the camp up close, Dreizil's brain froze up.

The pillboxes had interlocking fields of fire. If he tried to rush the gate from here, they would cut him apart.

Despite all the chaos Cavarra's men were evidently raising inside, the guardshack and the foxholes on this side of camp were occupied. The occupants might be scared out of their minds, but they were bristling with weapons. And even disregarding all that, he had no means of breaching the concertina wire.

Then something amazing happened.

An M60 came grinding out of the night and crashed right through the concertina. Antipersonnel mines blew under its heavy treads making for an awesome fireworks display but causing no damage to the tank. It ran over a foxhole and a couple defenders who didn't decide to flee until too late. It parked behind the southwestern pillbox and raised its gun.

It fired.

The shell landed amidst a formation of more M60s now plowing toward the camp.

The pursuing tanks fired back, and the earth in front of the pillbox shook furiously from a salvo of short rounds.

The southwest and northwest pillboxes opened up on the armored troop with rockets and machineguns.

This was beautiful!

Either Siyr was in that tank, or God Himself had taken a hand in the fight. Or both.

The renegade tank lurched from behind its concrete shield and went right for another string of foxholes. It fish-tailed into the concertina, shot geysers of sand behind it and straightened out. Land mines blew right and left. The concertina snagged on the track skirts. Wire snapped and the razor-tipped barrier was ripped from its place. The main gun fired again. The coaxial and cupola guns sprayed people fleeing from the iron monster.

The renegade tank turned slightly and bore down on the guard shack. The guards saw what was coming and bolted, only to be cut down by automatic fire. The turret rotated and the gun fired again. A direct hit into the back of the northern pillbox.

Now Dreizil had a passage into the camp.

47

THE SOUTHERN PILLBOX

Shells were blowing the camp to blazes now. Jet aircraft passed back and forth overhead, but these MiG23s were strictly fighter interceptors and carried no ground support ordinance. They came in for strafing runs, but the pilots were inept and hit nothing they were supposed to.

"Dog Team Six, this is Dog Team One. Over?"

"Go ahead Dog One," Campbell replied. "Over?"

"Get down from there and fall back. It's gonna get hot real quick."

"That's a good copy. There's not much live meat left anyway."

Cole tickled his trigger. The rifle barked and a shadow across the camp spun and dropped.

"They out in them there shadows," Cole said. "Cain't hardly get a clear shot."

"It's okay, Bulldog. We're done, here."

Campbell rolled over the side and dropped to the ground. Then a shellburst on the opposite side of the pillbox shook the earth.

"It sure did get hot," Campbell said. "This is no place for a sniper." He extended his hand upward, but Cole didn't take it.

Cole wasn't on the roof. Campbell looked around for his partner.

Something moved on Campbell's right. He turned and saw a dark figure writhing on the ground some twenty feet away.

Campbell felt sick as he approached. It was Cole, and he was in bad shape.

Campbell gently rolled Cole onto his side. "I know this is Gonna hurt, Bulldog. I'm sorry." With a groan he lifted Cole into a fireman's carry and range-walked as smoothly as he could back toward the dock.

Cole's legs dangled at queer angles. Blood dripped out of his nose and mouth. "T-twenty months..." he rasped.

"What?"

"B-been sobah f-fo' t-t-twenty months."

"I'll buy you a drink when we get back on the block. Okay?"

"Ah d-don't believe this shit."

"Hang on, Bulldog. " He carried him wordlessly for a moment, then heard weak sobs.

"D-doomed artillery shell? Ah'm a snipah f-fo' cr...cr..."

Campbell said, "It's okay. We're almost there."

THE COMMAND POST

Chin noticed that the machineguns in the nest had fallen silent. Probably because that idiot Ali had only provided one belt for each gun. Well, at least Ali's stupidity was working in his favor, now.

Chin shifted his remaining skirmishers over to the obstacle course. Too many had fallen to sniper fire. But he still had enough to take back the machinegun nest...and from there, turn the enemy's right flank. The enemy's force was small. It had to be. A larger force would have swept all the way through the camp by now.

These were commandos, here to steal the bomb. Commandos with a lot of firepower. But he had something just as lethal as firepower--he had fanatics. He could just keep sending his men forward until they overwhelmed the enemy. Just like his father had in Korea and Tibet. And whoever didn't go forward would be shot in the back as an example to the others.

THE MACHINEGUN NEST

DeChalk fired Zeke's gun until that belt ran dry, then looked again at the fallen sailor.

Lombardi wasn't answering the radio. DeChalk didn't even know if Zeke was alive.

"Dog One, this is Dog Two. Over?"

"Go ahead, Dog Two."

"Pappadakis is down and these captured guns are dry. Please advise. Over?"

"Zeke is down?"

"That's a good copy. Over?"

"Is it bad, over?"

"I think so."

Shells *whump*ed only a hundred yards away. Small arms chattered. Men screamed. Scarred Wolf's gun hammered methodically from over at the boathouse.

"Dog One, do you want me to hold this position, over?"

"Negative. Spike those guns and bring Zeke back here. Over?"

"Wilco. Out."

THE SUPPLY AREA

Mai looked down at Lombardi's body and jumped backward into the dark folds of the supply tent. He unsheathed his knife, slit the back wall open and squeezed through.

"What are you doing?" demanded a voice from above.

Mai looked up at Fava-Vargas behind the hasty sandbag fort atop the boathouse.

"Somebody just popped Lombardi," he explained. "I didn't see the shooter."

"You're gonna pull Lombardi out, right?" Scarred Wolf asked.

"He's dead."

"You're gonna pull him out. Right?"

"Sure. I just gotta be careful."

"Where's the bomb?"

"We couldn't find it."

"Well you **better** find it."

"Which way did the shots come from?" asked Fava-Vargas.

Mai pointed.

Fava-Vargas loaded a shell in his M203 and fired.

***

Bassam was rocked by an explosion on his left. He jumped up and ran to the right, and an explosion to his front knocked him back.

He had a few pieces of shrapnel in him, but nothing serious. He rose, spun and ran in a new direction.

THE DOCK

The news was relayed back to Cavarra that Lombardi was down and Mai still hadn't found the hot potato.

Cavarra found McCallum and asked about the dock and boats.

"Everything's good to go. But Terrell's hit in the leg."

DeChalk came running up with two rifles but no Zeke.

"Where's Zeke?" Cavarra asked.

"Back on the beach," the merc said. "He's just too heavy for me by myself."

"I'll go get him," McCallum said.

"As you were, Mac," Cavarra said, then faced DeChalk. "Can you carry Lombardi by yourself?"

"Yeah. No problem."

"Go get him. Chief says he's just the other side of that supply tent. But be advised: there's bad guys over there and it could be hot."

DeChalk grinned, dramatically drew his bayonet and fixed it to his rifle. He took off running.

McCallum shook his head, looking down.

"Terrell!" Cavarra called.

"Sir?"

"You done back there?"

"Hoo-yah."

"How's the leg?"

The SeaBee limped up to stand beside them. "I can still walk on it."

"Good." Cavarra pointed down the beach. "DeChalk left Zeke back there somewhere. Don't know if he's dead or bad wounded. I need you to find him and bring him back."

Terrell wore that same put-upon expression he had when ordered to work through the night on the rifle range. Cavarra thought he might groan or roll his eyes.

"Got a problem with that?"

Terrell hesitated, then shook his head.

"We're not leaving him behind," Cavarra said. "Dead or alive."

Terrell nodded and turned to go. McCallum patted his shoulder on the way.

"Bojado!" Cavarra called.

"Yes, sir?"

"Go cover Terrell. There's nobody to stop the bad guys on that side, now."

"Ooh-rah."

Cavarra turned back to the huge engineer. "I don't know what the hold-up is with Mai, but all we need is that hot potato and we can unass this place. Can you find it for me?"

"I'll do what I can, Rocco."

McCallum looked around, then took off at a crouching run toward the chaos of cracking rifles, screaming voices and bursting shells. Cavarra patted his shoulder as he left.

CAMP ALI NORTH

Siyr realized it was only a matter of time before a 105mm shell turned his tank into an armor-plated coffin, no matter how much they darted from place to place inside the camp.

He shoved the hatch open and was overwhelmed by the roaring of shells all around him. He stood up through the hatch, let the spoon fly on a smoke grenade and flung it toward the wire. He popped another and heaved it further out, then sunk quickly back inside the cupola and shut the hatch.

"My friends," he said, "it has been an honor to go into battle with you."

The men started to protest, but he cut them off.

"My name is Ehud Siyr, in case we ever meet again."

"Where are you going?"

"Somewhere you don't want to follow. I've given you a smoke screen outside. The enemy is buttoned up and can't see well as it is-- that's the only reason they haven't hit us directly yet."

"Stay with us," the driver said. "We'll help you."

"There is going to be a nuclear explosion here," Siyr said. "You must break through the wire out into the desert. Escape those tanks out there, then run as far and as fast as this thing will take you, in a straight line. Don't stop, and don't look back. When you run out of fuel, jump outside and run as fast as you can. If you meet up with your comrades, tell them to do the same."

He reopened the hatch, stuck his rifle through, then followed it outside with a cat-like motion. He rolled off the side of the turret, sprang off the hull and hit the sand running for the east side of the camp.

Shells sometimes came screaming down to tear at the earth where he had recently passed, but he didn't slow down to reflect on this.

The tank remained motionless for a moment, then plowed into the smoke, rolled over the wire and disappeared into the darkness.

48

THE PT PIT

Cavarra moved out to catch up with DeChalk and provide cover--or maybe carry Lombardi's body himself if the merc couldn't handle it.

Then Campbell came huffing and puffing along, Cole's body on his shoulders.

"Razorback!" Campbell called out.

Oh no. Not Bulldog, too. "Campbell! Over here!"

Cavarra saw the blood dripping from Cole's mouth and knew it was bad.

"I don't wanna put him down, Rocco." Campbell said. "It's gonna hurt him too bad to pick him back up."

"C'mon. Let's put him in the boat and make him comfortable. Have you dressed those wounds, yet?"

"Negative. I don't even know where he's hit, yet. But he must be cut up inside."

"Lombardi's gone," Cavarra said. "You're gonna have to take care of him yourself."

CAMP ALI WEST

Qawi's tanks rolled toward the camp slowly. They were no longer taking incoming fire. All the pillboxes had been wiped out, as far as he could tell, and not a single body twitched where his main guns, now silent, had swept over the camp.

He had lost another tank to a rocket from a pillbox. His Scouts had taken a terrific beating and he still didn't know who he was fighting, how they managed to fortify a place like this so far north, how they managed to steal one of his tanks, or where that tank had gone.

Hatches opened and heads popped out. They could hear sporadic small arms fire down by the shore. Qawi ordered his infantry to dismount their M113s and push through the camp on foot. He wasn't about to risk any more armor to mines or crazy men with rockets. His tanks would deploy a safe distance away, where their 105mm cannons could sing again if needed.

THE MOTOR POOL

The shelling stopped and the camp seemed strangely quiet. Even more quiet than when the men had first fallen from the sky.

Bassam survived the rifle grenades with only flesh wounds. But he knew where the grenadier was now--behind the sandbags atop the boathouse. It would be very difficult to steal into the armory without being spotted by that man.

But if he went to the spot where he killed the man with the loud radio...

They shouldn't expect him to return there. Then he could take out the man on the boathouse and proceed to the armory.

Bassam slipped between two of the Toyota Hillux pick-ups in the motor pool, and came face-to-face with DeChalk, in the process of lifting Lombardi's body.

DeChalk's brain was still groping for recognition when Bassam's rifle butt busted most of his teeth out. Bassam's dagger flashed in the moonlight. The Martyrs had taught him how to kill quietly, and he did so now.

CAMP ALI EAST

"Dog Four, this is Dog One. Come in, over?"

"This is Dog Four," Scarred Wolf said.

"Climb on down and bring your gun to the boat. I'm not sure why the shelling stopped, but it might be the best time for you to move that pig."

"Hup, sir. How 'bout my buddy?"

Cavarra thought about it. He didn't want to lose his last, and best, high ground position until they had the hot potato and were ready to didimau. "Have him stay put. In fact, I'm gonna have some extra LAWs brought up to him directly."

"Hup, sir."

Scarred Wolf cut off a length of 550 cord from the coil in his buttpack and tied one end to the gun. He detached the tripod, dropped it over the side, then used the parachute cord to lower the Dover Devil gently to earth. He slapped Fava-Vargas' boot and dropped to the sand, where he grabbed gun and tripod and trotted down the dock.

***

Chin and his skirmishers covered the distance between the obstacle course and the machinegun nest at a fast crawl. Once to the nest, they found only a dead comrade and empty guns mangled by a grenade blast.

A trainee spotted movement on the beach below and opened fire.

***

Terrell winced from the impact of the bullet and knew, this time, that a lot more than just muscle had been hit. His flack vest slowed it down enough that it lodged in his torso rather than passing clean through. Zeke's body suddenly felt about twice its normal weight. If he went down, he'd never be able to lift him again.

Bojado rose and fired one-handed at the ridge overlooking the beach, while digging for a 40mm shell.

Terrell staggered on, growing weaker by the moment. Then another bullet impacted him and he tripped over his own legs. He and Zeke sprawled across the sand, where random bullets riddled them both.

***

Bassam slipped inside the supply tent and immediately noticed the slit in the canvas. He put away his dagger and pondered Allah's curious ways. He changed magazines and stepped through the slit.

***

"I got enemies in the open!" Fava-Vargas yelled. "At the MG

nest!" He extended a LAW and fired at the concentration of enemy.

The rocket streaked straight at them and detonated at their feet. The concussion was terrific, tearing limbs from bodies.

Fava-Vargas dropped the LAW and picked up his rifle/grenade launcher. He clicked out his M203 sight and fired. The 40mm Willie-Pete shell arced in and cooked some more meat. He sighted down his rifle and stitched a burst along the ridge.

Bassam Amin emptied half his magazine up into the boathouse. The burst went through the wall and window and on through the roof. Some of the rounds sunk into the stack of sandbags. Some of the rounds sunk into the man behind the stack of sandbags.

Fava-Vargas, who had been up in a kneeling position, fell backwards and teetered for a moment on the edge of the roof, then slipped over and hit the sand below with a wet *thump*.

***

McCallum moved slowly and stealthily, all the more difficult now without the shellfire to mask his movement. He'd seen no trace of either Mai or the warhead, but now he saw the bodies of Lombardi and DeChalk.

The little know-it-all had bought it trying to bring a buddy back. A far nobler end than McCallum might have predicted. The engineer considered leaving them there for the moment and continuing his search. But if he himself bought it, that would make three bodies some poor fool would have to drag back through Indian Country. He slung a body over each shoulder and hauled them away, knees popping under the weight.

***

Mai hid in one of the Toyota "boxes," fuming. He was even angrier now, after the way Scarred Wolf had spoken to him. He didn't like taking lip off anyone, and the redskin had treated him like some Army private.

He wondered if anyone would suspect him of fragging that stupid prairie nigger.

He would like to kill them all. Especially McCallum and Cavarra.

Movement caught his attention. He looked up and who should he see but big Jake McCallum, trudging by carrying two dead bodies, completely unaware of Mai's presence.

Mai's heart raced. He slid down from the truck and crept out to where he'd have a clear shot at the huge sapper's back.

Bassam Amin was getting ready to do the same thing.

Mai and Bassam saw each other and swung their rifles to bear as McCallum disappeared around the corner. Both fired. Bassam was singed just below the armpit. Mai took one in the stomach.

Mai fell, clutching his stomach and shrieking. Bassam entered the armory.

49

While helping Campbell move Cole to a comfortable position, Cavarra saw Terrell and Fava-Vargas go down in quick succession. "Chief! On me! Campbell! Put some fire on that ridge!"

Cavarra and Scarred Wolf dropped what they were doing and ran down the beach, slinging Galils over their backs on the way.

Campbell stood, shouldered his rifle, compensated for the movement of the boat and began tapping men across the camp.

Bojado had drawn some blood, but a bullet grazed his leg and another round glanced off his helmet, knocking him cold. When he came to, bullets were snapping by and he had to roll down the dune for cover.

Bullets kicked up sand at Cavarra's feet, but he only ran faster. Halfway to Zeke's and Terrell's bodies, he saw that Bojado was still alive. "Bojado!"

"Yo!"

"Help me get these guys to the boat!"

"Ooh-rah!"

"Chief!"

"Hup!"

"Give us some cover!"

"Hup, sir!"

Scarred Wolf changed course, now charging straight up to meet the enemy.

He tore a grenade loose. Yanked the pin. Chucked it.

He kept running. Pulled another frag. Yanked the pin. Chucked it.

Dove to the sand. Unslung rifle. Flipped selector lever to rock & roll.

Frag detonated. Frag detonated.

Back up and running. Topped the ridge. Enemy silhouetted. Pulled the trigger.

Short burst. Body dropped. Short burst. Two bodies dropped. Dove to the prone.

Long burst. Three bodies dropped. No one left standing.

Flipped selector lever to waltz.

Tap tap here. Tap tap there. Here tap, there tap, everywhere a tap tap. Chief Scarred Wolf is bringing smoke, eeyai-eeyai-oh.

No one left moving.

Deafening quiet.

Scarred Wolf watched. Waited for anyone...anything...to move.

He loaded a shell in the M203, swapped a full magazine into the Galil and watched some more. Finally he rose and stalked to the last body he had dropped.

It was a rather fat body, armed only with a pistol. It looked Asian.

Scarred Wolf squatted, took the pistol and drew his Ka-Bar.

***

Aerial flares popped overhead. Blinding white light reached down to chase away the shadows. Oblivious to Chief's rampage behind them, Cavarra and Bojado hauled their dead buddies back to the dock at a gasping gallop.

When they arrived at the boat, McCallum stood wheezing over two more dead bodies.

"Find the nuke?" Cavarra asked, gasping for air.

McCallum shook his head. "Not yet. I found these two."

Zeke. Terrell. Lombardi. DeChalk.

Cavarra sucked wind and pointed toward the boathouse. "Fava-Vargas is down over there. Go see what you can do. I'll go look for it myself."

***

Bassam emerged from the armory with his rifle in one hand and the metalic suitcase in the other. He looked at the whimpering Mai and considered silencing him with a merciful shot to the face. But the fat infidel deserved to suffer. Bassam kicked the Galil out of Mai's reach and continued around the corner of the armory.

***

Cavarra unslung his rifle while trudging wearily past the PT pit, still breathing hard.

Around the corner of the armory stepped a thin figure with an AK47 and a suitcase, just as a flare popped directly above.

It was a boy.

A young boy.

He couldn't be a day older than Justin.

Fire spat from the boy's rifle.

Something like a red-hot axe chopped into Cavarra's chest.

***

Bassam caught the man almost center-mass. The man went down, but the magazine ran dry only a few rounds into the burst.

Voices yelled from down at the dock. A rifle cracked and the AK47 jumped from his grip.

The weapon lay at his feet, the metal receiver caved in. The hand which had held it hurt terribly, refused to function and was slick with blood.

The man Bassam shot struggled to rise and level his weapon.

Bassam lunged forward and swung the suitcase as hard as he could into the man's jaw.

Shots rang out. Voices shouted from the beach. Bullets kicked up sand all around him.

Bassam turned and ran back past the armory to the motor pool. He stopped and stood thinking for a moment.

How to get to the boat? There were enemy at the dock and along the beach.

He nodded to himself and climbed in the nearest "box" truck. He set the suitcase in the passenger seat and looked around for the ignition switch.

The sideview mirror darkened and Bassam looked in it. There stood Siyr with rifle leveled.

Bassam swung down from the cab to face Siyr, groping for his dagger.

Siyr shot him through the heart. Then in the head. Then twice more in the heart.

Bassam crumpled to the ground.

Siyr looked all around, patiently. The only threat in sight was a far-off line of infantry advancing toward the camp from the west.

He pulled the suitcase out and walked to the armory, where he sat down with his back to the wall.

He opened the suitcase and looked at the device inside.

How I wish no such thing had ever been invented. I wish it weren't even possible.

He stared at it. There was certainly no rush. In fact, the closer the enemy infantry got, the better. And the longer he waited, the farther away the Sudanese rebels could run.

Samson said, "Let me die with the Philistines!" Then he pushed with all his might, and down came the temple on the rulers and all the people in it. Thus he killed many more when he died than while he lived.

Siyr heard the whimpering sounds again.

He shut the suitcase, stood, and walked toward the noise with weapon at the ready.

There on the ground was Mai, gut-shot.

Siyr never thought such soft, pitiful sounds could come from such a cold, hateful man.

He thought back to the previous afternoon, when McCallum had beat him senseless. No one deserved the humiliation more than Mai. And yet, when he heard about the beating in detail, Siyr couldn't help feeling sorry for him. And being embarrassed for him.

Later that night, when he'd visited the tent to discuss something with Cavarra, Siyr had noticed Mai staring into nothingness with a hopeless look of utter despair.

Siyr looked down at Mai, up at the stars, and down at Mai. He listened to the American voices from the beach, rising above the gunfire.

Siyr grinned. "Stay right there, marine. I will return with some help. I know it feels like you are dying, but not all gut shots are fatal."

Siyr turned and carried the suitcase along the same path McCallum had taken earlier.

Mai fumbled the .45 out of its holster. "This one is fatal, you nigger kike weirdo."

Mai fired center-mass into Siyr's back.

**

Dreizil had climbed the tallest structure on the obstacle course so he could observe all that went on and know how best to secure the bomb.

What he'd seen had been breathtaking. More thrilling than Entebbe, because he'd been an active participant from beginning to end back then, not an opportunistic spectator.

Not that he didn't get the urge to participate tonight, more than a few times. But he was armed only with a pistol, and drawing fire wouldn't help his odds.

Most importantly, he witnessed the scene between Siyr and Mai.

Mai had the suitcase open, now, and was smearing blood all over the hot potato, trying to figure out what button to push.

"What are you doing, Mai?" Dreizil asked, from above and behind.

Mai flinched, but felt the silencer against the back of his neck, and didn't try for his pistol.

"Slowly take your hands off the device and shut the suitcase. I'm only going to tell you one time."

Mai hesitated. Dreizil shot him through the left shoulder, then the right.

The nuke slid off Mai's lap while he writhed and shrieked, now unable to use his arms.

Dreizil ignored Mai's screaming and said, "That's so you can't shoot anyone else in the back. Or in the front or side, for that matter. Now lay flat on your back."

Blubbering and convulsing, Mai did.

"What were you doing?"

"Dead," Mai muttered through his sobbing. "Blow you all up. All you haoles."

"What made you decide to blow us all up?"

"Go to hell."

"Hmm," Dreizil said.

Dreizil shot Mai once through the right kneecap, once through the left. He ignored Mai's screaming and said, "That's so you can't walk."

Dreizil reached down and plucked an incendiary grenade from Mai's ammo pouch.

"White phosphorous," he read aloud. "Don't Americans call this 'Willie-Pete'?"

Mai continued screaming.

"You could say," Dreizil told him, "this is so there's nothing left of you for the others to come back for. But if you prefer, you may think of it as a brief orientation for the place you're going to."

Dreizil pulled the pin but held the spoon down until he had retrieved the suitcase and walked a safe distance away. Then he let the spoon fly and tossed the grenade at Mai's feet.

Dreizil scooped up a fallen rifle and trotted between the supply tent and armory, around the boathouse, and to the dock.

50

0553 17 AUG 2002; NUBIAN DESERT, SUDAN
CAMP ALI EAST

When the Murahaleen Scouts reached the beach, they found nothing but thousands of spent casings and the splintered remains of the dock floating in the water.

When confident that the area was secure, Qawi dismounted and walked every square foot of the wadi and the destroyed camp. Mixed in with the Sudanese bodies they found a bound, gagged, white European evidently crushed to death by a tank. Among the casualties inside the camp were some who were still alive, and could talk. What they told him was perplexing.

General Rahim ordered Qawi to pull back out of the Hala'ib Triangle, which he did, missing almost half of his men and machines.

The army launched an investigation. Observation aircraft combed the western Sudan. A deserted camp was found along the Tekezze. Tents, cots, a fence, a fuel drum...they never were certain who set it up or how long it had been there.

Khartoum told Washington that, in cooperation with the international war on terror, an elite Sudanese unit had destroyed a terrorist training camp. They even videotaped the ruins of the camp for network news.

Washington praised Khartoum for showing initiative and promised a strategic partnership once Saddam Hussein had been dealt with.

Qawi was reprimanded for sustaining such heavy losses against an inferior force. For destroying the terrorist camp, or helping to, he was demoted and transferred to the regular army.

The war against the non-Muslim south went on.

1200 20 AUG 2002; LOD, ISRAEL
HADID MILITARY CEMETERY

Ehud Siyr's body was dressed in his old IDF uniform, with red beret, red-brown jump boots, and jump wings.

The Israeli paratroopers who composed his honor guard were too young to know who the Ethiopian was. No family or friends were present. Only Yacov Dreizil, Generals Dahav, Ben-Gadi and some other IDF brass knew anything about the deceased.

Dreizil felt a few drops of rain but ignored the gathering clouds as he stepped behind the podium and adjusted the microphone. He looked over the faces of the soldiers gathered for a hero's funeral.

Too young.

Too young to appreciate frequent rain.

Rainfall had increased over 400 percent since the children of Jacob regained control of their land. Israel had been reduced to a wasteland in the last 2,000 years, but diligent cultivation had reversed much of the damage in just over half a century. The desert bloomed again.

Too young to appreciate men like Ehud Siyr.

Dreizil tapped the mike and cleared his throat. "Nobody knows much about Ehud Siyr. That's because he gave up his life years before he physically lost it."

Dreizil had never been much of a public speaker. He wished, just this once, he had the sort of voice to captivate a crowd.

"He came here with nothing but a heart that loved Israel. That was all he had to give, and he gave it. He never had a home, a wife, or a family. The demands of his profession kept him from ever developing lasting friendships. He must have been a lonely man...but I can't say for sure, because Ehud Siyr never complained once in all the years I knew him. He was the best soldier I've ever seen."

Rain fell steadily now. Many officers looked more preoccupied with avoiding it than with Ehud Siyr. Dreizil could tell the real soldiers from the rear echelon clerks & jerks. The latter looked miserable while trying to shield themselves with clipboards or map cases. The former remained oblivious to the rain and studied the dark, rawboned man in the casket.

A lieutenant used a mirror to check her lipstick. Pairs of soldiers whispered to each other.

"Are you listening to my words?" Dreizil asked, with a sharp rise of tone that made some in the audience flinch. "My father jumped at Mitla Pass. I fought the Jordanians along the *Nablus* Road. It was because of my comrades that Moshe Dayan and Yitshak Rabin were able to march through the Lion's Gate and stand at the Western Wall. I lost brave troopers taking the Sinai back after Egypt caught our country sleeping. I stormed the airport at Entebbe with Yonni Netanyahu. I'm telling you there has never been a better soldier than Ehud Siyr."

He had their attention, now.

"You should have seen him when he volunteered for the paratroops—a wide-eyed teenager who weighed less than his uniform and not a single callous on his feet. He was so skinny a strong wind might have blown him out to sea! You wouldn't think he could survive the first hour of training. But he had something inside him that carried him along until the innocence was bled out of him and his body was as tough as iron."

Some of the soldiers chuckled. The younger generation thought everything was a joke. Did they have any clue how close the Iranians were to developing nuclear weapons?

"This man believed in God," Dreizil continued. "A devout Jew. I sometimes teased him for his childlike faith. Out of respect for my rank, I suspect, he never took me to task. But once he told me, 'Colonel Dreizel, the Mighty One chooses to remain unseen for His own mysterious reasons; but evidence of His intervention in the affairs of men is all around you.'

"At the time, I scoffed at this remark. Yet now I look back at things I've seen and I remember his words. And I wonder...if this very soldier was himself part of the evidence he spoke of."

Dreizil gnawed at a peeling cuticle. General Ben-Gadi wore a strange expression. The crowd was deathly quiet. Dreizil never thought aloud, preferring to measure his words carefully before uttering them. Yet here he was chattering like a school girl into a microphone with hundreds of witnesses. Their disrespect for a fallen hero galled him; but what good could a speech do? What value were mere words, however eloquent? He exhaled heavily and stiffened a bit.

"Not many people are strong enough to be like Ehud Siyr. But when I think of the next generation and what they will face...I can't urge them strongly enough: remember him."

1426 19 AUG 2002; MCLEAN, VIRGINIA, USA
"LANGLEY"

The Big Guy beamed at Bobbie Yousko from behind his enormous desk.

"Outstanding job, B.Y. I want to congratulate you on a first-class piece of work."

"Thanks, sir," Bobbie said. "There were lots of people who made it come off, though."

"Of course there were. Of course. It's all about teamwork, isn't it? Working together. And you obviously did an admirable job of delegation. The hot potato is safe on a US Navy vessel and some of your team even made it out of there alive."

Bobbie tried to smile, but all she could think of was taking some aspirin and lying down somewhere quiet.

"You were right about your ex-SEAL, I'd say," the Big Guy said. "We ought to keep him in mind for future work. What's his name--David Carrerra, right?"

"Dwight Cavarra," Bobbie said.

***

The following day the State Department breathed fire down the Big Guy's yellow stripe and he handed them Bobbie's head.

All the bureaucrats seemed to care about was the political embarrassment that could have resulted had the mission failed.

Bobbie stood by her actions, and John Boehm backed her up. This was help from an unexpected quarter, as Boehm had been furious with her upon learning what happened to James Harris. Boehm blamed her fit of panic for getting Harris killed, but recognized that Operation Hot Potato had prevented a catastrophe of unknowable proportions. Bobbie Yousko had been the only one in authority with the guts to attempt it, and he would stand by her.

Eventually, she was exonerated and the Big Guy reversed his position yet again.

51

1630 19 AUG 2002; INDIAN OCEAN

(At the quick-time.)
I dunno' why I left... But I know I done wrong
An' it won't be long... 'Til I get back home.
Mama Mama don't you cry... Your little boy's too mean ta die
But there's other boys... Won't be comin' home.

A cargo ship cut across the rolling waves, hauling tons of toys and electronic devices bound for the shores of America.

The consumer goods shared the hold with six occupied bodybags.

Cavarra, Scarred Wolf, Campbell, McCallum and Bojado basked in the sun and ocean spray up topside.

Bojado had a lawn chair. The rest had towels spread out on the wooden deck. All were wearing identical blue swimming trunks.

Campbell closed his eyes and hummed a melody he couldn't get out of his mind.

"Our house...
In the middle of the street.
Our house..."

"I think I liked the submarine better," Bojado said, rubbing his sore neck.

"Shut up or give me back the lawn chair," Campbell said.

"Naw. I just mean the food, man."

"Hey Rocco," Mac said, "this is all y'all do in the Navy, ain't it?"

"Only if you're an officer," Cavarra said.

They laughed.

Laughter hurt Cavarra where the bullet had glanced off his flack vest and cracked some ribs. It didn't feel too doomed good where the suitcase full of tactical nuke had crashed into his chin, either.

Cavarra looked back down at the letter he would never send. This one was for Mai's family. Jeez, it was tough trying to find something good to say about that dirtbag.

Years ago Cavarra had tipped a few cool ones at the officer's club with an old-timer who led a SEAL team in Vietnam. The veteran told him how writing the "we regret to inform you" letters to next of kin was every bit as difficult as having your child's puppy put to sleep. But it could also be therapeutic.

Cavarra had lost more men on this one mission than he had during his entire Navy career. He could use a little therapy.

It didn't help that he couldn't get the boy's face out of his mind.

"Charles Mai was an extremely confident individual. His belief in his own leadership ability was unsurpassed. It is no wonder the Marine Corps made him a non-commissioned officer..."

How much more could he stretch the truth about Mai without puking?

Mac cracked a joke and the others laughed. Except Scarred Wolf.

"You okay, Chief?" Campbell asked.

"Yeah..." Scarred Wolf said, and let some silence pass while he worked on his scrapbook. He arranged Sudanese Popular Defense Force uniform insignia around the accoutrements he'd cut off the chubby Asian corpse at the camp. "I was just thinking about Bulldog. I never did figure out what he was."

"You mean his ethnicity?" McCallum asked.

"Right."

"Me neither," Campbell said. "I was curious, too, but I never had the nerve to ask him."

Scarred Wolf nodded. "I tried to be slick a couple times, and use some Shawandasse phrases on him--just in case he was my long lost cousin or something. He didn't bite."

"He was American," Cavarra said. "Ain't that enough?"

"That's right," Bojado agreed, with gusto.

McCallum blew raspberries to the tune of "Stars and Stripes Forever."

Cavarra shuffled through the other letters he'd written. Lombardi's had been a challenge, too.

"...Greg Lombardi maintained an immaculate appearance at all times and displayed such attention to detail, it is no wonder the US Army made him a First Sergeant. Greg not only demonstrated medical competence, but proved himself in such diverse roles as jumpmaster and patrol leader. His courage under fire was never in question. Greg was an asset to my team."

The DeChalk letter proved to be a bit easier.

"Mr. and Mrs. DeChalk, you should be very proud of Samuel. When he first came aboard, he was definitely behind the power curve. But your boy never shrunk from adversity. He demonstrated a never-failing determination that has set American fighting men apart for centuries. Sam showed courage under fire when given the opportunity and, in fact, he died in the act of carrying a comrade to safety..."

Campbell sat up, thoughtful. "Everybody here fought in the Gulf. Right?"

Some nodded. Some grunted affirmation.

"Any of you keep in touch with the guys that were in your unit?"

All shook their heads, except Cavarra. "I tried, for a while," he said.

"Why do you ask?" Scarred Wolf inquired.

"Well, I haven't either," Campbell said. "But I don't know why, 'cause there's not a day goes by I don't think of the guys I went to war with. And if any one of them was to call me up out of the blue some day, needing a favor, or some money, or some of my time, or just to shoot the breeze with an old buddy...I'd do it without hesitation."

Mac nodded. "Even the ones I couldn't stand at the time."

Everyone seemed to agree with this.

Cavarra found the letter to Dwayne Terrell's family easier still to write. He praised the SeaBee for his physical strength, his job knowledge and technical proficiency, but mostly for his loyalty. The man didn't enjoy many of the tasks assigned him, but he fulfilled his duty and did it well.

The letter to Zeke's family was nearly book-length. The only difficulty writing it was in finding the right words to express his admiration of Zeke not just as a non-commissioned officer, but as a man, too.

"So why didn't we stay in touch?" Bojado asked, rubbing the bandaged dome of his skull. The helmet had saved his life, but he'd suffered a concussion and occasionally grew dizzy for no apparent reason. The wound in his leg drove him crazy sometimes.

"Maybe 'cause the Gulf War didn't last long enough," Mac said.

Scarred Wolf shook his head. "It's because you all feel guilty about what you did."

"I don't," Bojado said. "I didn't do anything to be ashamed of."

"I'm not saying you did, Carlos. Why do World War Two vets, Korean vets, even some Vietnam vets, still stick together?"

"I give up," Bojado said.

"Those wars were fought by draftees," Scarred Wolf said. "Citizen soldiers. They had to go. They didn't have a choice. So their consciences are clear."

"Not all of them have a clear conscience."

"Well, in general. But us...we volunteered. We asked to go kill people and break things."

"And here we just did it again," Campbell said.

"That kinda' sets us apart, doesn't it?" Cavarra mused. "But not necessarily in a good way."

"In a world without war," Mac said, "somebody might have to lock our kind up."

"Well, we don't need to worry about that. Do we?"

"Somebody definitely would have locked Mai up," Scarred Wolf said. "Maybe Dreizil. Maybe Siyr. Maybe me. The dogs of war are ugly up close."

"Dreizil," Mac said, shaking his head. "That fool was really gonna set off the bomb? Blow us all up...and himself?"

"That's what he told me," Cavarra said. "And for once, I didn't doubt him."

"What stopped him?"

Cavarra shrugged. "I guess he decided to trust us."

They fell silent. Campbell lied back down.

"...Pablo Fava-Vargas was an exceptional sailor and the model of a Special Operator. Physically, mentally and morally, Pablo was among the elite of the elite. His attitude remained upbeat and positive even after sustaining debilitating wounds in the line of duty. His cheerful singing is already sorely missed by his comrades..."

"You know, I could be wrong," Cavarra said, "but I really don't think Dreizil was made for this. Not like us. I think he'd just as soon settle down to some boring job with a wife, kids, a dog...same stuff that wasn't enough for us...and forget how to kill people and break things."

"I kinda' got that impression, too," Campbell said.

"Me, I always wanted a mission like this one," Cavarra said. "Well, maybe not exactly like this one. But something hairy."

"Me too," Mac said.

"Me too," mumbled Scarred Wolf.

"Yeah? Who here plans to volunteer for something like this again?" Bojado asked.

"I probably will," Mac said.

Campbell shrugged. "Maybe."

The others were quiet.

"I think I'm done," Scarred Wolf said. "I've still got the wife, the kids and the dog. Those kids are gonna have a dad."

Cavarra nodded. "Roger that, Tommy. Take me back to the land of powdered milk and artificial honey."

Somehow, for some reason, Cavarra had been given one last chance—or one last warning, depending on perspective. There was still time to become "Dad" to his kids. There was still so much he could, and should, teach them. There was lost time to make up for, but still some precious years left. Saving the world wasn't his job. There were men who lived to do that and they could get by without him.

"Audie Murphy called himself 'a fugitive from the law of averages'," Scarred Wolf said.

Cavarra looked down at the last letter.

"...I also regret that I never got the chance to know Robert Cole better on a personal level. A man of his professionalism, diligence and

can-do attitude would be a credit to any fighting force. I honestly
believe our great nation has survived because of men like Robert--or
'Bulldog' as we affectionately called him. He was humble and quiet,
yet motivated by the kind of mighty, gallant spirit found in the people
our society calls heroes. "

Cavarra puffed his cheeks, sighed and wadded up the letters. He stared out at the ocean and threw the wad overboard. The wind caught the paper and drove it out to sea.

Cavarra studied each face of the men around him and wrestled with whether or not to speak his mind.

"Fellahs," he said, "I can tell you right now, I won't forget any of you. As far as I'm concerned, you're family. If you ever need anything, or just have some time to hang out, I hope you'll give me a call. Any time, day or night."

"That goes for me, too," Campbell said, quietly.

"And me," Bojado said.

"*Nijenina,*" Scarred Wolf said, raising his water bottle as if to toast.

Mac nodded agreement. The resemblance to Eddy Murphy was even stronger when he smiled.

They listened to the wind over the ocean and watched the last crumpled letter sink under the blue-green waves.

Cavarra saluted from his seat.

"What were those?" Bojado asked.

Cavarra thought for a minute. "Memorials. Justification. Guilt. I don't know."

The others threw casual salutes seaward.

McCallum unboxed some cards and asked if anyone was up for a game of spades.

THE END

Made in the USA
Monee, IL
18 September 2019